MW01064999

BORDERLINE

by

Lynne Rike Herndon

Lynne R. Herndon

authorHOUSE™
1663 Liberty Drive, Suite 200
Bloomington, Indiana 47403
(800) 839-8640
www.AuthorHouse.com

First published by AuthorHouse 11/01/05

ISBN: 1-4259-0059-3 (e)
ISBN: 1-4208-7759-3 (sc)

Library of Congress Control Number: 2005907318

Printed in the United States of America
Bloomington, Indiana

This book is printed on acid-free paper.

Acknowledgements

I would like to thank my two families just for being here;

My sister, Corlyss, for her reading and encouragement;

William, my husband, for his knowledge and generosity;

Margaret;

Scott, Beth, Sally, Stephy, Shannon;

Nancy and Helen;

The support of Libby Leverett-Crew, Author of

Saturday Nights With Daddy At The Opry;

Ann, My First Friend;

Anna and Rebecca

Dear Robin;

Other wonderful friends for their interest,

My grandson, Aaron, for his urging me onward;

Christopher, Cory, Abby, Madeleine, Alexander,

and my friend, Joanne Johnson, for her valued help and research;

and especially Mother and Daddy, who are not here now but I have felt their nudging;

and the characters in this book in their beginnings and in their endings.

LIST OF CHARACTERS

Jessica Hastings

Daniel Cummings

Martha Horace

Debbie Hastings

Becca and Jon Robertson

George Shadowens

Maria Cadez

Dr. Jerold

CHAPTER ONE

I've come this far, I can't just leave.

This is so crazy but why do I keep hearing the sound of his voice? My mind won't quiet down and my hands are like wet crepe paper!

Wonder what he looks like?

This can't be me sitting here waiting, waiting to see a man I don't even know at all, except from a phone conversation. Jessica sat on a waiting bench in the front of the restaurant, letting her thoughts go in and out like any silly schoolgirl. *My guilt is hanging from me like moss on a tree! It probably shows on my face. Is anybody looking?* Her thoughts traveled back to the ad she had put in the personals. She wasn't courageous enough to do it by herself, but what fun Martha and she had had doing it. But now she chose to meet her recklessness head-on. Thinking back, she certainly knew why she did it; now she would try to be casual and not show her nervousness and anticipation. She felt a little like she had when she was a teenager in school and had to give a speech. Her palms were sweaty. The man who was supposed to meet her here had been the only one who sounded promising, and he held his cards. The others had sounded goony. But this one's voice kept ringing in her ears. What if he failed to show? She knew, though, she would look to him as the ad had read: "Cultured, attractive SWF, happy with all life has to offer," her ad began.

Not exactly true, for life had dealt her a blow that overshadowed her either its physical presence or in her thoughts, but now with that truth completely aside, the man, whose voice compelled her, would walk through the door at any minute. She sat there, hands in lap, contemplating how he might look, that is, if he showed up. He had sounded handsome on the phone and he told her how he looked, but she had been wrong about that disastrously one time. Voices don't always speak for a person.

She reflected on her conversation with Martha last evening. Martha, her jovial self, had said they were beating down *her* door. Then she acted serious and said she would have to lose ten pounds, have a facial, and buy a new outfit before she could see the pastor who had called. Then Jessica knew she was kidding, but she did wish her good friend could find a significant *other*.

Jessica and Martha had been friends since grade school. Jessica remembered that first time she had seen Martha, a new girl at school, she liked her immediately. They continued on through their teenage years and went to the same nursing school. Although Martha never married, she was always there for Jessica. Jessica's two daughters, Debbie and Becca, were very close to Martha and confided in her when Jessica, after a long marriage, divorced.

When Jessica became ill, Martha was the first to suspect multiple sclerosis. The two friends seemed to become even closer after Jessica's husband left her.

The idea that these two professional women would put an ad in the personals seemed hilarious, but—

Red shirt ... gray pants ... there he is! Her heart gave a little lunge. Although not exactly suave or debonair, he was the best-looking guy she had ever seen! She could feel the chemistry in the air before she even said hello.

Daniel looked around and saw her waiting on the bench at the front of the restaurant. He took her hand hesitantly and said, “Are YOU Jessica?”

The electricity went through her. Could he hear her heart pounding?

“Hello, Daniel. It’s really nice to meet you, in person. There are tables in the back where we can talk.”

Jessica tried to sound calm, but her mind raced forward and backward seemingly simultaneously. She had hoped to meet “Mr. Right” in the church she attended, but she guessed they assumed she was already taken; either that or they knew she had a health problem. She knew she was somewhat opinionated as well, and that might have pushed some away. Perhaps it was a combination of problems. But now she had done the unthinkable, which at the moment seemed very thinkable, very thinkable indeed. She would have to handle this carefully. She wanted him to like her. This time, her brain was almost numb and she felt speechless.

“You sounded very nice on the phone, Daniel; now I see you look as good as you sound,” she said.

Help! What a dumb thing to say.... He is going to think I’m desperate.

He elbowed her to a booth in the back and they sat down. He wondered why in the world this babe would put an ad in the paper. Maybe she had a problem, was a problem, or was on the rebound. He hoped he would not come across as too eager. *Wow! She is beautiful!*

His wife had died two years ago, *maybe more,* he thought. How long it really had been blurred in his mind since he'd been dumped out in this city completely confused. His kids had stopped caring about him he felt sure, so he needed someone, someone to fill the void.

Bonny had been always there; even though she had some flaws, they had stayed together through years of marriage and then her illness. He blamed her for not going to the doctor sooner. It certainly was not his fault. It was not his job to search for lumps. She didn't tell him. When he noticed her breast, it was already misshapen. He recalled the endless treatments, the wheelchair, frail bones that would break from any small pressure. Sometimes, he couldn't help but yell at her; she whined and complained so much. He never hit her, though; he felt proud of that. But he did mostly participate in her care. Someone had to, and during that time, they became strangely closer. Once in a while her sister would come to take some of the pressure off, but the kids were conspicuously absent. Bonny had not done a very good job with them or they would have turned out better. He'd been through too much. So much of it he didn't understand. Oh, he understood the fact that his wife didn't choose to tell him about her illness until it was too late, and the flashbacks from the war and that unspeakable horror with his boy it was too much. *Oh, Joey, if I only knew what really happened!* After that time in that awful place they called a hospital, he tried to get lost in the crowd after he landed here; here in the Queen City. Even the kids didn't know where he was, as if they would care. He had told Jessica on the phone he was financially secure. Well, he did get his Social Security check every month and had what was left of his savings. If Bonny hadn't gotten sick, he would still have a sizeable amount. Hell! The SS was more than it would have been, since they declared him unstable. He told them he was NOT unstable, but they didn't listen … when … he couldn't pull himself together.… He recalled the butterfly the day of her funeral. It kept hovering around him, then flying almost into his face. *Could it be? No, that was too weird.*

She ordered hot tea, he iced; they both wanted french fries, then came the small talk. Jessica became more intent; she wanted him to know he was making a good impression. He seemed to hang on her words as if they came from a goddess. She asked him about his family and told him about hers. He seemed somewhat hesitant; perhaps he didn't want her to know his family might get in the way of a possible relationship. That was all right. She told him she still worked the same place she had worked for twenty years. He said he was a writer. That would give him a lot of free time. He told her he was a romantic sort—he liked to send flowers and little notes. He asked her where she worked. She replied, "Christ, Christ Hospital. I'm a nurse."

"Oh, I think I know where that is—a pretty classy hospital, like you, Jessica!" flattered Daniel.

"I certainly like my chosen profession and usually look forward to what each day might bring. I guess in many ways I am more fortunate than a lot of other people," said Jessica, ignoring his compliment, not knowing exactly how to respond to it.

They ended their first meeting surprisingly by quoting poetry and then by quoting the soliloquy from Shakespeare's *Macbeth.* She was impressed that he knew it, since his English wasn't without fault. As they left the restaurant, he took her hand and walked her to her car. Jessica could not help but tremble a little. Daniel seemed too good to be true. A writer? A poet? Her kind of guy!

"Can I call you tonight?" he said.

She didn't want him to know what an effort it had been for her. She hadn't been getting enough rest with the anxiety about meeting him. She really didn't like to talk endlessly on the phone. She wondered why, if he liked her, he didn't just ask her for a date.

"Why not call me tomorrow or the next day?" she said.

He seemed very eager. She was, too, but felt she needed to pace herself. *Well, I will just have to wait and see if he calls.* Surely he liked her, but she was a little puzzled with his behavior. *He is a dream of a man, though; he has to call.* She imagined what he would look like in shorts with that physique.

Monday came—no call. Maybe she had angered him by making him wait. Maybe he wouldn't call. Her dream was to find a quality person who would love her before her illness became evident. She thought about him continuously like a long-playing record. She hadn't handled him right at all. If she had, she thought, *he would have called by this night.*

I know in my heart I am not being fair, but I don't really know the man. It just seemed we had so much in common, the poetry and all, and he said he is a writer. I wonder what he writes. Will I ever get to find out?

Tuesday evening, the phone rang. *Let it ring a little, be busy.* Then, "Oh, it's nice to hear from you, Daniel."

Be nonchalant and causal, she thought. It turned out to be a too-long but good conversation. He kept calling her "sweetheart." That bothered her a little. She wasn't anybody's sweetheart yet. They talked for about an hour, and still he didn't make a date. Finally, she mentioned that it was her birthday Friday. Then, he said, "Hey, let's go out on your birthday!" as if it was his original idea alone.

She dressed carefully Friday evening in anticipation. She tried on many pairs of shoes to see which ones looked decent with her blue dress. It was becoming more and more difficult to find the right shoes, yet still walk like there was nothing wrong. She had cleaned her fake solitaire diamond necklace and earrings (so small they looked real) with that new stuff she purchased at the mall until they sparkled. She laid them carefully aside as if they were real, until she put the finishing touches on her makeup. Then after putting on her "diamonds," she said aloud, "Yes, I guess you will do in a pinch." Jessica knew she looked young for her age, and heredity had been good to her. She sometimes complimented the pretty, curly haired girl that looked back at her from the mirror. It made her forget her problems.

Daniel drove to her place from his austere apartment in the country. Why had he ever rented that place? The one in the city was much nicer, but he just couldn't afford the rent indefinitely. Maybe this lady would have a nice house and if things worked out.... Well, she certainly was good-looking; beautiful, in fact. He pictured her perfect little nose, wonderful eyes.... *Maybe I should get her roses for her birthday.* He stopped at Kroger and purchased a dozen. That ought to impress her. He stopped out front of her pretty place that was also handily across the river. *Not bad, not a bad place at all; in fact, it's darn good!*

She heard the knocker, made sure it was him, and let him in. These days one couldn't be too careful. Debbie and Becca, her daughters, warned her repeatedly about opening the door even if she were expecting someone. She wasn't strong enough to fight off a possible intruder. "Hi! Oh, how beautiful! I love roses—they say so much!" She closed the door and he hugged her. Now she knew he really liked her. She found a vase for the flowers and then hugged him back. She guessed she had wanted to do that since she first saw him. They arranged the roses together until they looked lovely on the dining table. She put her cheek against his. She hadn't expected this miracle. Daniel was the type of man she had longed for, had dreamed about, even had made a list of the qualities she would expect in someone she could love.

"Where are we going?" she murmured softly as she put her hand on his cheek while thinking at the same time, *Don't be so forward!*

Daniel said, "I think it would be nice to drive across to the city, and how about going to Eden? It's early; why not make an evening of it? We can take a walk through the park and then go to one of the restaurants. It will be beautiful since the moon will be full tonight; do you think that's a good idea? I don't know about you yet, but I really enjoy watching the barges. I like to pretend they might be the riverboats of old and I'm the captain of one and writing about my adventures; you know, sort of a Mark Twain!"

"That sounds fine and I've always liked to imagine, too. I think I've been an imaginer ever since I was a little girl and would play alone in my mother's violet patch," said Jessica as she helped Daniel move over several pieces of stuff just to allow her to get in on the passenger's side. Well, not everyone kept their cars like she did, she mused. There was a faint smell of apples; could it be he threw a core or so in the back seat? Oh well….

She felt so content just riding beside him on the way to Eden Park. When they arrived and parked, he opened the door for her, then bent down and picked up a couple buckeyes, looked at them, and put them in his pocket. "You know," he said, "I've never seen two of these alike."

"Funny, but I guess I never noticed, they are so plentiful," she replied wonderingly. *Is he from here?*

The full moon's dim reflection at dusk on the river played havoc with her thoughts. There was no lull in their conversation. It was if they had known each other through time. Hand in hand they walked through the lovely park, taking in the red oaks, white oaks, buckeyes, and ancient maple trees. Jessica so wished she had continued with her art lessons of long ago; the park was, indeed, a picture in the darkening sky.

Suddenly, two yearlings crossed their path, surprising them both. After Jessica found her voice she said, "Oh Daniel, weren't they wonderful?"

He said, "And how could anyone kill anything like that? Some do it just for the fun of it, a sport, although I guess some people like venison!" Daniel seemed angry.

"They who do it say they must keep down the population, but they are protected here in the park, as is all wildlife. The babies are so sweet; I wonder where the mother is?" Jessica queried.

Ignoring Jessica's comment, Daniel proclaimed, "I would NEVER kill anything!"

Grasping hands, they shortened their walk, for the dark river could look ominous, and Daniel said, "I don't know about you, but I'm ravenous; let's find a restaurant and eat!"

Cruising in the car they found a restaurant that Jessica had heard good things about, parked, crossed the small bridge, and luckily found a booth where they had a wonderful view. Jessica realized Daniel had, as did she, an artist's eye.

He is such a sweet person, she thought—*can I be this lucky?* The service may have been good, but her appetite seemed to have left her. Daniel kept looking at her and picking at his food. Finally, he said, "Are you enjoying your dinner?"

"Yes, of course, it's very good, I think." She wiped her hands and reached for his hand.

"Well, it's good, but I can only look at the beautiful lady sitting across from me." They continued holding hands and looking at each other searchingly. Finally, he said, "Let's go." He left a less than ample tip.

On the way back he put in a tape. It sounded like country, but the person singing had a very good voice.

"Who's that?" she asked.

Daniel said, "Me." He looked sideways a little and grinned.

"You? That's wonderful—your voice itself is kind of mellow, and that carries over into music." Country was not her favorite music, but to know that he was singing it made it suddenly super.

"Do you like the lyrics I wrote?" Daniel was doing his best to sound modest.

"You did? Oh, Daniel, you write music? The words are like something you may have experienced!" She asked him to sing along with the music. He did and Jessica felt so much for him at that moment, so "in love"! One of the songs was called "Roses in the Moonlight."

"I've written stories, too," said Daniel. "I will show them to you sometimes if you would like."

"Oh, yes," said Jessica, "I would love to read whatever you have written. You are really talented, Daniel!"

Inside the house, they hugged and kissed—so many times that she did not want it to end. When he left, she knew he had to be the one for her. He was so cozy, so very warm as he held her close … and somehow familiar. How could that be?

CHAPTER TWO

While he drove home, he was thinking.... *Maybe, if I play my cards right she will be putty in my hands. Let's see, the money I receive, and her job—all I will have to do is stay home and write, if I feel like it, and make phone calls ... AND she is VERY pretty. There seemed to be a lot of passion there, but she could have been playing games. Women are like that.* His mind undressed her. She was well preserved for her age. *But wait a minute, she might eventually have her eyes on my savings (what's left of it)*, he thought disparagingly. *Women basically are all alike. They all want anything they can get. BUT she did seem like a nice person—I wonder if she would have an AIDS test.* He was so scared of AIDS. How could he broach the subject? It might insult her. *She did look more than okay, but I can't be too careful. Well, it's well into the next century and AIDS is a fact of life. She did appear to be open to everything I said. A good trait in a woman. I'm certainly attracted, that's a sure thing. I won't have a relationship with anyone without that test.* He would just tell her as a matter of fact, and while he was at it discuss his feelings about sex in general and one thing in particular. *Might as well set her straight*. He thought of all the women through the years ... but Jessica had admitted to another boyfriend before him—what if he had AIDS? No, she wouldn't have had relations with someone like that.... *I wonder what he was like.... No, you can't really trust anybody.*

Jessica, meanwhile, couldn't seem to stop smiling as she thought of him. The way he sang, and he was so romantic. He had just the most wonderful voice! She undressed slowly, taking off her hose and rubbing her legs. If they and the other things would just magically be all right.... She could remember how it used to be, how her legs used to feel, really feel, if she could just go to sleep and wake up all right. She could run the track for two miles without getting tired. But that was then, this was NOW. Her doctor had prepared her, saying that sometimes it gets worse. She knew that as a nurse and she had seen really terrible cases. Sometimes, though, it might level off and stay in remission for years. She apparently had the relapsing-remitting type of the disease. So far when it became worse, it had been of the mild variety but a wake-up call, nonetheless. She knew what the medical books said. If she could just think herself well, for now she had a dual reason to be all right. For herself and for HIM. He had the most arresting blue eyes. Even though he said he was from Illinois, she detected a Southern accent. Maybe it was his years in country music. She put on her pajamas, slid into bed, then hugged herself. How would it feel with his arms around her? With that thought, she drifted off to sleep. For some reason, she slept fitfully, and when she did sleep soundly she had the oddest dreams. In one dream she was running from him and her legs were all right.

He called again the next day at her work and they talked too long. He made a date for the following night. His plan was to mention his fear of AIDS. Even though she had said she had only one other person in her life since her divorce, could he believe her? No.

He thought of his long string of women. Bonny had not understood his need for variety. Men just evolved differently than women. He remembered the scene when he found out or thought she had been unfaithful. He pushed her to the floor and tore off her wedding ring.

She cried and said she loved only him and had just done it to get back at him. The man, she said, meant nothing to her, but he made her suffer for it. His face was a grimace of satisfaction. Yes, she loved me. She got down on her knees and told me how she loved me. Had she really had an affair? He doubted it. She only said so because she felt that might be what he wanted to hear. *Oh Bonny, what a relationship we had!*

Jessica dusted and vacuumed the house with a new fervor. She was through by 1:00 and had the rest of the afternoon to casually get ready for her date. The roses had opened up a bit more and were still pretty. She thought about his song about roses that he sang so beautifully to her. She pulled some candlesticks from the upper shelf of the closet and put those on either side of the roses. She had to go out to get candles. After they were put in the holders she thought of what he might say if she had the candles lighted when he arrived. She was being too obvious. This is not like me—why am I being so forward? How could she like him so very much already? When he got there, she would have Brahms's Second Piano Concerto playing softly. Well, he wrote country, but it wouldn't hurt to let him know the music she liked—or rather also liked. Somehow country music had taken on a new role in her life, a new appreciation.

She put on a short skirt and silk blouse. She could walk pretty well in these sandals and they looked good with the short skirt. After rubbing her legs with her favorite fragrance, she put on very sheer, thigh-high hose. She looked in the full-length mirror and the image looking back reminded her a little of a younger Elizabeth T. Not bad for a forty-eight-year-old! *Oh, stop it, Jessica—vanity does not serve one well—not a good trait.*

Daniel thought maybe they could just skip dinner, save his money, and talk. Even if she were willing—he would go no further. He remembered the doctor who had said AIDS was in the air around an infected person. It might be in the water for all he knew. They are not telling everything they know about AIDS he was certain.

Jessica greeted him at the door. The apartment was aglow with candlelight.

She said, "It's in honor of your song." He laughed and held her close.

He said, "Do you mind if we just sit down for a while and go out to dinner later?" She eased him to the couch and they held each other.

He said, "Hugging and holding close is better than anything."

Jessica held on to him so tight, as if she were afraid to let go. Much later, and bluntly, he said, "I am so afraid of AIDS. If I get a test, will you get one too?"

She said, "There is nothing wrong with me—I don't have AIDS—I couldn't have!" She did want to say about checking in with the doctor regularly. "We are not in the age group where it is prevalent, and aren't we skipping ahead pretty quickly?" They had given her every medical test imaginable and they certainly would not have omitted that one.

He was adamant. "Well, I won't go any further unless I know for sure and I know what we both want. You do want us to make love, sweetie, don't you?"

"We don't have to hurry anything." She pulled away from him and pushed herself to the end of the couch, feeling dismal and shocked. She felt the color reddening her face. After a period of shocked silence she said, "Well, if you feel that way, I must request the same from you. Oftentimes, they that insist on such things have something to hide. How can I be sure of you? This works both ways, and frankly I am shocked you would insult me like this; and furthermore, you are making an assumption!"

"Oh, sure, sure," he promised, "that goes without saying, and I didn't mean to hurt your feelings. It's just we can't be too careful, you know. Perhaps I am a clumsy ox—it's just that some doctor told me to be very, very careful about such things as that!"

"Just how many relationships have you had anyway? I'm the one that should worry about you!" Jessica said icily.

"Please, I guess I better go. I'll call you later sometime when I'm feeling like it," Daniel turned to leave.

Jessica took his arm and said, "Our first disagreement—I hope it will be our last."

"Probably," said Daniel, and left.

This unexpected discussion quickly ruined the evening for Jessica. Any ideas of romance flew out the window. *How could he?* She blew out the candles and switched on the lights. She was so pulled by his mere presence she would do almost anything to please him. He had such charisma, and the chemistry between them drew her to him with an almost irresistible force.

And I certainly don't know what to think about him. It's as if my prince charming has gone up in smoke. Of course, I believe I came on too strong, but I couldn't seem to help myself; it was just so there, so within me, and I don't believe his behavior tonight indicated any stop signs. But I don't like it; I don't like it at all!

Although very embarrassed about his unexpected request, the next day, she made an appointment with her PCP for an HIV test. Since she worked at the hospital there was no trouble getting in right away. The nurse said to call for the results and they would send her the written results in the mail. She wondered if her word would be good enough for Daniel. But, of course, he was right. If they had carefully planned to have a relationship, they had the right to ask about each other's health. But this was too much too soon. *Maybe I am being super-sensitive because I know I have something to hide about my health!*

Daniel called her at work and said he had to go out of town for a couple days and when he got back would have his test. Jessica said she had hers. What was he thinking about her?

Daniel, meanwhile, had no intention of getting a test. Why should he spend the money? He just wanted to give her time to get one. He called her on Tuesday saying he was back and everything was okay as far as he was concerned. She told him the results of her test. Then he said, "Now aren't you glad we both know we are in good health?" Jessica said that she already knew she was and she had hoped that he would have realized it.

"Now, honey, you know that it is a good thing that we did this, don't you? We should be careful and I certainly don't want to use any protection; that would take away from the joy and the love I feel for you all ready." Daniel's voice made her love him, although he seemed not to trust her with his unexpected request. Perhaps it was best that they had the tests. She, however, had not been concerned about him—after all he had been married all those years.

They made a date for the following Friday. Jessica felt that when they did eventually make love to each other, it would be a most natural thing. There was something so familiar about him—she couldn't explain the uncanny feeling. Except for the embarrassment of his demand, she felt that everything from here on out would be a growing relationship. She guessed he had a right to be somewhat paranoid since he didn't know the statistics of people in their age group. It just thoroughly surprised her—that's all. Couldn't he just look at her and know she would have no such thing? She guessed she couldn't expect him to be as intuitive as she. Most men just weren't intuitive. After all, they really knew only what they had told each other.

CHAPTER THREE

The next morning, Jessica awakened feeling dizzy. Something was wrong, very wrong. After making it to the bathroom, she splashed cold water on her face. The feeling didn't leave. Then, glancing at herself in the mirror, she noticed her vision was not right. Disturbed, she splashed more water and more water, rubbed her eyes, and looked again. There were little shadows around both eyes. Nothing was clear. *Oh God, please*, she nearly sobbed. Then, though, she noticed that if she looked straight into the mirror, she could see all right. It was her peripheral vision that was bothered, that was somehow not right. *Oh please God, not now! Not when things are going pretty much the way I envisioned they would. Daniel wouldn't want me if he knew I have something wrong with me. Not at this point, at least.* Jessica thought about her life so far and realized she really wasn't in control of what happened to her. She prayed. "Let me be all right—let this cruel horror go back whence it came!"

Work, always work, no matter how she felt. She took her shower, dressed quickly, then had the new job of putting on her makeup with frayed peripheral vision. Luckily, she did not need much help in that department, but thank goodness for magnifying mirrors. Out the door and into her car like any normal morning of any normal day. *I'm just Jessica Hastings the nurse, looking straight ahead, very straight ahead!* The car had made this trip so many times it seemed to take her there automatically. She turned down the side street and eased her car into the parking garage. *See, that wasn't so hard.* After she got to her work station she phoned her doctor and explained the situation. His explanation eased her somewhat; he said that the disturbed vision may go away as quickly as it started, MS is like that, and when it does remit, it may stay away for a long time. Jessica told herself to think positively as she had many times.

Daniel had told Jessica they would go to that German restaurant across town. But that meant dressing up a little. At least wearing a jacket. He didn't feel like dressing up. He was most comfortable in his favorite jeans. Might as well get her used to his favorite way of dressing. Oh well, he would wear his jeans, a white shirt, and a jacket. They would let him in if he had the jacket. His shirt didn't look too white. He really needed a woman to take care of laundry and the cleaning. He wouldn't live in a dirty house. If they lived together, she would do that; and since he had hardly any furniture, they would live at her place. After he pieced himself together he bought the computer and one easy chair and, of course, his bed. It wasn't very good stuff anyway and he couldn't stand to look at it. He burned up his guitar in a moment of anger; he couldn't quite recall what made him do it. What a wonderful guitar it had been. Jessica will wonder about that, probably. It would cost a bundle to replace it, but he had been upset. There were so many bad things, some remembered, some not: the flashbacks from the war, the stupid psychiatrist who attempted to treat him as if he had bipolar disorder, and then the doctor told Bonny he had a borderline personality disorder. Probably made it up—what a crock! Then the cancer, Joey's death, the hospital.... After he got dumped here by some creep from that place, it was a long time before he realized who he was—Daniel, Daniel Cummings.

Jessica would be gentle with him so he wouldn't have those spells. Maybe. Actually they hadn't known each other very long. He hoped she was the good woman she appeared to be. He was nervous about it. He decided to go get a quart of beer to calm himself.

When Jessica met him at the door, she thought she detected the smell of beer. He had said he didn't drink. She recalled his words on their first meeting—"It's unusual to find someone who doesn't drink or smoke these days." Well, maybe if he had had some beer, he wouldn't notice her slight dizziness. She had been practicing all day, turning her head and looking out of just her front vision field. He couldn't notice anything as long as she didn't say anything about it. She kissed him, which reinforced her thinking, "Yes, definitely beer." But she wasn't going to mention it. She suggested they wait a while before driving to the restaurant. Even without beer, she felt his driving deplorable.

They held hands on the couch; then she hugged him. He put his head down on her breast and she noticed a little tear making its way down his cheek.

"It's okay," she murmured. "I know you lost someone you loved very much. We don't have to hurry into anything."

He broke into sobs. "I've been through everything bad that you can imagine and it wasn't my fault." She didn't know quite what he meant. People die, life goes on. He wasn't the only one who had had a loss. She thought of some of her own losses—her divorce. A divorce is sometimes worse than a death. It happens. He cried and cried and couldn't seem to tell her what was going on in his head. She just held him close and tried to comfort him. Was he afraid of a new relationship? He finally pulled himself together a little. She got a damp cloth and wiped his face.

"Now," she said, "you'll feel better in a little while; there isn't anything you can't tell me." She had never seen a man cry so hysterically, so out of control.

Daniel told her that his wife had been sick for so long that it took a toll on him. He told about the last weeks when her bones broke at the slightest provocation. He would try to catch her before she fell, but oftentimes didn't make it. It was too late to set the bones—she just became bedridden. He declared that he could never go though that again with anyone. Jessica felt a lump begin to form in her throat. She knew she couldn't tell him about herself, and at this time she must focus only on him. She just had to pretend, and maybe if she pretended enough this disease would go in remission completely again. She thought, *I didn't do anything to deserve this illness. I just won't have it! I know I already love Daniel. He was so sweet when he cried.* Whatever demons were attacking him, she knew she would be there to help him.

He then told her a wild story about some crooked cops in Illinois who had doped him, put him in a compromising position, and filmed him while he was under the influence of drugs. He said they had done it so he would not file charges against them. He said it was so awful that he had buried it in his psyche, but he was now remembering a little. She only understood about half of it because he was still very upset and spitting out the words between sniffles. She wished he would gather himself together and be himself. Charming, unassuming, loving—he could be that. *Please come back, Daniel.* Finally, after about another bout of crying, he pulled himself together again.

He said, "Please just hold me and let me lay my head in your lap." She suggested they go in the other room and just lie together on the bed in the spare room and hold each other. They lay there until he suddenly snapped out of his morose mood and raised himself up on his elbow.

"Let me look at you," he said. "I didn't realize until this moment, this magic moment, you are so beautiful—there's nothing wrong at all with you, with your precious face. You, Jessica, are perfect! Your brown eyes seem to glow in their intensity. Let me see if your mouth kisses like it did before. Maybe like that first night I kissed you—mmmm—I believe it does." Daniel bent back her head and traced her face like a blind person would over and over again. "Your face is unbelievably soft, and not a mark on it." He then smoothed back her dark, curly hair and kissed her ears and said, "How do these ears hear, my dear? Let's see if you are as perfect the rest of the way, but I think I know the answer."

Jessica thought they might be going too far too fast, but she was speechless to stop him; it had been so long that she had felt the strength of a man against her. She couldn't say a word.

Daniel took off his shirt, then began unwrapping Jessica as one would slowly anticipate a candy bar.

"Oh Jess, you are unbelievable—but I don't want you to get chilled—let's put this blanket over you." Daniel finished undressing and crawled in beside her. He kissed her—then it seemed he couldn't get close enough. Their lovemaking became intense yet sweet. Almost remembered, it seemed to Jessica. They separated except for holding hands. They wordlessly cuddled each other. She basked in the wonder of it. He held her for a long time and she felt so content with his arms about her. Her whole body felt as if she were still attached to him, as if the feeling would last and last.

Suddenly out of the blue he said, "Your bed isn't very comfortable."

She asked, "It isn't? What is wrong with it?"

"It doesn't quite fit my back right," Daniel surprisingly replied. She had only had the mattress for a couple of years and had turned it faithfully, and why were they talking about her mattress?

"Well," she said, "if we decide to stay together, I guess we could go shopping for a mattress together."

Then he said in his mellowest tone, "Aren't you making an assumption?" But then he laughed, so she knew he was all right with at least the thought of it.

He put his head on her shoulder and seemed to sleep a little, but after a while he sighed and said, "I'm hungry. Why haven't we gone out to eat?" and laughed again.

She said, "Well, I guess we could now, but I'll have to fix up a little."

Then he said, "Woman, I like fried potatoes, why don't you just fix me some fried 'tatoes?" chuckling again, so she assumed he couldn't be serious.

"Daniel, we just made love. I just want to lie here a little longer," she sighed. "I'm zapped."

He put his arms around her again and said, "Of course, we can order out. I don't feel like going out now, but do you have some potatoes? I'll help you peel them."

She felt very tired, still aglow and filled with her love for Daniel, but puzzled with his seeming disinterest now. "Daniel, did our making love mean anything to you?"

He said, "Of course, sweetheart, it was great fun!" There was no indication of the teary tizzy he had had earlier, and his response saddened her somewhat.

She put on her prettiest robe and went to the kitchen. There were enough potatoes for one and a little more. She began peeling them. The peeling of the potatoes didn't match with the robe! Daniel said he would go get some Cokes and bologna. When he left, she thought, *Bologna, ugh!* Kind of a far cry from the German restaurant, but they were together—*that is all that matters.*

Jessica didn't have much of an appetite. She was very, very tired, but so much in love she tingled. Daniel ate all the potatoes anyway and she didn't want the bologna.

He said, "Boy, you cook a mean potato! How 'bout some more?" Daniel had not noticed that his beautiful lady had not eaten.

"Sorry, honey, those were the only potatoes I had in the house. That's it, kaput."

"Well, that's a fine how-do-you-do; I'm still hungry. Don't you know you should keep more potatoes in the house than that?" Daniel looked angry.

Then she could feel a few tears welling up and turned away, not wanting him to see them. "Sorry, next time I shop," she said in a small, barely audible voice.

Daniel abruptly got up, patted his stomach, and said, "That was good; better if there'd been enough—fried potatoes are my favorite!" It was around 9:30 and she hoped he would lie down with her again just to cuddle and to close her eyes. Her eyes had been under a strain all day. "Can we cuddle up on the couch for a while?"

He replied bluntly, "What do you think I am?" Jessica walked over to the couch and put her head in her hands. He could at least be kind. All she wanted was the affection to last a little longer. That was all she wanted in the first place. "Baby, I'm not a kid anymore."

Jessica really felt foolish—it had been so long for her, she had forgotten. "Daniel, I think I love you, already—I'm sorry you thought that. I just wanted to be hugged."

He thought, *There she goes, trying to put me on the spot.* He said, "Yeah, I guess I will leave—I have things to do."

He left with only a peck on her cheek. Jessica couldn't figure him out. Maybe he wouldn't ever call again. Maybe he got what he wanted and that would be the end of it. She lay on the couch and dabbed away the tears. Later, she realized that her vision was a little better, just not normal yet. A lot of the blurriness was caused by the tears that persisted to creep to the forefront of her eyes.

CHAPTER FOUR

The next morning the bed held her fast. She didn't want to face the day. She just wanted to lie there with her eyes closed. It seemed to take forever for her to calm herself from the previous evening. It had been so bizarre, then it had been so wonderful. Then, why had he changed so abruptly? Thank goodness she didn't have to go to work. What could she tell them about her vision? Maybe it would be better even than last night. She was afraid to open her eyes, then get up and look in the mirror. "Oh Daniel." Did he think ill of her because of making love? They hadn't known each other very long. What a mistake, but it did take two. She had been the one to suggest that they lie on the bed, though. And what was all that about the crooked cops in Illinois? What she could make out didn't make good sense. It also didn't make good sense that she could love him so soon. What did she know about him, really, except that he didn't have AIDS? She guessed maybe he wanted her to have a test so he could go to bed with her, no strings attached. But then his tearful attack showed a different man entirely. He needed her! She wanted someone to need her.

After she finally got to sleep in the night, she had slept like a dead person. But there had been another strange dream. A nightmare, really. It seemed she was living in a log cabin in another time, another place. She was tending her baby—a little boy. How she loved him—in the dream she was nearly overcome with the love she felt for her child. He seemed to be about a year old.... She gently laid him in his wooden crib, then lay down herself for a little nap. Her eyes were about to close when she heard a rustling in the cabin. Grasping her baby was another woman dressed in a long gray dress. She saw Jessica and ran out of the cabin—the baby under her arm. "Stop, you wicked old woman, stop!" yelled Jessica, until she woke herself up. The dream was so real that upon awakening, she still felt the fear, the awful fear. She shuddered.

Oh well, a new day. Maybe, just maybe, things were better. She didn't feel as dizzy, and upon looking in the mirror she thought her vision was a little better. She looked to the right and to the left: blurry, but certainly not as bad. She knew this particular illness could wax and wane. "Thank you, God!" She felt she shouldn't call Daniel because of the way he left last evening. *Give him a chance to think things over.* "I know I love him." She had told him, so he knew it. How did he feel? Maybe confused. And he might be embarrassed about the way he acted before they made love, although he had seemed to not give it a second thought. But maybe he thought she was too easy a mark. That was not it at all. She felt so much love for him, it emanated from her being. Then she knew she "overthought."

The phone remained silent the whole blessed day. Well, he hadn't said he loved her so why should she expect him to call? In fact, afterwards, he acted like it hadn't even happened. Making love had made her feel closer and closer to him. On Daniel, it seemed to have the opposite effect; it just made him hungry for fried potatoes! *Please, please call.* Well, she was not going to call him.

The evening dragged on ... but she knew if she called Martha she'd get a lecture and she probably would not be able to hold back the tears.

She thought back about how she and Martha had laughed about putting in that ad and considered it great fun! Well, this certainly was no laughing matter!

Monday came, the beginning of the work week. Her vision was definitely better, so she would not have to tell them anything. She disliked Mondays, but as usual, the day went quickly. Even so, Daniel didn't call. She was so busy she wouldn't have had time to talk anyway. She couldn't, however, seem to get him off her mind. He was always in there, churning around in the cockles of her heart, and she found it difficult to work with her patients. She thought continually about his crying jag and if she could help him. She knew it was not normal the way he switched gears and came completely out of it as if it had not happened. The word "mania" came to her mind. "Manic-depressive" maybe. As a nurse she was familiar with such things, but certainly was not an expert. It was not her field. *Stop it, Jessica! I love him—hopelessly!*

She couldn't appear to be preoccupied. Her job developed as important in many ways. It had proved to be a well-chosen profession, and now it took her mind off her illness. The doctors at her work knew about it, but as long as she could do the job, it was never mentioned. Her work satisfied her and them; she liked helping patients feel better. Sometimes, though, she became too attached to one or another. Some of the families were very supportive, but then there were ones who seemed disinterested in the patient and were just crankily and begrudgingly present. And then there were the very few that appeared critical of the way she did her job. If that happened, it could cause a particularly bad time for her. She must not let thoughts of Daniel affect her work. She did the best she could by telling her mind to stop thinking about it.

Monday night came and still no call from Daniel. She finally broke down and called Martha. Martha's remarks were as she expected: sympathetic, but she didn't understand how Jessica could fall so hard for a guy she barely knew. Jessica in talking to Martha left out the crying episode of Daniel's, out of loyalty to him, and because she didn't want to hear what Martha might say. They talked for about forty-five minutes and before she knew it, it was time to get ready for the next day. She took a long, hot bubble bath and lit an aromatherapy candle in the hopes it would relax her so she wouldn't have trouble sleeping. In a way, the candle was for Daniel.

When her head hit the pillow, she felt relaxed and sleepy, but before long her mind began to twist over and over. After lying there at length, she finally got up and went to the other room to read for a while. She opened the Bible at random, as was her habit at times when she needed solace. It fell on the story of Ruth and Naomi. "Whither thou goest, I will go, and where thou lodgest, I will lodge: thy people shall be my people, and thy God my God." Could that have meaning for her situation? She finally went back to bed for a night of fitful dreams.

Tuesday at work, Daniel called. "Hi, sweetheart!"

Oh Daniel, she thought. *My sweetheart*. However, she forced herself not too sound overjoyed. "Oh hi, what have you been up to?"

"Oh, things. I was shopping for a guitar. They are so expensive now I may have to go to a pawn shop."

Jessica said, "But what happened to your other guitar?"

Daniel lied, "I gave it to someone who needed it more." Jessica thought, *Well that was sweet—giving away his guitar would be like losing his right arm.*

Jessica remarked, "Honey, if you don't mind, please call me this evening. I am really busy."

"Okay, if I can find the time. I've been busy, too," he said in a somewhat sharp voice.

"I'll be waiting," she said. Why did she always sound so humble and meek? *Well, because I am*, she thought, *at least where he is concerned.*

That evening when it was almost time for her to go to bed, he called. Her heart gave a little leap. She should have been angry, but so what if it was late? Maybe her workday would be light the next day. They talked well into the night, mostly her listening to what he had to say. The gist of it was he was afraid of their getting involved too soon, before he was ready. There was no mention of his teary display of the other night. He didn't even say he sometimes got depressed because his wife died. She thought he would at least mention it. But they did make a date for Friday. Actually, he wanted to check out two more women on the list who had put ads in the paper. Who knows, they might be even better fixed financially. He doubted, though, if they would be as good-looking. One said that she weighed 166, but her height made up for it. He would have to see what setup she had.

Wednesday evening he met this broad. Yep, a good way to describe her. He was so disenchanted he didn't care to call for her at her home later, even though it was a fashionable address. He made a date with her, but planned not to show. That would give her the message loud and clear. Daniel looked at the other numbers he could call. Perhaps they were dead ends, too. Maybe he should just concentrate on Jessica, but leave his options open. She was, it appeared, nice and great under the covers! If he played it right she could be molded like clay. He hoped he would not have any more spells. He had hated it when Bonny made him take that medicine. But he would have to control himself or that could push her away. But she seemed to love him already. If he really had her love, she would put up with anything. One necessity—they must do everything together. Unless, of course, he needed a little variety. Even the best could become routine. Her routine might get tiring for him. It was important for him to be satisfied. Wives, if she did become his wife, should do their husband's biding. He knew a little of the Bible—the parts that would do him some good. Financially, it would be wise to marry. He could live at her place—rather, in that case, their place. She had said her house was paid for. How convenient! He needed to be comfortable—some things would have to go. He needed an easy chair in the kitchen area to make his phone calls. You never knew what you might find thumbing through those yellow pages. He just loved dealing with the world "out there." In case he got into an argument, they couldn't see him. Maybe the recliner he had would work. Those old-fashioned chairs she had about the table hurt his back. Yes, financially he would be much better off, but marriage was a scary thing. Maybe just live together for a while. She may not agree to that, though. She apparently had scruples. Marriage would make her more tied to him anyway. He wondered if she had any life insurance. Bonny hadn't, and then, because of her cancer, couldn't get any. *Great timing, Bonny!* Her illness took too much of a hunk of his savings. He would insist Jessica get some; maybe she had some at work. He thought of Bonny and the cancer. He wouldn't go through that again for anyone. He would just leave. First things first. A joint account. Jessica could manage it. He never had been very good at math—just so he knew what the balance was. She'd be working at least ten more years—that should let them save substantially, and if she didn't shape up like he wanted, he would just split and take the money. But he was getting older, too—if he became ill, she could take care of him. Daniel stopped with his thought rambling long enough to go to the bathroom. He caught sight of himself in the mirror. "Oh, you handsome devil, you!"

Somewhere in the fashionable part of town, a happy person, beautifully dressed, waited by the door … an empty feeling beginning in the pit of her stomach—a void she had not expected.

Jessica's day at work had not gone well. It rained all day—a perfect match to her too-tired state. If Daniel ever called again that late on a work night, she would just have to tell him. She couldn't lose her job! They might suggest she take a medical leave.

How would she explain that? Daniel didn't call that evening—she was almost thankful to get to bed early. But they did have a date for Friday, so there will be no real need for them to call each other. Thankfully, her Friday workday was much better, and she looked so forward to the evening. She wasn't even all that tired. Excitement could sometimes play tricks on a person.

Daniel arrived wearing a turquoise sweater and those too-roomy jeans. She would have to buy him some new jeans. But oh, what that turquoise did for his eyes. She held him a long time. She didn't want to let go. He kissed her and said, "My, you look great!" He was enthusiastic about their going to a nice place. He knew of a night spot with live music. It was mostly bluegrass, but he felt she would enjoy it. *Well, maybe,* she thought. She guessed she would have to learn to like it. Daniel was very charming and he gave her his complete attention. She would have liked to go somewhere to slow dance; she could do that. But one didn't dance to bluegrass. Well, hardly!

When they got home, he talked about their getting married, maybe, someday. She couldn't believe he was mentioning marriage so soon. She knew it was too early to be talking of marriage, AND, after what he had said the other night, certainly too soon to tell him about herself. But his talking of marriage reinforced that the other night had meant something to him, too, and was not just fun! It seemed they were so happy and content with each other, she could not imagine being without him—he was part of her and they would always be together. These thoughts tumbled over and over in her mind along with deciding to make an appointment with her neurologist as soon as possible. Just maybe, there might be a new treatment or breakthrough. Her vision had improved! That was something, but the numbness was spreading. Would it affect in all ways—eventually?

The contentment and fulfillment she experienced with Daniel was short lived. The following morning she awakened with this playing in her head. "God is my refuge and my strength." These scriptures, poems, or verses on awakening had been happening to her for more than twenty years and she was grateful for it. Why that particular verse now? No mystery, really, when she thought about it. Daniel had left in a huff last night. He had wanted to spend the night, but she was afraid of the possibility that something might happen and one of her daughters might need her for something. How would she hide Daniel if something like that were to come up? She would always be a good role model for the children, no matter how old they were—she had to be.

Daniel had said, "Well, I can see what is important in your life, and it's certainly not me. I had hoped you would take up for me against your family. Just who is important here anyway?"

"Honey," she had said in her gentlest tone, "this isn't against you at all—it's the principle. I can't let you stay here all night."

Daniel shouted, "There is a lot of shit going on here!" With that he grabbed up his jacket and left without another word. Jessica was shaken. *Does there have to be a choice here? My family wouldn't interfere with us if we were married, but I would want them as an important part of my life as much as they have always been. Does this have to be so cold-cut? I've never been shouted at or even talked to like that. Why is he doing this? How can he switch from being so loving to being so hateful?* She told herself, *I haven't known him very long. Am I in trouble for loving him?*

When Daniel drove home that night he was half on the highway and half on the shoulder. He was livid with anger. Luckily the hour was late and the traffic minimal. He thought of how selfish and uncaring Jessica had been. Did he want to be with her for the rest of his life? Her family would be a threat. She might want to see them once in a while. Of course, he would go with her, but what if she wanted to visit them alone? He'd put a limit on that to an hour or so. What if they talked about him? No doubt about it, they would, and she might not take up for him. He would just always insist on going with her. When they were married any contact with the family would be limited and the two of them would go for a visit only occasionally, together. He was almost home, but suddenly in the mist of the night he saw a shadow coming toward him. His driving became even more erratic—trying to avoid it. It would almost hit the windshield before it disappeared only to appear once again with a repeat performance. He thought about a poem his granny had repeated to him long ago when he was little. "And the goblins will get you, if you don't watch out!" *Please let me get out of here and home!* Then the shadow seemed to have a misty face on it. His son—Joey. Daniel shouted, "Go away, go away, go away!" He landed in the ditch—blowing out a tire. He was trembling. "Joey, Joey—I didn't do it!" He sobbed, his head falling to his hands.

The police officer found him that way—sobbing. "I didn't do it!"

"Sir, you obviously lost control of your car. Pull yourself together, man. Let's see your driver's license." Daniel immediately snapped out of the spell and presented his license.

The officer said, "How far do you live from here?"

"About a m-mile," replied Daniel.

"Get in. I'll take you. You can get that car towed to your place in the morning." A very collected Daniel rode home with the officer. Later in bed, he thought, "Joey?" No, that stupid cop forced him off the road.

And he told a surprised Jessica that story in the morning when he called her. "Honey, I had some bad luck last night when you made me leave—a stupid cop forced me off the road. Now I have to pay someone to tow my car here; except for the tire, which I can fix, I hope there's nothing else that joker did to it. It was a nice car when I bought it. Damn that guy!"

Jessica had felt so bad for Daniel and guilty that she had made him leave. She felt he wouldn't call for a while, or worse, not at all, to punish her for asking him to leave; so for that, she was relieved. She gave him the number of a tow company she had used in the past.

He snapped, "They won't come way out here! I'll just check the yellow pages 'til I get a reasonable price."

Jessica felt empty. It had nothing to do with her that an officer forced him off the road. She wondered how he had been driving, since he was clearly angry at her when he left. He had called about his trouble, though. Maybe he wasn't overly angry about last night and could be made to see her reasoning. She guessed he had never thought about how she might feel if she let him spend the night. Besides, with her trouble she never knew from one day to the next where it might strike. But that was negative thinking. She knew though that she'd lost weight since she met Daniel. She got on the scales—115, too little for her five-foot-nine, though small, frame. Their lovemaking last night had been great, though, and she loved how it made her feel so close to him—until … his quick mood switch.

Daniel finally found a tow company that would do the job for $25—but it was nearly noon by then. He would talk too long, asking questions, and saying others would do it for less. One company hung up on him, but he called them back and let them know what bastards they were. His car came chained to a tow truck around 1 p.m. The man yelled, "Hey, buddy—was your radio gone?" Daniel looked at him in disbelief and then saw the gapping hole where his radio had been. Daniel cussed him, said he was not his "buddy," and accused him of taking it.

The man said, "Calm it down, man—your car was setting there since midnight. Anybody could have taken it! If I took it—where is it? Search my truck!"

Daniel did precisely that; no radio was found. "You probably had an accomplice." The man shook his head and drove off.

Daniel yelled after him, "Never trust a smelly, lowlife like you!"

CHAPTER FIVE

Jessica awakened early Sunday morning in time to go to church. *This is what I need,* she thought. Church would put her mind on spiritual matters and less on her present troubles with Daniel. Somehow she felt she would need all the spirituality she possessed in order to cope with what seemed to be a roller-coaster ride. Daniel was so unpredictable, but she knew he needed her, and that was what loomed in importance—certainly more than her own well-being. Her appearance, even after she put on her makeup, startled her. As usual, whenever she lost weight it showed up first in her face. She called Martha to see if she was going to church and if she could get a ride. She just needed the comfort of her best friend. Martha picked her up and it was evident her appearance bothered Martha.

"Honey, no man is worth your health! Tell him to get a life, away from you."

Jessica just looked away, but said, "He can be sweet. He is just having a few problems adjusting to having somebody new in his life. He'll be all right, I know he will. If you could see how great-looking he is, there has to be goodness there and I know you would realize why I don't want to give him up."

Martha replied, "Well, you are great-looking, too, and you have your act together. At least…," she hesitated, not knowing what else to say. As a silent afterthought, *Great, that is, when you look well.* Martha, a nurse as well, stayed cognizant of all new findings in the literature about MS.

"I know," said Jessica, "at least I have my act together NOW."

In church they sang, "Be still, my soul, the Lord is on thy side." Jessica had always loved the hymn from Finlandia. "With Every Change He Faithful Will Remain." The words seemed to speak to her. She sang out with conviction. *Another message,* she thought. *I am really getting them lately.*

When she got home there were several messages from Daniel on her answering machine. He seemed so distraught that she wasn't home when he needed her. He had called repeatedly.

Martha gave a deep sigh when she entered her apartment. *Oh, poor Jessica—she has really fallen hard for the wrong guy.* Though deep in thought, she found herself almost automatically doing her usual Sunday afternoon ritual: she popped some corn in the microwave and settled down to read the paper … the headlines, a little of the "living" section, but her mind and heart could not concentrate. Her thoughts kept drifting—drifting to Jessica. Jessica looked awful! She knew enough about MS to realize how stress could affect the course of the disease. In her mind's eye, she saw Jessica in a wheelchair. *If she doesn't get some rest, gain some weight, and get away from that guy—* how her heart went out to her! They should never have put those ads in the paper. What had possessed them? *Now wait a minute, Martha, it was your idea. If Jessie gets worse, it will be my fault. My FAULT!* Jessica wanted to find love just like she did, but look what had happened to her. *This guy oozes poison.* She was glad her own contacts had turned out to be duds. She would

NEVER do such a thing again! Had she come across a Daniel type, looks or not, she would have told him to get lost, or at least she thought she would. She couldn't judge what Jessica was doing, because she wasn't in the situation. She had to say the right thing to Jessica. Her own health was great; well, a little fat maybe, and she had not cared if she found someone before an illness became noticeable. This Daniel was just tearing Jessica down. He must be some guy to get Jessica in such a state. The only way she could help Jessica would be to point out what he had done to her health. She needs a laid-back, non-elusive type, one on whom she can depend. Surely Jessica knows this. Martha wasn't sure how her interference would be met.

Daniel had sounded so upset with his continuous messages that Jessica wasted no time calling him back.

"Where were you?" he demanded.

"I went to church," she said.

"Church? You mean you wasted your time in a place like that? I can't stand the organized church. All those places do is try to get your money," he hastily replied.

"Daniel, I don't see it like that. Church calms me and I have met many wonderful people there and I have many memories; I was brought up in the church," she said.

"Well, I don't like it when I need you and you aren't home. Having you go to work is enough, and I don't particularly like that either. Sometimes I need you—today, I needed you and you weren't home. I want you always to be home for me, sweetheart," he said in his mellow tone.

"Sorry, honey, I know you had troubles with your car," Jessica said sympathetically.

"That's not the half of it; they stole my radio while it was in the ditch. Those smelly bastards did it," he said.

"Daniel, don't talk about people like that. There are good people and bad people in every race! Please, anybody could have done it. You don't know who did it." Jessica wondered about anyone who would say such a thing in this day and age.

Daniel said, "Bye," and hung up.

It was evident that Daniel had problems. Somehow this made Jessica love him even more. He needed her, certainly more than her ex-husband had ever needed her. It didn't take him long to leave when he found out about her MS even though it had just started with the mildest symptoms. If she could just go back to the days before her illness, she might better be able to cope with Daniel's sometimes erratic behavior with a position of strength. His eyes had looked so hateful that night he yelled at her. Those same eyes could look so loving—so blue, so tender, and then sometimes brimming with tears. It had been long enough since his wife had passed away that he surely could control himself better than that. Maybe the tears were caused by some other demons he carried. She realized in their short relationship that there was much she couldn't know and maybe would never know.

Daniel showed up on her doorstep Sunday evening unannounced. She was just ready to wind down for the evening and take her bath. She was dressed in only her robe. "Honey," Daniel said, "how could those bastards steal my radio. It was a good radio, too. The fidelity was great. You just can't trust anyone anymore." He put his head down on her chest and loosened her robe—it fell to the floor. Seeing her naked, he wanted her so much. He ran his hands slowly over her until she twined her legs around his body. He carried her to her room and laid her on the bed and began kissing her all over.

"Honey," Jessica sighed. "Wait a minute—let's get in a bubble bath. It will take just a minute." She put on the water full force, added the bubbles, and slowly undressed him. When the tub was full, they both stepped in, immersing themselves in rose-scented, bubbling water. She kissed him from head to toe. He could hardly stand the intensity of it. He had never made love like this before. When they joined together, it felt so wonderful—before long they were basking in their love for each other. Jessica let out the water and they cradled each other with their slippery bodies before they dried off so that they could lie down on the bed. Daniel immediately went to sleep. Jessica covered him up and spooned herself around him. His heartbeat and his regular, soft breathing made her love him even more—if that were possible.

Jessica, of course, was not sleeping. It was Sunday night—Monday was a workday and here was

Daniel in her bed. So much for not letting him spend the night. She couldn't make him leave after his last bad experience. He was sleeping so peacefully. The girls (Becca and Debbie) had their own lives and it was Sunday night—unlikely anyone would need her. He could just stay here tonight. She gave him an extra hug, got up to make sure the chain was on the door, then took a sleeping pill. She wouldn't be able to sleep with Daniel without one. Jessica wasn't used to sleeping with anybody. She put her arm over his peacefully sleeping body and before long drifted into a blissful sleep.

Sometime in the night, Daniel leaped out of bed, yelling, "Why did you claw me with your fingernails?"

With the sleeping pill in effect, Jessica couldn't quite focus, but did manage to say, "I didn't touch you, except have my arms around you."

"Yes you did!" shouted Daniel, and he proceeded to stalk around the room in his nakedness—yelling, "Why are you lying about it? You did too claw me—you must be weird! And you are pushing me into a relationship I may not be ready for, and I can't sleep in this bed—it's hard on my back!"

"Well, Daniel, if that's what you think, go sleep in the other room!"

Daniel muttered, "You did scratch me deeply—you just won't admit it!" He stalked out to the other room. Jessica, thanks to the sleeping pill, stretched out on the whole of her bed and went back to an untroubled sleep.

Monday morning, Jessica peeked in at the sleeping Daniel. *Maybe he just had a nightmare,* she thought. *I hope! He wouldn't have said all those things, normally, would he?* She closed his door quietly, washed and dressed, and went to the kitchen. The pill had given her a hangover. Except for the lovemaking, last night seemed a confusing blur. She drank two cups of coffee and started to put on her makeup. She felt hands on her shoulders; she trembled, gave a little scream, turned, and looked a disgruntled Daniel in the eye. She hadn't heard anything—he was just suddenly there, behind her.

Why in heaven's name did he sneak up on her? Shaken, she said, "You scared the heck out of me!"

"Now, look," said Daniel in a gruff voice. "Someone else is here—you had better get used to it!" Then he sat down in a kitchen chair with his head in his hands, mumbling, "I had a bad night—you scratched the fool out of me, then I couldn't stand to sleep with you."

"Next time you come downstairs, please, Daniel, make some noise—I didn't know you were anywhere around. As far as last night is concerned, you must have had a nightmare. If I scratched you, show me the marks," Jessica said emphatically. Daniel didn't move. She could tell he was going to pout about it. *I can't bring up his accusatory behavior of last night.* It was getting late and she couldn't be late. She showed Daniel the coffee and poured some grapefruit juice for him. "Cereal is in the pantry." She rushed out, without breakfast, but not before she had kissed him goodbye. He was like a stick in his response.

After two more coffees at work, Jessica was operating in her usual manner. Around noon she received a call from Daniel.

He said, "I'm leaving, Jessica, to think things over. I just think I'll drive out West, and maybe while I'm gone I can find a replacement for my radio. I can't live without playing my tapes. Besides, your house isn't that comfortable for me. We will have to make some changes."

Jessica's disbelief brought quick tears. "When will you be back?" Her voice sounded small, constricted, and weak.

"Oh, I don't know, maybe after Christmas."

"After Christmas?" Her voice shook in denial. "And you are leaving now without seeing me again?"

"Yeah, I'm going. I'll call you when I get back," he said calmly.

CHAPTER SIX

After Christmas! Jessica couldn't believe her ears. They had just loved each other so intensely last night and now he was leaving! Whatever for? He could get a radio here. She'd buy him a better radio! What was this about? Certainly not his radio. He said he needed to think things over, but did it take her life to think things over? Jessica had so counted on having her special someone for the holidays, after those years of being alone; she was already looking forward to trimming the tree together, buying gifts for him, and just sharing the magic of the season with him. She should not have projected so much in her mind. How could he do this to her? Last night he had said he loved her. Then today? Were those just words? That would mean he would be alone for the holidays, too. Or would he? Nothing rang true. Jessica couldn't console herself. The tears came. She took her purse to the restroom and locked the door. Her colleagues couldn't see her this way. Maybe he was angry because of her response to his sneaking up on her and the assertive way she spoke about it. But that would be a small reason to just leave like that!

In the restroom, she applied some coolly dampened paper towels to her eyes, then sat down and leaned her head back. *This cannot be happening—what else have I done wrong?* Perhaps he had felt pressured … she should not have let him share her bed so soon. Maybe it was too soon. But, no, it had been right at the time. When she thought she had pulled herself together and reapplied a little makeup onto her puffy eyes, she left the restroom and tried to continue her job. One of her co-workers said, "Have you received bad news?

What's wrong?" That burst the dam again and she had to retreat to the ladies' room all over again. Finally she felt she couldn't continue the day, as every thought brought a new cascade, so she pleaded illness and left. On her way out her friend Bea stopped her. "Jessica, what's wrong?" She knew Jessica wouldn't just leave in the middle of the day.

"Nothing," said Jessica, "or at least I can't talk about it." Jessica's voice betrayed that there was indeed something wrong; she could hardly get the words out.

At home, she lay down on the bed and cried 'til there were no more tears. Then she felt a little better. She pondered his behavior of the night before, his insisting she had scratched him for no reason at all. Was he dreaming? Well, that stalking around the room was no dream. She wished she hadn't taken a sleeping pill so she could better recollect just what had happened. All she knew was that her heart had pounded during the episode, whatever it was; and then his sneaking up on her this morning. He had made it seem like her fault that he scared her. Could that have been why he left, because she reacted in a frightened way at that behavior? But, after all, who wouldn't? She had no idea he was anywhere around, and in her hurrying to get ready for work, how could she have known when he stealthily crept up? He may have felt rejected. Must she consistently second-guess him? Well, he was gone now and it wouldn't do to continually make excuses in her mind for him.

• •

Daniel decided to drive west. It would calm him. He didn't know where he'd go—he'd just go. How dare Jessica shun him and scream like that when he only wanted to put his arms around her and surprise her. What was wrong with her, anyway? She must be crazy! "I don't know whether I'll ever go back to her!" he said out loud. *Funny, though, she said she loved me. She has a poor way of showing it.* All he knew was he had to get away. He drove 'til he nearly dropped. A motel sign beckoned him. "Adults Only—Massaging Beds—Adult TV in Rooms." It looked like a dump. Oh well, he must save money. The clerk growled, "How many per room?"

Daniel growled back, "Just me—no women."

"That will be thirty-nine dollars," said the clerk.

"Highway robbery!" replied Daniel.

"Take it or leave it!" sneered the clerk. Room 2 had a strange, deathlike odor to it. He thought, *Wonder what happened here?* The mattress was lumpy in comparison to Jessica's bed. Hers really hadn't been all that bad. In fact, it wasn't bad at all. He looked at the button on the foot of the bed and pushed it. *Oh God.* The bed came alive. *Could you even "do it" with that angry ocean?* He laughed at the ridiculousness of it, but then was suddenly lonely. He arranged the pillows to ease out the lumps. He wondered where he was … Texarkana, outskirts maybe.

He tossed all night long, not really sleeping well enough to start out again—but he must; he was driven by an inexplicable force, his awareness of it plain as the regular hum of the rolling of the tires.

I'll continue west to Fort Worth, then south to Austin, probable destination, Galveston. He pictured himself with his feet in the gulf—lying in the sand and soaking up the sun. He knew he was even more handsome with a tan. Perhaps he would meet some women on the beach. Yes, this was a good plan—perhaps he could forget Jessica. She was not for him—well, maybe not. But he pictured her beautiful face and the way they had made love. Of perhaps the hundred women he'd been with, she was clearly the best. Her participation—so actively involved—he really did feel she loved him. He wondered if she missed him. Well, just maybe, he'd go back someday. He needed a home. In any good-size city like Cincy, property was so expensive. Jessica had a house. He could make changes to suit him, if he decided to go back. But now, he needed time to think, and if he stayed away until after Christmas, he wouldn't have to buy her a present. She would expect one—all women do. *Good thinking!* Besides, some new adventure may await him in Galveston.

His gas gauge read on the wrong side of empty. *Lucky to have looked,* he thought. *Women will do that to you every time.* Jessica had made him forget all about filling up. Suddenly hungry, after filling up he bought some corn curls and a Coke. *Away to Austin I go.* He missed his radio and tape player, but after getting over being angry again, he began to sing. A song he made up about traveling to Austin. He did love to hear himself sing. "Oh, you are good!" he said aloud. He was hardly to Austin when his sleepiness overtook him and he knew he had to rest before going on. He pulled into a roadside park and his eyes immediately clicked shut. An awful nightmare awakened him. *Oh Joey, you are relentless, you won't leave me alone!* This awakening a couple hours later robbed the adventure and the rest he might have felt. *Why can't I just forget about it and you?* But it was two hours later and his stomach growled angrily. Wearily, he pulled into a Burger King and wolfed down a double cheeseburger, fries, and a large shake. *Well, that ought to get me along another 500 miles or so, and I don't want to sleep anyway.*

CHAPTER SEVEN

Jessica plunged herself into her work the next day. Only once did she demonstrate her sadness. Her friend Bea, knowing something was very wrong yesterday, embraced her and told her, "Time heals a lot, my friend." Bea had no idea what had caused the trouble, but somehow she sensed it had to be a man. Women generally know these things because of their own experiences.

Jessica tried to pull herself together, but when Daniel came so strongly into her thoughts—the tears would glisten in her eyes. Why, oh why wouldn't he let her help him? Clearly, he needed help; there was obviously something deeply wrong.... She felt so inadequate, and so very sad. If she could have only seen him before he left perhaps she could have talked him into going to counseling together. She couldn't just say, "You need help!" She knew how he'd take to that bit of advice. Well, he was gone—no doubt about that fact. She must get over this, but if she could just hear his voice—that wonderful voice, when he wasn't being angry, that is. That angry voice had such volume. Looking back, she had done nothing to cause such vehemence. She had only loved him. His complexity was like a giant jigsaw puzzle with so many small, blended colors that it was next to impossible to decipher which color went where.

No special someone this Christmas, AGAIN.... Would there ever be? Becca and Debbie were her family, but they had their own lives. If she did find someone again, it would have to be someone with a handicap, because who knows what would happen to her in the future? At least they could both be honest. She could see them dragging each other along … she with her walker, he with his crutch! *Oh stop it!* She wanted Daniel. "Oh please, Daniel, be okay." She thought of his driving—no comfort there. *God, please help him and keep him safe.*

She pictured a new ad: "Woman with MS needs gentleman. Your disability welcomed!" She had to laugh at that one. Well, good, at least she was coming back a little to her old self—the self that tried so much to be optimistic and happy no matter what. The workday went better after that—it helped to laugh at herself. Even the grumpiest patient didn't put her under stress. She thought about calling Martha when she got home. Martha would probably be glad that Daniel was gone.

Yes, Martha seemed sympathetic, but underneath it all she was relieved that he was gone. "Now, you can get on with your life," she said. "That guy was no good at all for you. You're not tough enough."

Jessica lamented at that, saying, "He had his goodness and that was the part I fell in love with. But I know I really didn't know him well enough to have fallen so hard. Maybe I was just in love with the idea of being in love."

Martha replied, "You know, I was thinking that same thing."

Martha and Jessica were such good friends that they sometimes didn't have to talk to know what the other was thinking. Jessica, however, felt that idea was just a random thought. Perhaps because he had many problems and because she had problems, too, of which he didn't know, is what drew her to him. Well, he was gone now, maybe forever.... Although he did say he would be back after Christmas. She knew she should be very angry at his behavior, but instead it seemed that perhaps she hadn't handled him correctly. And he did need to be handled! She knew only a little about psychology. Maybe if he did come back, she should confide in another friend of hers, who was a psychologist. Or they could go together for counseling; he might take better to that. *But wait a minute, don't cross any bridges—wait and see. Get a grip, Jessica and try not to think about him.*

But, when she thought about him and how he sang—sang to her—her eyes would mist up again. But she mustn't think about it, or him. Just push him out of her mind and heart now. Easier said than done, of course. Jessica slept fitfully that night, but finally toward morning and nearing time to get up, she went into a deep sleep. When the alarm went off, she talked herself into thinking she had slept well. She knew she could make it fine, at least through the morning. She had noticed a new weariness as the day advanced. Perhaps she was just emotionally drained. She told herself that she must snap out of it—she had seven more years until she could officially retire. Daniel had suggested she take early retirement, but she suspected that would be because in that way she would always be with him. *Besides I do have a life without him.* She couldn't retire early and have enough money for her retirement years. Even though he had a wonderful talent, he was in many ways like a little boy needing his mommy. He had retired early—she wondered what was behind that.

Actually, the truth is there are many mysteries about him. Could these mysteries be the cause of his erratic behavior?

Like Martha said, though, she must get on with her life and pretend there had never been a Daniel….

The workday went pretty well until around 3:00 p.m., when it seemed difficult to move or lift up her left foot. Another new symptom—this couldn't be emotional. She knew if she called her doctor she would get his famous pat answer, "MS manifests itself in different ways." She pictured herself with a cane. Oh no, she was too young for that; but MS did not respect age—it was a cruel war declared on her body. Where would it strike next? She knew emotional turmoil would also take its toll. Daniel, no matter how she loved him, was not good for her. If her limp didn't get better, if Daniel did come back she'd have to tell him. That would make him leave for sure. She should have been honest in the first place; then there would have been no Daniel to love. She was certain of that.

It seemed a long time 'til quitting time, but she somehow made it home. Thank goodness it was her left foot that seemed to want to be part of the floor, so she was able to drive all right. Perhaps after a good night's sleep, her foot would be better; she was just tired. She took a bath, washed her hair, set it so it wouldn't be too curly, had a light supper, and went to bed. She put her reading pillow behind her back and read a few meditations until her head began to nod. It wasn't long before she was in dreamland.

Suddenly she was back tending that baby again in the same log cabin. He was smiling at her, and again she felt the tremendous love.... Again she put him to bed and laid down to rest. She looked at her clothes—a long, gray dress—and there was a type of sun bonnet hanging on the wall. She looked around and noticed a fire in the hearth. Then the rustling in the cabin and the old hag of a woman snatching up her baby. She awoke with a scream, "No, not this again!" AND WHY?

She got up and took half a sleeping pill and knew no more until morning.

CHAPTER EIGHT

Daniel was driving down the coast looking for a cheap place to stay. It would be nice to be right on the shoreline— that way he could just look out the window and survey the babes that might be strolling along. He stopped by a dumpy-looking place, but the rooms were $20 a night. He had around $200 and his debit card. That wouldn't last very long. He was terrible with figuring math. He wondered what he had in the bank. Maybe he could find a job that would at least help pay for the room. He knew he was good at fixing things. He'd get the room first—it was obvious that this dump could use some fixing up. He was a good carpenter. First get the room, and then present a deal to the owner. The man at the desk looked out in space somewhere. *Better just get a room for the night and then see the owner tomorrow.*

"Say," he said to the man, "who owns this place?"

"Me," the man said. Daniel's face fell, but he was ready to sleep—he'd talk tomorrow. The room had tacked screens with little holes in them. Enough holes that there were four giant Galveston mosquitoes flying about, and it smelled not of surf but of fish. He couldn't sleep in the same room with those mosquitoes, so he asked the owner for some spray.

He replied, "I provide the room, not the spray—want a swatter?"

Daniel could hardly contain his anger but said, "Is there a convenience-type market around here?"

"Yep," said the man, "right around the corner." Daniel paid over three dollars for the spray and begrudgingly killed the invasion of mosquitoes. He would have to fix those screens—if he were to stay any length of time. The pillowcase was clean but smelled of something unidentifiable. The hard bed didn't bother him. He covered his head and went to sleep.

The next day he put on his shorts to walk on the beach. He knew he had a great build because he saw to it—if there were any women around they'd be certain to notice. He was strong, too; strong enough to replace screens or whatever else in that dump that might be his home for a while. He began hatching a plan.

There was only one fat woman on the beach with a kid. She had to run after the kid as fast as her porky legs would carry her. The little boy's fearlessness reminded him of Joey. *Oh Joey!* Daniel wiped a tear from his cheek.

Later he went to the office to talk to the man. "Say, ole fellow, I have a deal for you. If you would let me stay here rent free, I would replace all your screens for you and maybe fix up the place a bit."

"Can't afford it," mused the man.

"Look," said Daniel, "if this place were mosquito free, you could advertise it as such and go up on the rent to at least sixty-five dollars. You'd be ahead of the game!"

"Hmm mm, we'll think about it," replied the man as he stroked his chin.

"Do you have a hammer and some nails?" asked Daniel. When Daniel had one of his few real working ideas he became determined.

"Yep," said the man.

"Could I borrow them?"

"Yep. I see no harm in that," said the man. Daniel then drove around 'til he found a place that sold framed screens. He bought two for his room, took down the unframed decrepit screens, and put up the new ones. They looked so much better than just tacked-up screening. Boy, it was hot and humid, but there'd be no mosquitoes in his room tonight! Maybe the man of few words could get a better price on many screens and the place would at least look respectable. A paint job would help, too. Daniel went to the office.

"Look—I want to show you something." The man appeared impressed with the obvious improvements. "It would take me some time, but you would have a place to be proud of when I finish," said Daniel. "Hey, I'll drive you over to the screen place."

"What did you say your name was, buddy?"

"Daniel—Daniel Smith." Daniel didn't know why he lied; he just couldn't get over wanting to hide from something—someone.

"Well, Daniel, owin' to how much they charge me, you kin have the job," drawled the man.

"I can probably do two rooms a day and still have some beach time," said Daniel. After the business was worked out at the screen company—it was arranged that Daniel would pay no rent.... *This is a cinch,* thought Daniel. *I'll have all afternoon for the beach, to go into the city, and probably find just the right guitar.* He envisioned himself playing on the beach at twilight with beautiful women sitting beside him. He loved putting on the charm and being the center of attention. He craved it. He thought suddenly of Jessica. Jessica with her job could never give him all the attention he deserved. He was a talent—he could write—he could sing and play well enough to accompany himself. He imagined his next song would have the ocean as its theme.

Back to the reality of his room, he purchased a new pillow and an egg-crate foam pad to put on his bed. With those improvements, the new screens, and the song of the ocean, he slept but dreamed of making love with Jessica. He awakened abruptly—a clear vision of Jessica and her warmth. Did he do the right thing in leaving? He thought of her house—he did need a permanent place.... Meanwhile, however, he would stay here, maybe find another woman, and have a good old time. First, though, he had to get to work on the windows so the weird guy would see him diligently prettying up the dump.

After doing his morning exercises, Daniel put on his shorts and went shirtless outside, dragging four screens with him. It was early and not too hot, so he could get two rooms done and then a bite to eat. He decided to do the screens closest to the office first in case he decided this was not the place for him. He finished around 11:00 and went inside his room to clean up before heading to a restaurant. He always wanted to look his best. The shower wasn't half bad. After dressing he looked around the room. Maybe if he put some posters on the walls this place would look more like a home.

He felt ravenous, and his hunger led him to a feeding nook—a quaint little diner facing the sea. This beach was unspoiled so far and looked like a paradise when the sun shone on the water. The restaurant was fairly cool, and the smell of bacon made his mouth water. Evidently it was not too late for breakfast. He ordered two eggs, bacon, muffins, and coffee. After all that labor he could eat a horse. The bill came to $5.95. He realized he'd have to cut corners in the future. But here he might meet some regulars and maybe even a woman. He looked around and noticed a middle-aged girl at the counter. Her skin was darker than what he thought he preferred. *She may be Mexican or maybe a mixture*. After paying his bill he sauntered over to the stool next to her. "Would you join me in another cup of coffee?" he said.

"Well," said she, "who are you, foxy man?" She had no hint of an accent.

Feeling a bit more forward he said, "Daniel's my name—I'm the new construction worker at the Bay Motel."

"Oh—so you're not a drifter? Sure you can buy me a cup of coffee, and maybe a drink later."

Well, thought Daniel, *not a bad start on an adventure for my third day here.* Her name was Maria—she was not bad-looking either, plump in the right places, and had a nice butt, yet she couldn't hold a candle to Jessica. She dressed rather flamboyantly, with a ring on every finger. She might even be married for all he knew. *Better watch it with this one.* It was a little too easy and may be risky.

After leaving the diner, Maria invited him to her place. She produced a bottle of vodka and poured two paper cups full to the brim. "Hey, easy," said Daniel. "I don't drink that hard stuff, or rather, at least not 'til evening."

Maria shrugged and took a large gulp of hers, then put it down. "Okay, have it your way, but we have a beach date this evening."

Holy hell, thought Daniel, *straight vodka!* "Hey, Maria, I know what we can do this afternoon. You can help me pick out some posters for my room—that'll be fun!"

"Okay," said Maria. She took her cup with her. They were within walking distance to many tourist shops, so it didn't take long to find a store that sold posters. The ones Maria picked out were horrible. Dogs or cats with bad hair days or hair balls. "I want landscapes," said Daniel, "something to clear the mind and inspire me." He picked three Monet's.

Maria said, "You're a strange guy."

Daniel didn't like that one bit, but contained himself. *How dare she say I'm strange?* Quick anger turned his face scarlet. Maria noticed and took his hand. "Just kidding, foxy man." Daniel filed it away in case he would need it later. They went to his place. Maria laid on the bed while Daniel tacked up the posters. Against the rustic walls, they looked like windows to the outside.

Maria, sprawling in as sexy a position she could manage, exclaimed, "Hey, you did know what to buy. These really look fine!" Daniel was pleased with his choices and that she agreed. He thought, *Bet I could paint like that.* He had a sudden feeling of elation and well-being. *I've got a part-time job, a free room, and a new friend. What more can a guy want? I don't really need Jessica.* However, he managed to ignore the sexy-acting Maria.

"Maria, do you want to meet me later around sunset at the shore?"

"You bet!" she said as she pranced off the bed, skirt flying above her hips. *This way, I won't have to buy her dinner,* thought Daniel.

"See you directly down from my place," he said as she bounded off.

CHAPTER NINE

The sun was making interesting patterns of gold, blue, and purple on the sand as Daniel made his way down to the shore. He had on his swim trunks and a shirt because it could get a little chilly when the waves came in. He also brought an army blanket for them to sit on and a large bag of potato chips. He decided to skip dinner, since he had bought breakfast out. Maybe tomorrow he could buy a hotplate for his room and bring in a few canned staples. He'd go broke if he ate out every meal. Maybe Maria could cook. No sooner had he spread the blanket, opened the chips, and got settled than Maria approached, swinging her hips in a put-on manner.

"Hey, foxy man!" she chirped.

"Daniel, my name is Daniel!" *Better to nip that in the bud.*

"Sorry, DANIEL," said Maria, "but you are a fox."

"I'm glad you think so, but I prefer my name. Don't you prefer your own name?"

"Yes, I guess so," she said hesitantly. She had her bottle with her and two glasses. *Maybe I can pour some of it out on the sand,* thought Daniel. *I wouldn't want her to think I can't hold my booze.*

"Just look at the sunset—it's never, ever the same," Daniel said in a reverent voice.

"Yeah, I know, but you get used to it living around here."

"I will never get used to it," said Daniel. It was evenings like this that made Daniel think there might be a God. *If there is one,* he thought, *He is inside me and I am part of Him. He is me, I am He. Though, I doubt if I could paint anything like that.* Maria clearly wouldn't understand his sometimes philosophical thoughts. She was a sexy woman and probably with little more on her mind.

Maria took large drinks of her vodka. "This is the life," she said. "Here I am with a great-looking guy and my favorite beverage."

"Take it easy with that stuff," said Daniel. "I don't want to carry you home."

She put her hands inside his shirt and ran them up and down his muscular chest. Then suddenly in a quick gesture began stroking him. Daniel put his arms around her and said, "Oh, yeah, do that some more." She did until he was thoroughly aroused. He turned her over on the blanket, kissed her on the lips, and proceeded downward to her neck and then her breasts. His lips hesitated there. Suddenly, he jumped aside and said, "You're doing your best to trick me! How do I know what you are! You probably have AIDS!"

"Foxy man! I'm okay, really I am—I've been married to the same jerk for a long time. You just got to me, that's all!" gasped Maria.

"Well, get away from me!" said Daniel. "I am not doing anything with you—I don't know anything about you, and quit calling me "foxy man!"

"Well, foxy man, I just happened to bring one along—how do I know about you?—but I'm out of here NOW!" With that, she rolled off the blanket and headed quickly whence she came.

Daniel put his head in his hands. *I really messed that up,* he thought. *She might have been at least someone I could have, and maybe as even a friend. Why can't I ever trust anybody? Well, I know why! She said she had protection. I will be lucky if she speaks to me if I see her tomorrow. But it's obvious she's a slut. She tried to seduce me.*

The sun was a large ball on the horizon, leaving only a hint of the sunset. He thought of Jessica. *Jessica is a good woman and so beautiful.* He thought of himself strolling down the street with Jessica on his arm. *She could help me, too. I know sometimes I need help. Why do I feel so good sometimes and at other times—I just don't know. Well, my stepmother never did anything to make me feel good about myself. It's all her fault. It's everybody's fault. No one asked me if I wanted to be born!*

Daniel put the blanket around himself like a cocoon. It felt good listening to the waves come in and yet being protected. No one could touch him here, not those crooked cops, not the hospital, not Joey—of course, not Joey. Daniel knew he hadn't done anything. Joey, fearless Joey, had always been a problem. And then, when he had discovered Joey had been using crack, all he did was knock him down. *I knocked my fourteen-year-old kid down. But I hadn't done anything any father wouldn't have done.* Joey had gotten up and laughed at him, called him a stupid old man. How dare he? That was the last time he'd seen Joey alive. *No, what was it? Another time?* In his mind, he saw Joey's unseeing eyes staring back it him. He cried out.... Then, he'd been hysterical. They put him in the hospital with all those crazies, or so they said. *I never saw one crazy, though. They said I had done it. I wouldn't have killed my own son! The cops threatened me to keep my mouth closed or I'd be sorry. Why can't I remember what happened?* His painful thoughts wandered back to Jessica. He needed a wise and caring woman. Someone who would shelter him from all of this. But could she? He said aloud, "Jessica, I'm really sorry about what happened tonight, I really am...." He rocked more in his blanket cocoon, protected from all wrongs.

A sole figure on the beach, Daniel picked up his blanket and headed for the motel and his much-improved room. Maria had praised him for his choices. Maybe she wasn't so bad—perhaps he'd see her at the diner in the morning and they could make up and have a new beginning. He needed someone, at least while he was here.

Maria finished the bottle. *That crumb,* she thought. She lay on her bed, eyes closed, but still awake. She heard Carl come in—bouncing into the walls as usual, then a thud. He didn't even make it to the bed this time. Oh well, even after all the vodka, Maria was still horny. Daniel was such a fox. He just didn't appear to know the ways of the world. Where had he been all these years? She guessed him to be around fifty. Fluff, her cat, jumped on the bed and settled down in the crook of her arm. Fluff always knew when she was about to drift off.... *Maybe I'll see Daniel, the crumb, tomorrow,* she thought as Fluff's purr lulled her into dreamland.

CHAPTER TEN

The sun coming in the window awakened Daniel. Somehow he had slept well, although he didn't know how. His mind had milled around from one issue to another for some time last night. But this morning, he hoped to see Maria again. A few compliments might make things okay. That usually worked with women. Guess they were basically all alike, especially slutty women. Except Jessica. Jessica had class and substance.

He sang while he exercised; yes, things would work out one way or another with Maria.

After his workout, he took four more window screens, his tools, and moved again to the front rooms of the motel. Better to make the front look good first. Maybe the guy could start charging more already for the finished rooms. That would put him in even better stead. He hurried through his job in order to get to the diner. Maybe Maria was a regular. He hoped he'd be able to patch things up. He felt it all her fault but he needed her friendship, and again his mind slipped to the scene on the beach. Sex.

Maria was sitting in the diner, drinking tomato juice into which she had discretely poured a little vodka. She had learned to drink it slowly to ease her pounding head. She was seated in a back booth so she wouldn't have to make small talk with anyone—and she could keep an eye out for Daniel. Carl had fallen across the doorway last night and she had to rouse him and ease him into his bed. What a drunk he had turned out to be! At least she could hold her liquor. He was the one that got her to like the stuff when she was just sixteen. He was twenty-six and had introduced her to lots of stuff and sex. Oh, how she liked it! When she became pregnant, they got married. Guess you could say that for him. Marri the kid had left long ago—they never got on good. She was an impossible kid and a worse teenager. She ran off when she was thirteen. Maria was almost relieved, but she hoped she was alive. Life on the streets was rough, but after all, she was part of her. She thought back to when she had first held her in her arms. Her baby. As she grew, everything went wrong. That girl would never listen to her. The vision she had now of her—perhaps mistreated by a pimp—meant she might come home someday. What, then, would she do?

From her booth vantage point, she saw Daniel come in. Damn, did he look good. He had on a blue T-shirt that matched his eyes. He was evidently searching for her as he scanned the place. She tried to be aloof, but it didn't work. Their eyes met and he slowly walked over. "Hey, don't I know you from someplace?" he said.

"I wouldn't know where," she replied. She looked down into her tomato juice.

"Hey, honey, sorry about last night—I wasn't myself. I had too much to drink. Let me buy you breakfast." Maria knew that was a lie and said she wasn't hungry—to Daniel's relief. "Well, I'm going to order something—you will sit here with me, won't you?"

"Well, I guess, but after last night—I didn't think you liked me." Maria looked very sullen as she spoke. "My old man was drunk as usual last night—he doesn't care what I do or who I'm with. You don't have to worry about him caring. Besides, you could knock him over easy with one hand. Of course, I would protect myself. AND I had hoped it would happen with us so I came prepared, foxy man." Maria couldn't resist his penetrating eyes, but Daniel cringed at the name. However, he contained himself. She was such a dumb broad.

"Do you want to spend the day together again?" asked Maria.

"Sure," said Daniel, relieved that she didn't stay mad at him. *It's my charm,* he assumed. "Well, I would like to go guitar shopping and maybe pick up a hotplate—how does that sound?" Maria said fine and remarked he was a man of many talents.

Since everything seemed peaceful with Maria, Daniel's mind leaped ahead to whether he should have sex with her. He doubted she limited her activity to her drunken husband—no matter what she said. He was scared she might give him something, but if they used protection—at least it would give him a release. He thought of Jessica and their lovemaking. That ideally was the way it should be, but Maria was a sex pot and it might prove pretty fine, as long they used something.

"Hey Maria, climb in. Let's go look for that guitar and see what else a pawn shop might have." Daniel's car had seen its better days, but Maria didn't seem the type to care about a few apple cores here and there, and the less-than-optimal upholstery.

"Okay," she answered, "but first let's drive to my house; I need to get something." While Daniel waited in the car, Maria quietly entered her house to get a glass and pour a little vodka. Carl was still snoring away. *The lush! Wish I could just get rid of him,* she thought. Luckily he had inherited some money, but that wasn't going to last forever. Carl, when he wasn't drinking, was a talented potter. He would order his clay in great galvanized cans from some company located around the Mississippi. Tourists would pay heavy prices for his art. She didn't know what the big deal was; they didn't look that great to her. But she wished he would snap out of it and do something. He'd better or his liver would be dead meat. Would he even miss her if she disappeared with Daniel?

"Okay, ready," she said to Daniel. He looked at her longingly—then gave her a quick pat on the butt. She eagerly responded, cuddling up against him. They drove into the lower part of the city, where pawn shops abounded. After trying many guitars, Daniel found one that pleased him for only $250. Surprisingly, it was quality and had a wonderful resonance; easily $1,000 anywhere else. Usually Daniel had a difficult time making up his mind, but this one sold itself. Maria, after hearing him play a few bars, said, "My foxy man Daniel knows how to make that thing sing!" Daniel beamed with pride. She spoke the truth—he was a talent. He was born with talent, thank the gods! Maybe soon his new song would come to him, but he needed to be alone for that.

They walked farther until they were almost back to his car when Daniel saw the park across the street. His fingers ached to play his new guitar, really play it—it was if they were reaching down in the case and drawing it out. He could see himself sitting on one of those benches, playing some of his music—his, only his.

"Maria, let's go over to that park for a while."

"Why? I'm starting to get hungry." Maria wondered why go to a park when they have the whole ocean at home.

"Because I want to and said so." Daniel started walking rapidly to the park with Maria following.

No sooner were they seated on one of the benches than his guitar was out. Before Maria had time to compliment him on the scales, he started his repertoire. A crowd gathered when he began to sing. Maria could not believe her ears; all she could do was smile at the crowd to let them know how happy she was to be with HIM! Some of the people asked for other tunes. Daniel just said, "Not now. Maybe at another concert."

Daniel soared with feelings of grandiosity. There he was—where he belonged, in front of an appreciative crowd. If Jessica could only see him now!

"You're my man, aren't you, foxy man?" Maria whispered in his ear, then, "Oops, sorry—my man, Daniel."

With that, Daniel put his guitar back in the case, and said, "Let's get out of here." The crowd that had gathered quietly dispersed, some saying, "Don't go!" others saying, "Come back!" It was enough to keep Daniel in a good mood, even though he wanted to shake Maria.

Maria sat so close to him in the car he could hardly breathe. "Move over a little, honey, I've got to drive." Maria sighed, hoping there wouldn't be a repeat performance of yesterday. They drove back in the direction of the beach, but then Maria spotted an adults'-only bookshop. She'd been to the Black Carnation before. In the back room they showed erotic films. "Daniel, I'm hungry, first for food—it's almost 5:30. Let's eat and then check out the Black Carnation." Daniel locked his guitar in the trunk when they stopped at a Burger King. *This man sure knows the classy eating places,* thought Maria in disgust. They ordered fries, burgers, and Cokes. Daniel hoped she wouldn't want dessert. He saw his money flying away—if he knew his balance, it would distress him. He would have to visit the ATM and find out the bad news. His money had to last until his next SS check was deposited, or he'd have to dip into his savings. He didn't want to do that. He wondered if Maria ever worked.

They went into the shaded Black Carnation. There were lights only above the bookshelves. Some disreputable-looking characters were looking at peep shows. Daniel was disgusted. There was a disheveled-looking man sitting by the back door, saying to whomever would listen, "Give yourself to the Lord. Have you been saved?"

Maria laughed at that and said, "Once saved, always saved." She touched the rosary around her neck. "Let's view a film." She hugged him. "It will be fun!"

Daniel reluctantly said okay and shelled out seven dollars. *Don't want her to think of me as cheap.*

The film was hardcore. He was already planning his evening with Maria, and this only intensified his desire, even though the film somewhat offended him. Nonetheless, he was thoroughly turned on. Other couples were making out in the darkened room. "Let's get out of here!" growled Daniel.

"Aw, honey, come on!" urged Maria.

"Not here." Daniel nearly shoved Maria out. "Let's go!"

Maria was all over him in the car. "Stop it!" he said. "Let's go home." Daniel drove down to the beach and parked. They moved over to Maria's side of the car and hungrily searched each other. Maria unbuttoned his shirt. He nuzzled her ample chest, thinking it much too large for his taste. She covered him first with her mouth and then with her body, not forgetting the protection. She thrust at him with a vengeance. Daniel felt he was in a dream. What a tiger she was! Daniel blissfully cradled her in his arms. *So this is what it's like to be completely taken over*. She did it all. *Perhaps for a living?* With that thought, he eased her aside and tried to gather himself. He was exhausted.

"It's still early. I don't want to go home yet—except maybe to get a drink," she said.

"Okay—but can't you make it though a day without that stuff?" Daniel didn't want a drunk on his hands….

"Aw, yes, but it makes my day more delightful. I know not to overdo it, mostly. Last night was an exception and I paid for it dearly with a sorry head this morning. Please, honey, just drive me home for a minute." So they drove to her house, where Daniel waited in the car while Maria went to the kitchen to get her bottle and usual paper cup. Her supply was diminishing—*must remember to go to the liquor store tomorrow*. It looked like Carl hadn't touched anything. Maybe he'd just gone out on another bender. A sudden chill ran down her spine. "Carl?" He was still in the bed. "Oh no—Carlos. Oh Carl, Carl!" She stood over his stiffened body. "Oh God in heaven! Hail Mary—full of grace!" Maria fell to her knees and crossed herself repeatedly. "Oh God, God—oh Jesus—take him out of here!" She gulped down the vodka and ran to Daniel's car. "Oh Daniel, he's dead, Carlos is DEAD! What do we do?"

Daniel sat bolt upright. "What do *you* do—he's your husband. What do *you* do?" He began to shake. He couldn't stand it! Death, death, always around, haunting him. *Oh Joey, why?* He got out of the car and began swinging his arms and pacing up and down.

Maria went over to him and held him. "Daniel, I need you—pull yourself together. We must call the police first, then the undertaker."

"The police—not while I'm here! I'm out of here!" Daniel jumped in the car and ripped away, sand flying.

He left Maria standing there in disbelief—crying. He went to his motel and turned on the TV loud to stifle his thoughts. *I'm not going to be around any police crooks. No way. They must have set it up for me to go to the funny farm. They must have—if I could just remember! There's probably a network of those crooks all over the U.S. of A.* Maybe Carlos wasn't really dead; maybe Maria is in on it with them. They were after HIM! He hit the wall with his fist. It really hurt. *Enough,* he thought, *I can't stand any more.... No blinds at the windows! Thank the Lord it is dark. They don't know where I am—they can't see me. Maria KNOWS where I live. Wait a minute, I didn't do anything.... Maria knows I didn't do anything. I wonder how he died. Stop this crazy thinking—I KNOW I'm not crazy ... but what's wrong with me?*

After much pacing and pulling at his clothes, Daniel calmed down. *Why do I have to go off the deep end? I DIDN'T do anything. There is nothing to implicate me in the death of a drunk.* He thought of Maria's crying and the way he left her. *She will think I am crazy, but I'm NOT. I just react badly because of that blank part of my life—because I can't remember—because they did something to me. Those cops did something to me and I don't know why or what happened. Joey, please don't haunt me like this! Go away from me.* Daniel slumped on the floor beside his bed, his head cradled in his hands. *Get it right now; don't think these thoughts. Joey was then, this is now. Maria is now.*

Maybe she needs me. The cops are probably gone. Should I drive over there? Now, tonight? I don't want to lose the only friend I have here.

Daniel stopped at the convenience store and purchased one of those artificial roses that looks as real as real. Then he went and gently knocked on Maria's door. "It's me, Maria."

"Go away, you slime!" She spat out the words as she pushed on the door.

"Please, honey, let me in—I'm sorry about what happened—about what I did." The door opened a crack. The face Maria presented was a combination of puffiness and mascara streaks. "Please let me in." Maria saw the rose and burst out crying again, but she let him in.

"Daniel, I think it's my fault. I wished him dead today and I got my wish. I will burn in hell!"

"Honey, there's no hell—we make our own." Sometimes it seemed to Daniel that just the right words were put there; they fell from his mouth. "I'm sorry I reacted the way I did; I should have stayed with you, but I can't stand death. Something happened to me that was very bad, and it was not my fault; that's why I acted that way. Cops are bad news for me, but I really don't know why. Something happened years ago that I can't talk about because I don't remember—that's the horror of it!"

Maria said, "Why, what did you do?"

"NOTHING! I did nothing, but got blamed for something I didn't do. I don't ever want to be around when cops are around—they are all crooks!" Daniel was nearly in tears.

"Well, those guys were very nice to me when I needed someone. More than I can say for you, Daniel. You just fell apart. Do you do that often?" Maria queried.

"NO, I told you, do I have to tell you again?" Daniel shouted out his angry words.

"Daniel, calm yourself! Carlos croaked because of the booze. But I shouldn't have wished him dead.

Let's go to the cathedral and say a rosary. I don't want to be in endless purgatory when I die. Who would pray me out? Certainly not you! I must see a priest and confess!"

"Okay, okay," Daniel said reluctantly. He hated churches. They drove several blocks to a massive cathedral. Even though it was late, the front doors were open. Candles were burning in the back, which gave the place an eerie presence. Daniel could feel himself tensing up. *Come on, relax. I can handle it; it's just a drafty building.* There were statues all around. In the dense light, they took on an otherworldly effect. *I'm surrounded by the Other...,* Daniel shuddered. Maria went to one that must have been meant to be the Virgin Mary and said her rosary, he guessed. *How is that going to help her soul? What stupidity!* Then she went in one of those booths. He kept a safe distance.... He thought of the little church to which his stepmother would send him when he had no choice but to do what she wanted. They would speak in so-called tongues—a fake if he ever heard or saw it. He recalled Amy Jo, who supposedly had the gift. She was speaking that gobbledygook and he reached up under her skirt. She came out of that trance fast! Daniel smiled at the thought in spite of the surroundings.

The church couldn't help but have a somewhat spiritual quality about it—spooky described it better, as the images made their shadows on the cold floor. Maria left the booth, he took her icy hand, and they walked silently out. Maybe he could stay with her and forget the Bay Motel. "Daniel," she said, "I've decided just to have a graveside service. Carl didn't have many friends—he stayed crashed much of the time. Will you come with me?"

I didn't even know the bastard, thought Daniel, *and I sure as hell wasn't his friend.* "Sure, Maria, I'll come with you." Daniel's mind leapt ahead to living with Maria. Maybe the guy at the Bay would pay him for finishing the job, and with Carl's insurance money, if he had any, they could live pretty well … so maybe he wouldn't have to finish. "Maria, as far as picking out the casket and so on, I just can't do that—you understand, don't you?" he asked.

"I guess," she said. Maria looked very small and pale as she faced him.

Daniel and Maria stood hand and hand the next afternoon as the priest read a few words from the Bible. "In my Father's house there are many dwelling places—if it were not so, would I have told you? I go and prepare a place for you…." Daniel wondered if he had a place. He had a sudden vision of Jessica—was that his place, at least for now? He wanted her. He envisioned her curly, dark hair that framed her face and gave her a beautiful, regal quality. The priest's voice again broke into his reflections….

"I am the resurrection and the life. Those who believe in me even though they die will live...." Her brown eyes and long lashes—he wanted her, only her, in the worst way. He looked down at the small, wet hand in his. *No!* his heart told him, *not Maria! Maybe I should give my real woman a call.... I told her I'd be back....*

"'Will never die?' He's dead, isn't he? I hope that jerk in the coffin's dead!

Sudden tears came to Daniel's eyes—Joey, as far as he knew, had no beliefs, so where was he now? In his death where was he? Where is his son's dead body? *Someday I am going to find out—I don't know how, but someday.* Maria looked up and noticed Daniel's glistening eyes and said, "I know this is hard for you, too; we can leave as soon as I settle with the priest."

CHAPTER ELEVEN

In Galveston, the seasons don't change much. Same sand, surf, hot sun—Daniel was getting very restless. It wouldn't be long 'til the first of December. Maria and he had had Thanksgiving together, and then he asked her about bunking with her for a while. Two can live as cheap as one, he had said. "I will keep working at my part-time job and we can have the afternoons for fun," he had told her. She looked at him in her flirty way. Maria, after she had gotten over her initial shock of Carl's death, seemed happy. At least she was happy with him as a man. That much he knew for certain.

"Well," she said, "we do get along well together. Carl and I were essentially roommates." That evening he brought his meager belongings over to her place. In the morning, they went out for breakfast at the diner. He didn't show for his job. Maria asked him, "What about the Bay—did you quit?"

"No," he said, "just taking a little vacation to celebrate our being together."

Maria beamed at him. "I don't have a lot of money—Carlos didn't have any insurance, but I do have what's left of an inheritance he had. Since paying for the funeral, I have only around $8,000 left." It was more like $28,000; intuitively, Maria felt she shouldn't tell Daniel everything. "You probably should hold on to that job so we will at least have some new money coming in." Maria had more womanly intelligence than Daniel could possibly know.

He hated to be told what to do by a woman. He said, "You mean that louse didn't have any insurance?"

"No, he didn't care about me really, and when he appeared to, it was only for himself. You know he never thought about death; he stayed plastered too much—guess he thought he could live plastered forever." Maria looked far away in thought. That statement burst Daniel's bubble. Guess he needed to work a little to keep up appearances … at least 'til he decided to take off. New Years would be a good time to call Jessica—start the new year right.

Daniel didn't want to go back before Christmas. He hated Christmas! Remembering all those gifts that the others kids got, it plainly wasn't fair. If he went back before Christmas, Jessica would probably expect that present. Well, he wouldn't play that game. He recalled one Christmas when he was a small boy. He had asked for a GI Joe and instead he got only a pair of jeans, and those weren't new. He remembered the teasing from the other kids—"Is that all you got, Daniel?" Then they continued to play their war games, excluding him. He hated them all. They did have a good dinner that Christmas, though, looking back as if yesterday to the Christmas he didn't get his GI Joe. Harriet, his stepmother, could cook and sometimes put together a meal even when only meager food showed up on the shelf. For Christmas, they had his favorite: stewed chicken and noodles. There was even an apple pie for dessert, and she had to save up for that. Many a night he went to bed with his stomach rumbling. Oh, how he remembered being hungry! He wanted to belong with the other guys, but without a GI Joe, he just didn't. After that, he never asked for anything. He saw himself as a lone figure, playing under the house with some marbles he had stolen from the other guys. He dug a perfect, round hole there, where he could keep the marbles and no one was the wiser. Then he would shoot into the hole all by himself. There was just enough light and he had become pretty good at it. Too bad he couldn't have shown his skill to the guys. The memories came in painful spurts. He had a part in the school operetta because of his singing voice. He didn't have to have a costume because his own clothes were perfect for the vagabond part he played. He didn't need a special costume, the teacher had snapped at him. He remembered the teacher's pointer that she used not just to point out lessons on the board, but also on the backs and butts of the poor kids when she took the notion. He wiped a tear away. Why was he so emotional? That wouldn't do if he were to win Jessica back.

He may already be in trouble. A looker like Jessica may have someone else already. But she did say she loved him. Did he love her? He really didn't know, and did he know how in his heart? A broken heart was part of him. A loss he couldn't make right.

Maybe he should call her before New Years. He would put on the charm.

Maria and Daniel went Christmas shopping on Christmas Eve. Since he lived with Maria now and he was receiving slightly above minimum wages for his work at the Bay Motel, he saved a little money as he plotted his trip back northeast. Maria was in a happy mood—anticipating her Christmas present, no doubt. "Hey, Maria, you know how much money I make;

let's don't go overboard on each other this year. We're together, that's what's important. Maybe after we shop, we can pick out a little tree and decorate it together."

"Okay," said Maria softly. She had already learned to be agreeable because the least little thing could set him off. BUT, sex with him was great! Daniel seemed drawn to the toy stores. Maria finally said, "I don't believe we will find what we are looking for in these places."

"Oh, come on, Maria, Christmas is for kids anyway. I just like to look." There they were; he found them. In one bin were several GI Joes, updated and clothed in the most modern fatigues. "Maria, I want one of these. It's all you need to get me."

"DANIEL, come on!"

Daniel raised his voice, "I SAID, I WANT ONE OF THESE, OKAY?"

"Right," said Maria, "and that is ALL you get!"

After leaving the toy store, Daniel left Maria, saying he was going to find a surprise for her. He picked out a blue glass ring in a gold-plated setting, thinking she would like it a lot. He felt happy with himself and he thought about holding his GI Joe and running his fingers over it. Maria's heart fell as she thought, *If I spent only twenty dollars on that stupid GI Joe for him I guess my present will really be something!* She had lots of evidence of how cheap Daniel was. *Oh, well....*

Later they went to a tree lot where the trees had already been marked down. Daniel bargained for a little more than a twig for two dollars. *This is a*

Christmas tree? thought Maria. Anyhow, it didn't take long to decorate with the ornaments Maria had. The ample amount she had left she put in a clear glass bowl and they lit a candle.

The candle glow on the ornaments created a festive impression. Daniel got out his guitar and sang "Silent Night." It brought tears to her eyes.

After Daniel finished with his song, he gave the little box containing the ring to Maria. It really was pretty and the man at the pawn shop had wrapped it in Christmas paper for him. When Maria opened it, she surprisingly said, "Oh, honey, it's so pretty—I know you didn't intend it as an engagement ring, but can I wear it as one?"

"Oh, sure," said Daniel, "whatever you want." It just fit on the ring finger of her left hand. Daniel really didn't intend for that to happen; all the more reason to make his plans to leave. He felt sullen, but he ran his fingers over his GI Joe and thought, *Better late than never.* He put his arm around Maria, then wordlessly they made love.

CHAPTER TWELVE

Jessica awakened with an awful cold. She felt she might be getting one last night, but then this morning she could hardly talk. Well, maybe it wouldn't hurt to just stay home today and get some much-needed rest. Not that she had been burning the midnight oil or anything—she just would get so tired just doing the ordinary work things. The limp was no worse, but it just made her tired dragging her foot around, and not feel as normal as she used to be. Anyone looking could tell something was wrong. She wondered what was next. No, she couldn't think that way. She would just stay in bed today; with no voice it would be difficult to call in and make them understand who it was. She called and they knew; even with a squeak for a voice they recognized her. She put on the tea pot and looked in the refrigerator. Nothing looked good, except a tin of Scotch shortbread. She knew the rules. Drink lots of juice or fluids and don't forget the chicken soup. Of course, shortbread wasn't mentioned, but the thought of juice made her sick. She would take a hot bath later; that might warm her up. She was freezing. It took her warm robe and a blanket to even get halfway warm. She turned on the TV and nibbled on her shortbread. The tea tasted strange.

Unfortunately, a day didn't go by that she didn't think about Daniel, and being at home sick made it worse. He really was a world-class jerk, but why did she continue to think about him. Was he still thinking of her? She had learned through the years that her intuition usually had merit. If so, why in heaven's name didn't he call or write her? Anything. Just to have him disappear like that made her realize more and more the problems he had. Well, his problems weren't hers. After all, he chose to disappear from her life, so why not let him be gone from it. He did say, though, that he would be back after Christmas. It seemed she always would get a cold or flu right around the holidays. More people were out in the stores shopping and spreading around their germs, and she was more prone to having those germs land on her. As usual this year she would be having Christmas with her family—no significant other. That was just fine. She KNEW her family loved her. She didn't need Daniel, or anybody else for that matter. If her MS got a lot worse, she would just investigate an assisted-living facility. She hated herself when she thought like that.

She wondered why Daniel decided to stay gone 'til after Christmas. Was Christmas too painful for him? Yes, that may be it. But, if he did call, she wasn't going to be available. Besides, how would she explain her limp? She twisted her ankle? No, she wasn't going to be available and that was that!

She had had a couple dates with a guy from her church that knew about her MS. He was kind and gentle, but the chemistry left something to be desired. He had sent her a very sentimental birthday card last week. It wasn't her birthday, but he had said he liked the sentiment and just wanted to send her a card. That really was sweet of him. There were sweet people out there. After seeing her stepfather at the nursing home, she had gone out for dinner with Martha and discussed this new man with her. Martha had said, "He sounds like everything Daniel wasn't! Why not give him at least a chance, and you wouldn't be hiding anything."

Her thoughts shifted to George and his residence at the nursing home—now there was a subject she could think about for hours. She and her stepfather had not been especially close, that is, until that last visit with him which opened her eyes to an entirely different man – a man she never knew.

Previously she had gone to see him because of loyalty to the memory of her mother, now things would be different. George had always seemed glad to see her, even though thoughts of the conflictive years still haunted her. Back then, he had tried to be her father in her important teenage years. A heart attack took her father when she was just thirteen and nobody, but nobody could take his place in her mind. George Shadowens.. She had laughed at his name - ("The Shadow knows"). Jessica was never sure her mother loved him. How could she have married him? They did have fun together and traveled; that was it. He wanted Jessie to call him Dad. No way—she rebelled at that. Her memories of her father were sacred in her mind. No one could take his place. When George would even attempt to tell her what to do, she turned a deaf ear. Somehow through all of it, she and her mother remained close until her mother died two years ago.

George had had kidney failure and was on dialysis. At seventy-seven, his mind was okay, but he was so feeble. His primary diabetes had initially caused the kidney problem. At his age kidney transplant was impossible. As always, there were too many patients and not enough kidneys to go around. Besides, he was on Medicaid, which obviously deleted him from any list. The room smelled strongly of urine. He shared it with another man, who had no lucid moments that she knew of. Jessica visited every Wednesday after work and would bring him a fast-food treat she felt he looked forward to, probably more than seeing her, but now she wasn't sure that was true at all. She always brought anti-bacterial wipes for his hands, as she questioned the cleanliness of the place. Growing old in this country was close to scandalous. She knew it would just be a matter of time. Her mother would have wanted her to see about George; she felt that deeply.

She replayed in her mind the scene of her last visit with George. It had been so strange, yet seemed to bring her closer to him. As usual she ran into elderly people either walking slowly or wheeling or being wheeled in their chairs. Some, though, recognized her and stopped her. When it was obvious that they knew what they were about, she would stop and talk for a bit. There was one lady in a wheelchair who continually shouted, "I'm ready to go home, Lord, I'm ready; come get me!" She had been doing that the whole time Jessica had visited the home—almost two years now. Although deeply religious herself, she wondered why things had to be like this. Where is God in this kind of situation and in the many more like this? Obviously, this lady's soul had been gone for a long time.

"Come in, honey," George had said; then almost simultaneously, "What did you bring me? Oh, that smells like heaven!" George smiled a broad smile and then said, "I am so glad to see you, Jess; you are the sunshine of my day!" Jessica handed him a double cheeseburger, small fries, and a sugar-free Coke. "You always know what I like, Jessie."

"Yes, Dad, I do." She didn't know why she had suddenly called him Dad.

George looked at her strangely. "That's the first time you have ever called me Dad." He looked a little misty-eyed. Jessica took his hand only briefly, knowing it was needed to devour the food. But George didn't eat it right away. "Jessie, what is wrong? You look like you are carrying the weight of the world on your shoulders."

"Oh, not much; just the usual things and then some, but go on eat your burger."

"It's the *then some* I'm asking about," he said. "Have you met someone interesting?" Before Jessica knew it, she was telling George a lot about Daniel, how he left—almost the whole story. George, instead of discouraging her, said "Well, there is usually a reason when a person can't get another person out of her mind. He has treated you like dirt, I would say, but still you can't get him out of your system—might be a far-life memory of some sort."

"What in the world are you talking about, George? Have you lost it? Please don't get like some of the others!" Jessica exclaimed.

"Look, Jessie," George said, "some things are hard to explain—such as great likes, dislikes, the inability to get certain people out of your system—it's all far-life memories."

"George," said Jessica, "all I know is this life, and right now it's rough for me but I'm doing the best I can."

"Sure, you are, honey, but there is more to this life than meets the eye. Even this moment is already gone, and all we have is the future and the past to think about. You see, our lives are made up of many facets and our brains are filled with memories that are sometimes hidden, but sometimes they come out when we least expect them. Sometimes they are soul memories or just an awareness that we can't put our fingers on, but they are there, nonetheless."

Jessica had never heard George talk so profoundly. Since he had mostly finished eating, she took his hand again. "Dad, I've been having dreams, too, and they really bother me."

George looked so tired then, but he was still bright eyed with his subject, saying, "Your dreams may have a message." Jessica didn't know what to make of it—was he failing or what? She got a washcloth, dampened it, and washed his hands and face. "Do you want to brush your teeth?"

"Yes, I better. Wouldn't want them to find me with burger on my teeth; they might call in the guards!" he joked. Jessica stayed a little longer, but changed the subject from Daniel to other things. It troubled her to listen to such strange talk—what indeed had he been talking about? He seemed about to drift off, when she had kissed him, said goodbye, and slipped out.

Though Jessica didn't know it, through sleepy eyes, George noticed her limp before he let his eyes close and behind the closed eyes was the thought, *My poor girl has a challenge she must work through—I pray that she makes it....*

Jessica was grateful that George had his right mind, especially when she walked by so many folks who had completely lost their light. But then again, George had said some strange things … maybe his mind was beginning to go. He had never talked like that before. What did he mean when he said "far-life memory"? She had no idea about that one, but for some reason, the word Dad fell from her mouth, twice, and for some other reason she had strangely felt closer to him. It didn't seem like a duty to visit him that day, but why had she blurted out the story about Daniel? Oh, her thoughts were tumbling one on top of another since she had this day alone. And Martha would wonder why she had told the story to George. She just plain didn't know. Her habit had been not to share anything really personal with George.

But she had talked to him about Daniel, and that caused him to talk so strangely. Daniel was gone and she would never see him again and that was that. He hadn't called or even written; it was obvious he had forgotten her. Perhaps he had found someone new, someone who didn't disturb him like it appeared her very presence did. No, it had not been her presence; Daniel would fly off the handle at nothing. He obviously had problems she had not caused. She knew a great deal about misdirected anger from some of her patients.

George said we only have the past to think about. Well, I am thinking about what he said and we have the future . . .

And I am feeling nauseated. Oh, how her head hurt! Obviously she might be getting some sort of flu, for when she took her temperature it read 99.5˚. This was really a fever, because for her, normal was 97°. The chilling was worse even in her flannels. *Maybe if I take a hot bath and wrap up good afterwards, I will break this fever.* She put some bath oil in before she drew her tub then lit an aromatic candle. "I need all the help I can collect," she thought aloud. She knew she should be careful of the water temperature, but the hot water really felt good. She decided to wash her hair, too, to make herself as germ free as possible. All that steam would help her throat. She had been blessed with carefree hair, not that it made any difference today with this flu bug. All she had to do was wash it, towel it dry, and it would curl up just like she wanted it. After her bath, her throat did feel a little less husky. She bundled up in a clean robe and went to the kitchen for some more Earl Grey and more shortbread. *I'll heat some soup after that,* she thought. However, she didn't have the energy, and before long her head had fallen into the couch pillows and she was nearly asleep.

Partially in and out of sleep, she was looking at the walls of the log cabin. It was getting dark; it might rain. She hoped it would be a gentle rain, without wind, and that the chinking between the logs would stay in place. She was holding her baby, looking at the dismal sky before she put him in his basket. *I'll get a little shut-eye while baby sleeps,* she thought. She lay down on the cot and felt so drowsy she was about to go to sleep. Suddenly, into the cabin came the old witch woman, who grabbed up her baby in her apron, gave a harsh laugh, and ran out of the cabin. Jessica ran after her, yelling, "Stop, DON'T TAKE HIM! YOU WITCH!" The woman ran into the dense thicket with her prize bundled in her hands. Jessie fell to the ground just as the thunder and lightning crashed about her. "My child, my little boy!" she cried out—then she was fully awake, her head pounding. "The dream," she said aloud. "The same dream! But I wasn't really asleep; I knew I was here on the couch." In her somnambulism, she remembered how the baby looked, his penetrating blue eyes—how somehow familiar he was. *Why is this happening?* she thought. *WHY? I never before would have recurring dreams! Maybe it's just the fever, but I've had it twice before with no fever. What is this dream or this vision trying to tell me?*

Jessica felt so overwhelmingly sad that her eyes filled with tears. *I've lost him AGAIN. Now that was a crazy thought—where did that come from?* She pondered that for some time, and then realized the baby's eyes looked like Daniel's! *I'm just sick,* she thought, *and when I'm here at home with this flu, I just have too much time to think and then I think about HIM. I must realize he's gone and that is that. Besides, if he does come back, how am I going to explain this stupid leg? I'll just lie, if he comes back—when he comes back.... I sprained my foot.... Stop it, Jessica! You don't lie. He's NOT coming back. You have got to get better so you will have other things to think about ... to dream about! Why is this happening now? And what did George mean by "far-life memories"?* She was so cold and shivering—maybe the heating pad would help.

I'm probably going crazy and will end up in a home like George. Will I ever end up like that? She had been saving systematically through her employer's retirement plan—saving more than she really could afford. Years before her diagnosis, she had subscribed to a catastrophic illness insurance plan, so she felt somewhat secure. With healthcare costs the way they were, how long would that last? Hopefully, until she went to the great beyond. Jessica hated it when her thoughts ran to the negative.

Daniel, when he was here, took her mind off thoughts of herself. *Where is he?*

She looked in the pantry and found a can of chicken noodle soup. While it was heating, she poured herself some orange juice and forced it down along with four vitamin C tablets. *I must eat right or I never will get back to work.* She knew the flu would run its course, but when? If she was going to dream or hallucinate like that, she'd rather stay alert constantly, but that wouldn't help her get well. *I'll just go back to work tomorrow anyway—flu or not. My voice is better; that steam seemed to help that.* That day had vanished—she looked at the kitchen clock, which read 5:30. She dug out the heating pad and put it around her shoulders while she ate her soup. Maybe Jewish mothers knew what they were talking about when they advised chicken soup for colds and flu. She settled down into the small folds of the heating pad.

Every time she got up she found herself heading back to the couch. She was just too weak to do much of anything. She had always thought that lying around made a person even weaker, but the cozy couch kept calling her back into its overstuffed comfort. *Don't go to sleep,* she said to herself. She flipped on the evening news and watched it through feverish eyes and a pounding head.

CHAPTER THIRTEEN

Jessica couldn't make it to work as she had planned. Her fever had broken in the middle of the night, causing her to throw off her covers and change her gown, which was sopping wet and clinging to her skin. She put on a lighter one, took a couple more aspirin, and went back to sleep.. A hard chill awakened her. This time she was trembling with the cold. More blankets and a quilt eased her back to sleep, but the fever was even higher, over 102°, when she hobbled out of bed and managed to take it. They would know she was still sick, so she didn't bother to call.

The phone by her bed jolted her awake. It was Debbie, her younger daughter. "Mom, I tried to call you at work, but they said you were sick. What's wrong?"

"Flu, I guess." Jessica's hoarse voice didn't deny that she was very sick.

"Mom, you've got to go to the doctor. You know you always get worse after an illness. You will need to be on some antibiotics!"

"I can't go," croaked Jessica. "I can't get out of bed."

"Well, I'll call your doctor and pick up something for you—he knows how you are when you get any kind of illness."

"Okay," Jessica said weakly. She knew she had to get well and back to work, as Christmas was in three days. She hadn't been able to make her usual cookies that she brought in to the people at work. Feverish as she was, it didn't seem to matter. She drifted back into a fitful sleep.

Debbie called Dr. Amish right away and talked to his nurse. The nurse, however, after conferring with the doctor, said he wanted to see her mother—he couldn't diagnose her situation until her saw her. They were able to make an appointment for 10:00 in the morning. Luckily someone had canceled, or she would have had to take her to the emergency room.

As soon as she left work, Debbie went home and searched her larder. She had some chicken broth and a little celery and a potato. *I'll stop at the grocery and get some chicken breasts to make some real soup.* She found a basket and put those things in it and also some aromatic massage cream and some mentholated salve for her mom's throat and chest. What a mixture! At the grocery, she found some Walker's shortbread (she knew how her mother loved it) and two boxes of herbal tea (Orange Spice and Tension Tamer). She purchased two pink grapefruit and a couple navel oranges. Then she stopped at the beauty salon and got some Aveda shampoo and rinse. That would be a treat. She arranged everything in the basket and covered it with a red napkin and tied a little holly on top. After all, soon it would be Christmas. This might help to make her mom feel better. Debbie knew an infection could make her mom's MS worse, and she was so worried about her. She packed an overnight bag and decided to call Becca, her older sister, to let her know what was going on. They were a close family. It seemed her duty to call Becca, who was a stay-at-home mother. Her twin boys kept her hopping.

Debbie arrived at Jessica's around six that evening. Since Jessica had expected her, she had made her bed on the couch again so she would hear the knocker. "Don't hug me," said Jessica, "I don't want you to get what I have."

"Gosh, Mom, I'm not worried about that—I'm worried about you! Now lie back down while I get your supper." She put the basket down on the coffee table in clear view.

Jessica, sick as she was, could not help but notice the cute basket with all her favorite things. "Honey, you didn't need to do that—I still had a little shortbread left."

"Mom, as soon as I get supper on, I'll brush your hair and rub a little of this mentholated salve on your throat and chest." She could easily see that her mother wasn't up to a bath and a hair wash. Debbie chopped the chicken, celery, and potatoes; sautéed them briefly; and added several cans of broth. When she had put the soup on simmer, she boiled some water for the tea. She knew her mom liked Tension Tamer, so with that tea and a piece of shortbread, she carried a tray into the living room. Debbie remembered when her mom had done such things for her and clearly loved the role reversal. "Here, Mom, let's prop you up so you can have some of this tea." Jessica didn't object; she liked having Debbie with her. "Mom, I was able to get an appointment for you in the morning at 10:00."

"I don't think I can drive, Deb," said Jessica. "I'm so weak—this stuff smashes a person."

“It’s okay, I’m spending the night; then will drive you in the morning.” Debbie was a take-charge individual and generous almost to a fault.

“But honey, you need to be at work, not tending to me,” Jessica said as strongly as she could.

“I haven’t taken off work for a personal day for ages—they will understand.” Debbie was a supervisor in a real estate office, so it really was no problem to take off a little time when necessary.

In about half an hour, the soup was ready to eat. She put that on the tray along with some of her homemade bread. Debbie was on a health kick—she always made whole-grain breads—it was easy with her bread machine. Jessica ate about half the soup and really seemed to relish the bread. “This is a treat, Deb; you are such a good cook!” Jessica’s voice was breathless along with its husky sound; it seemed a lot of her congestion had moved to her chest.

“Mom, in the morning I’ll fix your tub and maybe if you feel a little better you can use this new shampoo I got for you. I really love it myself. I know I could wash your hair for you this evening, but I think you need your rest more. Having had your fever go up and down has made you one big sweat bead!” Jessica had to smile at that. Debbie could be so descriptive, and she hit that one right on. “Come on, now,” said Debbie. “Go get back into your own bed. You’ll be more comfortable in there.” Jessica replied that she would as soon as she brushed her teeth. She thought that it seemed not too many years ago when she was putting Debbie to bed. Debbie was such a nurturer; she’d make a wonderful mother some day.

Easing down into her feather bed, it wasn't long before Jessica was asleep. Debbie decided to take her shower and at least get ready for bed, then read a while. She had started a new Stephen King novel and was eager to get back to it. She curled up in the chair closest to her mother's room and began to read until she too got sleepy. Just as she was shaking off that somnolence, she heard her mother cry out, "Oh no, no—don't take him!" She ran in her mother's room and found her nearly hysterical.

"What is it, Mom?" she exclaimed, feeling shaken and now very awake. *What is wrong with her? Maybe the fever is up again,* she thought as she felt her mom's hot but clammy head.

"Oh Debbie, a dream, a dream—that's all, but it's too, too real!" Jessica collapsed into Debbie's lap, still in tears. "It's like—like I'm in another time, another place, but it's still ME! I'm wearing an old-fashioned long dress, and somebody, like a witch-woman, takes my baby from me. I run after her, but she disappears into a thicket or woods, or something! Honey, I've had this dream too many times before and it's like it is me, but back then—like I'm really experiencing it!"

"Mom, you're sick, that's all, and fever makes the mind play tricks. Don't worry about it; it was just a dream," Debbie said in her most reassuring voice.

"Debbie, I'm beginning to think it is more than a dream. I've had it when I wasn't even sick!" Debbie cradled her mom and tried in every way to console her.

Finally she said, "Well, let's get you over this flu first—and then, if it still keeps happening, maybe you'd better go talk to someone."

"You mean a psychologist—I'm not nutsy!" Jessica was on the defensive.

"Of course you're not." Debbie regretted she had said that—her mom was so feverish. "All I meant was there are usually reasons for recurring dreams. I remember I used to have one about not finishing school, not graduating … you know, one of those frustrating things that you are so glad when it's over and it was just a dream. Dreams are messages—like maybe something you didn't do, or forgot to do. I wouldn't take it seriously."

"I know I shouldn't, but it's so real, like it really happened," said Jessica.

"Come on now, Mom, lie back down on your stomach and I'll rub some of that massage cream on you—that will relax you. Then I'll get you a cup of cocoa."

"Debbie, you need to get to sleep, too—don't do that, honey."

"I can't sleep for a while anyway—I'll have some cocoa with you, then we'll both go to sleep." Debbie was insistent.

The next morning, Jessica seemed a little better, so was able to take a shower and use some of the new shampoo before her visit with Doctor Amish. Debbie rubbed some more scented massage cream on her back and chest, so at least she would feel fresh. Jessica's temperature was still elevated, so it was difficult to be appreciative. But she did so appreciate Debbie's being there with her. *I know I will get lots better after I see the doctor,* she told herself. After all, she had to; it was almost Christmas. It was always her practice to do her Christmas shopping in October, so at least that was done, thank goodness.

Debbie went with her into the little room to wait for the doctor, after her vitals were checked by the nurse. Debbie noticed that her mother was not as stable on her feet and that she seemed to drag her left foot a little. *Oh no,* she thought, *it's already worse.* Debbie didn't know that the left foot had been acting up before the flu.

Dr. Amish came in with his usual "I'm in charge of the world" demeanor. "Well, Jessica, what are we up to this time?"

"I just have a fever, that's all," said Jessica, who usually downplayed her symptoms.

"Let's hear what we are dealing with," he said as he quickly listened to her chest. "It would be a good idea to get an x-ray; you have a rattle. I don't like that."

While Jessica was putting on her x-ray gown, Debbie said, "Mom, do you feel so weak that you have to drag your feet, or rather, one foot?"

"No, honey, that's been doing that."

"Well, then, tell the doctor, and why didn't you tell me? I didn't notice anything until now." Debbie was so afraid for her mother.

"It started about a week before this flu," replied Jessica. Debbie felt very frustrated that her mother would just let things happen and keep it to herself. But then, she probably didn't want to worry them.

After Jessica's x-ray, in a short time Dr. Amish came in carrying it. "At this time, you just have bronchitis, but we don't want anymore trouble than that! I'm going to start you on a round of antibiotics, assuming it's bacterial."

"Okay," said Jessica, weakly. "Wish that would help my foot as well."

"What's wrong with your foot?" said the doctor, knowing full well that it was the MS.

"It's just been dragging a little—it started before the flu," said Jessica.

"Let's see you walk," said Dr. A.

Jessica walked to the length of the room, her weak foot demonstrating her lack of control. Sick as she was, Jessica felt ready tears come to her eyes.

"Okay, that's enough. I'm going to start you on a course of prednisone in a rather large amount right now and then taper it off. You know how I feel about steroids and we don't want to use them unless we have to. In your case, however, we will do it just to get you over the hump—just 'til your symptoms improve. It won't hurt your other condition in the slightest, just make you better faster!" In some ways, Debbie didn't like his superior countenance and wiry smile. Jessica knew full well what he meant, but her doubt was *How long? How long will it help?* But then she knew of cases that remained in remission for years—in fact, she knew a lady in her seventies who had been diagnosed when she was twenty-six, but had remained for the most part in remission until just recently. There are many good cases on record, not the other kind. If they just knew more about it, about the cause or perhaps many causes.

"And you know how I feel about steroids as well, but as long as I get off it as soon as possible, the good it does is many times counteracted by the injurious side effects. I've done my homework," Jessica added to the conversation.

To Debbie, the doctor said, "Go straight to the pharmacy, then get her back home and into bed! Call me tomorrow after she has had the first dose of meds, okay?"

"Right!" Debbie replied.

Debbie talked emphatically on the way to the pharmacy. "Mom, please let us know if you think your MS is getting worse. Don't let it go just thinking it will magically disappear!"

"Deb, I would have gone to see him if I hadn't gotten this bug. Really, I would have."

"Mom, what I mean is—let us know, okay? We're a family. Becca feels the same way. We need to know if you think you are worse!" There were lots of things in Jessica's life that her girls didn't know about and wouldn't know about. Some things are better not shared with daughters. But yes, if the MS became worse, she owed it to them to let them know.

"Debbie, sometimes I don't want you to worry. But I'll tell you girls first when I get better," Jessica said dryly. She didn't have the energy or the animation to express herself anymore.

Debbie settled Jessica on the couch with a bed pillow behind her head, turned the stereo on low, and went in the kitchen to get the first dose of medicine for her. The steroids packet read take six today, five tomorrow, four, etc., and when she got down to one, stop. With the antibiotics she was to take one now, then two more before the day was over, and three a day until the ample bottle was gone. Since it was a little confusing for a sick person, she laid it all out on the coffee table in the correct doses. She wished she had one of those graduated pill boxes. "Debbie, you are treating me like an old character," Jessica objected.

"Mom, you know how much you have been sleeping and you know this is important!" Then she filled an ice bucket and surrounded a carton of orange juice with ice. Last, but most important, she got her a large glass. "I want you to stay down as much as possible and I'll call you this evening."

"Yes, Doctor," said Jessica. Debbie patted her on the cheek, fixed the door lock, and left.

After Debbie left, Jessica relaxed completely on her familiar pillow and closed her eyes. "Unchained Melody" came on the stereo. If she hadn't been so sick, how she would have loved to turn up. "Oh, my love, my darling, I hunger for your kiss...." *Daniel's, no, certainly, not! Oh, I am hopeless.*

The ordeal of the visit to the doctor over, Jessica fell, this time, into a dreamless sleep. When she awakened it was beginning to get dark—*must be about 4 o'clock.* She appreciated the sweet gestures of

Debbie—there was no doubt as to how much medicine she would need to take before the day was over. And Debbie was right, she needed help right now; she had brain-fag, or so it seemed. Since Debbie was going to call tonight she would have to have a good report that she had followed orders. She gulped down the medicine with the orange juice then went into the kitchen to put on the water for tea. She went to the bathroom and washed her face and hands and felt more rested, even though her cough sounded gruesome. It seemed the medicine was already beginning to loosen things up. After the tea steamed hot and ready, she added a slice of shortbread to the plate and carried it in the room.

At 6:00 on the dot, Debbie called. Jessica told her in no uncertain terms that she had been following orders and then some. Debbie stated that it would be necessary to get a good night's rest and let the medicine do its job. Jessica knew that, of course, but she let Deb expound all she wanted.

"Mom," said Debbie, "I'll check on you tomorrow, and don't worry a thing about Christmas. Becca and I will do the turkey. We've watched you do it a million times, but I'll have to run over sometime and get your dressing recipe. We can't have Christmas without it."

"Maybe I'll be better enough to do it, honey; it's not difficult," said Jessica.

"No, I need to learn how anyway. You just be a duchess and lie on your bed of affliction," replied Debbie. At this point, Jessica was relieved to just sit on the sidelines.

After settling back onto the couch, she went to sleep as Debbie ordered. No dreams that she could remember, thank goodness for that.

The next morning she called in to work to let them know she wouldn't be in again but that she had gone to the doctor and was now taking medication. It was a usual occurrence the day before Christmas to have a little open house in one of the break rooms and her cookies were always held in high regard. She talked to Bea, her special work friend, who said, "We'll miss you very much AND your cookies! But you take good care of yourself. Some of us have been doubling up, and you know things are always slow this time of the year. The most important thing is for you to rest—you've been under a strain lately." Bea didn't really know the strain she had been under; she just guessed.

That afternoon there was a knock on the door. She got up in her robe to find a florist bringing a poinsettia and the largest Christmas cactus she had ever seen. How very lovely and thoughtful! It was from the blue team at work. The card said nothing about "Merry Christmas," only "Get well soon—we miss you." She put the poinsettia on the dining table and the cactus on the bookshelf. That gesture alone made her feel better. She dug in the closet and found just the manger and the baby Jesus figure and put that on the bookshelf as well. Just doing that small gesture made it look a little like Christmas especially along with the cactus and beautiful poinsettia.

Lying on the couch still felt so good. The very thought of doing anything other than what she was doing did not appeal. *Maybe tomorrow I'll put on some clothes and act like a human being for a change. Well, I'd better*, she thought—tomorrow was Christmas Day. She wondered if Debbie or Becca would come pick her up and take her to one of their places. Where would Christmas be this year? Debbie was coming over this afternoon to get her dressing recipe; maybe she'd then break the news. If she had her preference, she didn't want the twins running all over the place. At their house, they had room to play.

A light knock at the door forced her up from the couch to let her daughter in. Debbie looked like an angel holding six beautiful red carnations. "Oh honey, how sweet of you! They are lovely!" Debbie carefully cut them in different lengths and, along with some holly and fern, put them in a white vase and placed it on the coffee table.

"Now, all I need is your dressing recipe and I'll get a move on." Debbie handed her the favorite recipe box and Jessica found it quickly. She was organized anyway. Debbie left without saying if Christmas would be at her house or Becca's.

Becca called later to say, "Mom, Merry Christmas Eve and feel better tomorrow!"

The next day, December 25, Jessica awakened around 10:00, took a long bath, put on her makeup carefully, dressed in a red caftan, and deposited herself back on the couch. *I will rest until Debbie picks me up and then try to feel like a new person,* she thought. Debbie came by at one p.m. and took her to Becca and Jon's place. Jessica had made a grand effort: along with her red velvet caftan, she wore three necklaces and some red earrings. She might feel like an invalid, but she wasn't going to look like one. The twins, Greg and Eric, came bounding toward her. "Granny, Granny!" they said and gave her a big hug that nearly knocked her over. As cool as she tried to be, her cheeks felt red and feverish with just that boundless energy. The house was the epitome of Christmas, hosting the aroma of turkey roasting mixed with cinnamon-scented candles and pine. This had to be her favorite time of year. Her girls seemed to have inherited her love for candles. The tree was very artistically decorated. Both girls seemed to have a flare for such things. Jon said, "Here, Jessica, your place is here, on the couch—we don't want you doing anything but recuperate." Jon was everything Jessica had wanted in a son-in-law. He is such a good father and always so thoughtful and sensitive.

"Mom, you're pale as a swan, but how do you feel?" said Becca

"I think I am better, honey; just still pretty shaky. Call me the wavering woman but I'm willing myself better. After all, it is Christmas." From her perch on the couch she watched the twins zoom around with their shiny new trucks—at least the trucks didn't make a noise, but the twins provided their own. Becca and Jon didn't believe in going overboard for the boys at Christmas or anytime. They could afford it certainly, but felt too many things were overwhelming for children. Better to put the extra money away for eventual college.

Jon had put her modest gifts under the tree. At least they were wrapped prettily. She had purchased heavy wooden puzzles for the boys and two books, each beautifully illustrated. She loved to have one or the other boy on her lap pointing out different pictures, and recognizing their names with their limited vocabulary. She had given them each a Beanie Baby on her arrival, a lion for one and a lamb for the other. She would tell them that story later when she felt better.

The dinner was wonderful; even though she didn't have much appetite for it, it pleased her to see everyone else digging in. Even the little boys were not as picky as usual. The girls had done everything without her help—the younger generation had taken over. It made Jessica glad and a little sad. It would be difficult to explain.

In his prayer before dinner, Jon thanked God for family and for health. He was one that would not accept illness in anyone. *He feels we are all perfect in the eyes of God,* she thought. *How I wish it were so. Think health, think miracle, think perfection.* She knew she loved God, at least the Jesus/God in the Gospels. The forgiving God, the God of love. Her thoughts wandered to Daniel. She wondered if she would be forgiven for loving a sometimes unlovable man—a man who clearly had problems. *Now, wait a minute, Jessica, he is gone—gone from your life, perhaps forever. Stop thinking about him!* She felt a little ashamed that she had not told her daughters about Daniel. Why? Because they clearly would not approve of him. She knew that in her heart. They would want her to be happy, but they would readily pick up on his problems. If they knew him, she knew what their collective opinion would be. Where was he now? Well, he had gone from her, so why should she even think that he would return. She shuddered about the dreams and how the baby had Daniel's eyes.

"Mom, you are miles away. Did you like everything?" said Debbie.

"It was all wonderful, honey. I think you girls can do it from now on." She smiled to let them know next time she would help in her usual way.

"You do feel a little better, don't you?" queried Becca.

"Oh, yes," she replied, hoping it were true. "Just being here with all of you and out of my soulless house helps immensely." She knew she was still a little feverish because of the clamminess that would hit her every so often. It had been long enough for her not to be contagious, and she was so thankful she was able to spend Christmas with her family.

"You won't have any more of those dreams, Mom, and then your house won't seem so soulless. You know you love your home, you always have!" exclaimed Debbie.

"What dreams?" Becca wanted to know.

"Becca, you know sometimes you have recurring dreams—well, it was one of those. Nothing to be concerned about—it was probably just my fever." Jessica knew better, but she tried to sound convincing.

"Oh, I see, and yes, I've had those before, but they were not too disturbing after I awakened." Becca and Debbie were busily cleaning up the kitchen while Jon supervised the twins.

"Now it is tree time," announced Becca after they had finished. They had decided this year to buy only one stocking gift and to exchange names. Jessica had drawn Jon's name, but she wanted to get something special for her girls' stockings. Stocking gifts were to be slipped in when no one was looking. For each girl she had purchased tiny diamond earrings.

She felt good about Jon's tree gift, a beige cashmere sweater. Men always looked sweeter in a sweater, she thought. She anticipated how he would like it. But then her thoughts shifted to Daniel. He could be sweet … so sweet, but then, out of the blue …

Before the tree, though, as was their family custom, they held hands and sang "In the Bleak Mid-winter," not so much for what the words said, but because of the beautiful tune. Under the tree for her was a slinky, long navy skirt. It was just beautiful. Debbie knew what would look good on her. The girls were thrilled with their diamond earrings. At the very bottom of her sock was an interesting-looking long box. In it was a sapphire bracelet from Jon and the girls. They had broken all the rules. Stocking gifts were supposed to be small. "Oh, you guys, thanks, thanks so much—it is so beautiful! You know how I love sapphires! Didn't you break some rules here?" Jessica was thrilled and put it on right away. Her mind wandered back to Daniel and dressing up for him. As quickly as that thought crept in, she pushed it away. *I am going to enjoy my loved ones, here, now, today!*

Becca seemed happier with the cashmere sweater than Jon did. "Oh, Mom, it is so soft! He has never had cashmere before!" She held it up to him and Jessica could see it would look great on him. *Jon is so handsome and such a good person,* she thought. *I could not have picked a finer son-in-law.*

Jessica felt very happy and so grateful for her family when Debbie took her home. But it would feel good to get into her feather bed again and just be alone. She still had on her bracelet. She felt like a queen or at least a duchess in it. "I'm not sure I can take this off, Deb—it is too beautiful!"

"Mommy, I'm so glad you like it!" Debbie's inner child came out; she was excited about the bracelet as well.

She took off the necklaces and washed her face, but she was too tired to take off the caftan. She put on the stereo, turned it way down, and stretched out on the couch. Toward morning, she had the dream again—wearing the bracelet didn't help that mystique. She cried out in her sleep, awakening severely shaken. Her thoughts returned to George's remarks and what he had said about far-life memories. The baby's eyes were clearly Daniel's. Could she have lived before this life? No, that was crazy thinking. You live, then you die. Maybe you go to heaven. But that is the mystery; no one really knows. Maybe you just die and that is it. No, she had faith that she was going somewhere. As soon as she was completely well, she was going back to see George, whether it was the usual day or not, and make him explain himself. She got up to microwave some milk—milk usually helped her get back to sleep, although she didn't like it much. She noticed her foot seemed a little better; she could walk carefully without dragging it. Steroids are wonderful in small doses and as long as you eventually stop taking them. After slowly drinking her milk, she thought what a bonus that would be—to have her foot behaving! But for how long?

CHAPTER FOURTEEN

Daniel was feeling suddenly trapped. Having Maria even pretending that ring was an engagement ring made him VERY uncomfortable. He was thinking more and more about Jessica. Did he love her? Well, it certainly seemed that absence from her didn't take her from his thoughts. She was a lady, a real lady … and besides that she had a house and a good job that would bring in income. All he would have to do was write when he was inspired and felt like it. He was just wasting his time here with Maria, who wasn't much more than white trash. AND she wasn't all that white either. He hadn't ventured even close to his job since Christmas, and when Maria asked him about it, he lied that he had received a Christmas vacation until after New Year's. Oh well, it didn't matter; lies came in handy. Sometimes he couldn't recall the difference between truth and a lie. Through the years, it had been easy. At first, he recalled lying to his mother and what would have happened if he hadn't; then his stepmother—oh, it was easy to lie to her.

By New Year's Eve, Daniel had his plan hatched. He would wait until Maria had passed out and then he would make his move. He'd take everything that he had and put it in the trunk of the car. "Here, honey," he said, "let's have another toast to the new year together."

Maria's love for vodka surpassed any clear thinking by that time and she drunkenly made another toast. "Here's to us, Daniel, my foxy man, ole man…." Her voice trailed off. Maria had finally realized how

Daniel had hated that name, so she was about gone. Daniel had hardly had a drop to drink. While toasting with Maria, his supposed vodka was water. She had started early with her binging, wanting to wipe out any unhappiness she had felt with Daniel. He was so unpredictable; maybe the new year would be better. Around 4 p.m., she had brought in shrimp, crackers, and cocktail sauce to go with their drinks. The food didn't last long, and any effect to temper the drinking had long since vaporized. She laid her head down on the bed and said, "Come to me, lover—ole guy," she slurred. Daniel lay down with her until he was sure she was completely out of it. "Well, Maria," whispered Daniel, "it's been fun—sleep away now, tomorrow you'll have a surprise. Happy New Year, woman." With that, he crept out to the car and quietly opened the trunk. He put all his belonging on the plastic he had prepared that day and closed it up. He went back in one more time to make sure he had everything. He took a couple boxes of crackers in case he got hungry and some bologna to go with it. Looking at the bed, he noticed the ring on Maria's hand. *I can't leave that,* he thought. *After all, it cost me thirty dollars.* Maria made a little sigh as he inched it off her hand.

Daniel drove as far as Dallas before he felt he needed to take a break. It was after dawn in the Texas sky and he felt so elated and free. *I'll take a sleep here in this park, then call Jessica.* Maria was probably still passed out and wouldn't notice he was gone until noon. *Well, little girl,* he thought, *you're in for a bombshell. I'm going back to a real lady—maybe, my true love. Maybe, just maybe ...*

Daniel awakened around 11, feeling refreshed and hungry. *I'll just go to one of those quick markets, buy a package of sausage biscuits, and then a phone card. I know Jessica will be happy to hear from me.* He didn't search long until he found the familiar 7-11 sign. Some fat lady was ahead of him, taking her good old time with her hands full of purchases. "Hey, lady, will you hurry your fat ass up!" snarled Daniel. "Some of us have important things to do!"

The woman turned around glaring at him. "And who do you think you are, bum?"

The clerk, having been trained in confrontations such as these, wasted no time in addressing Daniel with, "Sir, the guard will have you removed from the premises unless you quietly wait your turn in line." Daniel stared at him with a look that said, "Don't you mess with me, boy…," but said no more and waited until the woman moved on and out.

"I'll take these and a ten-dollar phone card—gotta call my lady," Daniel said in a much-improved tone of voice.

"Oh, I guess that's why you was in such a hurry," the clerk said knowingly.

Daniel left and drove to a talk-from-your-car telephone. Lightheartedly he pushed in Jessica's number. He let it ring off the wall before slamming it down. *Well, of course,* he realized, *she's at work, but why no answering machine?*

• •

At the beach, Maria had awakened holding both hands on her head, saying, "Oh, Happy New Year," and called, "Daniel, Daniel, lover, if you're in the kitchen, would you mind bringing me some ice for this killing-me head?" Even to her throbbing head it seemed too quiet. "Daniel?" Only Fluff the cat seemed interested in Maria and her aching head, as she rubbed up against her. "Daniel?" Maria called again. Still no answer. *Where did my guy go?* "Daniel, Daniel, love?" A chill made Maria look at her naked left hand. "He took my ring! It's gone.... The dirty louse is gone.... How low is that? How low? How could he?" Maria put her poor head down on the bed and cried and cried. "He could have at least left the ring he gave to me. It was mine, mine...." Finally she sat up in bed and said, "I loved the louse, Fluff, I loved him, no matter what, crazy as he was ... but if I see him ever again, I'll kill him. You know, Fluff, he never told me where he was from—never! He had a lot to hide, that guy did; why did I ever take him in? Because I loved him, that's why, and who couldn't? Even though he's so difficult, who couldn't love the guy? Well, it's over now and he showed how little he loved me!" Maria buried her aching head in her pillow, steeped again in a waterfall of sobs. "I'll never drink again!"

****

Jessica was able to go back to work the day after New Year's. She felt considerably better, though still a little shaky. The steroids worked a miracle on her leg. She was walking like any other normal human; again she wondered, *How long?* It really felt great to be back at work, doing the job she loved. Everybody seemed glad to see her, and she had to admit it was so nice to be wanted and liked by her co-workers. And she liked all of them, too—it was such a good feeling to belong to a group of people who were nearly all competent and had the best interests of the patients uppermost in their minds. On New Year's Day, she baked a batch of the cookies they had missed at Christmas and put them in the break room. She had written a note thanking all for the gifts at Christmas and tacked it on the bulletin board. Work with her patients placed any thoughts about Daniel on the back burner.

Daniel felt furious when Jessica's phone rang off the wall. There wasn't even an answering machine so that he could leave a message. *What had she done with it?* he wondered. Where was she when he needed her? Well, he could call the hospital, but he had lost that number. Of course, she would be at work—what was he thinking…? He called information and then hospital information. He was using up too much of the calling card, but he finally got Jessica's number. He wrote it down hurriedly, then punched it in. A crisp voice answered. Daniel said, exasperated, "Let me speak to Jessica Hastings!"

"I'm sorry," said the voice, "she is in with a patient."

Daniel nearly yelled into the phone, "This is an emergency!"

"Just a minute, then…," said the voice. Bea quietly went into Jessica's patient's room and said with a look, "You have a call—it sounds important."

Jessica excused herself and said she would be back shortly.

"Hello?" said Jessica, who couldn't keep the worry from her voice, thinking something serious might have happened.

"Jessie, oh Jessica, it is so great to hear your voice. It's been so long!" Daniel quickly shifted gears and verbally put on the charm. "I've missed you so much! I never stopped thinking about you; night and day, you have been with me. I just had to find myself, honey. I'm okay now...."

"Daniel, oh Daniel," Jessica was shaking, but she quickly shifted gears, knowing she had to be firm, as with a child. "Daniel, you have been gone too long. What nerve you have—calling me after all this time!"

"Please see me, Jessie, please, just once. I will make it up to you, I promise!" he pleaded.

Jessica spoke determinedly, "No, Daniel, it's too late now."

"Jessica, you can't mean that—you know you love me! You said you did!"

Jessica was melting, hearing that voice that only Daniel had, but she couldn't see him; no, she couldn't, she mustn't. "Daniel, you have taken me away from a patient and I can't talk now anyway."

"Can I call you this evening, sweetheart? I just have to talk to you, to SEE you; then you will understand!" Daniel was crying into the phone.

"No, Daniel, don't call. Goodbye!" Jessica put her head in her hands to stop the tears. *Why do I still love him?* she thought. *I am such a fool where HE is concerned.... Why he is here now, I was beginning to get over him. Oh God, help me to be strong!*

Jessica told Bea, who was still at the main desk, that she wouldn't take any more calls; that she was having a busy day. Actually she was going through the motions only, thinking, *I can't go home tonight. I could go to Martha's.... NO, I'll go see George—I need to hear what he has to say.*

The main desk phone was busy as usual, and when it rang this time it was another call for Jessica. Bea, still at the desk, told the caller that Ms. Hastings wasn't available. The weak-sounding voice said, "All right, but will you see her today?"

"Yes, sir," said Bea.

"Then would you tell her George called and could she come this evening?"

"Yes, sir, I'll be sure to tell her," said Bea. Without any hesitation she found Jessica—something about the man's tone made Bea realize that this time, this was the more important call. "Jessica, it sounds like an old man—do you know a George?"

Jessica thought, *How strange, I was just thinking of George.* "Yes, did he say what he wanted?"

"No, only that could you come this evening?" A little chill came over Jessica—as she had fully intended to see George that evening and not go straight home. George NEVER asked her to come to see him—perhaps he was worse.

"Thanks, Bea. Yes, George is my stepfather. This is not my usual night to go over there, but funny thing, I was going to see him tonight." Jessica's worried look made Bea concerned as well.

Bea said, "Maybe he especially needs you tonight."

"Yes, maybe," mused Jessica. In the forefront of her mind was Daniel and his call. How she would love to see him! But no, she could not—would not—he was not right for her and she knew it. Thinking ahead—*should I get my phone number unlisted?* She was completely torn about the right thing to do. Daniel had sounded desperate, and if anybody needed her, especially Daniel—her heart was pounding. Now, what about George? The urgency … *I must leave now and go over there immediately.* "Bea, I'd better go now."

She pulled into the parking lot at the home and nearly ran to the elevator. Her foot worked like new. *Those corticosteroid drugs are miracles, but I can't take them forever ... and Daniel is IN TOWN. Almost like it is a plan. I couldn't have let him see me limp too badly. Now wait a minute—you are NOT SEEING HIM.*

An IV was dripping into George's arm and they were giving him blood as well. George's eyes were closed and his breathing was uneven. *Oh God, George, don't leave me now—now that we are just getting to know each other.* He had been in pretty good shape the last time she saw him. She picked up his chart, and read, "Pt has taken a downward turn—keep him comfortable." She remembered how years before she and her mother had discussed living wills, she and George had made one together—neither wanted to be kept alive by artificial means. She quickly went to the bed and took George's hand and thought, *No burger and fries needed now.* George opened his eyes. "Jessie, you CAME. I knew you would, honey."

"Of course, Dad, I'm here. I was coming anyway tonight—we were thinking about each other."

"Jessie, I'm glad to see you and I need to tell you something. You know about the living will, don't you? Well, that is what I want definitely want for myself. None of this bringing-back stuff. You see so many folks here that they have brought back and then they die again before very long, and maybe lose some of their marbles in the meantime. There's a time to be born and a time to die. The way I see it, why suffer twice? Honey, I am not suffering now; they have given me something for the pain and that's all I need." Jessica's eyes filled with tears—remembering the last time she stood by the bed of a loved one. Yes, she realized then, she did love George.

"Dad, you are not going anywhere. I won't let you! I want you still to be HERE."

"Jessie, I know you have always been religious in a churchly way—well, I need to tell you something. I am not sure about what the church has taught—heaven or hell—all that stuff, but I KNOW we go somewhere, else why live at all? Maybe a cosmic consciousness or something, close by, but I KNOW also we come back. What we have accomplished here isn't lost—or what we haven't accomplished. We somehow meet it again and maybe the circumstances are turned around. What I mean, honey, is we may be with people, or souls that we have been with before, because we need to work out something or maybe failed to work out something, so we meet it again." George paused and sighed. "Even when I was a small boy, I knew I had been here on this Earth before." George was rambling on weakly, but like he really believed what he was saying.

"Dad, I have never heard of such a thing—I just want to be me and you to be you!" Jessie said, tearing up.

"Jessie, I won't be here in this body much longer—it is worn out. But my soul is not—it will go on and on until I get it right and then I haven't figured out the rest…." He looked at Jessie with continued interest. "That guy you have dreamed about—there is a clue for you there. I've been thinking about it."

Jessica thought, but I didn't tell him, *It was a baby I dreamed about—a baby with Daniel's eyes—I didn't tell him THAT!* "Dad, please don't wear yourself out by talking so much—please rest—I will be right here." Jessica pulled up a chair and sat down and patted his head. He felt so cool and clammy, his breathing labored….

George's attention suddenly shifted from Jessica to across the room. His dark eyes stared seemingly at something. "Go away now," he said and he tried to move in the bed and throw up his free hand as if to stave off something.

"Me? George, I am going to stay here. You don't want me to go away, do you?"

"No, not you, honey. THEM, over there … see?" George obviously was hallucinating. Jessica had seen it before with very ill patients. She was afraid for him. She hoped he would go to heaven, but if he didn't believe in heaven—where would he go? She thought about what he had said about Daniel and the dreams. How did he know? George looked back at her and patted her hand as if he read her mind. "Jessie, I am getting very sleepy, but don't let me sleep—I need to talk a little. I need to tell you that for each life there is a plan—my plan is almost over for this life, this time—you need to find yours and make the decisions, the right choices. You have an illness, but your illness isn't YOU—it is your shell acting up—just as mine did—but I am old; you have many years yet—you may need to do something—play your hunches, okay?"

"What should I do, Dad? I need you."

George trailed off. "If something or someone keeps coming into your life, it is for a reason—don't turn your back. I feel I need to tell you that—we haven't really had too many 'heart-to-hearts,' have we?" He smiled faintly and Jessica slipped her hand up to his pulse and it told her he was talking too much and overtaxing himself.

"Dad, please don't try to say too much—please let's just be together for a while."

"I'll see you in a little while; guess I need to rest a little." George looked at her and Jessica hugged him and kissed him. His eyes closed and Jessica sat with him until he seemed to be sleeping peacefully. A nurse came in and said, "He is a fine old gentleman."

"I know, and I wish I had realized that sooner," said Jessica as she put her head on his chest, unable to hold back the tears. Jessica knew this would be his last sleep. "I'll never ever forget you, George." Into her mind came, *"His soul will not sleep…."* Where did that come from?

Jessica stayed with the sleeping George for another hour or so, holding his hand. His hand seemed to give a little jerk and she slipped her hand up to his pulse, which could no longer be found. *Wait, please, George!* Her heart seemed to leap from her chest. *Finish helping me, if you can.* "I love you, George," she said out loud.

Jessica sat by George's bed weeping; she couldn't seem to control her grief. Why had she not realized sooner how she and George connected? It had been a waste, such a waste! And it had been her fault for being so stubborn. She had let her adolescence carry all the way to adulthood and then some. One should never harbor a grievance. It leaves a scar. She hoped George knew that she loved him now and would take that love to heaven.

She finally called her girls and together they made the arrangements for her stepfather. He had been such a fine man, a deep-thinking man, a philosopher…. *Why did I not know that sooner? We make so many mistakes in our lives. I have made my share. George, please know how I did care about you. Somehow, take that with you.*

Then, *Home, I must go home!* It was very late—too late. Oh if she could have just talked a little more to George. What did he mean with his strange comments?

Daniel. He would be there looking for her. She couldn't cope with that now. Too much too soon. She called Becca again and told her she didn't want to be alone tonight. Becca said that certainly she could come there. Becca's house had a wonderful guest room with an attached bath. It would be no trouble at all for Jessie to spend the night with Becca, Jon, and the boys. No Daniel tonight.... *Oh Daniel!*

CHAPTER FIFTEEN

George's private graveside service was the day after he died. He had no other family except a nephew in California, who was notified but did not have the time to come. So Jessica and her family stood quietly as the minister from her church said a few comforting words. George had not been a church member.... Jessica and the girls each put a rose on his coffin and walked away to be together at Becca's house. Jessica told her girls about the George that they had not known, a dear person, the deep George, the philosophical George, the stepfather she had not allowed herself to really know until too late. "Don't be so hard on yourself, Jessica," Jon said. "He is in heaven now and his memory will always be with you."

"Mom, why not stay here again tonight?" Becca asked. Jessica gladly consented—she did not want to be alone with her thoughts.

Meanwhile, Daniel drove like a fiend to Jessica's: 500 miles of speeding, no stopping to eat, rest, or anything else. Finally arriving well after dark, he circled the block around Jessica's house for what seemed like hours. He was furious ... where the hell was she? His mind was in turmoil. "I know she was at work yesterday—she has to come home some time; she can't be staying away on purpose—she loves me—she said she did before I left—I know she still loves me...." He visualized Jessica's black curly hair and beautiful eyes. Then, he thought of her in bed with him—*she is mine,* he thought. *She'd better not be seeing anyone else!*

Finally, though, tired of circling the block, he thought, *I'll show her. I'll just cross the bridge, go to a bar, and have a couple drinks; then surely she will be home.* Daniel crossed the Ohio and before long was in the heart of downtown Cincy. He began looking on Vine, but waited until he found a hole in the wall at the end of Vine in a dubious part of town. Like any large city, the Queen City has its objectionable areas, but Daniel wasn't thinking too clearly. He entered the seedy-looking place and located a table in the corner of the room. Looking around and seeing the crude-looking guys lounging there—regulars, he assumed—he felt a little afraid. A waitress with a bosom that nearly hit him in the face took his order of a beer. She swung away, hips swaying, then busied herself with the keg until she came swinging back. He thanked her and laid his money on the table. He would have liked to put it in her hand, but was afraid she might belong to someone in the place. He took a long pull on his beer, staring at the different people as they came in, but cast his eyes away as soon as one might look his way. *I don't belong here,* he thought. *This place is for the hardcore; maybe I'd better get out of here. There might be trouble here,* he thought. Almost simultaneously with that thought, a hostile-looking reprobate shoved he way inside. He looked Daniel's way. "What ya staring at, buddy?"

"I'm not your or anybody else's buddy," snarled Daniel.

"I can see that, and I don't like to be stared at, imbecile!" said the man.

"Nobody calls me an imbecile, you creep, and gets away with it," yelled Daniel, although more than a parcel of fear measured up his spine.

"Get up, you son of a bitch!" barked the man.

Daniel slowly got to his feet and met a fist that had the strength of a professional fighter. He hit him repeatedly—in the face and chest. Never skilled as a fighter, Daniel helplessly slumped over. The man was unrelenting. Two men came from behind the bar and yelled, "Stop it, Gus, you'll kill him!" The men picked up Daniel like a sack of feed and threw him in the alley.

A curious rat sniffed his face and crawled the length of him several times before Daniel regained consciousness. He picked himself up and limped through the alley to the street, found his car, got in the front seat, and managed to lock the doors. He lay down on the seat and passed out again.

Nearing 2 a.m., a patrol car noticed dirty sandy license plates on a car parked out in front of the bar. Most of the habitués of this joint were well known to the cops. They stopped to investigate and found Daniel in a state of collapse, slumped almost to the floor. They knocked on the window. Daniel, so suspicious of the police, nearly started the car to make a run for it, but he was too weak from loss of blood. He unlocked the car door and an officer opened it. Daniel fell into his arms. "Who did this to you, sir?"

"Don't know," mumbled Daniel.

"You need some help—I'll drive you to the emergency room at UCMC." He took Daniel's keys and got in the driver's side and drove him to the hospital, with the other officer following in his car.

At the hospital, the officer stayed with him for what seemed an eternity before a nurse came to check on him. She put him on a cot. As he lay there, he occasionally felt the length of his sore and stiff body. Nothing broken it seemed, but he was afraid his face might be garbage. The officer seemed almost human. He asked Daniel if he would like to press charges. Daniel knew he would never be in that place again and said, "No." The mere presence of the police made him shake.... He would not want to face anyone in that place again. Finally, the clerk came in.

"Could I help you find your insurance card, sir?"

"Don't have one," said Daniel

"Okay, you have no insurance?" retorted the lady. Apparently, they were used to treating people off the street.

Then a different woman came in. "Do you have a nurse called Jessica here?" Daniel asked weakly.

"No, we don't," said the nurse.

"You don't know?" mumbled Daniel.

"Look, this is University of Cincinnati Medical Center on Goodman; she doesn't work here. You're going to need a workup on your face—your nose and your cheekbone on the left are broken; that gash on your cheek is nasty. We will need to do the surgery now before it swells more, or we will have to wait until the swelling subsides."

"Will I have to have a shot?"

"Look, honey, you won't even know it until we are through," the nurse said kindly.

A doctor came in. "Looks like you ran into a wall, mister—don't worry; we'll take care of you." The nurse brought in a form for his permission to do the surgery. "Just sign here if you will."

"I'm not signing anything. Just do it, but I want to be awake; don't put me to sleep. I won't have it!" Daniel cried.

"You have to sign this or we won't DO it and you will go out of here looking like a bulldog." She guided Daniel's hand to the form and he signed "Dick Jones." *My face,* he thought. *Will Jessica know me? She should have been home. Why did this happen? Why? Why?*

"Okay, honey," said the nurse. "Let's get those clothes off, get you cleaned up, and put on a nice gown."

What next? thought Daniel as she held out his arm and started dabbing alcohol on it.

"What's that?"

"We're starting an IV in your arm—you've nice veins. Hold it straight now!"

"You're not putting that thing in MY arm," yelled Daniel.

More people in white gathered around his stretcher, held him down, and helped the nurse position the IV and then start wheeling him down the hall.

“What’s your name?” asked one of the white-clothed people.

“Daniel’s my name, just Daniel.”

“Someone really did a job on your face,” one of the white-clothed people said.

Into a cold, bright room they wheeled him, and then the stretcher stopped under bright lights. He was surrounded with more white people wearing masks and gloves. The drug was put in his IV. “Okay, Mr. Daniel, start counting backwards from ten.”

“Don’t think you are putting me out! You are NOT putting me to sleep! No way! They did that to me before and I am not going to let you!” Daniel started up and off the cot until several helpers saw the commotion and helped hold him down while his arms were restrained. The doctor proceeded with the anesthesia. Whether Daniel knew it or not, he was soon in Never-never Land. It took the surgeon, Dr. Patrick, over an hour to repair first the cheek before even starting on the nose; then, began the intricate work around the eyes and finishing with his mouth. So many bones were broken it was a tedious but skilled job.

The next thing Daniel knew, he was waking from a drugged sleep. *What is real the clouded Daniel thought. Is this a room or…?* “Where am I?” he rasped. “Wha … did ya do to me? What did YOU DO TO ME?”

“Are you waking up?” A different nurse was by his bedside and he was in a long, anesthetic-smelling room with one bed after another. His face felt the size of a basketball. “Oh God, what did you do to me? What did you do to my face? It's like before—it's true. I'm telling the TRUTH!" Daniel didn't know what he was taking about, but in a way, it was familiar; he had done this before. The bed, the nurse—he remembered, he had done this before. *Where? What truth? What the devil am I here for?*

The nurse patted his hand. "It will be okay, Mr. Daniel. The truth is you were in a fight and we had to do a little repair work on your face." Daniel reached up to his face and felt nothing but bandages.

"My face, my face. What does my face look like? I'm a handsome dude … or I was…." He trailed off—nearly asleep again.

The nurse smiled. "You will be a handsome dude again. Dr. Patrick is the best plastic surgeon we have on staff." Daniel could feel the tears through the gauze dressings as he went back into his drugged sleep and he bounced on a pink cloud of heaven.

Later, he grabbed at this bandages. "Take these off!"

"Now, Mr. Daniel, I will stay with you until you get out of recovery, but I can't let you take off the bandages. It's too soon."

"It hurts so much, I can't stand it!" cried Daniel.

"It is a little early to give you a shot for pain—the anesthesia hasn't worn off completely, but I'll ask the doctor." The nurse disappeared.

"Where did you go?" yelled Daniel. "I need help! I hurt bad, really bad—but no shot, no you don't!

Where is Jessica? I want Jessica!" Daniel was sobbing under his bandages.

Finally the nurse came back. "Look, honey, you are going to have to keep yourself under better control. I know it hurts, but there are people in here in a lot worse shape than you, and you are going to have to stop clawing at those bandages. You want to be a handsome dude again, don't you? Well, leave them alone!" she said sternly.

"I'd like you to be here and see how it feels!" snarled Daniel, pulling at his bandages. "Let me out of here!"

"Stop it, I said! Out of here and you really will hurt!" the nurse replied loudly. "Turn over now—that's it…," and shoved a needle into his butt a little harder than was necessary. She had told the doctor about the difficult patient who might need something more just to control him.

The doctor said, "No way."

"I SAID NO SHOTS!" The tears welled up again under the bandages

In what seemed like minutes, Daniel's thoughts soared. *Oh, this cloud I am on is better than life—was this what Joey felt…? Is this why Joey used that stuff? Oh, Joey. I know I didn't do it; they said I did, but I know I didn't, I didn't, I didn't—THEY DID IT, THEY DID IT….* The cloud of euphoria made thoughts tumble over thoughts…. *I wonder what happened to Maria.… Why wasn't Jessica home? Will Jessica still want me? I want her, only Jessica—if I get out of here—what if I look like garbage…? Jessie may be scared of me.*

Oh God, I am not a bad man ... I am a good man ... God, just let me out of here okay and I will prove it to You. I know You exist. I might even go to church even though I know you aren't there.... I didn't ever really do anything bad. I really am a good man ... I will make Jessica want me back ... but what if my face is gone...? I had just a great face.... Daniel finally drifted into a restful sleep ... until the stabbing pain jarred him awake.

"Please somebody help me! I'm about dying in here...," moaned Daniel in a yell that made the nurse quickly come to his aid.

"I know it hurts, honey, but you will have to be brave a little longer. Since you hate shots so much we will put the medicine in your IV, okay?"

"Yes, no, no shots, but anything for help—it hurts too much—what did that doctor do to me? My whole face is burning up and hurts like hell! Anything for relief—I want what I had before. I want to go to sleep and not wake up until this pain is gone. Please do it, anything, NOW!"

The nurse, realizing the type of patient she had on her hands, came back in a hurry with the medicine and said in her most soothing voice, "Okay, here, no shot—into the IV it goes, but it will take a slight bit longer for you to feel the effects of it. I'll stay right here until you ease up a bit, okay, feller?"

"Yes, please don't go. You help me by being here. I can see you here and I would know if you left. Please don't go, please!"

CHAPTER SIXTEEN

Most of Daniel's days in the recovery room were blurs of in and out of what was real to him, the pain, and his special times of soaring into a dream world. The staff's decision to apply his pain medicine into his IV proved useful to both them and Daniel. His bouts of dismay and near hysteria were too much. His fear was real to him. He was so afraid there would be a repeat performance of something he only sensed. This vague remembrance, what was it? He was sure it had happened when he was in that institution or whatever. It brought back half a memory that he had not done something, but was being blamed for it. Joey, it had to be about Joey, but what had really happened?

In three days he was wheeled down the hall into a ward of six beds. He kept crawling around the bed, nearly losing his IV, and clawing at his bandages. Then, not only did the staff bother him about that but also the guys (other losers, he supposed) yelled at him to stop. There were only occasional nurses in the ward, who tried to calm him.

He finally settled down, convinced he was there to get better and that he had better, for his own good, cooperate. He had lost all track of time, and knew only that he had been there too long. Occasionally, he would cry salty tears into his bandages. Would he ever be the same? Would he ever see Jessica? *Jessica will not know me. I will have to sing to her. Please God, let my face be all right. I will thank you over and over again. I didn't do anything wrong to deserve a messed-up face. Why, why did I go to that bar? Jessica didn't come home, and where was she? I merely wanted to get even with her for not coming home. But it wasn't her fault. I know it wasn't. It was me, me, me! I just had to blame her! I was at the wrong place at the wrong time.* His IV was gone and if he asked for pain medicine, it came in pill form. No more soaring—no more pink clouds.

Under his bandages, his face began to itch. He had enough sense at that time to know not to scratch or tear at the bandages. Itching was good; it meant healing. He needed to exercise his body or he would get soft, and he needed to take his mind off the awful itching. He began doing push-ups beside the bed.

"Look at the show-off!" one of the men said.

"The headless Hercules!" Another said.

Daniel growled back, "If I ain't got no head, at least I can whup you. You better shut up!" It became strangely quiet in the room. Nobody but nobody wanted to cause any trouble, and besides since he couldn't see well. Who would he choose to hit?

A nurse finally came to his bedside with the then-familiar Dr. Patrick. "Okay, Daniel," he said, "this is your big day. Let's see my handiwork." Slowly the nurse began to unwrap the bandages from his face in a long trail of gauze. Daniel wanted to pull them off but he contained himself. Dr. Patrick said, "In time, you will look as good as new."

"In time?" said Daniel. "I want to look the same now!"

"In time, I said," repeated Dr. Patrick. The bandages finally were off and thrown away. "Now, Daniel," said the doctor, "there is still some bruising and you will see a few stitches, but the stitches are the kind that dissolve. Also, we will give you a laser treatment this morning, which will reduce most of the scarring. We will treat only the scar, so that the healthy tissue won't be damaged. Then, I want you to come back next week for another treatment, if we think it necessary, and that should do it. You will be able to leave the hospital by tomorrow."

Daniel jumped out of bed and ran to the mirror that was used by all the patients in the ward. "Oh God!" yelled Daniel.

"Again, Daniel, you will look completely normal, in time. Actually, it is wonderful surgery considering what you looked like when you came into the ER. This bone on your cheek…," Dr. Patrick gently touched his still-bruised cheek, "… was a compound fracture; it was sticking out of your cheek, "he said in his kind but still condescending voice. "We set that back in place, then did a heck of a repair job to make your cheek still look like your cheek. Your eyes were punched up terribly, but they are normal now with only a few slight bruises left, and, as I said, those stitches will dissolve. Your lips had to be stitched, but they are almost normal now and you will be able to eat solid food, same as always. Your nose is nearly back to normal. We had to take a special instrument and put it inside to set what would have been all over your face. I am really proud of the job we did on you, Daniel; you will look fine and completely healed in a couple of weeks. I am not sure at this point that you will even need that second laser treatment. You look fine, comparatively speaking."

"Doctor, you say the bruising will all go away?" blurted Daniel. "Those stitches make me look like Frankenstein! God, what am I gonna do!"

"You don't have to DO anything—your healing mechanism will take care of you and, as I said, you will be good as new; listen to what I am telling you!" Dr. Patrick knew the difficulty Daniel had caused and he was growing weary of him now. He would be glad when he could release him. The more he thought about it, one treatment ought to do it and even if it didn't….

After the doctor and nurse left, Daniel ran again to the mirror and gazed at himself. He began to see that he would look like himself again when the bruising left, but those stitches were ugly sons of bitches. Those laser treatments would have to work miracles. Some guy from across the room said, "Oh, look at him; boy he is a handsome creature!" This was not said unkindly and the voice it came from was hooked up to all kinds of machines. Daniel looked around, seeing fully now without all the bandages blocking his vision. When he looked at the other patients in the ward, he realized they would not be as lucky as he to get out tomorrow. They may never get out, alive anyway. Basically, he felt good—good to be alive and free from all the mess of the hospital. He thought back to the bar and the beating that put him there. *Oh, what a fool I was. Would Jessica even remember me? She knew I was in town, and then it was like I had gone away again. But she wasn't there. Purposely I guess.* He got back in bed to await his lunch. He would be able to eat like a normal person without all those bandages. *Oh, God, please let me heal fast so that I can find Jessica again. Maybe she is sick or something; maybe she has moved or something. I can't stand not knowing. I think I really am in love with Jessie. Always have been, ever since I first saw her in that restaurant—there is something about her that I can't put my finger on. Something that makes me feel so close to her and no one else. But why did I leave her? If I hadn't left, we would be together. I am so stupid. Guess I just didn't want to get too close too soon, and then I didn't want to get too close because I was afraid to love her because I might lose her. I couldn't stand the thought of that. She is mine. She will realize that when I am with her again. I do love her. I do, I do. I will do everything to prove to her that I do. Why is it that when someone is within your grasp, you blow it? I blew it. Maybe she will never want me again. I must somehow convince her I am sincere now. What can I say? I will sing to her. She has always loved my singing. What can I sing to her that will be the right song? Maybe that beautiful song "Hello, My Friend, Hello." That way we will take it slow again—not like before. Go slowly and not look back, but only ahead. That way, she will know I don't just lust for her; I want her first as my friend. If we cannot be friends, we cannot be anything. But I want everything, everything. I can almost feel her close to me ... where she belongs....*

Daniel was lost in his thoughts when the diet people brought in his food. Real food this time, and it looked good. The girl looked at him with surprise and said, "Well, hello, handsome!" Daniel smiled, then got out of bed and looked at his face again. *It will be all right,* he thought, *all right.* He touched his face gingerly and resisted the urge to rub the scar. It itched horrendously.

That afternoon Daniel was wheeled down the hall and taken by elevator to the basement into the laser room for his treatment. "Is this going to hurt?" said Daniel.

"No," said the doctor, "only a little sting. Put on these goggles to protect your eyes and we will work only on the scar. This isn't bad at all. One or two treatments should fix you up good."

"Can't you work on the bruises, too? I gotta go see someone."

"Those will be gone as soon as all the hematomas under the skin dissipate. It should be another week or so and you will be good as new. Remember, you are lucky to be alive. It says here in your chart you sustained a severe beating. This light will work only on the scarring. That's good, we're finished. See, that didn't hurt much at all."

The next day they took Daniel by wheelchair to his car. It seemed to him strange to be in the real world again as he slid behind the steering wheel.

"Don't you have anyone to drive you home, sir?" said the attendant.

"No, nobody likes me," replied Daniel with a surprising grin. He felt so free and happy to be alive that the euphoria that came over him was a surprise even to him. He carefully drove out of the parking garage and into the street. It felt funny to be behind the wheel. *Home,* he thought, *where is that?* So here he was, without a home, and even without Jessica until his face healed completely. He looked in the rearview mirror to catch an image of himself. He hoped those jokers at the hospital knew what they were doing … what they were talking about. He couldn't even try to see her now. *What can I do?* he thought. He drove to the river, parked, and got out of the car. It was a sunny day, though very cold; his jacket proved not warm enough since he was so used to Galveston. He got back in the car, looked at the peacefulness of the sun on the river, and pondered what he should do. *I need to at least try to call Jessica and find out if she still cares about me, then find a place to stay. This car is a mess and Jessica is a lady. Why didn't I notice this wreck before? I guess 'cause I am a wreck. I'm not feeling so hot. I need to find a place to stay now. Then lie down a bit. Yes, that is first thing. Lying around so much has made me tired. I wonder if they did anything to me at that hospital. No, they were kind—they fixed me and I didn't even have to pay. I paid last time—paid with whatever they did to me, to my head. Oh, why did it have to be, and why did they blame me for Joey? I KNOW I didn't do it—they did it to cover themselves.... Joey was my kid. I wouldn't kill him; I just hit him. I know they did it, I know they did, and then put me in that funny farm....* It all came back to him in a rush, tumbling in his mind like a whirlwind.

I can't do away with that now. What is, is. I have to get my face well and then see Jessica; I have to see her. I know she will still care for me. She has to, she just has to ... I won't have it any other way.

Daniel drove around 'til he came to a fashionable neighborhood. He soon found himself on Mehring Way and then arrived at a beautiful apartment complex, One Lytle Place. He brought the car to a quick stop. *I can't afford that! But I'm recuperating; maybe for a little while, and maybe if my face heals fast I can invite Jessica here and she'll be impressed.* Daniel took a quick inventory of the outside, then went in. The woman at the desk looked surprised. Surprised to see someone, or maybe surprised to see his ugly face. "What can I do for you?" she said in a weak, trembling voice.

"As you can readily see, a lot," said Daniel. "Do you rent by the week?"

"No, sir, only by the month," she said. "These are luxury apartment dwellings, well worth the price." She indicated the price of the one-bedroom.

"That is highway robbery!" exclaimed Daniel. "But let me see one."

"Come this way, sir. Down the hall, up the stairs, and to the right, and I will point out all the amenities—I know you will like it." The girl sounded enthusiastic. It seemed to Daniel that she was trying not to look at him.

She unlocked the door and let him go first. It really seemed spacious for a one-bedroom. Daniel crossed the large room to the balcony and looked out at the bustling city below. In his mind, he put himself out there, guitar in hand. In the evening, it would be quiet enough for him to write—write a song for Jessica. Yes, he could do that. That would open the door for him. "I'll take it," he said. He had enough savings for at least some time, and then he could make do until Jessie took him back. "I'll pay you your money, but will I get any back if I don't stay for a month?" asked Daniel.

"Probably," said the girl. "We can take that up with the manager, but you will like it here; everybody who lives here does!"

"Time will tell," answered Daniel.

CHAPTER SEVENTEEN

Jessica spent a third night with Becca and Jon, and then went in to work. Word had spread about her stepfather's death. On her desk were a beautiful hyacinth and several sympathy cards. She was so thankful for the harmonious situation at work; the people were so caring and considerate. She knew not all hospitals were so peaceful; in fact, not all departments in her own hospital had folks that got along so well on a daily basis.

Her flu had finally gone and she didn't feel weak from it anymore. The after effects had persisted far too long, but now she felt just fine. Even her leg remained better, but she was still taking a small amount of the steroids. She knew that when those stopped, her MS might take a turn for the worse, again, but she would pray. Prayer maybe did help, or then again maybe it just helped to not feel so helpless against this monster. *Please, God, let it remain in remission. It can, you know, because You know all things, right?*

And what about Daniel? What do You know about Daniel? She had the feeling he was close by, but if he was, the phone would be ringing off the wall. Maybe … maybe since she had not been available maybe he gave up, and maybe he found someone else. She had a strong feeling that this was not the case; he was waiting for something.... *Play your hunches....*

George said, "Follow your intuitions." Well, she had those for certain. Maybe as a courtesy or perhaps in remembrance of him, she should see if the library said anything about such things. "Far-life memory," he had said. Reincarnation? That was crazy! She had no idea what it would be called. It certainly wouldn't be anything scientific. Maybe a librarian would know. Rather than buy books, she still had her library card, even though she hadn't done much heavy reading lately. This was heavy. *Too heavy for me.* Magazines had been her genre. Magazines on how to modernly spruce up the house, or fashion magazines. She always wanted to look nice, to somehow compensate for her illness and for her house to reflect her personality or maybe her soul. Her soul? That sounded like George. Maybe George was somehow leading her. George was a good man; he had probably gone straight to heaven. Maybe. Did you go to heaven if you didn't believe in it? Ministers, who were supposed to know it all, were pretty vague about heaven. They just cast their eyes upward and gave assurances. Well, the truth of the matter is, nobody really knows. But the Bible said the sheep were separated from the goats. She knew she couldn't be a goat, although those scenes with Daniel may have made her borderline! Then, one couldn't take the Bible word for word anyway; there were too many contradictions. She needed to look somewhere in the library where there were no contradictions, if there were such a thing.

Why did she feel Daniel was close at hand? After that desperate calling, there had been nothing for over three weeks. *I hope he is all right. I wouldn't want anything to happen to him. Now wait a minute—you gave the idea firmly that you did not want to see him. Perhaps it sunk in and now he doesn't want you. Well, maybe that is for the best. Oh God, I wish I could just see you one more time, Daniel. I do love you, even though things are not at all right between us and you need help! Then, there is this stupid MS. I should have been honest from the very beginning. I have never been dishonest; well, not since I was a teenager anyway. This was crazy of me, crazy to want someone, then tell him later. Maybe I am a goat after all!*

Jessica looked fleetingly behind her as she entered her car. *Now just who am I looking for?* she thought. *I need to find a hobby! Why think about someone who will never, never be right for me? And besides he must be gone again. For one thing, my dishonesty would catch up with me, and then what will I do? I will have to fess up and say, "Daniel, I have been lying to you all along. I have an illness that may get worse, has gotten worse, and then you won't want to be with me. I know that because you have problems of your own. You will not want to live with the problem that I have. You will not want me and I love you so much. But, I cannot help it. I didn't ask for this, but I am asking for you. Even though I know you will be better off with someone else, someone who is strong and healthy. As well as someone who can cope with your ups and downs. Your strange behavior, that at times scares me. Where are those demons in your closet and why are they there? Daniel, I know you have had a difficult life even though you pretend it is not so and that everything is all right. Then you shift gears and suddenly everything is all wrong. What is it, Daniel, and where are you, my love?"* Jessica knew she was almost crazy with worry. *Daniel, you were here; now where are you? You are not right for me. Not right in any way.* Those dreams, his eyes, and George's beliefs. Does everything have a plan to it? Should she really follow her clues from her dreams? Maybe it would be for naught. Maybe he had disappeared again—and yet she felt he had not. She felt he was close by and just not calling for some reason. *God, I hope he is all right!*

I am thinking crazy thoughts. I told him to leave me alone and he obviously is. So be it. My life is better off without him.

But he needs me!

She drove to the downtown mission, with her mind on little more than her dreams and their significance, to her bimonthly work as a volunteer. Her job assisted poor human beings down on their luck and others who were unable to make it through the day without a bottle. What a life! She could not decide whether those who were alcoholics merely had a bad habit they could not break or if it really was a disease. The disease idea certainly gave them the benefit of the doubt. The truly sad cases were whole families without a shelter other than the mission. Many churches had a program called "Room in the Inn" that was very helpful by providing ample nutrition and a warm place to stay during particularly cold nights. Some refused to go to the churches, and it was those that she helped at the mission. Did they not believe in God? Perhaps they thought God had turned away from them.

This evening, through, her thoughts ambled to wondering how these people began their lives—had they been cute babies with parents who cared? If so, then what happened with them? Surely they wouldn't just have always lived on the outskirts of society and would continue to do so. Usually, she just dished up the food, was pleasant to them, but never really wondered what their history might be. She thought about the baby in her dream, the baby she lost—could something like this have happened to any of these unfortunate people? Everybody had a history; could there be more of a history than people are consciously aware of? George seemed to think that there was.

Maybe she would get some answers when she visited the library. There might have been others who thought the same as George. George, she had found too late, thought deeply about these things. Could he be right? No, it was too crazy—at least it seemed crazy to her. Except for the recurring dreams—the dreams that began when Daniel arrived on the scene. Could there be a connection? The baby's face had the blue eyes and features of Daniel, even though it was a baby. That too was absurd!

After finishing her job she went on home to her own little nest. Since she had been away for a while, things looked a little strange. She made a cup of tea and sat on the couch. *Home is the best place,* she thought. *Alone, to think.* She wasn't with her thoughts very long before the phone rang. She inwardly groaned. *It's nine o'clock and I don't want to be on the phone now. Hope it's a telemarketer or someone else I don't know—I don't want to talk to anyone now; I've got to think about what to say to a librarian—she will think I am harebrained.*

Jessie walked slowly to the phone and lifted it with no anticipation. The phone's ring stopped and there seemed to be no one there. However, a chill went down her spine. It was Daniel. *I know it was and why didn't he say anything? I am glad he didn't, but why call without talking to me? Now wait a minute; it was probably just a crank caller. Why must I always have him on my mind? If I could just turn off this CD player of a brain—just quiet it down ... it is driving me nuts!*

CHAPTER EIGHTEEN

Daniel peered into the mirror. *Oh God,* he thought, *it is getting better. Why couldn't I say anything to Jessica? It just wouldn't come out—like I was tongue-tied or somethin'. I wanted to; I just couldn't. Could I be ashamed of myself? I don't think so. It wasn't my fault she wasn't home before and I had to go to that bar. But did I? Did I have to? Now look what I have done to my face. But I do think it is getting some better, and the scar is fading. The bruises are almost gone. Even the woman at the desk said I looked better. All I needed to do was say hello to Jessica, then talk for a little bit, see how she is. That is all I needed to do; but no, I had to hang up like a nut. Now look, I can call myself a nut, can't I? Would she talk to me?* Daniel was having a long conversation with the mirror. *Maybe it's a good idea to look at myself and talk. See what I really see, sort things out, and try again to call. Not tonight. Tonight she will have thought it was just some crank caller, some creep. Yes, that is what I am, some creep!*

Time. I may not have much time! A looker like Jessica might find someone any day now—someone she likes better than she likes me. Someone who wouldn't just take off. But hey, I did tell her I would be leaving; it wasn't like I just left. I told her and I remember how she reacted—she loves me, I know she does. I just needed time to think things over—she will understand that—I can make her understand. Daniel stroked his scar gently and then covered it up completely with his large, muscular hand. *Okay,* he thought, *it will be okay. I can call her before I have my last treatment.* He put his hand on the phone and began to punch in the number, then stopped midway. *No, not now; not tonight.*

Daniel lay down on the bed, clad only in his shorts. He preferred to sleep in the buff, but not tonight. Funny how the mind is. He thought back to when as a small child, his real mother caught him touching himself and what happened to him. She had said she wouldn't whip him, but she did anyway. His remembrance of her was that she was a very pretty lady, but she shouldn't have done that. She wasn't brunette like Jessica, but blonde, with his coloring and his blue eyes. That much he did remember. Then, she died and his father went away. A couple years later, he came back for him from Grandpa's with a new mother. He would have liked to have known his father before this new mother. He remembered more of his stepmother than his mother. *Guess I might have been four or so when she died. Life has been rather mean to me. I need to change things—make them better for me, and one way will be to get Jessica back.*

Daniel couldn't sleep. He thought back to the hospital and being put to sleep, then waking up in pain. The worst pain imaginable! His mind wandered back to that other hospital or whatever it was; being put to sleep and waking up not in pain but confused, so very confused. Each time had been like a small death. How many times did they roll him into that inner room, and why? Each time, he was a little more confused. Finally, he had no remembrance of a block of time of his life. Now, though, he did realize that not all hospitals are bad. This one fixed him up. That one messed him up. It had something to do with Joey. A weird scene floated into his mind. He saw himself awakening with a gun in his hand and Joey's body lying beside him. In the scene, the police came rushing in. They told him he killed Joey. *NO—I KNOW I DIDN'T KILL MY OWN SON!*

What happened there? Why did they ship me off to the funny farm? I don't remember enough. I must remember. I do know I was put there. If I did something bad to Joey, why did I not have a trial? Something's very rotten here, but I think I am beginning to remember a little. It is so foggy. Big tears ran down Daniel's face. *I need to remember—I must remember! I do remember leaving that place. They blindfolded me, but I still knew it was nighttime. I couldn't move. No one talked, so it must have been just one person who drove. I realized I was tied up. We drove quite a distance and I was unbound and dumped out here. Someone said, "Good luck, Cummings."*

I had my identification and my bank book, but I was afraid to go back there. The ATM told me my bank balance, so I established myself here. Strangely, I remember things pretty clearly before that block of time, and especially things about Joey.

Bonny and I needed help with Joey, impossible almost from the beginning ... looking back, Joey was always difficult. Even as a baby ... as soon as he could pull himself up in his crib, he was out of there. "No" meant nothing to Joey. The doctor said "hyperactive" and told them to put a fish net over his crib so he couldn't get out. That didn't contain Joey—no, sir. He figured that out in no time flat and was out from under, crawling down the stairs to get into the first thing he came to. Even spanking didn't faze him. The only way bedtime came would be if it were Joey's idea. He would finally fall asleep on the stairs from sheer exhaustion.

Joey lived on the edge, a daredevil when he got older. "Joey—don't swim so far out in the lake—we don't know what's out there!" The next thing I knew I saw this distant figure far out—too far out.... I went after him in a boat, but Joey refused to get in—eventually swam back to shore. That boy never seemed to wear out. Secretly, Daniel had been proud of his exuberance and strength, but he was so exasperating.

They wanted him to have friends, but other parents feared their kid would get hurt. Daniel thought Joey may have wanted friends, but he only seemed to interact by being too rough.

He became a disruption in all his classrooms. Parent-teacher discussions were a farce. Bonny would cry. Daniel would get mad.

Finally when Joey was twelve, the principal said he would be expelled if they didn't get counseling for their boy, and recommended a counselor from the police department after Joey ended up in juvenile court several times.

What was it with Joey? Why could he not be a normal kid like other kids? I am a good man. Bonny was a good person—was it genetic?

Daniel remembered his mean, sadistic grandpa, who beat him for fun, just to see how much it would take to make him cry. Two years he stayed with him—two long years, waiting for his dad to come get him after his mother died—two years of hell.

He eventually drifted into a fitful sleep, his arms around his pillow, a pillow that was wet with his tears. He dreamed about standing with Maria by the grave of her husband. No grave for Joey. He needed to find Joey's grave, but blocks were always put in his way. Obstacles from nowhere, out of nowhere, but where was Joey's grave? He woke with a start. *My son must have a grave somewhere!* Distraught, he jumped from the bed and, throwing back the covers, he thought, *I'm his father—I must know, I need to know.*

They did get the counselor from the police department. He was someone that seemed to care about kids but who wouldn't take any nonsense. He had been recommended by the school, so he must have known his stuff. Joey, though, didn't get any better—worse, in fact.

Daniel's mind flitted in and out. *Why do I hate the police? Is it because they made Joey worse?*

We were up north and I played solo guitar, a short gig—Joey came to the performance—high. Fourteen years old and high on something. I remember his face, acting so cool, like he knew all things possible in the world. I asked him where he got the stuff and he said what did I care...? No, not my boy—high on crack. I lost it then, and hit him. Then he backed away and said, "I'll show you, I'll tell what you had done to me!" Then, I shook him 'til his teeth shook in his head, but he got away and ran. Then what?

Other people may have blanks in their memories, but why me? I'm intelligent and have always had a good one. I know it was what they did—those jokers at the hospital. I'm sure, now, it was not a real hospital and maybe there weren't any other patients, now that I know how a hospital operates. It's the police, though, that I couldn't stand. Why was that? He remembered how he acted when Maria's husband died. *Why did I act like such a clod—a jerk? It was only something that had to be done, a death report. Nothing serious, but I bolted like a wild horse from a cougar. Maria took me back, but it is a wonder she would have had anything to do with me from then on. It was only after my beating up at the bar that I began to think that not all policemen are bad.* That guy even came to see how he was doing at the hospital and asked him if he needed anything. He knew that Daniel couldn't see very well out of the bandages at the time and brought him in a portable radio. Later he told him he could have it. Daniel, though uneasy, thanked him and thanked him for coming to see him.

He thought of Maria and how he took the ring. *I gave it to her as a present. I just didn't want her to feel engaged. I'm a real clod, but knowing that little butt, she probably has another dude by this time. I had to get away, though, I need to be here. Jessica has missed me, I know she has.* He put his hand on the telephone again.

CHAPTER NINETEEN

As Jessica was rushing out the door on her way to work she heard the phone. *Oh no,* she thought, *I can't be late. If it is someone I know, they can reach me at work or this evening.* She was on the interstate when floating into her mind came Daniel. *Yes, I know it's Daniel. It has to be him. Oh Daniel, I want to see you so much. I want to see you! Maybe he is different—just maybe. Come on now, you know that Daniel will need help before he will ever change. Well, I'm a nurse—maybe I can help him. You know, though, you must take care of yourself, and Daniel tore you down before—his behavior was so strange, so very strange. He needs me, though. Or he needs someone. If my MS gets worse there will be no hiding it from him. Wait a minute, Jessie, the MS—you don't own this disease, nor does it own you.*

Jessica thought back to the strange dreams she had had since Daniel came into her life. *I should tell someone, perhaps speak to a counselor or my minister or someone.* And what was her stepfather talking about—that we have a far-life memory and what is that? *I remember a lot about my childhood, but only scatterings; not many specifics, though, until I started school and related to other kids. Of course, I remember earlier little things with Mother and Daddy. Mother taught me Bible verses and some poetry. I was very small then. I remember hitting each step when I fell all the way down, but that is a blur, a scattering in my brain. George must have meant something else. Are we blank sheets of paper when we arrive here as babies or do we come with a history?*

Could my dreams be a hint of what may have been for me before? If so, what can I do about it? Or, so what!

It's uncanny that the baby in my dreams had eyes like Daniel. I'm thinking about this too much, wasting time with these thoughts. One thing I know now for sure is I should not see our minister about it. Someone else. I should go to the library and see if there is anything about so-called far-life memory (whatever that is). I don't think he knew anything about psychoanalysis—George was an intelligent man, but the medical field was not his forte.

Could a librarian help me out? I have no idea what category THAT would be. Of all the subjects there are in this world, there could be something on far-life memory, but I surely never heard of it until George's strange words—it seemed urgent for George to tell me, even in his frail condition. Dying, hallucinating, but he had to tell me. Too many words for a man not long for this world. It was so important to him and I know he must have really loved me because he became desperate to tell me.

The day seemed longer than usual—although she was as busy as ever. *I must go tonight, right after work. I will go to the new downtown library; if any library would have a book on far-life memory they should.*

Jessica turned back on the interstate, but instead of her usual route, she headed downtown toward that tall building that had been erected recently and become the new library. She parked in the garage and took the elevator to the first floor. Then fear came out of nowhere. She recalled suddenly how her minister had warned about anything that might be different—of the devil, he had said. She turned abruptly around, took the elevator down, and headed for home. *I must do this, but I must be protected if it is anything "of the devil."* The vision of an old movie came into her mind. *I don't have on my cross. Mother gave me that cross. If anything will protect me, a cross given by my mother will.* Jessica thought about her mother. *Mother loved me and she loved George. Some thoughts of mother from heaven may reach me and protect me. I cannot test these waters without my cross. I will need to wear it every day. Even thinking these thoughts might be wrong whether there is anything at the library on that subject or not. It can't be all wrong, though, or George would not, on his deathbed, have been so determined to tell me!*

Jessica entered her home to a ringing phone. *Oh no,* she thought, *it's him again—it's Daniel.* She waited until her answering machine came on. "Jessica, it's Martha, where have you been keeping yourself?"

Jessica picked up. "Oh, Martha—lots has happened since I last talked to you, and we need to talk! I'm so confused with this life of mine. I was about to go to the library to see if I can sort some things out."

Martha said, "The library—it's dinner time. I've never known you to miss dinner, and it's late to be going to the library. I'd go with you if you would wait until Saturday."

"I can't wait this time, Martha, though I appreciate the offer of having you with me," Jessica said.

Martha could clearly hear the anxiety in Jessica's voice. "Well, I can be there in about twenty minutes—wait for me, okay?"

"Martha, you will probably think I have lost it completely, but yes, I'd like to have you come with me." Jessica was searching for the cross in her jewelry chest as she talked.

"See you, good friend." Martha hung up.

CHAPTER TWENTY

Jessica sat on the couch to wait for her friend. Her fingers fumbled with the clasp of the gold chain that held the cross. She remembered how she admired her mother's silver cross of the same design, and then for her birthday, Mother had given her the gold one. Always so generous, her mother had been. *I don't know why I don't wear it every day!*

Why do I feel so tense? The last time had to do with Daniel, I suppose, and now because of Daniel, I feel about the same way—the way I felt when he had gone into a tangent of sorts. No mystery here. She fingered the cross, outlining its shape with the sensitive tips of her fingers. She felt somewhat protected from the unknown territory she was about to enter. If her mother were here—would she understand? Yes, Mother would have understood and perhaps be interested over time, but she would have to be satisfied that it was right.

The wind was blowing so strongly outside that it made the shutters on the windows quiver and hit against the house. This did nothing to offset her mood. Then came a crack of lightning that made the lights flicker, followed by the expected blast of thunder that shook the whole house. "Gads, I hope the electricity doesn't go off!" she said aloud. She went to her cabinet where she kept all of the emergency supplies, her flashlight, a ready candelabra, and her small, transistor radio. If the electricity did indeed go off, she wanted to be sure of the time since tomorrow was a workday.

She heard Martha's car pull in the drive, tires crunching against the pebbles that she had many times regretted, especially during lawn-mowing time. Raincoat and umbrella in hand, ignoring the ringing of the phone, she made her way as quickly as she could to Martha's open door.

"Glad you brought the umbrella—my hair couldn't stand it. Yours, of course, would get curlier. Sometimes I envy you! Now, what's up?" Martha said in her steady voice.

Jessica quickly plopped down beside Martha and closed the door. She didn't really know where to start and how to explain it in the brief time it took to get to the downtown library. "Martha, you are such a friend! I'll tell you when we get there. We can go to the café and have a hot chocolate or a cappuccino … okay?"

"You know me, always ready for liquid or solid intake." Martha laughed, thinking of the many diets she had been on through the years.

They were there before long, even in the rain, and took the elevator up to the main floor and went straight to the café. Jessica noticed a woman at the desk that she hoped would be of eventual help, but that had to wait until Martha (whom she hoped would understand) was brought in on the plan. Actually, she was glad Martha was here—maybe like she had been before as with the personals, a partner in crime.

Martha ordered a frozen cappuccino with lots of whipped cream. Jessica found them a table in the farthest corner of the café, steadying her coffee and hopefully her nerves. After they were seated, she thought she might as well get on with it, see Martha's face, and then know whether this was something she could do with her friend or needed to do without her. Her hunch was that Martha would not turn her back no matter how strange it all sounded.

"Martha, you remember how sick George was before he died. I made it to the hospital just in time—you remember that, don't you?"

"Yes, of course." Martha looked interestedly curious.

"Well, I had told him about the strange dreams that I had been having repeatedly, and then it was as if he had to tell me something. Although the time I had seen him before—before he was critical—he mentioned something about far-life memory. I thought he might be talking about when I was a little girl or something, but it appears that wasn't what he meant. He meant something strange, like the reason I was having the dreams may be a memory from a past happening I know nothing about. He was hallucinating at the same time he was so far along the path toward death, but still he had to tell me, like he thought it so important. Martha, I think he meant something before this life. I know it sounds crazy … is crazy, but I thought if there would be something anywhere about such a thing, it would be here—in the library. Martha, do you think I'm bananas and it is just a crazy notion? What makes me want to take it seriously is—the dreams, Daniel, and why I can't get him off my mind. He is in town now and I should just tell him to get lost; but Martha, I can't—for some reason I can't. It's like I might lose him again. I feel I couldn't stand that!"

"Well, if you ask me, it would be good riddance! That man has been nothing but trouble for you—you look so much better now—let him be gone. He left you, remember! That would be a good excuse to just tell him to leave again!" Martha's words were stern, but she went on.

"Jessie, the man is bad news, but I think I know what George might have been talking about. I read a book once that supposedly was about the far-life memory of a woman. In fact, I believe she wrote many books. Then there was that man that grew up in Hopkinsville, Kentucky. There has been a lot written about him. I went through a phase when I was interested in such things. However, I finally decided nothing could be proven, so I gave up on it."

"Martha, you mean there are books on the subject? I didn't tell you this—whenever I have one of those dreams, the baby that is snatched from me has eyes like Daniel. I know this is getting bizarre, but I'm relieved you don't think I'm crazy!"

"Never, honey, never, but as far as the baby in the dream having eyes like Daniel, that could be your subconscious mind overworking!" Martha continued. "One of the reasons I was interested and still am a little bit is that when I was a little girl, very little, around two or three I guess, I would keep repeating my name to myself, saying is this really my name and what am I doing here. I thought as deeply about it as my limited vocabulary would allow at that time. Then later, when I started to school at five, it seems I got more into living my life and those memories faded."

"You mean you think you were having far-life memory and it got in the way for a while? Why haven't you ever told me these things?"

“Oh, you get into life as it is now and you eventually don’t think too much about it.” Martha spoke somewhat excitedly as if Pandora’s Box had been suddenly opened. “Another thing that would happen to me when I was very little—in fact I would like to know if there is anything concrete about this. When it was time for bed and Mother turned out my lights, I would lie awake for a while. I would look at the ceiling and there would be mists up there that would churn around. In their churning they would form into figures and those figures would come down to the floor and bend around my bed. I couldn’t make out any definite, recognizable shape, but they had form that would resemble the form of a human being—heads, noses, shoulders, you know. Then after milling around my bed for a while, they would seem to gather together and go back to the ceiling and mill around as mist again. Only they would re-form for a repeat performance. I never said anything to anybody in the family about that; I just figured it happened to everybody when the lights went out. Did it ever happen to you?”

“Martha, I’ve known you at least forever it seems, but you never saw fit to tell me any of this!” retorted Jessica.

“Well, Jess, you have always been so faithful to your church and to your religion that I didn’t feel it would be right to rock the little boat you were on.”

“Martha—get a grip—why not?”

“I’ve certainly felt for a long time that there is so much more to be discovered and it is not that neat little picture that is narrowly expressed in church.

Together we may find some answers. Those dreams you have been having since Daniel entered your life may eventually prove, I hope, that he is not right for you. But it may take a long time and we may never prove anything, though I hope for your sake we do prove that!"

"Martha, I loved and lost this baby in the dream, and that is why I cannot seem to turn my back on Daniel."

"Jessica, I want what is best for you, but from what I have heard of Daniel, he tears you down and is a definitive jerk. However, we will not find out anything just sitting here wolfing down cappuccinos. Let's go talk to the librarian before it gets too late."

Martha sucked up the rest of her whipped cream and together they went to the desk. The librarian seemed deep in thought before looking up.

"May I help you ladies?"

Jessica and Martha looked at each other; then Jessica blurted out, "Yes, ma'am, do you happen to have anything at all about far-life memory?"

"I believe you want something about the occult. That section is called parapsychology. It's on the third floor in the section by psychology, you can't miss it."

"Occult?" Jessica looked disturbed, knowing what her pastor would say about that.

"Occult just means hidden. There are a lot of things we cannot readily explain. If you find any books that interest you, you may take out as many as eight at this library and turn them back in when you are through with them either here or at one of the branches." The librarian seemed to sense Jessica's unease.

"All I know about occult is that it is something to be left alone," Jessica said softly as they took the elevator to the third floor.

"Jessica, I cannot believe that you have lived this long and never read anything about predictions, mediums, and the like. Why, I saw something just the other day about people who believed in reincarnation. Like Poe, Ford, Benjamin Franklin, to name just a few."

"But what about far-life memory—do some remember, while others, normal people, forget? And you seemed to have a little far-life memory—do you think everybody does, then they just forget?"

"William Blake said in a poem, 'Our birth is but a sleep and a forgetting,'" answered Martha.

"All of this is blowing my mind and filling my head with a headache." Jessica lowered her head in her hands.

"Come on, honey," said Martha. "Here is the section we want."

There were three stacks and several rows of books. Next to those books was a section on astrology. Jessica thought of that as pure nonsense. *Also unknown,* she thought.

"Psychoanalysis, and here is one about religions," said Jessica. "Do you suppose one can have a religion that admits to far-life memory? It seems that in order to delve into memory, you would have to be psychoanalyzed. I thought that was just for people that had anxiety or depression problems."

"Jessica, we may have come upon something. Maybe you could be psychoanalyzed and just see if there is something more to be remembered." Martha's eyes sparked with excitement. "What if we both have something previous to be remembered that makes us what we are now? I know this person I was talking about believed the soul has many life experiences, but the soul remains a distinct entity. Your soul enters your body and takes on a lifetime; the brain develops the personality of that lifetime. If your brain, say, happens to be mentally retarded, your soul, then, has the experience of being mentally retarded. This man believed what we are now is what we have been, only totaled up.

"Oh, here's *Venture Inward*; now, I've read this book! It was written by the son of that man I was telling you about from Hopkinsville. The man's name is Edgar Cayce. Look, here's a whole section on Edgar Cayce. His son was Hugh Lynn Cayce. Both are deceased now, but they have systematically kept all his readings in a place in Virginia. Virginia Beach, I think. Early in his life he was fundamentally religious, but through trance he found out about reincarnation. Maybe you can find out something about those dreams by psychoanalysis and maybe trance."

"Trance? Martha, I would be afraid of that—what if I said something I didn't mean to say, or would be embarrassed?" Jessica seemed excited though wary.

Martha said, "We can inquire around and find out about someone with a good reputation, and don't worry—I will go with you."

"Martha, you amaze me! You knew all this stuff and you never told me a thing about it!"

They checked out *Venture Inward, Psychoanalysis and Religion,* and a large volume on reincarnation. The librarian smiled and said that they would certainly find a wealth of information in those books.

It had stopped storming by the time Martha dropped Jessica home. Luckily the power had not gone off.

"Martha, dear friend, get a good night's sleep after I pulled you out on a night like this!"

"You didn't pull me, I wanted to come—the storm made it more fun!" replied Martha.

Jessie didn't relish the idea of a dark house. She needed light. *I really need light,* she thought. *What am I getting into?*

She took a warm bath and gathered herself in her coziest flannel nightgown. *I think I will look at one of these books until I get really sleepy.* When she had positioned herself, book in hand, she noticed the light blinking on the answering machine. *Oh no, I don't want to talk to anyone—it is too late....* But she pushed the button to hear Daniel's voice:

"Honey, it's me. I want so much to see you, please see me. I've had a terrible time. I need you Jessica; you know I need you and love you more than life. Please call me at this number: 298-3232. Please Jessica, I have to hear your voice—it's all I ask—please call!"

Jessica noted the time—he didn't call until 9:00, but he did sound desperate and so loving at the same time. She decided it wouldn't hurt to give him a short call—she missed him so much, too—that voice, oh God, that voice, like none other. She held and cradled the phone for a minute before she punched in the number, determined to make it brief—but she had to call, she had to....

"Daniel, it's Jessica."

"Oh, my love, you did call. I've been sitting by the phone just waiting. I have a lot to say and I know I have disappointed you, but I can explain it all!"

"Daniel, you will get the opportunity I promise you that, but I don't promise it will make a difference. I will see you, but only when I can manage it. Tonight is too late to talk about anything—anything about us, for that matter. I must sleep now. Perhaps I can see you Friday night; will that work?"

"Jessica, I've had an accident, but I am better. I have a cut on my face and I don't look so good. Will that be all right?"

"Oh Daniel, a cut doesn't do anything to you—what is inside you counts. I will listen, but not until Friday. I'll see you at 8 o'clock."

"Oh, Jessie, I love you and I know you have every reason to hate me!" Daniel was almost crying.

"Bye, Daniel." She slowly hung up the phone. Then, uncharacteristically, put her arms around it. Tears came to her eyes. *He's been hurt? How? Where?*

She leafed aimlessly through the large book on reincarnation, thinking how could that be, how could that work—but eternal life in heaven or in hell didn't make sense either. So she finally settled down under the covers—sleepy eyes, but still too many waking thoughts. She fingered the cross around her neck, Mother's gift—would she want me to take an unknown journey? Into her mind came "I shall fear no evil." *Where do these thoughts come from? They just roll into my mind. She put her face in her pillow with the hope for sleep.*

....

She was feeling sad as she bent over and stirred the pot on the fire. Potato soup again. Ulysses had to leave or there would be no meat for the long winter ahead. She smelled the leather of the heavy clothes, which all the men wore for the hunt.

The odor of the leather made her knees weaken. She always hated seeing him go, and especially now since she would be alone with their son. *John won't be contained much longer in his cradle, he is already pulling up—his gown alone dissuades him and that won't last long. He is the image of his father—is that why I love him so much.* She blushed at the thought of their lovemaking—could any couple love so much and so well? Her mother had said it was something she must tolerate—well, she did, oh, she did!

Ulysses held her long and hard. "Darlin', I shall miss thee but be back in the wink of a sheep's eye, you'll see. Wait, I shall come down the path." She held him as a tear ran down her face.

"Oh Ulysses, I love thee too much! John and I are with thee. Godspeed."

The door of the cabin closed and she watched him through the window until he was out of sight. John called out. *He is a bright penny,* she thought. *He'll be talking soon.*

John held up his little hands. "Mum-mummy."

....

Jessica, who awakened only a little, tried to push herself back into the dream—she could almost smell the leather, even though Ulysses had gone from the cabin. She could see him in his tattered suit and the baby in her mind. This couldn't be true, but it seemed it had really happened; that it was so much more than a dream. The cabin—the cabin was the same as in the other dreams. But this was not a nightmare. She felt love, love for Ulysses. *Come on now, Jessica, get a grip on yourself. Of course, it was a dream.*

Now completely awake, this definitely was no nightmare—this did happen. Ulysses had the same build, the blue eyes of someone very familiar—the familiarity of Daniel. *Oh Daniel—we just have one life, don't we? We don't come back; we don't have a history—do we?*

She turned on the light and looked at the clock—5:15. *Maybe I can fall asleep again and find out more.* She turned off the light, closed her eyes, but she couldn't even get drowsy. When she closed her eyes, they seemed closed too tightly; all she could see was a blurred redness of closed lids. She tossed a few times, fifteen minutes passed, then she planted her feet firmly on the floor. *No more of this,* she thought. *Might as well get up. This is useless.*

She ran the water in the tub instead of her usual hurried shower. *I must look a fright—living two lives at once,* she smiled in spite of her worry. *I can't believe such a thing, but now a man in my other life—and it is the same life, the same baby!* The love she felt for this man, this Ulysses, was still fresh in her mind. She put on the most refreshing Clarins facial mask before stepping into the water. One life is enough, too much, but the dreams were so vivid, and why, other than they have to do with Daniel. They started with Daniel. All of this started with Daniel, and when George said, "Play your hunches."

I will see him on Friday. I need to find someone to talk to about the dreams before I see Daniel, if I can. That would be a miracle, though, at this late date. Maybe if Martha could find someone reputable today—she has freedom with her schedule. I could possibly get worked in before Friday. She dressed hurriedly, then called Martha. Martha sounded excited after hearing about last night's dream and said, "I will be on the phone all day—whatever it takes, and I'll find the right person; someone open, but honest."

Jessica had difficulty at work. The idea of going to an analyst seemed so foreign to her. However, this last dream was so different and it seemed to be leading somewhere—somewhere in her past of which she had no conscious memory. Her dream world was completely different—a different place. But since this was not a nightmare but almost pleasant, there may be some meaning to it. She thought again about George and how it was so important that she know something, at least enough to make her investigate. *But I am me,* she thought, *only me. I cannot see how I could be anyone else. Martha will be happy as a lark if I find out something—something deep in the recesses of my mind. Martha is turned on to this stuff. Funny, I've known Martha all these years but didn't know that about her. I guess it is not the usual over-the-coffee-cup chatter!*

When she returned home, there were messages on her answering machine. Martha had indeed found an analyst, an M.D. Ph.D., who was into past-life regression. It turned out that his specialty was relieving pain in the present life by uncovering what appeared to be in the past. Well, the dreams were painful, but only when she had them. The miracle was that she made an appointment for right after work on Thursday, before she would see Daniel on Friday. "But," said Martha, "call me. I need payment for this miracle."

Jessica thought, *You are a great friend, Martha, I'll pay!* She punched in Martha's number and Martha answered right away. "Well, guess what, friend—I have to go with you or he won't see you."

"Really? Why?" said Jessica.

"It seems the secretary or girl-in-waiting leaves on Thursday and there won't be anybody there. He won't see you professionally under those circumstances."

"But he will see me if the circumstances are right, that is, if you come with me, right?"

"You guessed it." Martha seemed to have a grin in her tone of voice.

"Well, old buddy, I'll meet you at the coffee shop if that is convenient, and I know you are just dying to come!"

"Can't wait. It will be another learning experience, and don't worry, honey, see you then," Martha said before ending the call.

Another pleading message from Daniel awaited; she listened to his voice twice, but she would not call him back. He knew they would see each other on Friday and a conversation on a work night would only be upsetting. He could be so emotional.

There was not an opportunity to dream the night of Wednesday. Try as she might, sleep was a foreigner. No sense in even trying—she got up and took another bath, walked around, looked out the window at what was close to a wind storm, ate at least five of the muffins she had made on Sunday, helped herself to too much ice cream, played solitaire on the computer, laid on the couch to watch TV, and tried to read but her eyes were too heavy—heavy. Instead she was seeing Ulysses in her mind. What happened to Ulysses? She seemed to sense that something had happened, something bad, that she had lost him, too. *Now how could I know anything like that—I know nothing about him, other than that I loved him very much and someone took our baby—a weird woman, who seemed like she was a nomad or gypsy, or worse, a witch. I have to get some sleep or I will be a zombie at work tomorrow.* She looked at the clock: 4 a.m. *Maybe if I take another bath with that relaxing stuff, I can get at least an hour or so of sleep.*

Jessica nearly went to sleep in the bath, crept to bed, and did sleep like the dead for an hour or so, until the alarm went off. *I could call in sick, but they count on me. I have to be there.* She put on her mask around her eyes and almost went to sleep again. Wearily she put hot, then cool cloths on her face before she put on her makeup. *I will just have to pretend I got a full night's sleep.* She put on a fall jumper and comfortable shoes, set the alarm, and smiled at the world. It was a beautiful day, and the leaves were dancing in the yard synchronized with the wind—*I slept, I slept, that was a wonderful hour that I slept! Aren't I lucky?*

CHAPTER TWENTY-ONE

Once Jessica got to work and the usual things began to happen, she found she rallied around and before long her talk to herself began to work. *Thank goodness my foot is still working okay; Daniel would not understand a girlfriend with a weird foot. But why do I care so much? He left me and then turned up almost a year later and expects me to take him back. What gall! He said he had been in an accident, though; I at least have to hear what he has to say about that. Jessica, who are you fooling? You know you still love him, still care so much. You know that when you hear his voice your heart will leap! "How do I love him, let me count the ways." Now where did you come from, Elizabeth Barrett Browning? Things seem to be planted in my head out of nowhere.*

She met Martha at the appointed spot and gave her a look of unspoken words.

"Gosh, Jessica, were you up all night?"

"Oh no, I spent a good hour sleeping soundly." Jessica smiled grimly, "Work was a breeze!"

"Oh, honey, I wish you wouldn't stress yourself out so much—I'll be with you and maybe, just maybe, we will find out some answers. It might be very, very interesting," said Martha.

"That may be what I'm afraid of." Jessica looked away.

"Look, let me drive. I don't want you sleeping at the wheel; then, we'll come back and get your car and I'll follow you home, okay?"

"Sounds good. I'll sleep while you drive over there."

Dr. Jerold was located not too far from work in a cottage-type house, painted white with red shutters. Cheerful enough.

"I wonder what will happen behind those red shutters," said Jessica as she struggled to open her eyes.

They both walked in and Jessica said, "Dr. Jerold, my friend Martha here called about me. I'm Jessica Hastings."

"Ah yes, Jessica and Martha." He held out his hand to both. "My secretary has gone for the day; we will get the information on you, Jessica, next time. Have a seat and tell me a little about why you are here." Jessica liked his manner immediately and his charisma seemed to dance around him. She breathlessly told her story or as much as she could think to tell. Also, she added that she might not make much sense because she had not slept due to her apprehension about coming.

"Well," said the doctor, "when we get to know each other better you will see you have nothing to be concerned about—actually sleepiness makes one easier to be hypnotized."

"You are going to hypnotize me then? Martha said something about that." Jessica wasn't sure she would care for that. "Can't we just talk some more?"

"You will not say anything under hypnosis that you would not say under normal circumstances. Some people are not good subjects and can't be hypnotized anyway. But I have a feeling, due to those troubling dreams, that you will be a good subject."

He asked both Martha and Jessica into an interior office. Then he asked Jessica to get comfortable in his overstuffed chair. He then said to her, "You may hear yourself talking—just let it flow.

"All right, Jessica, I would like for you to clasp your hands together and look at your thumbs. While looking at your thumbs you will become sleepier and sleepier, sleepier, and sleepier."

Tired as she was, only a minute passed before Jessica could feel herself begin to breathe very deeply; her head nodded and fell forward. Martha wondered if she was asleep or hypnotized.

"Now, Jessica, I want you to go back in time until you see yourself in school. Do you see yourself."

"Yes, I do, sir."

"Now, let yourself go back until you see yourself in a particular grade in school. You are just a little girl. Do you see yourself?"

"Uh huh, I am at my desk behind Jimmy," said Jessica.

The doctor gave Jessica a large tablet and pencil. "How old are you, Jessica?" he said.

"Six. We aren't s'posed to talk in school," she answered a childlike voice.

Martha was fascinated; the little voice had her convinced....

"Okay, I'll talk quietly and you can just follow my direction like you would in school. Write your name here on this tablet, Jessica."

Jessica printed her name in large, manuscript printing.

"All right now, Jessica, I want you to go back even further in time until you see yourself somewhere else and tell me about it," said Dr. Jerold.

"I'm getting my hair washed. Gramps is holding me over the sink in the kitchen while Mommy washes my hair. It will hurt, but I'm being brave. I'm a big girl. This part doesn't hurt; it's that hurt comb takes FOREVER."

"Is your hair long, Jessica?"

"Uh huh, long and very curly, but Mommy won't cut it. Too pretty, she says." Jessica tossed her head and shook her shoulders as if showing off her hair. She smiled and giggled. "Mommy puts a big bow in it on Sunday."

"All right now, Jessica, I want you to go even further back in time if you can and tell me where you are," Dr. Jerold said in his friendly but insistent voice.

Jessica's eyes were blinking as if she had difficulty placing herself, but she finally said in a small voice, "Waiting, waiting…."

"Waiting?"

"Yes, waiting to be born…." She began to cry.

"Why are you crying?" Dr. Jerold said kindly.

"My mother, my mother … because, because of her pain."

Dr. Jerold had been taping the session, but this surprised him, even though his practice had produced many surprises. "Because of her pain?"

"Yes," said the little voice, "she doesn't deserve pain."

Martha remembered Jessica's mother and tears came to her eyes as well—it was a very emotional statement and so true.

"Oh, yes, I understand what you mean. Now I want you to move away from there to another time another place—do you find yourself?"

It seemed to take no time at all until Jessica's voice changed and she said, "Aye, sir, I bid you, to move from the door is not within my power. I am as one possessed. But I bid you speak nothing of it. I am as one possessed by unnatural cause. Ulysses won't come, he won't come!"

"What is your name?"

"Sir, I am called Elizabeth. Who be ye, sir?

"I am here to help you, ma'am."

"I find it late to be Elizabeth now, so old am I. I were wife of Ulysses. I know how old I am—these craggy hands were as any lady. Ulysses held them." Jessica put her hands up to her eyes. "And my eyes hurt, so blurred are they. I can't see across yonder where he disappeared, and who, pray, be ye?"

"The doctor sent to help. Why do you not want to move from the door?"

"It be necessary at dawn and dusk according to custom. Though my eyes hurt, Ulysses may come back. The village cares for me, but speak nothing of it and of his walking to yon woods. Lost in the hunt they say. I can't believe; only truth I believe, so I keep waiting, waiting.… I have had wickedness fall on me. Ulysses would not have let us lose our child. In my heart, here, sir, I know he's gone!"

"Tell me about it."

"They, in the village, think I may be possessed but protect me all the while. They come to my aid. Every time there is a hunt they bring me parts of deer or bear to smoke. 'T'weren't for my neighbors, I would only have roots an' berries. I tire so of taters, but they keep well in the ground. Can't wait for spring of the year, though old am I."

"Tell me about Ulysses."

"Aye, Ulysses, my husband, sir, gone for years and years. He disappeared in the hunt. They told me the story. They said he got lost from the others. This can't be the truth. I know truth. Ulysses loved me. He would not get lost. He were the leader. And, and…," Elizabeth put her face in her hands, "… while in dense woods, a witch woman took John."

"Oh, I am sorry, Elizabeth. So you live here all by yourself?"

"Yes—all I have, had, is my hope. Am strong though or I wouldst not live through my grief." Elizabeth motioned as if she were picking up her dress to wipe her eyes. "Only the good Lord knows about these things. He must know why I have had to suffer. I have stopped going up to the church. My health goes; my knees can't go to the Lord's House.

"Elizabeth, it sounds like Ulysses must have been a fine man and you loved him very much. It must have been terrible to lose your baby while Ulysses was away; that must have been terrible for you," sympathized the doctor.

"The good Lord knows. I lost the two most beloved of my life—no one couldst know how I suffer—how I feel, and I don't think the truth be told to me. Amos—you know Amos, do you not? Amos were jealous of Ulysses. He could never win at targeting and he would get furious. Like spurs of a rooster! He wanted to fly at him; you could see it in his eyes. He were so hateful when we had our son—he had two baby girls at the time; he looked at Ulysses with hate, with meanness in his heart. I just know he did a terrible deed. Ulysses would not disappear from sight and leave me. But here I wait—for a dream, a dream that won't happen now. Faith somehow sustains. Without faith I am nothing. How I grieve—my tears are for naught. They are gone—my life is destroyed, so why can't God take me? It is a cruel God—I know Him no more. If He cared He would take me from this cold, damp place. I long for spring—just one more spring. Death will come soon—my rest will come, but just one more spring. The wildflowers 'round the oak tree, you know that do you? I want only that—the waiting is nearly over—I am old. Look at these hands—veins, that's all. Ulysses were such a man, a fine man, and I loved him so, so much. At least I have my senses! What a wonderful man, wonderful, he was, you know?"

"Yes, Elizabeth, I know how you must feel, so lost and angry. Now, though, I want you to move forward in time. Where do you see yourself?"

"I cannot see the door anymore. Ulysses will not come back if I can't watch. I desire aloneness. The Lord taketh me to die. I seeth the river." Elizabeth's voice sounded crackly and she could barely speak.

"Where are you now?"

"They carry my box up the church hill. Look't, the tulips and daffodils be up! Springtime of our year is here! But I smell not the daffodils. I am here." Elizabeth's voice had become different.

"Where do you mean?" said Dr. Jerold.

"I float along with the box. They do not know about things as this. What I am cannot be in that box. I am tired of waiting for Ulysses, so I will not be around long.

"I was an old, old woman when I died there, so Ulysses must have died in the woods."

Elizabeth begins speaking in a voice suddenly stronger. "Ah yes, I need to be warm again—warmed by the Light. The Light is everywhere, but when you pass over it becomes so bright, so warm. The Light is True—True Existence. It is Home, but only for a while. I will see many I knew and cared for in this chapter of my Being. Then I will have a little help hashing it all out. This is the way it is—I will have some help, but I will decide whether or not I have made any progress. It is always one's own decision as to how long to stay by the warming Light or whether to go right back. We always have that freedom. If we have made progress, we get to stay and help out others who may be groping for answers, but you have to earn that."

"How do you do that?" queried Dr. Jerold.

"Some of us get to be guides and we go into the mind of someone who will ask for help, but only if they ask. I've been a guide many times, but I doubt if I will get that privilege this time."

Martha was completely fascinated. Jessica's subconscious seemed so knowledgeable, but she wondered if she may have read it....

"Why do you say that?"

"Too much sadness and not handling it well." Elizabeth's voice was strong and knowledgeable. "I may stay a while, though; I need the warmth—I got so old and cold." Elizabeth/Jessica suddenly laughed.

"Oh how the Light warms me! I see Ulysses, but he is just an image for me. He's gone back. You know, been reborn. Why did I wait so long for him?

"What has always been, remains in the Cosmic Bank of Consciousness—my guide thought to tell me that." Elizabeth/Jessica laughed again, like that is just the way it is. "I remember things here, but when I have to go back, I only have an awareness, because my soul will eventually take on new responsibilities—my soul will always be my soul, but it will have new material added to it—hopefully I'll make some progress and not fritter it away waiting for a man—a man that never came back."

"Let me get this straight, Elizabeth. Ulysses is there, but not for you—I don't understand," said Dr. Jerold.

"Well, he has gone back to the Earth plane—I guess he wants to find me again—he grieves, too, and we, we missed each other. His personality in the life of Ulysses is stamped in the cosmic world, but the soul is out searching again in a new form. He may be a baby or small child now with lots of memories, not just from his life as Ulysses, but bits and parts of everything that has ever been for his soul before. But according to the circumstances, those memories fade and are easily forgotten when he lives as a new personality. Then when that lifetime is over, he will have a new summing up to add to the other memories. The potential for growth is always there, although some do not take advantage of the opportunities. Everybody's progress or failure to progress is up to the individual soul. Some never forget and are very aware." Elizabeth seemed to become very expert.

"Do you think you will ever forget Ulysses?" asked the doctor.

"He has gone back out looking for me—souls that have earned choice have choice. Ulysses and I could have had a joyous meeting. At this point I know I wasted what could have been a productive experience grieving over him and over our baby. Very self-centered I was in that lifetime."

Martha knew then she could not have read that somewhere....

"We should learn living is about helping others. That's it. The secret of life—to love others. I was stagnant, feeling sorry for myself. I shall not do that again." Elizabeth wiped tears from her eyes.

"Remember, you will never wait that long again—not again—not again. I will snap my fingers and you will wake up, Jessica. Jessica, wake up now and look around the office to get your bearings."

Jessica rubbed her eyes, blinked a bit, and said, "I've been away, but I'm ME. What can it all mean?"

"But do you remember hearing your voice?" Dr. Jerold asked.

"Yes, and it was me, but it wasn't me. My voice was so old and strange." Jessie put her head in her hands. "I'm not sure I want to remember any of it!"

"Jessica, I've regressed many people. Some feel as you do; others are quite excited to finally get answers to problems—and problems such as yours, recurring, troubling dreams. Of course, I have your tape for you. You may listen to it when you are ready, or you may decide you don't wish to, but that is for you to decide. I would advise keeping it in any event. Of course, I will have a copy here as part of your record. Would you like to come back and talk about it some more?"

"Doctor, I just don't know yet. I need to think a lot about this. It goes against what I've always believed. I don't know what to think." Jessica's tiredness crept into her voice. "I just need to go home."

"Yes, go get some rest, Jessica."

"I understand," said Dr. Jerold as he ushered them to the door.

Martha took Jessica to her car, talking excitedly the whole time.

"I'll follow you home, Jessie." Martha felt she needed to make sure Jessica got home safely. When Jessica crawled into her car, it seemed that her car drove her home on automatic pilot. Her hand automatically hit the light switch inside the door to her house. Martha beeped and went on her way.

The tape was clutched in her hand, for it seemed too precious to slip into her purse. *Should I face it now?* she thought. *It cannot be a dream, though I know the mind is capable of many imaginings. Even Freud said, "There are many rooms yet to be investigated." What, though, do I know but what I, myself, experienced this night, this very evening? I heard my voice, a strange one at that, but I know it was my voice and I had no control over the sound. This other woman, this Elizabeth, this other ME.* Wearily she laid her head on the couch and fell into a deep, dreamless sleep.

She awakened in her dark living room and flipped on the light. Blinking to get her bearings, she glanced at the clock—2 a.m. *I've got to get in my bed, but what a sticky mess I am with these clothes still on.* She got up and, unlike her usually orderly self, threw her clothes in the hamper and got in the shower. The warm water splashing on her face felt so good. Elizabeth would not have had such luxury, but then Elizabeth would not have known about it, so she wouldn't have missed it. *Stop it, Jessica. You are to live one life, okay? Oh, the tape. I can't lose the tape.* She rearranged her underwear over the tape in the top drawer of her dresser, then slipped on her nightgown and slid under the covers for a few more hours of sleep. Before the images came, she told herself severely, *I'm only me, only me.*

Martha woke at 2 a.m. and suddenly wondered about her friend. *Oh, I hope Jessie is sleeping. She certainly uncovered some pertinent information. Something surely is there.* She got up and looked out the window, musing before she returned to her bed.

Across town, Daniel tossed and turned in his bed as if having a nightmare.

CHAPTER TWENTY-TWO

He could not make it through the thick brambles, the darkness of bushes; sharp stickers tore at his clothes and surrounded him. His clothes were of skin and dark cloth, foreign to him and yet remembered. Through all of this dark forest with lowered limbs he saw blue sky ahead and the beautiful face of a woman known to him, looking distraught and frightened. She seemed to hang tantalizingly on the blueness of sky. He knew he must somehow make it to her—she was his; she belonged to him. Stickers tearing at his clothes, he hurried to her but then he fell, fell, fell, down, down into a pit of more brambles, stones, and dirt. More dirt caved in, falling on top of him, suffocating and drowning him.

Daniel sat straight up in bed, sputtering and shook himself. "My God, thank you, I'm alive!" He jumped to his feet, shaken, and took out a silver cross from the bureau drawer. "God, if there is a God, I need you!" Daniel paced back and forth, back and forth, back and forth several times until he began to feel calm again. *What in hell caused a nightmare like that?* he thought. *I've had nightmares before, but this one is worth writing down.* He scrawled down the dream as best he could remember before settling back into his bed. It came into his mind, *I didn't die in the pit; someone shot me. When? How? This is crazy! But it connects with the dream in some way.*

Daniel had noticed a tiny, cheap metal cross in the drawer when he first moved in and thought little of it. He felt like he needed it now for whatever comfort it gave. He held it to his chest, but felt foolish; still his mind refused to quiet enough to sleep. *Maybe I could use that dream, embellish it a bit, and write a good short story. It's been a long time since I've written anything but lyrics for my music. That was a humdinger.* He thought about it more, but for the most part drew blanks when he tried to add a sentence and develop his character. *Hey, the woman—she seemed to be the focal point of the dream, and I couldn't get to her. She needed me, but then I fell in that pit. Almost a message it seemed for me. Could that woman have represented Jessica? She needed me and then I left her. Now, I am back "from the hole" and she is reluctant to take me back. Could I blame her?* He threw the cross on the table, then as an afterthought he wrapped it tenderly in his handkerchief and placed it in the drawer where he had found it.

Friday is finally here and I sure can't sleep now! Daniel looked long and hard at the face that looked back to him in the mirror. "Well," he said aloud, "I've healed pretty well, maybe still a little redness, but she will know it's me! I am a lucky man to have come back from that mess alive not dead." Daniel wondered about "dead" as he had in the past. *Are we ever really "dead"?* He thought back to the dream and the strange clothes he wore in that scary scene. He had never owned any clothes like that, so how could they be in his mind? The "forest primeval was there all right"! Now, where did that come from—evil forest, for certain. Maybe "forest primeval" came from school a long time ago, but he couldn't remember.

Jessica will be glad to see me. I know she will. After all, part of my trouble came because she wasn't home when she should have been. All of this wouldn't have happened to me if she would just have been home. But then, I chose to go to a wrong place—I can't blame her for that. Daniel combed his face with his hands, again looking in the mirror—*the scar is barely there now, imperceptible—but I can trace it with my hands and she will be able to see what I went through. Don't think I'll need another laser treatment; it will just make me redder. Besides I don't like to be labeled indigent—I'm just as good as anyone—better than most. Why, look at this place? I'm living the life of Riley, you might say.* Daniel shook at the thought of the money this place cost!

After taking a quick shower and pulling on his clothes, he looked again in the mirror. Thinking aloud, "You're all right, guy, foxy man!" He laughed, remembering Maria and how furious that name made him. *Hey, though, maybe I ought to get something new to wear, something Jessica has never seen; maybe the woman in the lobby knows where I can find some better clothes that don't cost a fortune.*

Daniel's thoughts shifted back to that troubling dream. He'd had dreams of falling before, but he always jerked himself awake, almost to the point of falling out of the bed. He was certain he died in this deam. *Maybe we do live before and maybe we do live after and on and on, but how could we stand it—life over and over, or rather, continuously in some form or other, like, well, maybe the Hindu belief—that a cow may be your great-aunt Charlotte or something, or whatever that is they practice in India or other places. Do Buddhist's believe that stuff? Well, nobody ever comes back to say, "Hey guys, this is the way it is—climb on board!" I've thought it really doesn't make any sense to be a spot on the planet and make your mark just once, now does it? There my mind goes again—it just takes off sometimes....*

Daniel sat on the couch again with his hastily written note of a dream clutched again in his hands. *Now let's see what I can do with this.* Every thought Daniel had found a dead end. He kept seeing the face of the woman, the blue sky behind her. Suddenly his pen took off as if it had a mind of its own; a force somewhere outside Daniel, outside himself, pushed the pen and wrote Jessica, Jessica, Jessica, again and again as if possessed. Daniel dropped the pen, threw on his coat, and went to the lobby. He sat down by the crackling fire and looked deeply into the flames. *What came over me? Something—IT came over me!*

After a long while he asked the girl at the desk where he could buy some decent rags. She smiled, sucked in her breath, and said brightly, "There's a mall just up the street and if you want me to, I could take you. I'm off at 2:30 today—uh—that is if you would like some female advice."

This gal had had her eyes on Daniel ever since he had started to look human again, handsome, and less scary, he had felt. Actually when she had first seen him, she did not know quite what to think, he supposed. Daniel winked at her. "Guess I need help. I've got to impress a million-dollar gal. I'll meet you down here at 2:30, hon, if you really don't mind." Daniel certainly wanted to be upfront with her—no more Marias in his life, no, sir.

He walked out the front door and the cold air blew its welcome in his face. *I must have imagined what happened up there, but it seemed my hand wrote "Jessica" larger and larger, nothing else, all by itself. So much for that being the beginnings of a short story—creepy. Maybe it was the pen! Now how could it have been the pen, tell me? I feel like I did when I went with Maria to her scary church with those images placed strategically in dark corners. How were those to make a feller religious? Beats me; it could scare a kid to death. But whatever that was that happened upstairs—it might make a believer out of a person—like there might be something out there beyond us. Do you just die or do you go somewhere and hang around a bit? I've read someplace that dreams are always about the dreamer and I've thought that before. Now I am wondering if there may have been something more to that when I couldn't develop it into a story; it certainly had the makings or the shell of one. I never had trouble before. Maybe it was because I definitely died in that dream. How can the writer write if he is dead? Daniel, you are being morbid. A dream is a dream is a dream. Stop the weirdness; don't lose it now, especially now!*

The beautiful snow of yesterday had turned to part slush, though it was still beautiful in his mind. He reveled in it, remembering how the city had turned pure overnight—a magical quality—covering the dirt with its pristine coldness. Now this, well, beauty can be short lived. He thought again of the dream, the beauty of the woman, yet she appeared so apprehensive. That scene, before the falling in the pit, and then the death.

Bootless, he made his way through the slush and the ice past an outlet mall. His stomach suddenly signaled hunger, although his mind kept drawing back to the incident in his room and the lively pen.

If that mall is where the woman is planning to take me, well, I could find that by myself. Best not to get her hopes up—he chuckled almost aloud, thinking about how he almost scared her when he arrived there. *Well, no scary Daniel now. Fortunately, by the skill of doctors, I look like Daniel again. I must never forget that—these were the good guys, not like those others!*

Hmmmm, Cracker Barrel. Wonder if they still serve that great apple strudel pie or the apple dumpling? That is a meal! I could have that without taking much from the money I've been saving for taking Jessica to a really nice place for dinner. She will be more open to everything I have to tell her if I treat her like the lady she is.

Nothing would satisfy him but one of those Cracker Barrel apple dumplings, so he sloshed back, got his car and took it across the river to Florence, luckily got right in, and savored every bit of the apple dumpling with ice cream on top. My, it was good, and with Cracker Barrel's coffee, the perfect complement. He leaned back in the chair, content, momentarily forgetting the weirdness of his pen, hand or whatever it was.

The clock on the wall said 2:10. *Better get a move on if that woman still wants to take me shopping. At least, I will keep my promise and be there. This is a new Daniel. No more broken promises. We are not in this by ourselves. At least, I don't think we are anymore. There is something.*

He made it to the lobby right at 2:30. The girl was gone. *Oh well, when she knew there was someone else in the picture, she opted out. Guess I don't blame her for that.* Daniel went to his room, then to the bathroom, and again looked long and hard in the mirror. His face seemed to change a bit. He shook his head. Daniel is with us again. *What was that?* He combed his hair and put a warm washcloth on his face. *Oh Jessica,* he thought, *be with me when I pick out just the right clothes so that you will find me more than welcome tonight!* He glanced down at his GI Joe that was sitting on the towel rack. "How's it going, Joe?" he said aloud. "Now don't let anything foreign in here while I'm gone, okay?" He shivered.

He came back from the mall with a Fair Isle-type sweater in a light green and a pair of khakis, unlike anything he had and unlike the old Daniel. *Jessica has to think I have changed in every way. She has to love me again,* he thought almost desperately.

As he was dressing in his new clothes he thought again back to the dream. *Why can't I stop thinking about that dumb dream and then the weirdness when I tried writing an augmented story? Do you suppose I am losing it again? No, I'm even more trusting now. That policeman that helped me and took me to the hospital showed they are not all bad, only some. I wish, oh how I wish I could remember the whole thing, the truth! Then, I would feel that I am a whole person. I think, though, that even as a whole person there are many facets. Perhaps I will never know all those facets.*

Jessica, please love me when you see me. I won't be able to stand it if you don't. I know, I just know we belong together. If she rejects me I don't know what I'll do. Daniel's thoughts clustered together like a tumultuous storm.

CHAPTER TWENTY-THREE

If Jessica were the type that had headaches, she would have one tonight. First and foremost, Daniel would be there in a little over an hour. That alone was enough. The fact that he looked so much like Ulysses in the dream/vision and later under Dr. Jerold's regression of her again pointed to why, in her heart, she could not give him up. No matter how she tried, she couldn't tell him what he really deserved to hear. He had treated her like a piece of garbage, just left when she needed him so, loved him so much it hurt. Then not even a call, a note, until he suddenly shows up acting as if she should just forgive him. Just like that!

Jessica turned off the shower, rubbed down with her bath blanket, then wrapped up in it and laid down on the bed. What had she been thinking of anyway to agree to see him? Well, she knew—how could she not know?—she loved him twice. The first time he had been a wonderful man, stable, loving, not prone to go off either physically or verbally or disappear for about a year, or shout and talk of strange things she knew nothing about.

But he said he had been hurt. Not for that huge block of time he had disappeared had he been hurt—*he can't expect me to believe that nonsense! I wonder how hurt? I should have been with him if he were hurt. Now, you couldn't have been. You didn't even know where he was!*

Jessica got up from her reverie and laid out her clothes carefully on the bed. These were the clothes she had worn the first real date she had had with Daniel.

Oh, how excited she had been! He sang to her. She remembered the warm, unexplained feeling of love that seemed to permeate her being. How when she took his strong hand, the current of strength and warmth went through her, as if they belonged together. This had never happened with anyone else, not even her husband. What could she call it? They belonged together even then, that connection. The sheer happiness, a contentedness that she felt he returned equally then, that magical night. He was so romantic: his singing, his holding her close later as if he couldn't break away.

Then … but no matter what his behavior had been, how erratic, how strange, she knew she loved him as Elizabeth had loved Ulysses and that she would stand by the door waiting for him as Elizabeth had, maybe waste a complete life pining for a person who would never come home. An analogy, of course; Daniel was home, but in his mind or brain would he ever really be home unless he received help? Maybe from Dr. Jerold?

Dr. Jerold had told her she might want to play that tape sometime when she was ready. *Well, I remember enough of it—Ulysses in that life looked like Daniel or at least strongly resembled him, but in another time, another place. I'm me. I just want to be me! This is all so strange—too strange, but yet at least part of me was Elizabeth—so alien to my beliefs.*

She dressed quickly after carefully putting on her makeup, knowing she wanted to look perfect for Daniel. *Daniel, my love....*

The jewelry was the same she had worn previously except for her new sapphire bracelet the girls gave her for Christmas. She lovingly went over the stones with her fingertips—maybe it would be her good luck for this evening. *Daniel, please be as you were that first night!* She knew she should be stern with him and let him know in no uncertain terms how he had hurt her; *a living, breathing paradox—that's me.* She loved him and she knew no matter what, she would take him back. He needed help and she would see that he got that help. *I wonder what he's been up to all that time?*

She had not been honest with him and he had not been honest with her. What had happened in his life to give him the skeletons he carried around? What would he do when he found out about the MS? Since she hadn't told him, it was the same as a lie. Maybe he would leave when he found out; her husband did. What a basket of variables!

Yes, for a while, when the girls were still in school, Jeb seemed to be as puzzled as she about her mysterious illnesses, and very supportive. She would be ill for a while and not even go see about it because it would go away as quickly as it started. Then, the vision problems began. She couldn't ignore those, and they frightened her; sometimes her vision was so blurred that she couldn't see what orders she had written at work. Finally after two years, the diagnosis came. Jeb may have been looking for an excuse all along, because a sweet, young woman suddenly appeared on the scene. He said he had been "in love" for a long time. He was at the age that some men cannot face their own aging, but she was certain he couldn't stand the thought of what might be ahead for him when the MS got worse. If that were the case, perhaps she had already forgiven him for that. Some men envision the worst possible scenario. The young woman, who was barely older than their own daughters, hurt them, and that took longer for her to forgive. Because of her girls, Jessica sometimes wished she had not divorced him. The young woman didn't last long. If she had simply refused, there would have been no Daniel. She had been so hurt and rejected at the time and hurt for her daughters. She wanted to hold her head high again. Jeb had an apartment by himself now and she wondered how he really felt since she certainly wasn't much worse. Well, he had to live with his decision, but Becca told her once he still loved her. Too late for that.

Unless Daniel had changed—*No, don't kid yourself Jessica. When he finds out ... but I am stable right now. Maybe it will be a while before I have to tell him.*

Fifteen more minutes before he would arrive, she got out her Bible. She searched through the Gospel of Mark, where Martha had told her was a passage that could be interpreted to mean reincarnation, and there were others in both the Hebrew Bible and New Testament. *Let's see, chapter eight; yes, here it is in red like all of the words spoken by Jesus:* ("8:27. Who do people say that I am? 8:28 And they answered him, 'John the Baptist; and others, Elijah; and still others, one of the prophets.'") Jessica didn't recall that ever being read as part of the lectionary, but even if it had, would she have thought it meant anything. *No, of course not! It's just that now I will probably be thinking everything means "something."* But her whole life, she had had poems and bits of scripture just seemingly put there in her mind and she always thought it significant; however, she had never thought of anything like reincarnation until Daniel came into her life, the troubling dreams, the not troubling but loving dream/vision with Ulysses, and then her regression. *I will want to listen to that tape eventually even though I remember so much of it. Too much sadness for the Elizabeth part of me. There, I said it as though I believe it....*

CHAPTER TWENTY-FOUR

Daniel headed for the lobby and out the door, not even looking to see if the woman was at the desk. *Who cares about people who don't keep their dates!*

I used to be like that, but not anymore; no, sir. His car in the parking shed had been hastily cleaned out, but he realized with a start that it needed washing and vacuuming. *Why oh why didn't I do that—there has got to be a car wash place on the way!*

Meanwhile, Jessica, wearing her blue dress, small diamond-like necklace, and her new bracelet, felt elegant. *I want to capture the magic of that first night. It would be wonderful to erase the pain of his illness and the secret of mine. Could Elizabeth's wasted life somehow give me this? No, that's crazy!* She thought and thought about Daniel—how he would look when he walked in the door—memory traced the contours of his face, his brilliant blue eyes, those baggy jeans. She laughed about that. How she wanted to take him under her wing and fix him—certainly not just those clothes, but fix all the demons he carried with him, find out what caused those strange emotional outbursts that.… *Oh, admit it Jessica, your heart pounded nearly out of your chest that one time he paced, raved, and stalked around like a mad man over nothing. Admit it, tell him how you feel. Tell him you are through with all that. Then you won't ever have to tell him about the MS; he will be gone from my life.*

Something tells me he won't be. Even if I let him know how I feel, he will keep coming back.

Will I have time to listen to the tape? No, I won't. I won't this time. All depends on how I feel when I see him.

There was a gentle knock at the door. Jessica sucked in her breath and slowly walked to the door.

She put her hand on the knob, slowly turned it, and opened it only to the crack that the chain would allow. "Daniel?"

"Yes, it's me, my love. Please let me in. I want so much to hold you in my arms, please, Jessica." Daniel's voice, the remembered mellow tone, the pleading, made her knees weak. There and then, time stood still.

She unhooked the chain, stood back from the door as it swung open, but put up her arms in defense. "No, no, Daniel—we cannot just pick up as if you never left me, as if you never hurt me; no, you walk in here like you own me, when I am owned by no one, no one, do you understand? You lost any privilege with me when you called out of the blue and just left. Do you realize how much I was looking forward to spending Christmas with you? I wanted you to be with me so much. I wanted to pick out the perfect gift for you and I wanted us to be together. I would have introduced you to the family for the first time and they would have known what was going on in my life. My family means a lot to me and I mean a lot to them! They seemed to be a threat to you when all they wanted was for me to be happy." Jessica took a breath but wouldn't let him get in a word. "At first I thought I had found that happiness in you, Daniel, but I was wrong, so very wrong! Anyone who could have just used the phone to tell me he is leaving is not right and needs help! If you think that shows love, Daniel, you don't know the meaning of the word."

Daniel felt like he had been slapped, but somehow he kept control. He knew she spoke the truth, other than that he knew he loved her. "Jessica, I will admit I am all mixed up—but I do love you. Please believe that, and believe anything else about me that you want, but believe me when I say I love you."

It seemed he followed a script. She couldn't believe he would ever admit that he had a problem, but there it came, right from his mouth. What had happened? Had he changed? "Daniel, you said you had been hurt—when did that happen?" A much gentler Jessica spoke those words. "Let's sit down here and you can tell me about it. Let me look at you. You look different, somehow, more polished. You certainly don't look as if you've been hurt."

"Well, to begin with, I found out that not all cops are sleazebags. I know how I've been before about them, and since you have known me how you knew I felt about them, and I only vaguely know the answer to that. But honey, I know there's a reason; but anyway, I got in a fight in a bar on Vine, Jessie, when I was waiting for you to come home. You didn't come, so I thought I would show you. I would go to a bar and have a drink. I found out quickly that I bit off more than I could chew. This bar, it was in the wrong part of town and the people there were snakes. I got beat up, nobody helped me, and they threw me in an alley after some weirdo knocked me out. I don't know how long it was before I woke up a little and eventually crawled to my car, but I passed out again. A cop saw me there in my car and took me to the hospital. I had a major patch-up job and later plastic surgery. The cop even came to see me at the hospital and had my car brought there. They aren't all bad like I thought, Jessie."

"I don't know how you ever thought they were ... there is so much I don't know about you, Daniel, and until I do, I cannot see a serious relationship developing between us. It just won't work. Since you left me like you did and now expect to pick up where you left off, is completely amazing. I am sorry, though, that you were injured, so very sorry. If I could have been there to help I would have, but I didn't know where you were; that just shows the real kind of involvement we have, Daniel. NONE!"

"Just to hear you say you would have been there if you had known makes me feel there is hope for us. There must be!"

"It's not just that. You need some help with your emotions. I cannot put up with not knowing from one time to the next what is going to disturb you and make you lash out at me for what I saw then as nothing—nothing at all, and where did you disappear to all that time? I would like to know." Jessica's tone was demanding.

"Well, it's a long story, honey. I just drove and finally ended up in Galveston and got a cheap place to live on the beach. Driving calms me when I don't know what to do. I didn't just loaf around in Texas—I had a job as a handyman at a motel. You should have seen the place; it needed help and I suggested some changes to the jerko that ran the place. Eventually, I stayed there rent free. Jessica, please believe me, I left here afraid of getting too serious too soon, but I never stopped thinking about you, never. You are my pedestal lady." Daniel held both her hands. "I always envisioned you—how you would be, what you might be doing, thinking; you were always first in my mind."

"And was there a second, Daniel?"

"No, never, not really, that is, you were always there in my thoughts, honey."

"So, you were not exactly true to my memory the whole time, is that right?" Jessica teared up at the thought but quickly gained control of herself. "Daniel, how could you and then expect me to take you back?"

"Jessica, I'm not going to lie to you. The old me would have. I did mess up a couple of times, but it didn't mean anything to me; it wasn't anything but sex. I know now; the difference is a real connectedness. I love you, only you; please let me prove it to you! Please give me another chance. I was lonely and it just happened. I'm so sorry, Jessica. Forgive me, please." Daniel was close to tears.

"How can I trust you, ever? Ever! For starters, one thing that is wrong with us and a possible relationship is that you see too many other people in a bad light. That woman, whoever she was—you may have hurt her and just cast her aside. And that man who gave you a job? He wasn't a jerk, so why call him that? He gave you a job, didn't he? There are just too many things about us that are different, don't you see, Daniel?" sighed Jessica as she looked him straight in the eyes. "As for me, yes, I thought about you, but I didn't have just sex with anyone that didn't mean anything. Yes, I was lonely, too; lonely for that man who just left me! Sex for me, even that first time, made me feel love for you. That is another way we aren't alike—I don't just do those things. It has always meant something to me!"

"I'll change, Jessica, you'll see. I'll change. I'll show you I can. Just give me a chance, please, please, honey, let me prove it to you. I've been sick and I know I've been sick in other ways, too. Something happened to me. I just can't tell you everything about it because I don't know enough about it myself. I do know now that I have to find out what really happened to me. I just don't know all of it, and until I know all of it, it would be as confusing to you as it is to me. I do know I trust you more than I have trusted anybody in my whole life. That's a beginning for us, isn't it, Jessica? We loved each other in the physical way; now maybe, step by step, we can learn to be best friends, and then go from there." Daniel just lightly kissed her on the check. "Friends now—just friends, okay, Jessica?"

Jessica couldn't believe her ears. It was all she could do to keep from throwing her arms around Daniel in a solid embrace that would last forever. How she loved him. It didn't matter about that woman. She didn't care about her; she would forget about that. She loved him deep inside herself to the point of weakness.

"Daniel, before, you talked to me about things I didn't understand—maybe it's time that we begin to understand these things together. Maybe let me think about it. It's late now, and I need to get my sleep for many reasons. I cannot say that I've lost all feelings for you, because I haven't. I have a bit of a puzzle myself and maybe together we can find some answers." Jessica thought of her own secret that she needed to tell Daniel and she couldn't wait too long. He needed to know, not so much about the regression but about the MS, if they were to pick up any pieces.

Hand in hand they went to the door. "I'll call you tomorrow, if that is okay, Jessica?"

"Yes, okay. We can both have a day to think about going slowly. I do want to hug you in spite of everything," said Jessica, as she reached out her arms. They hugged for a long time before Daniel pulled away.

When the door closed on Daniel, it was to Jessica as if Ulysses, too, had walked out the door. Jessica had a sinking feeling. Ulysses, so lovable and caring. Could Daniel carry those traits? Could Daniel have lived a life as Ulysses? It was all too much to grasp. *My life is complicated enough with the Daniel of the here and now, and furthermore with myself in the here and now.* Daniel might, as Ulysses did, disappear and never come back when he found out about her MS. The MS! *Why do I do this? I must not own it nor does it own me! I must tell him now while the symptoms have lessened and when it seems nothing is wrong. That will seem almost as if I were truthful from the beginning. Being "friends" as he put it does lessen the pressure, but what a turnaround; although you might say "turnaround" is his middle name. With him it's always surprise, surprise! It can be a step-by-step process—just learning to be friends and not let our attraction for each other get out of hand. But what did he say before I opened the door?*

He wanted to put his arms around me. Did my lecture change all that? Perhaps, but he changed quickly and if I admit it, I didn't really want that much of a change.

He seemed so normal this time and so logical. We never really gave ourselves time to know each other last time, before rushing into a relationship, except for that test he insisted on. That really was completely logical, too, though looking back—it just surprised me that he would be the one to insist upon it. I'm the nurse!

And as a nurse, I am going to insist that he have a test if we ever get beyond the friendship stage! But at least he did tell me—he didn't have to. Maybe he really has changed. I wonder what she was like. I know there is a difference in the sexes and that it is harder on a man, but I still don't like it one bit!

Is it because of this reincarnation thing that I can't give up on Daniel? It probably does make a little sense, but how confusing it is! But wouldn't eternal bliss get old pretty quickly? Or just sleeping until the trumpet sounds and the graves open up? Wouldn't that be a scene! But if a soul does travel through time, better to forget than remember. Just think, if Daniel and I had not met, I would not have started having those scary dreams. I certainly don't need to go into any therapy because of it now that I understand about the dreams. I certainly won't tell anybody about it. Martha, naturally, won't tell anybody. Now wait, Jessica, is it such a sin to be reincarnated if everybody is? It's just that not everyone knows about it—not everyone has been taught such things, so not everyone would think I was daft. "Poor Jessica, she's lost her marbles, they say people with MS sometimes lose them ... oh well, it's to be expected! We'll just talk about her behind her back." Jessica was so tired so very tired, but her thoughts continued their tirade.

Now wait a minute. Nobody knows, really knows anything about anything. We have been taught beliefs and it all started with some inspiration by the early church that was written and we followed those rules. But they were beautifully put, so they must have been truly inspired by God. But then, much blood has been shed because of beliefs. That is so confusing, what humankind has done through centuries in the name of the peacemaker Jesus. And all religions think they have the real truth. That's all. Nobody really KNOWS anything.

It could be that some people do just live once and die and go to heaven—if there is a heaven. I have always thought of heaven as a uniting place ... a place to see all the people we love who have died. It has been comforting and, let's admit it, simple to think of it in that way; but maybe some people do just live once and die once, and that is part of free will. There I go, getting into beliefs again, not what anyone really knows. No one has died that I know of and then come back and told the world about it. We were taught Jesus died for us and was resurrected from the dead so we wouldn't really die, but we still die biologically; but what did Jesus mean when he said, "I came that they may have life and have it abundantly," or something like that. Jesus is all of God to be put in a human being that we Christians know. But from my experience with Ulysses—we live and live and live. Is that living life more "abundantly"? I just don't want to do this anymore. I want just this life, just my family, and maybe I want to love Daniel again, but I have to really know him first.

However, I cannot deny the regression experience and the dreams of far-life memory. The life I lived back then is recorded on the tape. I know, though, that the mind is capable of all sorts of imaginings. It is just that there are too many issues here, the dreams that suddenly started and then they continued even in my waking state. The session with the doctor just iced the cake, so to speak. I don't even have to listen to that tape. I remember the whole thing clearly. It was as real as I am. I really was Elizabeth and I wasted that life waiting day after day for my beloved Ulysses to come home.

Do you suppose that is why I have MS now? I had a long life as Elizabeth and I could have been out helping others, but instead I self-centeredly wasted my life. Now my life may be withered away too early by illness and I won't be able eventually to do life's purpose. We are here to nurture and recognize the beauty of others, to almost forget the self. Or practice the Golden Rule at all times. One life goes so quickly. There is so little time. Some never get an opportunity in a lifetime to learn these things. Some have everything and never learn them. Some have nothing and learn them. Some because of brain dysfunction don't know what I'm even thinking about. Why? And while I am on the subject, as that Jewish author said, "Why do good people suffer?"

Haven't I always intuitively known we are here for others in a way? Could we just call it a conscience and deal with this life? Even thinking about reincarnation is just too bewildering. I'll just not let it affect me, or affect me much. I can make it go away at will and pray about it if it bothers me too much.

Thank goodness it is Friday night and I won't have to get up in the morning. Jessica stepped into a hot tub of water, thinking that soaking a bit would soak all of her cares down the drain. *First, I must realize that the only important thing is the here and now, no matter how real all of that other is to me. All my life with Ulysses shows why I cannot give up on Daniel. If Daniel were Ulysses, I know deep in my heart that there is good in Daniel, even though at times he just plain seemed off his rocker.*

It's conceivable we were brought back together to iron things out that previously we didn't have a chance to do. I know now that there is a reason why I can't just tell Daniel to get out of my life. Reason one: I love him. Reason two: I knew him as my husband in a past life and lost him somehow in a strange way. Reason three: He needs me. Reason four: I must tell him the truth, as it is not me when I am not honest, and I should have been honest from the beginning.

Jessica ran some more hot water in the tub and added a little more bubble bath. She laid her head against her bath pillow and nearly went to sleep. *Guess I'd better get out of here before I drown, literally,* she thought. She wrapped up in her bath blanket and rubbed down. She put on her prettiest nightgown before slipping under the sheets.

Daniel seemed somehow different this time. He was dressed differently for one thing. No baggy jeans! He really looked nice—like new somehow. It is going to be difficult for me to just be friends when I want him here, right now, beside me. I want to curl up around him and treasure him as mine. But Jessica, you have so many worlds to conquer before you can do that. First, you must tell him. Jessica put her arms around her pillow and drifted into a troubled sleep.

CHAPTER TWENTY-FIVE

She dressed just like she had for our first date. She's a romantic like I am. I know she did it for me and I went out and bought these new rags. I wonder if she noticed my attire. Of course she did. Jessie would notice—she was just determined to let me have it straight out. And I let her. I have never let a woman talk to me like that. I must have handled it right—I had her eventually purring like a kitten. Guess I really do love her. Daniel chucked at the word "attire." *Somehow, Jessica brings upscale words into my mind.* In this attire, he felt like a WASP instead of a product of the crummy neighborhood from which he came.

Well, with my music I came a long way from the poor white neighborhood; and although I had some bad luck, I felt almost rich at one time, I did. Then so much happens to a guy along the way. Bonny, I never really loved her—I did the right thing, though—when she got herself pregnant, I married her. Then the kids, and Joey's problems. I'll not rest until I find out what really happened.

Jessica, oh Jessica—you are everything I have ever hoped for—why did I mess things up and leave? I now will have a lot of catching up to do, and as I promised her—first be friends, only friends. Why in heaven did I say that? I have no idea, for we both have such attraction to each other, it will be hard. First, she will have to learn to trust me again, as I trust her with all my heart. It is so wonderful to finally have a person in my life that I really trust. I've had a bad problem with that. I can't trust so much because of what's happened to me in my life. I especially cannot trust policemen.

The trouble is—there is where that blank, that blackout is. I don't know why, because I never had problems with cops before that. I am an honest guy. I do remember them rushing at me and taking me to that place. They did that—they made it seem like I had killed my own son, and I didn't! I didn't! How could I do such a horrible, terrible thing?

Daniel's mind was suddenly besieged again with malignant thoughts. *I know now that other place was not really a true hospital.* In and out of Daniel's mind had been thoughts about the other hospital since he left Jessica, when he wanted only to think of Jessica. He couldn't make his mind stop. He knew he would not have a chance with her unless he could solve the mystery of what happened with Joey and why he landed in that place. The function of that dirty hospital—he knew it was an awful place—was to give him treatments to make him forget things. He remembered being continuously moved into an inner room on a narrow cot. He dreaded it—all of the wire and then that first shock. All then went black or blank as if he had died for a while—been plucked out of the universe. He wondered if that was like death—nothing—a void.

That was artificial, whatever they did. Death would be living, I just know that; living and traveling somewhere. But not that junk about heaven and seeing your loved ones again—hogwash made up by some committee in the early church. I know there is something else, though, or why be at all? What loved ones? It sounded nice. My mother died when I was four.

I wonder if my ma loved me. I have a vague recollection of being held on her lap ... her smell, not perfume, but a clean kinda castile soap smell.

Grandpa would call me downstairs to fight with the bigger boy from next door. I can still feel the fear of it. I would always get beat up. Grandpa would cheer. I can see myself standing, standing, just wanting to stand by the upstairs window, holding on to the curtain. The curtain was some kind of security and I could watch for Dad. Those two years of waiting, waiting ... with mean Grandpa, dreading to hear his voice, calling, calling, and then finally seeing Dad drive up, bringing a stepmother who treated me like a wart. But I wasn't hungry no more. She fed me.

But back to the now, I need to remember what really happened before they took me to that place. I need to know because I won't be a whole person until I find out the truth. Now I know I was made to think I killed Joey, but why—then, instead of a trial, I was railroaded off to this loony bin. I know I didn't kill my son. I maybe wanted to strangle him sometimes, but not really—I wouldn't kill anybody—never, ever!

I realize now more than ever that until I find out the truth, no matter what it is, Jessica will be far from my reach. Jessica is a true person. No more playing games. But this is no game; I just don't know what happened. How will I be able to find out? And will I be able to stand it if I do?

I remember that back in Illinois I was doing pretty damn good; they even played some of my songs on the radio. By damn I was proud and Bonny beamed. Then, if Joey hadn't continued with his acting out, it would not have cost me my career. Why, Joey? The other kids weren't that bad; just the usual stuff, but almost from the beginning Joey lived on the edge. But God help me, I didn't want him to end up dead. His drug use nearly killed me and we got help for him, or we thought we did—was it wrong? Was that the big mistake? The wrong help? The wrong kind? I can't remember and I'm trying to so hard! I do remember what I now think must have been shock treatments and that is why I was made to forget. Please, I've got to somehow bring it all back into my mind. I can, when I think strongly about it, still feel the coldness of that gun in my hand.

I don't have or ever carry a gun, and Joey, my Joey's body lying warm, so close to me; but I reached out to help him and these cops came rushing at me.

Joey, I loved you, I really did. I wanted to help you. God, you were my own flesh and blood. Joey, you looked so much like me; my blue eyes, but yours were taunting, that look of "dare me not to do it and I'll do it." I had a mean Grandpa. Maybe that's where it came from, but sometimes I swear it was as if a demon possessed you. You were only fourteen years old, a kid, when you started with those drugs, and why? No puzzle here: because I warned you that I would whip you if you ever touched those poisons!

But they gave me drugs when they diagnosed me as having a mental problem or whatever. They said, "A borderline personality disorder," Bonny told me, whatever the heck that is! Now who do you suppose thought that one up? Some idiot who was trying to psyche out his own head I guess. If I had a personality disorder do you suppose Joey may have gotten it from me, or Grandpa, or who knows? I don't think I am sick except once in a while I get those crying spells, and I guess I get mad sometimes, but it seems like mad does have to come out. I just feel mad and I act mad. Is that so bad? But I can't do that with Jessica ever again. Maybe I should go see a doctor – see one now! I certainly don't want to ask Jessica, or do I? With a developing friendship, friends ask for help from their friends some of the time, don't they? I've never really had a real friend. Do you suppose Jessie might know of someone who might help me? I cannot see how she wouldn't want to help and maybe, just maybe, there is someone who would help me remember. How will I bring it up? I can't let her think I have anything really wrong with me....

If I am sick, those years with Grandpa and then that bitch of a stepmother did it to me. I read somewhere that if your first seven years are messed up, you somehow get messed up. Daddy was mostly an okay guy, though he had to go and get killed. But I'm really okay, though; most of the time I am just fine, just fine. It's just that sometimes peculiar things happen. That time when I kept seeing Joey's face in front of the car, and I don't understand why I can't control those sad feelings I get. I know it's because of Joey, though; I could control it better then, but I guess I was taking that medicine then maybe. I can't remember much about when I took it or when I didn't. I do know that when Bonny was here, she saw to it that I took it.

I don't know what happens to me sometimes, but I know if Jessica and I are to be together I will have to control the demon within whatever or whoever caused it to happen to me. But why do these things happen? That weird thing when I was trying to rewrite my dream! It was great material for a story or perhaps background for lyrics to a song, but no, I couldn't write—just Jessica and more Jessica like a SOMETHING took over my pen. I've been a good guy, an honest guy anyway, perhaps; I haven't treated everybody wonderfully through my whole life, but I've been honest. I'm not proud of what I did to Bonny, tearing off her rings and all. I'm not even sure she had an affair. I kinda made her say she did, or I wouldn't have been satisfied. I just had to even the score whether she had had an affair or not. I really, looking back, don't think she did. I don't think she would have dared. She would have been afraid to. She never knew what to expect from me. I did, for her sake, go to the doctor after that.

People haven't treated me right. If my dad had lived, things might have been different. If he hadn't gone hunting that day, things would have been happier for me. An accidental shot and he left me—gone from my lifetime.

Why did I say lifetime rather than life? Do we have a time for life, then something else, then life again? I can't say death. Beats me, but that makes sense if anything does. My daddy showed me I had talent. Just as a little guy, we would sit and play and sing together. He gave me the only self-esteem I have. I'm a talented guy and he showed that to me. Then boom, he was taken from me. But the talent, that didn't get lost with what happened. That shadow that makes me not as I want to be, though, has been with me since before Joey died. I know that. I can't hide behind that, no matter how I try; that horror is lurking about and comes out when I least expect it. There, I said it. So what do I do? Do I ask Jessica for help? I told her we would first be friends, so if we can keep this new relationship, this friendship relationship—dare I ask for help? Do friends admit to friends that they may have a problem? I have never talked to anyone about this before except Bonny, and that doctor she made me see? He was kind of a creep, but his pills did help. They helped somewhat, I kept better control and didn't get that overwhelming sadness. I'm not sure I want to come right out and tell Jessica that a part of my life is missing and that I might need to see a doctor. I know she loves me, though; she should stick by me. "Should" and "would" are two different words, though. I just don't know. I just don't know what I should do.

Of course, I had to blow my mouth about having had a little sex while I was gone. That may have been a big mistake. Even though she seemed to understand it a bit, after all, a guy like me can't be away that much and not have a little; but she is going to think if I really loved her, I wouldn't have touched another woman. Jessica is a real lady. When she thinks it over, she may not want to be even friends! I probably blew it! What a dumb ass I am. I didn't have to tell her, but I did because I have reformed. Daniel put his head in his hands and before long he yelled out to no one in the room, "I DIDN'T HAVE TO TELL!" His body shook as he lay on the bed and cried. "Why am I me? And what a jerk I am! Maria was little more than a slut! Why did I have to have her and why did I leave in the first place? I ruined everything! I wouldn't have gotten messed up and we, Jessica and I, would be close and secure. Oh how sweet it could have been if I hadn't messed up, if I hadn't left her. Now it will be like building from the foundation up, and she may not trust me now. I don't know whether to tell her or not…."

It began to storm outside in keeping with Daniel's mood. "Go ahead," he yelled to a crackle of lightning, "take the power, put me in the dark. I'm in the dark already!"

Eventually when the storm subsided, he pulled himself together, undressed and hung his new clothes on the bedpost, got in his bed, and pulled the covers up over his head.

"Jessica, please don't let it be ruined."

No, if it's ruined, it's because of me—of what I am—whatever that is. I know there is something wrong with me or I would have better control. Most guys are not like me. Jessica could have a normal guy. She could have anyone she wants. She is so beautiful, and why she still cares for me I don't know. I can't—I cannot have another spell in front of Jessica or she will go away. I know she will—after I left her and all, she will not stand it anymore. How could she love a guy like me?

Try as he might, Daniel just couldn't sleep. He thought back to that dream he had that clearly represented Jessica and then the strange writing he couldn't control. *Spooky, that's what it was. I'm just one big, handsome spook, a creep. I think I will play a little. Maybe a new song will come to me. A spooky, creepy song.* He laughed aloud.

His guitar seemed to call to him as he went to the corner and picked it up. He played a few dissonant chords, groping for a song, groping, more chords, a few runs—nothing came. He began playing "Unchained Melody" until tears came to his eyes. He wiped them with his sleeve, then gently put his guitar back in the corner. No song, no new song, for Jessica.

Compulsively, Daniel thought about the medicine he used to take—could I have some? *I've got to do something—without pills, I'm this weirdo. I just better admit it. Something is not right in my brain. Could I possibly have some of those pills? What did I have on me when they dumped me?* He looked through his belongings and found the coat jacket he thought he had on. In the inside pocket he found a small bottle that said "Take with food BID." His hands shook. *I remember Bonny had me take those with breakfast and with dinner. It can't hurt to try. There's nothing in the apartment. I'll just go get a hamburger and take one.*

When he got back, it was after 1 a.m., so he wasn't much in the mood for eating and he was so tired. He took a few bits of the burger and downed the pill. *Now, I have to take one in the morning—gotta remember.* The pill put him in dreamland in no time flat.

CHAPTER TWENTY-SIX

I know I had sort of a night's sleep but I feel like I am living in a dream world. If I could just figure him out. Sometimes, we don't really know ourselves, though, and how we don't know ourselves! I cannot conceive of it. Part of me wants to forget all of it, but part of me wants to find out more. I find now I'm a lot more complex than I ever knew, and Daniel and I, if I am to believe all of what happened, have been linked together for a few 100, give or take. Just what is time anyway? One thing I must try very hard to do is live in the present and deal with what I have to deal with NOW.

Inequities have probably plagued Daniel all his life or he wouldn't act as he does against minorities and people that he seems to see as lower on the totem pole. There must be so much in his life that needs examining. He seems okay now ... but I know better.

Jessica stretched out as she always did first thing in the morning and felt all her extremities as she habitually had come to do. *Still okay, but I must tell him about this as soon as the time is right! Could I wish that the steroids I took during the flu and for a while after might make it stay in remission indefinitely? What a stroke of luck, although at that time I was sicker than a dead cat. No matter. Daniel told me that he trusted me more than he ever trusted anyone. I must be worthy of that trust. If it causes him to leave again, I will at least be able to live with myself. After his statement of trust, of course, I have to tell him.*

My Daniel is back, but everything is different. It makes me so unbelievably happy, but I'm different. He seems different. He even confessed to me that he had had an affair while away. That's just dandy! I don't think the old Daniel would have done that. And he looks so good—almost too good, and I know it is going to be difficult to take it slowly, at least for me. I wonder if the woman took him under her wing.... He can't believe I am so naïve as believe it was a simple one- or two-night stand. He said he never stopped thinking of me, though—poor other woman. Maybe it was the "other woman" that made him come back to me. Not literally, but maybe by comparison ... but maybe just fate. I'm beginning to believe in fate. Life has really changed for me and maybe him as well.

I certainly know he had been in a fight because I could see the faint marks on his face. What a reason to go to a bar. I guess he won't be doing that again for a good little while. Yes, the old Daniel would do that. Somehow in the interim, there has been a change and it seems for the better.

What I really have here with Daniel is that I plainly don't know him, not like I seemed to know Ulysses before. It seemed our love was perfect—no stumbling blocks, but that was the dream. Previously, Daniel could be so changeable, and how do I know any of that has improved with just one meeting after all those months? Oh he was charming, oh yes, but he could be charming before. Then my heart would beat out of my chest during one of his tizzy fits. I would have to admit it didn't do me any good when that would happen. However, I know he is very full of goodness, kindness, after all. I know what I know, but

I don't choose to think about it right now. I will see my beloved Daniel this evening and look only for the good. It's there. I know that facet is strongly imbedded in his personality, complex as it may be. He's troubled, that's all.

Jessica looked in her closet. Everything looked ordinary, but at least she fit in her clothes now. *I lost weight when Daniel was here before with just the stress of dating—dating him and caring for him so much took its toll. I'll have to admit I look better now and I cannot let him tear me down again. His leaving was a wake-up call—no matter how it shattered me at the time. Am I too dumb to resent him for it or is it that I realize resentment only goes inside and hurts the person who is resenting in the long run? Yes, I'm mad he had an affair, but that's over, he's back, and perhaps in a while the pieces will fall into place for us. He's here for a reason—like we need to play out our parts.*

Now I sound like George.

"George, I never really knew you until the end. How I wasted what would have been a good father-daughter relationship, and that's a good example of unneeded resentment that I carried from when I was a teenager. Why is it that people sometimes wait until it's too late?" Jessica continued her conversation with George as if he might be in the room.

"George, what you said to me at the end opened up a whole new avenue of thinking and of meaning for me. Thank you, dear George, wherever you are!"

The closet seemed to be a good place for conversations with the deceased and smatterings of the mind, but then her thinking shifted back to Daniel.

What great outfit can I come dancing out in tonight? There isn't any...? There's nothing dripping with sex appeal! Maybe I'll go the basic black route with a new scarf. I've just enough time to run to the mall—maybe something plain blue to match his eyes. "Vanities of vanities; all is vanity." All to meet a friend for a movie, right? Right!

When Jessica let Daniel in, she was very composed and beautiful in her black dress. Daniel held both her hands for a moment. The warm contact went through her, but then he dropped them rather abruptly as he helped her with her wrap, which enveloped her several times.

"What kind of thing is this?" he asked.

"It's the style. I rather like it, don't you? It's always so cold in the movie house that I freeze and don't enjoy the movie if I get too cold," she answered.

"I've been away too long—but you look great in it! It looks like a robe for a princess. Very fitting, I would say. Now, what movie shall we see?" he asked.

"How about *A Beautiful Mind*?"

Daniel wrinkled up his nose. "What's it about?"

"I'm really not sure—only that Martha said it was good. She said he was a genius but he had mental problems. It's based on a true story, so we ought to like it, I would think, don't you?"

"I guess, as they say, 'Truth is better than fiction.' Well, okay, honey, get in, Your Highness," he said as he opened the door to his freshly reformed car.

How could Jessica not notice Daniel's car had been cleaned and polished! Not an apple core in sight! Somehow with Daniel a core or two had not bothered her, though. *Has he really changed or is this the influence of "the other woman?"* His driving, however, had not improved, and she found herself tensely holding on to the seat belt. It was a rather somber ride, as it seemed like words escaped them; quiet except for when he would come upon a traffic light too quickly and have to screech on the brakes. She seemed to be listening to a quiet Daniel and thinking, "And miles to go before we speak…." It seemed he was speaking volumes without a word.

They held greasy hands in the movies after they finished their popcorn. Jessica had somehow managed to keep the popcorn in the bag and not on her stole. The movie was very intense, and for a while Jessica wasn't entirely sure what was happening. When she did comprehend the story, she wasn't sure this choice would do much for Daniel's psyche or sense of peace, or hers for that matter.

On the way home she was thinking this might be a good time to say something about how she sometimes worried about him, when he got so upset sometimes, but no, perhaps not. *How in the world would he take my saying something? He might flip out. That's not good—I shouldn't have to feel this way about someone who has been my lover, and I still love him, even though things are not as they ought to be. It's because of Ulysses—the past that I don't want to think about—but it keeps cropping up, sneaking into my mind. He was, I know, Ulysses when I was Elizabeth. Now stop that! It's not that important. I don't know enough about the other anyway. I sometimes cannot control thinking about it. And Daniel's so quiet tonight and my small talk sounds inane. It shouldn't be this way. So uncomfortable!*

Daniel finally spoke up. "Honey, that guy in the show was really mental, wasn't he? He really thought he saw those people, didn't he?"

"Yes, he was seriously ill with schizophrenia, but mental illness is a chemical imbalance of the brain and can't be helped, just like some other illnesses. By taking his meds, though, he led a productive life. It was really wonderful how he had the strength to conquer his disease. You know, mental illness should be treated just like any other illness and should not have any stigma attached to it, like it has in the past. He was a brilliant man. He won the Nobel Prize. That proved he triumphed over his illness, didn't it?"

"Sometimes even talented guys can have something wrong, you know, Jessie; maybe even guys like me. Of course, I'm not a brain like that guy but there is something wrong—wrong, very wrong, and I feel I need to tell you something about me—me, Jessica, me! I hafta tell you, but I'm not crazy, you understand that, don't you? This is serious and it's really awful. Awful things happen to me. Have happened to me. Even in the past, I have done irrational things. Bonny made me get on medicine for a while and I found a bottle of pills, but I'm not sure it is still good. Even when I was a kid I think my step-ma thought I, as you say, 'had an illness.' Like the guy in the movie, she thought my talent would get me through. Of course, I have never been really nutsy like that guy; I just let my emotions run away sometimes and I don't know why,

Jessie. Jessie, I don't know why it happens. And then, something really bad happened to me, and Jessica, I can't put it all together because there is a blank there, like a part of my life has just been scooped up and thrown away. This I somehow have to remember, and I would hope, maybe, you might help me!"

Daniel looked at her so intently in the way that she loved, but at the same time so pitifully, urgently that it frightened her. She couldn't believe what she was hearing, that he was actually bringing it up, but she took his hand and said, "Of course, I understand that there's nothing wrong with your mind; but there were times, uh, times we've been together when you were here before that I've worried when you would get so upset and I wouldn't understand—I know now, you don't mind my mentioning this. It would bother me more than you know, that is, more than I let you know, and to be completely truthful, I was a little afraid of what you might do, uh, when you got like that. It would make my heart pound, Daniel. Of course, I will do anything I can to help. I am seeing someone now who has all kinds of knowledge about different types of illness. If you will consent to see him, I feel sure he would be able to make a diagnosis and put you on the right medicine. I can't help you myself; you will have to go to a doctor who is certified in psychiatry."

"You mean a shrink? I thought you, as a nurse, might have some medicine that would work. I believe I brought it up and this isn't easy for me, not easy at all, telling you this, Jessica! But I'm not crazy like that guy—I don't see things, hear things, or nothing! I don't want to go to no shrink!" Daniel retorted sharply.

"But listen to me, Daniel; if I didn't feel that unexplainable way I feel about you, I would have broken up with you long ago, when you were here before, because of the way you behaved, out of the blue sometimes. It wasn't easy. If anybody should have been concerned, it should have been me. Of course, you are not like the man in the movie. You somehow seem different now, or maybe I'm hoping you will not get so upset and uptight like you did when we were together before, uh, that is, you seem calmer to me." Jessica didn't stop to take a breath until she had said what she needed to say.

"I have to tell you this, Jessie, you don't know the half of it and you have every right to worry. I didn't want to tell you, but you being a nurse and all and since we are working on friendship and all, I probably do need to go see a doc and take some meds and all. Maybe, okay, you know who I should see. Would you fix it up?" Daniel rambled on. "But way before I knew you and before Bonny died and before Joey...." Daniel began to tear up. "I've had problems more than you know, then this awful thing and this blank spot in my life and—I can't be telling you this, but it's true, it's true, and it's time I tell you. Can you believe it? That's where the weirdness, the blank space happened. They planned it. Somebody planned it for a purpose, Jessie!" And the worse part is after they let me go I was here in this city just knowing who I was, that's all, but afraid to go home—paranoid as a cat—I know I'm from Illinois but I can't go back until, until—"

Jessica interrupted, "You mean that you just got here by accident? Someone put you here? This is bizarre; undoubtedly a very evil person did this to you, but when you got your bearings, realizing who you were, you answered my ad. It's almost fated, mystical, even though we have had our problems…."

"I can hardly believe it myself," Daniel answered. "Here's the part I can't stand to have to tell you, but I must, so you will understand. I was found by the body of my son with a gun in my hand. My Joey! Somebody drugged me and somebody put that gun there. I barely opened my eyes and there I was by Joey's body, my Joey's warm body … and there was this gun in my hand and Joey, Joey, and before I knew it these cops rushed in the room, cuffed me, knocked me out again with a needle I think; the next thing I knew—the funny farm." Daniel stopped the car. "I can't see to drive the damn car—you drive, okay?" Daniel's shoulders shook as tears streamed down his cheeks after he pulled over and handed the keys to Jessica. Jessica put her hands to her pulsing head and leaned down in the seat, disbelieving.

Then, realizing how much he needed her, she reached for him and put her arms around him and said as steadily as she could, "Is this what you started to tell me a long time ago, but didn't? How terrible! Are there policemen that rush you off without any rights?" Jessica stopped abruptly, thinking, *Too much, too much for him, too much for me.… Stop questioning now, wait.* "It's okay. Please know that I know you couldn't have done such a thing; you did not, you couldn't, I know you couldn't." She crawled over on top of him so that he could scoot over on the passenger's side and she could take the wheel.

"I don't even own a gun—I wouldn't own a gun—I hate the things. A gun killed my daddy. One shot took away my daddy, and I think he loved me. I really think he did. The only one in my life who did, besides you, Jessica—you, my sweetheart. Daddy taught me to sing. Showed me that I had talent as a little guy, and then that one shot, when he was out hunting, took him away from me. So why would I have a gun? So Jessie, someone else put that gun there, and then those cops ran in and the next thing I remember is that funny farm or freak hospital, where they would put me in a room to black me out. Again and again, they did it! That's why I don't remember, I don't remember why I would be lying by my son's dead body. Jessica, I've got to remember what happened to Joey." Daniel shook into sobs again, saying, "Joey was a problem, a bad problem, and I got so mad at him I may have felt like killing him; but I loved him, he's mine—even though he's dead, he's still mine!"

"We're going home. Just talk to me about it all you want, Daniel. I can listen and drive, too."

Somehow with grim determination Jessica managed to drive the broken Daniel home. *Is this something in his mind or can this awful story be the truth? Real? When he calms down, if he switches to something else, I will think it is a mind thing. Am I being influenced by that movie? But God, please help me with this—it sounds almost like that crazy story he began to tell me early on. He seems so sincere, so troubled, but if he just has this in his mind, we are really in trouble. We will work on this together, whatever is the answer. We must. I will listen carefully, as it sounds like he may have been railroaded or something. It's so terrible. I don't want it to be real, for his sake and for mine. God, I don't know what I wish—every avenue is bad. Things like this don't happen in my world, my little protected world!*

"Come on in the house for a little while, Daniel, while we clear our minds a bit." Jessica measured her words. She didn't think Daniel should drive to his apartment in his present state of mind. He might not make it! She knew if all of it were true, it would have taken its toll just for him to tell her. *Friends,* she thought. A "friend" would help another in this state of affairs and console him and listen to him if he still wanted to talk. *Keep your head on straight, Jessica; don't be more than a friend now, no matter how you feel. This is an awful, awful thing—a terrible story. If it is a delusion, you will have to go along with that as well, you know; that is the way a professional would do it, right? Dr. Jerold? He asked for a doctor. Maybe, just maybe Dr. Jerold could help him. He is an M.D. He can prescribe meds.*

A calmer Daniel said, "I feel awful that I told you. Now, I have us both stressed out; but it happened, Jessica, it happened. I have a blank space because of what they did at that hospital, and Joey is dead. I know Joey is gone. I remember his body lying there, but that is it, except those cops rushing in and the funny farm." Daniel wiped his eyes on his sleeve. "Can we just talk for a little while? I know what happened with Bonny. Bonny desired cremation. As far as I know there's no grave for Joey, cremation, anything. I just don't know what happened and I guess it has become an obsession of sorts with me. Christ, he was my son!"

"Of course, we can talk; or rather, you talk and I'll listen," replied Jessica. "But first I'll make us some coffee. We need to relax our minds with a little coffee." Jessica needed to distance herself from thoughts of that horrible story with something normal. Coffee is normal.

"That might help," said Daniel. He laid his head down on the couch pillow and thought, *She doesn't really believe me. She is putting me on. I can tell by her tone. It's true, it's true ... if she doesn't believe me, the one person I thought I could trust doesn't believe me.* He could feel the tears beginning to well up again in his eyes when Jessica came in and set the coffee on the coffee table.

He was about to jump out of his skin.

"How long ago did this happen, honey?" Jessica said as she sat down beside him.

"Well, I think it was around two years ago that I arrived, but you said it correctly: it took me a while to find myself—I was a stranger in a foreign land."

"Daniel, we have to get to the bottom of this and I think I know someone who can help."

"If not you, who?" Daniel said suspiciously.

"Oh, I will help as much as I can, honey, but I think it sounds like we need professional help to help you fill in that blank space, don't you?" Jessica tried not to sound condescending, nursey, or the like. "It could be possible with the right kind of assistance you would begin to remember."

"Jessica, I thought you didn't believe me! You do believe me. You do! Oh, Jessie, I've got to find out what really happened or it's like a noose around my neck."

"It seems to me I remember a long time along you told me fragments of a story about some crooked cops who filmed you. At the time, you changed the subject, so I didn't give it much thought after that until now."

"Filmed me! How could I have forgotten that? That's right; they filmed me with that gun in my hand so I wouldn't tell." Daniel stood up and began pacing. "Wouldn't tell—but for Christ's sake, I don't know what! But I know why I didn't finish the story—we had just started dating, and I don't even know why I fell apart like that. I guess I do need help of some sort, Jessie, and it wasn't just what they did; I took medicine before—Bonny made me, if you wanna know."

"We can cross that bridge when we come to it, I think, but the story you are telling me sounds like blackmail, doesn't it to you? But until you remember all of it, you won't know why. A little information is helpful, though; at least we are a little farther along. Daniel, Dr. Jerold, is a psychiatrist and he specializes in regression. That is, if someone has a problem that worries them, he can hypnotize them and take them back and help them remember."

"Hypnotize? I don't know about that—I don't want someone messing with me—with my head!" Daniel held up his hands and placed them on his head and continued his pacing.

"Daniel, I was hypnotized, but that is another story that we can talk about some other time. It's late now, but I can tell you I trust Dr. Jerold completely. Think about it and think about how much you want to know the truth.

"Now, tonight, I'm going to bring you a blanket and pillow and you can sleep on the couch, I don't think you should drive home tonight—we are both upset."

"No, Jessica, I think I'd better go to my own place—I'm okay now, now that I know you believe me. You're right, I need time to think, and I do that better alone. I love you, though." Daniel headed for the door, and Jessica held on to his coat to try to dissuade him.

"Really, Jessica, I appreciate it but I need to be alone to think; and besides, it will be better that I don't stay here, remember?"

"Yes, indeed, we both remember," said Jessica as she let him out the door.

CHAPTER TWENTY-SEVEN

Jessica bolted the door and stood there in thought for a few minutes until she heard his car turn the corner noisily. *Oh, it's late and I shouldn't be going out in the night air.* However, she went through the house and kitchen, out the back door, and onto the patio. She wrapped her shawl around herself a couple of times and settled in its folds in the rocking chair. *What a dreadful story! What will be the best approach to this? I simply don't know! Maybe the darkness of this night will help me think.* The wrought-iron fence made strange shadows on the stone after her eyes became accustomed to the moon-slivered night. *Strange as the story may sound, I believe it. I believe him. Why do I? I know it's because I'm reaching into the core of Daniel—his very soul. And that soul is basically honest. For one thing, he didn't have to tell me about that other woman, but he did. For some reason unknown even to him, he had to be honest with me. There is an undercurrent here. I don't think the old Daniel would have been truthful. His time in a real hospital has changed him somehow and given him more depth.*

Then again, what should a person like me, who hopefully has it together, do in a case like this? What do I do? If I had any common sense, probably run like everything! The trouble is he needs me now more than he ever did. And I know his life has been difficult this time, so different from mine. This time, how easily I say that! Mine has been, until the MS and the divorce, all roses and glow until the bottom dropped out. Even though he hasn't told me a lot about his early life, I know he came from a poor family and has had a hard way to go for most of his life. But with his musical talent, he did pull himself up out of it, and I certainly admire him for that. His painful life no doubt left its mark mentally. Even if we do make it with each other, it will be difficult unless he keeps whatever is wrong with him under control. Poor Daniel. I used to wonder if I loved him because I realized he needed help and I needed someone to need me. Well, we both need someone, don't we?

It's evident I will have to talk him into seeing Dr. Jerold. I need to find out more about people who believe in reincarnation and why. I cannot conceive of my telling Daniel why I went to see the doctor unless I know more about regression and reincarnation myself. How will I tell him that I think we were together in a former life? Anybody would laugh at that unless they knew others who had the same experience. Maybe I should ask Dr. Jerold if he believes all that stuff. He certainly acted as if he did, but what do I really know about him. Maybe Martha and I should go over there and discuss it with him before I even open my mouth about it to Daniel. Martha certainly thinks it probable and is so persuasive, and I know what I know now; there's no going back to how I used to think.

But most important, we must get some help for Daniel, and that will be to find out what really happened with his son.... No matter what pictures whoever had, I know Daniel; even though he does have problems, he would not have done anything to his own son—especially the way he feels about guns. He couldn't have made that up, that story about his father—he was as sincere as I am, as anyone I've known for years. Remember how in the beginning, I always felt that I KNEW Daniel and how uncanny it seemed at the time?

And even though his behavior occasionally seemed irrational to me, I could never seem to turn my back on him. I couldn't because of the dreams, and now the answers were with Dr. Jerold and my regression. We may find some answers for Daniel in the same way and a puzzle may be solved.

With new determination, Jessica tried to clear her mind before she went in, but when she did it was to a ringing phone. Before she picked it up she knew who it would be. "Daniel," she said.

"Jessica, I hope I didn't wake you, but I got to thinking I laid a lot of bad stuff on you tonight and so much of it is a puzzle, but it means everything to me that you do believe me and I just want to say I love you for it and good night, that's all."

"Goodnight, I love you, too." Jessica couldn't talk, only say what she felt.

Although she thought a warm bath would do her some good she was too weary to even run the water. She quickly creamed off her makeup, put on her gown, and got into bed. *Oh, there's nothing like this comfortable bed. Hmmm, Daniel said he didn't like it. Well, just another one of his THINGS.* The phone rang. *Oh no, let the machine answer it....*

"Mom, Momma, if you're there, please pick up!" Debbie's voice sounded worried, almost frantic.

"Debbie, I'm here, honey, what's *wrong*?"

"Oh, I'm sorry to be calling so late, but I called a few nights ago and you weren't home, and then I called repeatedly tonight when I thought you would be home for sure and it's just that it's so late and you are usually home, and I just got worried, that's all!"

"Debbie, I'm a big girl, I can take care of myself; but honey, I'm sorry you worry. Please don't do that. I'm in bed now, all safe and secure, but we do need to talk one of these days," Jessica said gently.

"Mom, do you know it's after midnight?"

"I was out on the patio just thinking about what a nice family I have! Please, Deb, let me get to sleep; we'll talk soon. I'm so sleepy now, okay?"

"'Night, Mom. Get some sleep; talk later," Debbie was sleepy too, but relieved.

Debbie immediately got on the phone and called Becca and Jon. Becca had been waiting by the phone. "She's home and she wasn't out that late; she was out on the patio—thinking. Something is going on. I can feel it; she sounded strange."

"Well, maybe she was just sleepy or asleep when you got her," replied Becca.

"No, she was in bed but awake, but she wasn't going to answer the phone—I know something is going on. Maybe the MS is worse and she just didn't want to tell me!" Debbie blurted out, "Oh, what are we going to do if she gets worse, Becca?"

"Debbie, you don't know that, so don't borrow trouble." Good advice from the older, wiser sister but not well received.

"Becca, you didn't hear her. Something is going on, I tell you, and she even said we had to talk and she wouldn't have said that if something weird weren't going on. I'll be over tomorrow and we'll go see her, okay?"

"Yes, I think so, but let's get some sleep. Give me a call in the morning before you come so I can have things picked up a bit." Becca thought of the mess the twins had made that hadn't yet been touched.

"That's not the important matter, you know, but okay. 'Night, Becca."

"'Night, Deb. I'm thankful she's all right," replied Becca.

"Maybe all right." Debbie hung up the phone.

Debbie, single, no children, the worrier, imagined her mom in a wheelchair. *Well, we could lower everything in the house so she could manage somehow and have someone come in every day to see if everything is all right. Oh, what a horrible disease, and why? My mom doesn't deserve such a fate. Becca is right, though; I am borrowing trouble—she just sounded like she needed to get something off her chest, something said, maybe a problem she been having, maybe not the MS, hopefully not that....* Debbie drifted into a troubled sleep.

When Debbie awakened it was with "Oh my God, it's 10:15—I've gotta get out of here and over to Becca's!" She jumped in the shower, first warm water, then cold to wake her up, jumped out, dried off, put on a sweat suit, and was out the door.

Becca had everything fairly neat when Debbie arrived looking halfway put together. "Well, guess we're just going to Mom's, uh, have you called her?" said Becca.

"No, you do it, and tell me if she sounds strange." Debbie put on her lipstick while her sister made the call.

Becca picked up the phone and gave her mother a ring. "Mom, Debbie's over here and we haven't had a good ole girl tête-à-tête for a while. Can we play come over and see?" (Becca and Debbie used to play as children "come over to see," and it became a family tradition.)

"I'd love that—I could use another cup of coffee, so I'll put on a fresh pot, and I have shortbread!"

"Made with brown sugar? We'll see you in a small bit." Then to Debbie, "She sounds fine to me—just because she wasn't there when you called, you had to get all worried—just the very fact that she went out should tell you the MS is not worse. Get a grip!"

When the girls arrived all seemed quite normal at Jessica's. Debbie noted that the limp was still gone and breathed a sigh of relief. She made a second breakfast of the coffee and shortbread as they sat around the kitchen table. "Nobody can make shortbread like you, Mom; mine never turns out," said Becca.

"Thanks, but only three ingredients, honey."

"I know, but it's a failure when I make it—I just need to have the knack!"

"It just has to feel right," replied Jessica.

"Yeah, right, spoken like an older, wiser generation," said Becca, disparagingly.

Debbie could contain herself no longer. "What was it you wanted to talk about, Mom?"

"Well, guys, this is going to sound strange or completely crazy to you, but you know before George died, he said something to me about far-life memory, and playing on your instincts, so I've been doing some investigating—investigating because I have a sort of friend."

"Investigating? And a friend? Who? What?" quizzed Debbie.

"Investigating what? And you have a friend—am I to presume a man?" chimed in Becca.

"It's rather a long story, but I have the answer to those dreams that I was having."

Both girls looked at each other, then said almost simultaneously again, "How?"

"Mother, I can't imagine you had a boyfriend and didn't tell us about him! You know I would tell you if I had someone on the fence just waiting for me to give him the eye," retorted Debbie.

"Debbie, if that's all you've had for breakfast, you're going to get a low blood sugar attack," cautioned her mother.

"Come on now, Mom, don't change the subject; let's hear it," said Becca while she looked at Debbie with the wish that she could eat like that. Becca had had trouble with her weight since the birth of the twins, and this time was on a low glycemic diet. Debbie it seemed never gained no matter what abuse she heaped on herself.

"Well, it could be explained easily by this tape that I have, but you still would have trouble believing it and you're certainly not ready to hear anything like it yet without explanation. First of all, I haven't told you about this friend of mine, but I was going to; the time just was not yet right. Then he left and went to Galveston, so I thought it wasn't necessary. Anyway, occasionally, I would still think about him and apparently he thought about me, because he came back. His name, by the way, is Daniel. But before he could see me, he was in an accident and had to go to the hospital and have plastic surgery. Then he didn't want to see me while he was healing up from that because apparently his face suffered more than anything else. But when his face healed so that he looked like himself again, he came to see me, and our feelings about each other are the same as before he left. He left because he was unsure and didn't want to become involved too soon."

Becca said, "Well, that sounds like a mean thing to do, to go so far away. I'd be leery of him if he were my boyfriend."

"I know that sounds a little crazy and it was, but those dreams I had while he was here before and even when he left were so real and really bothered me. Then what George said about far-life memory before he died took root in my mind. He planted a seed that I couldn't shake away."

"Cool! So what happened?" Both girls hung on her intriguing words.

"Well, you know, Deb, you seemed to think those dreams were just imagination—well, they were not. In the last one, I seemed to really be living it. I was not really completely asleep; I was in that half-awake state. I was really THERE in another time, another place. That's when I really began to take things seriously."

"Oh, Mom, you can't be in another time, another place when you are here; that's not possible—unless you live in Gotham City...," Becca said disbelievingly.

Jessica went on, undaunted, "This dream was almost a vision. I know it sounds strange—weird, to you girls, and it was the strangest thing that has ever happened to me, but it followed a pattern—the pattern of the dreams, only it wasn't frightening but loving.

"I understand why you wouldn't understand, but keep open minds. I was half there, not awake, and I actually saw that log cabin in another time and I knew it was myself—me—that is, I had lived there in this other time, so I told Martha and Martha thought it a clue and not so strange."

"Martha is willing to believe anything," Becca said again. "Really, Mother!"

"I always thought Martha had a good head on her shoulders; now I wonder." Debbie was not being taken in either.

"Just listen, please. Martha heard good things about this doctor, a Dr. Jerold, and arranged for me to see him. He does hypnotic regressions to see if there is something in your past that you have suppressed but that may be troubling you now. I was hypnotized."

"You were hypnotized? I always thought you thought stuff like that was hokey," Becca queried her mother.

"Well, I have the tape of my hypnotic regression, but I don't think either of you are ready to listen to it now. Apparently, I haven't told you enough or I haven't handled this correctly to make you open-minded enough or even curious enough to listen to it. You are right, though; I did think things like this were hokey, until George opened my eyes and made me realize there is another world to conquer out there. It certainly goes against what I have always believed to be true and what I have taught you to believe."

"Oh, Mom, please let us listen to it. I'm curious, I'm curious," said Debbie.

"So am I—very interested," chimed in Becca.

"Oh, so you want now to hear it? I'll see if I can locate it."

Jessica went about opening several different drawers pretending as if she had misplaced it, but finally said, "Here is the tape. It's my first time listening to it—but I really don't have to. I remember hearing my voice and what I said; I remember saying those things. All I ask is for you to listen to it with an open mind, that's all. Even I can't believe it sometimes, but I know now it is the reason why I couldn't just tell Daniel to get lost and not think about him another minute. Daniel, that's his name, or did I already tell you that?"

"Well, Daniel is a nice-sounding name. Come on, let's listen to the tape; you've got our curiosity way up there now, that's for sure! And I'm just so glad it's something hokey like this instead of your health being worse." Debbie leaned back in her chair and took another shortbread.

"I hope you won't think that after you hear it." Jessica went to her refrigerator and got her daughter a large piece of cheese. "Here, eat that," she ordered. "I don't want you falling out in the middle of the tape. I want your attention!"

Jessica put the tape in the player and her voice and Dr. Jerold's began.

All three women eventually got up from the table and walked around the kitchen, but listened intently.

When the tape finished and Dr. Jerold had told Jessica, "Remember, you will never wait that long again—not again—not again," the silence in the kitchen seemed to pound in on Jessica's head. I *said all that and I believe it whether they do or not.* Finally the first one to speak was Becca. "Wow, Mom, I don't know what to think, but the part that really got to me was Elizabeth between lives. She didn't talk like you really, but she WAS you. And she seemed so knowledgeable, like she really knew the scoop; and the part about waiting to be born ... and you crying. I know you didn't make that up in your mind. I know you didn't. And that doctor. The doctor really knew what he was doing. How many other people has he regressed? I have to say I am impressed, though I can't believe you did that!"

"Well, all I have to say is, if we live more than once, we have been sold a bill of goods for over 2,000 years; and I don't think that has been wrong, but this gives me something else to think about—and since it's you, Mom, to worry about. I don't know how you could have done this without letting me know, or us know!" Debbie was perplexed, to say the least.

Becca chimed in, "It's so awfully believable, Mom, and I know you think you went through all of that, but how can you be so sure?"

This put Jessica on the defensive. "It's not think—I know. It all adds up—the dreams—this and that—and I've never been able to give Daniel the shove, and there were times when I could have, maybe should have."

Debbie then said, "The shove, that's interesting … but I'm also intrigued with Elizabeth and the between-life stuff. 'We are here to love and do for others'—that's simple enough, but I'm sure there's more to it than that. And Mom, couldn't you maybe have picked that up as loyally as you go to church?"

"No, Elizabeth worded it differently, uh, me—now I'm getting confused. Well, I think we get an assignment like in school and then we have to discover that assignment by living, because as babies we don't have the language skills and we have to get into our new situation, our new environment, and it's veiled somehow. I know it's very complicated. I do wish I understood more."

"Now Elizabeth didn't say all that!" exclaimed Debbie. "How do you know that, Mom?"

"Well, I sorta seem to know more now since I was regressed." This surprised even Jessica.

"Mom, the Great Guru. But really I'm not making light of this or fun of you at all. I think it's neat, although an unbelievable experience. What does Daniel say about it?" asked Becca.

"Well, he doesn't exactly know about it yet." Jessica couldn't look her daughters in the eye.

"What? He doesn't know? What nature of a man are we dealing with here? What is this play all about?" Debbie couldn't believe especially this.

"Now you're being sarcastic. I need support, not sarcasm. I need to wait. There are a few problems."

"I knew it! Mom, I don't care if he is Prince Charming or the prince of Wales, you don't need a problem man."

"Debbie, all of us have problems. No matter how far back our problems are seated, they can affect the present at times. You'll have to admit that, honey."

"'Tomorrow and tomorrow and tomorrow.' Listen, gang, I've got to go before the twins awaken from their naps. They can be a handful. Bye now," Becca said as she hurried out the front door.

CHAPTER TWENTY-EIGHT

Before long Becca arrived home to Jon and the boys; after she had hugged Jon, he said, "What's wrong?"

Jon and Becca had been together long enough that they almost began to look alike, like many married couples; perhaps it was more gestures than anything, but they did seem to look alike. They weren't able to conceive the twins until seven years after their marriage; they had eventually gone through fertility treatments until finally Becca became pregnant. They were elated when they found out she was carrying twins. Jon thanked God. It seemed an answer to the prayer they prayed fervently night after night and at breakfast. The boys were a gift from God.

Jessica's MS had taken a back seat to their desire for a family, but Jon tended to see everyone as healthy. Those seven years of waiting put a strain on that concept.

Becca hardly knew how to approach her husband with the news that his mother-in-law had dabbled in the occult, although she found Jessica's story somewhat fascinating and mysterious.

"Jon, Mother has a boyfriend."

"Oh good!" said Jon. "But what's wrong? I can tell by your look—you look funny."

"You've heard of hypnotic regression, haven't you?" Becca smiled a little.

"Well, yes. Sometimes some psychiatrists will use that to uncover something in the patient's past to heal headaches or whatever. Don't tell me Jessica is trying to be healed that way? If so, it is certainly unconventional," Jon jumped the track.

"Not exactly." In the bright light of day and with Jon, Jessica's regression seemed to Becca a possible fixation of the mind because of that boyfriend, who didn't sound like someone of whom she or Jon would approve.

"Jon, brace yourself. Our mother has gone a step further. I would say a giant step further into the past. Now, if it hadn't been for Martha, she wouldn't have even investigated this route. It seems she had been having strange dreams since Daniel, that's his name, came into her life; and then George, before he died, talked to her about far-life memory. She took him seriously and talked to Martha about it. Martha found this psychiatrist for her and he hypnotized her."

"Well, what did they uncover?"

"Jon, he took her back all right!"

"Back to where," Jon queried.

"You'll never guess! It seems back to early New England." Becca was really feeling foolish now. Jon was an elder in the church.

"Back to early New England," Jon repeated.

"Yep. She was named Elizabeth. And for Mom's sake, I'll have to say it was very believable. Debbie and I listened to the tape. The doctor recorded the whole session so she would have it. She said she really didn't need to listen to it because she heard herself talking the whole time. It was she, she said, and it was, Jon, only that she talked in early English. It was like listening to a play and she was the main character!"

"Becca, perhaps she had been rehearsing; if not, you are buying into a cultish idea."

"Jon, don't make me mad! I'm telling you this is the way it was, and you know Mom would not make up such a thing. The part that really fascinated me was the between-life stuff, when Elizabeth died. Jon, there was more information there than the church has ever given us—not that I say that it's right. I just wish you would listen to the tape."

"Becca, I am not listening to any evil tape that puts your mother in a bad light! You know how I feel about Jessica. She's our family! I am really surprised that your mother would get into such things, you know, without asking how I feel about it. What caused her to do it?"

"Well, that boyfriend doesn't even know, so I can't blame him. It was those repeated dreams she had, Debbie told me, about a baby being taken from her, and the baby's eyes were Daniel, the boyfriend's eyes. Then one of the dreams became like a vision. She was half awake, a happy dream with her husband back then. She could see it plainly and she wasn't really asleep. That's when she called Martha, and Martha talked to her about it. If we can blame anyone, let's blame Martha, but I do like Martha. Martha, though, is a free-spirit type. However, why blame anyone? It's not like us to blame people."

"I wish she had talked to me first. That's an occult belief!"

"Jon, I knew you would be like this. Completely closed on the subject. Well, I was as well until I heard the tape, and the between-life part is fascinating, I want you to hear it. At least I think there is more to life than we have always been taught. Go to the library and see for yourself!"

"Nothing, but nothing will destroy my faith in my God—not you or anyone else. I know where I will go when I go to the library. I choose my reading carefully." Jon turned his back on her and started walking from the room.

"Jon, please, honey. Jon—I'm not going to let you just turn away from me and walk away. You said it yourself, 'Mom's family' to you—well, then, be open at least to this. Your God doesn't belong just to you, you know. God is the God of everything, everybody, not just what you choose to believe—not just what you choose to put neatly on one of your shelves. I realize this is strange to you.... Well, it's strange to me, but I'm not going to slam a door on my own mother when she is going through a difficult time. Maybe, just maybe she is discovering something about life that we need to at least consider." Becca felt like screaming but was not at all surprised by his attitude. She pulled him to her. His face was red.

"Becca, nothing is going to make me entertain such a concept, no matter what is going on with Jessica. I realize Christianity is not the only religion, but it is the only religion for me. I will be sympathetic, only that; and I am just sorry about this and sorry that she can be so easily bent, and I'm sorry for her!"

"Jon, her heart is torn—she doesn't know. Just give her some support. Do you have a pipeline to God?"

"Now Becca, you are making me really angry! You have a way about you that can grate!"

"Oh, I do? I didn't realize that. Just what is it about me that can grate?"

"Sorry, I didn't mean that like it sounded, Becca. I just can't conceive of this whole thing—it's beyond me!"

The twins came rushing in from their naps and broke the argument, hugging Becca around the legs. "Mommy, Daddy!" They broke her pensive mood and her disagreement with Jon. She thanked God for them even though they nearly knocked her down. The four of them made a circle and hugged each other. She and Jon were so close that no argument lasted for long.

Daniel wasn't feeling well.

No, I'm not feelin' good. What's wrong with me? I'm shaking like a leaf about to fall from its tree. I was fine when Jessica and I went out, just fine—now this. I'm sicker than a dog!

And why did I tell Jessica all that? Maybe that's why I'm sick! But she did believe me; I know she did. I trust her more than anyone I've ever known. Maybe I trust her more than I trust myself. If I would have trusted myself, I never would have left her in the first place and maybe this awful mess would have already been solved. Joey! I know in my deepest heart, my very soul, if there is such a thing, that I did not have anything to do—do with what happened to you. I can't even say it! They did it somehow, but how, and why?

Jessie does have an idea about it that may help, though. But it sounded so weird. Now, I'm not doing anything weird! I've already been through enough weird stuff to last a lifetime and then some. But Jessica is so sincere—so sincere. I can't imagine her putting me through nothin' weird. She said she did some regression. Let this doc guy regress her; she said that, I heard her. I think I know what that is, but why would she want to do that, put herself through something like that?

Daniel's stomach began to roll. *I hate to throw up. I'm not gonna do it! Why am I coming down with something now? I just want to be with her.* Daniel hugged himself, mistakenly thinking it would help his chill that definitely had arrived. His hands and feet quivered, then his teeth started to chatter. *Oh God, I felt fine yesterday, now this.* He began to feel queasy and automatically put his hand to his mouth. *I can't throw up—I hate it! And I might have given this to Jessica!*

Daniel hovered over the john, but nothing came. He didn't have a robe, so he put on two shirts and wrapped himself up in a blanket that encased him like a mummy before collapsing on the bed. Still, he shook. *Please don't let Jessica get this,* he spoke to his unknown god. *We were together all evening.*

I can't remember ever worrying about anybody but myself. Survival, most of my life it's been survival. Even when I had Bonny.... For a minute or so, Daniel allowed himself to think of his life with Bonny.... He could see her plain as day when she was in good health. How she would yell at those kids! She had the voice of a fish wife at times: harsh, unyielding where they were concerned, but with him, a marshmallow. *Being sick makes me think of Bonny—sicker than a dog like her—but why am I even thinking about the past? I have the future, our future to think about, I think. But my past is me. I'm sick. I'm so sick and hot, it feels like my head's going to burst and I'm not sure I can make it back to the john!*

Daniel's chill became relentless and he could feel the heat radiating from the bed, but he was cold, so cold that the bed shook. *I don't even have a thermometer to find out just how sick I am. Should I call Jessica? No, but yes, I should or she will think I've disappeared again. I can't let her think that. She doesn't even know where I live and I can't stay here forever. This place is costing me a fortune, but I can't expect her to take me in. I might be very contagious at this point. I need a fireplace somewhere to get warm like the one at Jessica's, but I just need to sleep.*

Daniel's eyes burned yet were so heavy, but he made himself fall off the bed, mummy encasement and all; the jerk of the fall hurt every bone in his body. He rolled across the floor and reached for the phone. *What in hell is Jessie's number? I can't think.* He punched in what seemed like it; his burning eyes were itching and he could barely see, but he heard his hoarse voice say, "Jessie, Jessica, honey." She sounded like an angel—her voice so sweet to him. "Jessie, I have a bad bug or something and I need to tell you where I am—my apartment is at One Lytle Place, 621 Mehring Way, I think—stay away. I don't want you to get this. I called because I didn't want you to think I disappeared on you again—I do love you, you know...," his voice trailed off.

"Oh, Daniel, you sound just awful!" Jessica's then-worried voice came over the phone. "It was right of you to call. Are you running a fever?"

"No, no thermometer—I'm freezing and hot and sick at my stomach—bad sick."

"Have you vomited?" Nurse Jessica spoke.

"Had to—couldn't—stay away, though—don't want you to get it. I need to sleep. I'm going to hang up. I'll call you later on." Daniel dropped the phone and stumbled for his bed. The chill continued, as did the rising fever. The nausea abruptly had its way as Daniel barely made it to the bathroom to lose what seemed like everything in his stomach, and then some. He continued with dry heaves; there was nothing left, but he held onto the john afraid there would be. With closed eyes, he eventually crawled back to his bed, still feeling the urge to vomit. "God, make it go away," he murmured into the covers.

CHAPTER TWENTY-NINE

"Daniel?"

Daniel was obviously not at the phone anymore. "Oh, he needs me now. I must go over there!"

"What's going on, Mom?" inquired Debbie.

"Daniel's sick! He sounds awful!"

"Oh, now it starts. Mom, you stay right here—you don't need to play nursemaid to him. You've got to think of your own health. You get exposed to enough stuff while on the job without purposely taking that kind of risk. You have no idea what he has," Debbie said firmly.

"Well, I've probably been exposed anyway—I was with him all evening."

"With him? And I thought he is just a friend!" Debbie rolled her eyes.

"Well, he is just a friend who I happen to be very fond of. He did say to stay away, so you see, he's thinking of my well-being," Jessica retorted.

"Even if he just has the flu, you know you will need to go to the doctor first thing Monday and get a shot to keep your immunity as strong as you can." Debbie had read a lot of literature about MS.

"Yes, I know, but what about Daniel?"

"Well, most men act sicker than what they really are. Can't one of your nurse friends check on him?"

"He might not like that!"

"He might not like that? What have we here, Mom? In the first place, you are the one who is sick, as I see it, and you have been exposed to something. We don't know what it is ... so we have to find out what the guy has got!" Debbie's voice always got high when she became excited or, in this case, angry.

"Well, maybe...," Jessica's mind was running a mile a minute, "... maybe, I could get Martha to check in on him. She knows about him—I have told her about him, confided in her a little."

"Yeah, I know what bosom buddies you two are; she would hear about a boyfriend before we would!" Debbie exclaimed.

"Now Debbie, please. I am worried about him; don't make matters worse with an attitude.... I know that tone." Jessica got up as if to leave the kitchen; she was so worried and felt drained of all energy.

"Look, Mom, don't. I didn't mean anything. I'm just concerned you'll go sneaking out of here after I leave. Please promise you won't do that!"

"Okay, I promise. I'm calling Martha just as soon as I figure out how to word it to her. I will, but I will try to call Daniel again first."

"Well, he's probably asleep. You might want to wait a while and lie down yourself; you know you try to rest on weekends, and don't forget to see the doctor first thing Monday,"

Debbie hugged her mother and left.

Outside and in her car, Debbie called Becca on her cell phone. "We have to talk about this—the plot is thickening!"

"It is? I don't see how it can become any thicker! Tomorrow's busy for me, but I'll see if Jon will take the boys out after lunch for a while. I'll call you."

Jessica put the coffee cups in the dishwasher and the shortbread away, although there wasn't much left with which to bother, then went in the living room, sat on the couch by the phone, but put her feet up on the couch and laid her head back on the pillows. How grateful she was for its overstuffed softness at this particular time.

If I were Daniel and I were sick, what would I expect from someone I loved at this time? I would expect to see her tout de suite! He will expect to see me—I know he will. He sounds so sick and he sounded so sweet when he said, "I do love you, you know." But I do have to listen to my girls and to do what I know to be right. I can't go over there now. I did promise Debbie. Maybe if I can get Martha to go check on him, I can at least know he's all right. I know most men do sometimes sound sicker than they really are. But he doesn't know Martha from Adam, and Martha doesn't like him, even though she doesn't even know him. Jessica compulsively picked up the phone and called the last number on the display. She got the busy signal.

Of course, I should expect that. He dropped the phone on his way to bed. Should I just wait 'til he calls me? I don't know—it's probably just the flu, but it might be something really serious. It could be anything! I have to call Martha. She has to go over there!

Jessica picked of the phone and punched in Martha's number as fast as her fingers let her. "You have reached the Horace residence. We are away from the phone presently. Please leave your name and number and we will return your call ASAP. Thanks."

"Martha, call me as soon as you get this—it's important!" *Where is she? She always stays home on Saturday and cleans up the house—so that it looks like you could eat off the kitchen floor. Where is she?*

This Saturday, Martha had promised her doctor, the one she works with, that she would look up some things in the library for him. She had finished that, and got stuck in the neurology section, and was reading about a fairly new non-interferon drug used in the treatment of MS, Copaxone. One investigator had high hopes, as he had many patients who seemed to have benefited from its use. It would divert immune cells from attacking myelin. The interferon drugs were immune regulators. *I wonder,* she thought, *if Jessica's doctor knows about this. For sure, they are not gods on Mount Olympus! I'm going to tell Jessica about this and just see if her doctor has mentioned it. She seems to be doing all right at the present, but now dear Daniel has entered the stage again and I remember how she lost ground last time. She got so thin, then that limp; but that happened after our boy disappeared on her, or did it? I can't remember. Oh, look at the time! Guess the house will get a lick and a promise this time; all this research has worn me to a frazzle, but it certainly has been an interesting time. I love the library!*

As Martha drove home she pictured Dr. Amish, Jessica's doctor—how he walked around with his thumbs in his pocket like the cock of the walk. He might be difficult to tell anything to, but she had just seen him that one time when she went with Jessica. *Oh well, Jessie is doing pretty well right now. I'll just keep this information to myself for just in case.*

Martha drove past the supermarket then realized she was out of milk, turned around, parked and went in, picked up the milk, saw several other items (maybe not necessities), and before she knew it had spent over thirty dollars. Budgeting was not Martha's strong suit. "Milk, I needed milk!"

Home finally, Martha heard Jessica's urgent message and called straight away. "Jessica, what's going on?"

Jessica sounded out of breath when she answered. "Oh Martha, finally! I need you to do me a favor in the worst way, but I'm afraid you won't like it much and I haven't yet been able to get in touch with him! Daniel is sick and Martha, could you, would you go over there and check on him for me?"

"Where? Go over where, Jessica? Where shall I see my favorite person? And what's he sick with?"

"That's just it, Martha, I don't know and he has the phone off the hook. He said he would call—I assume he meant when he felt better, but I don't know if he has the flu or what. It could be something serious. From what he said, which was brief, it sounds like he has chills and fever and is sick at his stomach, but hasn't thrown up, just feels like it. That's all I could get out of him; he sounds just awful, so hoarse—his voice is gone."

"Jessica, it's probably just the flu or he may be putting on, but calm down, I'm coming over. Lie down or something—don't you get sick on me!"

Jessica met Martha at the door and it was obvious she hadn't been lying down. "I still can't reach him," she said as she hugged Martha. "I'd go myself but I promised my girls. Now I see why I should have told him first off. Since he doesn't know you, he might freak! Uh, that is, he might not open the door to you with open arms."

"You know I don't want to do this, but for you, of course I will. Where does the guy live?" Martha suppressed the word "jerk."

"He called from One Lytle Place. You know where that is, don't you?" Jessica seemed surprised at the address.

"Oh yes, I certainly do. Pretty fancy, I would say. What room number?" Martha asked.

"Well, I don't know; it's the first time he has called and he didn't give me the room number, just said he would call back. But he hasn't—that's what worries me, Martha; he just hasn't called. He really must be sick!"

"Jessica, you know as well as I do that this, this Daniel, isn't actually what I would call responsible. Now look back, and not too far, I might add." Martha knew she spoke the truth and so did Jessica.

"I know what you think, but he's changed. I know he has, and now he's sick. Oh, I feel so helpless!" Jessica's eyes filled with tears.

"Don't worry, honey, I'll go check it out—him out, that is. Off to the river I go and I'll find out something, uh, I mean, I'll find him for you." Martha put her coat back on.

"It's pretty late now, Martha. I wouldn't think of your going there now. It's dark; wait 'til tomorrow and maybe he will call. Surely he will," Jessica's face felt hot, not with temperature, but worry and concern.

"Right—although that's a safe place, it would be okay; but I do need to drag some rags from the closet to wear to church in the morning. I'll just go to church early, though, and give you a call right after that," replied Martha. "Now get as good a night's sleep as you can!"

"I promise."

CHAPTER THIRTY

Daniel's head felt like it was going to explode.

I may be sick in the head. A tumor in there or something. What's wrong with me? Why the fire in my furnace? Need more blankets. Head's throbbing like a beating drum all the way to Africa—not right to be shaking like this then getting hot. I'm not sure how many times ... doesn't matter. If Jessica were here I could tell her, but I don't want her here—can't give it to her.

Daniel drifted off into somnolence again with cold inside of cold. Jessica, Jessica, why can't you bring me more blankets? You can't touch me, though—I want you, though—the devil is in me.... I'm so hot! I'm not good, I've been found out! "Daniel, Daniel." He heard Maria's voice. "You bastard, you took my ring!"

"No! Oh no! Maria, I'll send it to you, I will, I promise! Maria, I'm not going in that damn church—you can't make me—with all those spooks lurking about. Take me out of here, Maria! Bonny, you're so sick, I'm so sorry for you—so sorry I yelled at you!

"Jessica, what awful ghosts! Joey, I love you—I always loved you, maybe best—maybe that was it. I shouldn't have loved you best. What was it? What happened with you? Why did I love you best? That was wrong, wrong; that's why they took you from me! They, yes! The counselor, that filthy pervert! It was him!"

Daniel's mind suddenly switched to the war zone. *Oh, the stench, the dirt, the bodies—oh God, get me out of here.* Tears ran down his hot, fevered face and he drew his legs up to his chest in a fetal position and cried until he could cry no more.

Daniel's fever raged as did his nightmares and hallucinations. Finally at its peak, the fever broke and he began to break out in a cold sweat—his bed became soaked as his mind began to clear. "Jessica? What time is it?" He glanced at the digital clock: 10:15. *So there went my day.* He looked again—after 10:15 a.m. The blinds were closed. *I should have realized—I must call Jessica—I told her I would call her back and now it's the next day! Will she even be home? Probably not. It's Sunday now, but I'll try to call her anyway. Oh God, I must have died a little last night. Like a scroll of my life sorta. Well, now I know I must find Maria and at least send her that cheap little ring. I've got to find it!*

He rose up on his elbows, but fell dizzied back into the shambles of his cold, damp bed. *No, not ready yet, but I have to call Jessica and at least leave a message.* Daniel reached for his phone. The phone had been off the hook for too long.

Jessica had just finished trying to call and put down the phone, discouraged again. Her tumultuous thoughts led in too many directions. Why would he have the phone off so long? Wouldn't he know how worried she would be? Was he too sick? Then, the phone rang....

"Jessica, it's me. I guess I've been awful sick, but I think I'm a little better," groaned a weak-voiced Daniel. "From the way my bed feels, I would say I had a pretty high fever that has come down—the fever came out and soaked my bed."

"Daniel, honey, finally. I've been worried sick! Did you know you had the phone off the hook?"

"I didn't know much of nothing. I was visiting the past, and Jessica, I may have dreamed this, but it was awful—the counselor—it was Joey's counselor from the police department he went to—that the school recommended. We did it to him. Bonny and I didn't know. It can't be true! It must have been just a dream. I was going back into the past a lot, but that was something new. Jessica, you don't think…."

"Daniel, you need to see a doctor and you shouldn't be talking so much. I can tell. Your voice is barely a trickle. Did you have chills and are you still having them?"

"Too many, I guess. This bed is soaked like someone took a pump to it. But I may not be contagious anymore. Maybe it would be all right for you to come over now," Daniel's voice that wasn't Daniel's said.

"Daniel, I would like to come over; there is nothing I would like to do more than to be at your side right now, but I cannot and I will explain in a little while when you are feeling better. Right now, though, I'm sending Martha over. I've mentioned her, I know I have. Anyway, I know I've said that she is a very good nurse. Please understand, without understanding for the moment why I cannot come. What is your room number so that Martha will be able to find you, okay?"

"I really don't want any Martha in my room—besides, I am a mess."

"Honey, please, I want to know you are going to be all right, and the only way I can know that for sure is to have Martha see you!" Jessica was close to tears and Daniel picked up on it, although he was gravely puzzled.

"I don't know why but okay. I'm too beat to argue with you. I'll deal with you later, Jessica, but you are being weird." Daniel couldn't talk any longer.

"Daniel, please, I need your room number," Jessica pleaded.

"I would like nothing better than to give it to you, but not to some Martha person I don't know from Adam. But look, you are the only person I really trust in this evil world and now it seems I might have been wrong about that. Why, Jessica, why is it? Now I'm going back to sleep and hopefully dream about the Jessica I used to know … that is, if you don't give me any good reason to hang on to this phone."

Jessica's tears did come then as she clutched the phone. "Okay, all right, this is it … I know you feel that way, that you can trust only me and that's the way it ought to be; and after I tell you, it can be that way again because everything will be out in the open—everything will be true, truthful, like we both want it. Daniel, I have MS. I have to tell you and it's been dishonest of me to keep it from you. Now you can trust me in every way. Now that you know."

"You know I won't believe that! Why would you tell me such a story? It's not true. It's not!"

Jessica replied, "I wish it weren't, but somehow it is easier for me to tell you over the phone. We must talk about it. Daniel, I am not on a contagious ward at my hospital; they wouldn't put me in jeopardy. I've worked there forever and I have to have the health insurance, it's so important, now more than ever. I will come over as soon as I can, Daniel, when—if you want me to." For an instant, Jessica thought she heard Daniel's real voice, a little of the mellow tone coming through, even though she wasn't sure they would ever be together after finally telling him the truth.

"Send your fat friend over—room 23!"

"She's not fat! Oh Daniel, it's been so difficult for me to tell you, but remember I love you, and as soon as I know you are not contagious with anything I'll be there. Keep warm 'til Martha gets there." Jessica's voice trembled when she hung up.

I can't do this. After she said Martha again, she realized that her place was with Daniel. Martha could not take her place. *After all, if we live through eternity, what's a little MS this time around?* She ran her fingers through her hair, looked in the mirror, put on her lipstick, and went to the closet and found her jacket. She nearly ran out the door. "Daniel, I'm coming. I won't leave you lying there sick without me!"

Jessica knew in her deepest of hearts (hearts felt from generations?) that she couldn't send a substitute in her place. Now, that's near to blasphemy! Daniel, no matter how messed up he could be at times, was hers, her soul mate. *Of course, everybody belongs to himself, makes his own decisions, just as I am making this one. MS be damned! Now where did that come from? I don't curse.* Jessica pulled into Mehring Way to One Lytle Place. Here would be Daniel. Poor, sick

Daniel, who needed her so much. Her Daniel. Her heart seemed to swell in her chest as she walked into the lobby, though she had nearly run out of steam. The girl at the desk looked at her curiously. "Hello, is room 23 on the second floor?

"Yes, it is," replied the girl.

"My friend is ill. I may need a pass key. May I have one?"

"And who are you?" the girl suddenly turned sullen.

"I'm a nurse. I'm Jessica Hastings. Daniel Cummings is my friend."

"We will go up together and I will see if it is all right to let you in, Miss Hastings. Mr. Cummings will have to give his approval. I have to make sure he really does know you—you understand, don't you? We can't just let anyone come in here claiming to be a friend of someone."

"Of course, I just need to see if he is all right since I am a nurse as I first told you." Jessica was losing her cool.

They arrived at room 23 and knocked. No answer. The girl used the pass key and opened the door a crack. "Mr. Cummings, there is someone here to see you."

"Go away," answered a husky voice.

"Daniel, it's me, Jessica."

"Jessie?"

The girl from the lobby took her leave, not bothering to hide the smirk on her face as Jessica quickly entered Daniel's suite of rooms.

"Daniel, are you back there? It's so dark in here, I can barely see," said Jessica.

"I'm here, honey. I don't understand why you came, but I'm so glad it's you and not some know-not poking around who doesn't know nothing about anything. I'm just sick, Jessica, that's all. I tried to get up, sit up, that is, and the bed just seemed to want me back."

"Oh, poor baby, you've been through it all right; this bed is soaked. You need to get out of it and get some dry sheets, but first I need to see if you have a fever or not. I think you are cool now, but sometimes it's difficult to tell." Jessica gently put the digital indicator in his mouth and held his pulse. Oh, his warm, clammy hand felt good, even then. Daniel looked at her with those beautiful eyes and she nearly melted.

"You weren't going to come—did the MS go away?" Daniel queried weakly.

"We'll talk later—let's see about you now. 'Whither thou goeth, I will go.'" Jessica thought back to that scripture and said it to Daniel....

"What's that?"

"Oh, a scripture that I just thought of. Daniel, I had to come. You need me—not a friend of mine. I don't think you have a fever now, but it might go back up the way your skin feels. Where are some clean sheets?"

"Probably in that drawer over there, but I'm a dirty mess."

"Daniel, I've give you a bath in the bed and then we'll change the sheets. Where is your clean underwear?"

"Top drawer—thank you, Jessica, you are my sweetie. But no bath-in-bed stuff; if you just fix the shower I'll get in. I know it's going to feel so much better to be cleaned up, but you're not doing it, understand? I'm just weak right now. I'll be okay soon. It's just a virus, but a doozie."

"Plan changes, if you think you can do it. I'll change your bed while you are in the shower. I'll be right here to hold you up if you need me, and as sick as you are, you might—but I see your point. Sit up on the edge of the bed and I'll fix your shower and help you in, okay?"

"Okay," Daniel replied with a slight smile.

CHAPTER THIRTY-ONE

Martha had begun to pace. Could Jessica have gone out for a little while? Surely not. Pacing again—she wished she would get over that nervous habit. Why has she not called? *I've been home from that boring sermon for well over an hour and no call. I should have just stayed home. Why do I go? Loyalty to my friends, I guess, but there is never anything new to really stimulate the mind—at least not this mind. I've heard the same stuff since I was a child. Well, children grow up and I've put away my childish things. When had it happened that easy answers no longer satisfied? I guess gradually, or maybe I was always a questioner. Jessica was always a believer. Yes, Jessica the believer, and how I upset her kettle! I was the culprit that led her to the psychiatrist. The whole episode of regression convinced me.*

But where is she? Doggone it! Surely she wouldn't have gone over there by herself, or would she? Darn right she would! That Daniel guy has her wrapped around his little finger. That is where she is. I know it! Know it! Know it!

I'll try one more time. No, still no answer. Maybe Debbie knows something. Martha tried Debbie's number and this time was successful.

"Debbie, do you know where your mother is? I've tried to get her many times. Uh, we were to do something today."

"No, I've no idea, but I certainly hope she didn't go to see HIM," said Debbie. "I cannot believe she would, because she promised me that she wouldn't go because he is sick and who knows what he has."

Martha, surprised at this news, still used her most reassuring voice, "Debbie, some things are out of our control and we just have to accept them. Your mother is living her life as she sees it. Now, I don't know that she has gone there; she may have run out of something and just went out for a while."

"Fat chance!" Debbie's tone sounded both worried and appalled. "Martha, I'm so afraid she'll get worse. Who knows what he has and she's so frail. She was so sick at Christmas and I was so afraid for her, but the steroids helped even her limp. I guess we shouldn't borrow trouble. I just found out about him. Martha, is he right for her? You would know, and what about this regression stuff? Never in my wildest imagination would I think my mother would get into anything weird like that. She's a Christian!"

"Debbie, I have a confession to make; I found that doctor, Dr. Jerrold, the one who did the regression. When Daniel came into her life, she began having these disturbing dreams that she had never had before. I guess I was a partner in crime, because I don't think reincarnation is such a far-fetched idea. It's better than any I've heard since the gods on Mount Olympus!" Martha said.

"But Martha, you have gone to the same church as we have for years and I just assumed you believed everything that we believe!" Debbie exclaimed into her ear. "Mom told us you found the therapist. Well, I knew about the dreams, but of course didn't take them seriously enough, I guess."

"Well, let's say that the church has never really given me the answers that I needed, and I have wanted more. Not that this regression will give all the answers we need, but it does fill in some holes, for me anyway," answered Martha.

Debbie remarked, "I'll have to admit I wasn't bored at all—I listened to every word; shocked, though, you better believe. It is fascinating, but I can't put stock in it. However, it does make some sense, though, and answers some questions. Eternal life and such—I always thought you could never be very blissful playing a harp or whatever through eternity."

"Ah, yes," said Martha. "It does give one changes through time and more chances, but it is mind boggling—no way to figure how it works."

"Well, Elizabeth, uh, Mom seemed to know a lot, and in fact, Mom surprised us with some of what she said after the regression; but of course, you two may have been talking on this subject for a long time, for all we knew," Debbie's voice softened.

"Debbie, not that long; let's say it's a seed that has been growing. Don't get tense or be sad about it, please; we will get in touch with your mom very soon, I know. We better get off this phone before our ears drop off."

"Right, and I have to call Becca."

"Okay," answered Martha, thinking, *Yes, better worry your sister as well.*

Meanwhile, with Daniel, Jessica did think about Martha. *I do need to call her now before she thinks I've completely left the planet. I am not being fair to her, but poor Daniel, these sheets are completely soaked—what a time he has had. Fresh sheets on the bed will be so inviting,* she thought as she jerked off the old and put on new. There were even clean blankets in the drawers. *This is really a nice place. How can he afford this?*

"Here you go, Daniel. Take my hand and ease down into the bed. This ought to feel a lot better, sweetheart."

"Jessica, you are my jewel. I am a weak cat, but I do think I will be on the mend soon. It helps so much having you here. Guess I just have a flu bug that hit me big time. But I am starting to get a little hungry; my stomach has hit my back bone. I think I hear a different kind of rumble," Daniel groaned in his returned mellow voice.

"Now, that is a really good sign. Is there a cafeteria in this place?"

"If there is, it would be too expensive. I have always gone down the street to one of those fast-indigestion places. A cracker with peanut butter sounds okay. You could just get one of those thingies in a little package."

"Yes, if that sounds good, but does any juice sound good? After what you've been through, I'm afraid you might be dehydrated," said Jessica.

"No, but if you say so, maybe Gatorade or lemonade—lemonade, I mean, something not sweet. I might throw up again, ugh. In fact, I think I just want a cracker and a sip. Cracker sounds best," said a sleepy-eyed Daniel.

Jessica thought it best to just go to a grocery and get a few items, some chicken soup, peanut butter, Vinta crackers, tea, and some lemonade mix, but then she thought of Coolbakers Deli. She had remembered seeing the sign on the way over. *I'll just call in an order.* She ordered chicken soup, sandwiches, ice tea, lemonade, extra bread, and extra cold cuts. *That ought to do it.*

"You just rest, honey, I'll be back in a sec," said Jessica as she quietly slipped out the door. In the lobby the girl at the desk glared at her. She picked up her order at 705 Central. Coolbakers were fast and efficient. She hurried back. Surely Daniel had ice. Daniel's deep breathing let her know he, at least, would be getting needed rest.

I must call Martha, who is probably ready to scream at me! Martha will know; she knows me like a book, but I have some explaining to do.

Martha had been reading a boring book about research on the psyche—at least she thought it boring—and her head had gone down into the book, glasses at a rakish angle, when the phone rang. She felt like she jumped a mile in the air, but she knew who it was. "Hello, Jessica? What a nice surprise," she said in a slightly sarcastic tone.

"Martha, I know how late it is and please forgive me for not calling sooner, but there just wasn't any opportunity. He is starting to get better; he just had a nasty flu bug, that's all. I really do appreciate your offering to come over here, but I just realized Daniel wouldn't understand. And besides, what about you? If he were really sick, you might have taken it as well!"

"Offering? Pardonez moi? You drafted me! Jessica, you know I'm healthy as a horse! But never mind making me wait on your call. I was training a gang of overweight nurses to run in the next marathon—you wouldn't think I would just sit around and wait, would you?"

"Sure, Martha, guess that was more fun than coming over here anyway," Jessica laughed.

"Oh, it was; you should have seen some of them go bouncy, bouncy, but I'm afraid most of the bounces came from my fat thighs! Where is lover boy anyway?" Martha said, getting serious.

"Lytle Place."

"He really is at Lytle Place! I thought it would be a wild goose chase. And when's he moving in? Not exactly where my friends stay—guess you pick them rich!"

"Hardly—I'll explain."

"Jessica? Why are you on the phone? Did you bring any chow?" Daniel had awakened.

"Gotta go, Marth."

CHAPTER THIRTY-TWO

"Why are you on the phone?" Martha couldn't help hearing the male voice in the background—nothing especially kind and considerate about that demand! *Just who does he think he is anyway, King Tut? And what does Jessica do but run—just what is this relationship anyway? Even Jessica's ex-husband did not talk to her in that tone, as far as I know. He was a wimp, though, to run out on Jessica. I bet he is sorry for what he did!*

But what does Jessica see in lover boy anyway? Soul mate somewhere in time or not, he is not good for her now. And I helped with this soul mate business. Why didn't I just keep out of the whole of everything? But no, I just had to stick my nose in and make matters worse. But I'm being hard on myself. Jessica would have loved him no matter what I did.

What to do, or is there anything to do? Maybe I should just go over there unannounced. No. Maybe I should call Debbie and let her know I've found her mother. Oh, groan, this is a mess! For sure, though, I need to call Debbie, but I wish we hadn't talked at all about him. I feel like a traitor to Jessica. Wait now, they knew anyway. I just wish we hadn't talked about it.

Martha picked up the phone and put it down several times until she finally did call Debbie.

"Debbie, I've found Jessica. She did go over there—over to Daniel's. But he's not very sick anymore. In fact, I would say he is on the mend. I heard his voice in the background and he sounds just fine to me."

"Well, I cannot understand why she went there unless—unless she really does love the guy or something. She promised she wouldn't go. Promised me! I cannot ever remember my mother breaking a promise, but I am really glad you called and really glad to know for sure where she is. Where is he, Martha?"

"Well, Deb, One Lytle Place."

"Lytle Place? There how? Where'd he get the dollars?"

"Debbie, she didn't say—didn't have the chance—but seriously I'm a little concerned about the way she ran at his ever beck and call, such as when he chirped his baritone from the other room. Sheesh, it became 'Gotta go, Marth.'"

"Martha, my mother is too nice a person, but still I have never seen her be pushed around either. I think we better go over there as soon as possible. I know it's a drive, but can you pick me up?"

Martha was feeling terrible and in fact scared for her best friend. "Of course, Debbie, I drive across the river every day, no trouble."

"I'll throw on some clothes that look decent and be watching for you, Martha."

Martha didn't know why she had this uncanny feeling—this sort of scared feeling....

Meanwhile, Jessica had made Daniel comfortable in one of the chairs in the sitting room, thinking it would be therapeutic to have his soup and juice sitting up and that it would make him feel stronger to sit up for a while. Daniel said, "You are really quite a little nurse, aren't you? And this soup tastes good. You never did tell me who you were talking to on the phone, did you?"

"Oh, Daniel, that was just Martha. Remember, at first I had wanted her to come here and check on you, but you didn't really think that a good idea," Jessica said diplomatically.

"Uh, yep, bad idea—don't want no stranger poking around here and me."

Jessica thought, *I do have friends—I do have family. I hope that some day soon, you can meet them.* She felt it best to remain silent on that subject for the moment and just play "nurse."

"Jessie, I don't know whether it is your presence or what, but my head is feeling clearer and the soup feels like it is going to stay where I put it. Thanks, honey, for being my friend and my sweetheart. We can't get away from that, no matter how we are trying to be just friends. It seems so natural for you to be here with me, helping me out at a time when I really needed you. It's like we are husband and wife in a way, you know. I realize we have a lot of baggage, or at least I do, that has to be worked out and you perhaps need to come clean about what you told me. I can't believe you, that is, why would you tell me you have MS?"

Jessica sat down and said, "Because I have it, Daniel. I promised my family I would not come here, because of your illness. They were afraid for me because we had no idea what might be wrong with you, you were so sick, so I broke a promise and came anyway. I had to come; it seems my place is with you,

MS or no MS. I have it and you must believe I have it. Why would I make something like that up?

"Because you really didn't want to be with me, that's why."

"Daniel, I know that you know better than that! I feel terrible that I was not completely honest, because either you are honest or you're not. In fact, I've been lying to you—not lying really, but not telling you something I should have told you a long time ago. But I would have, Daniel, I would have, but then other things happened, and then you were gone from here for what seemed like forever, and when you came home there never seemed to be the right time, and I had other things I wanted to talk to you about as well. I never wanted to lie to you."

"Well, so what? I'm sure there have been some things I haven't told you. It can't be that bad. What is it now, Jessie? You know how I feel about you—it can't be that bad, not from you, sweetheart. What? I know it can't be MS."

"Daniel, I had wanted someone to love more than anything and no one that I knew would let themselves love me, because they knew about it, about me. It was hopeless to ever find anybody in my circle of friends. So that's why I put that ad in the paper and we found each other. We've had problems—problems sometimes insurmountable, so I felt I needed my head examined to want to be with you. But I still wanted you. I should have been extremely angry with you and never wanted to see you again, but somehow I couldn't do that—ever. I wanted you so much, I was afraid to tell you about me.

"I know why I love you even though you left me, and there's so much I need to tell you other than this; well, there are far-reaching things about us, but you will probably not want to be with me when you realize the MS is true."

"Jessica, tell me, sweetheart, I'm so tired—please don't beat around the bush. I'll so sick, please tell me. It can't be that bad or any worse than this!"

"I told you, Daniel, I have MS, and that's what I should have told you long ago, and then you never would have come back from Galveston and we wouldn't be having this conversation now.

"Even when we talked about just being friends for a while, I wanted to tell you, but I couldn't seem to find the right time. Now this is it. I have an illness that might get worse; that's why I want to make sure what you have. I had to promise my family I would stay away and not expose myself until we find out you're okay. So, in a way, I've been forced to tell you—forced to not lie anymore." Jessica could hardly get the words out.

"God, Jessica, you work in a hospital, and what's your family got to do with this? How should they have anything to do with us? MS! Multiple scleroses—not that! I've seen people with that. Not that! Maybe you just don't want to be with me. I've told you too much. You're okay. You've got to be, understand me? I'm the sick one. You look perfectly fine. You can't be the real sick kind; not that, Jessica." Daniel's disbelief made his voice falter.

Daniel continued, bringing the conversation again back to himself. "I have trouble all my life trusting people and when that awful, terrible thing happened to Joey, that just about did it for me. Trust completely went out the window when they put me in that place, that awful place. Jessica, Joey was dead; my Joey is dead, and they made me think I did it by erasing what really happened. I know that now. So you have made me believe in people, uh, somewhat again, and now you tell me you have MS. You are my perfect girl. A goddess in my mind, so how can you have such an awful thing? I just won't believe it!"

"All right, Daniel. You believe what you want. But remember, I did tell you. I know you will believe only what you want, but when you can accept the truth, that is it."

"If that's the truth, I'd be afraid to make love to you ever again, and I would rather not ever talk about it! Don't bring it up again!" he retorted.

Daniel's mood had become agitated, and Jessica, remembering, feeling that fear she had felt at other times, quickly changed subjects, "Daniel, you probably have sat up enough; don't you think it's time you rested more in bed?"

"I will go back to bed when I feel like it. Right now, I don't. Jessica, when I had that fever I think something came back to me. I think I took Joey to a counselor because the school would not let him come back unless I did. And this counselor was from the police department, because Joey had been a truant many times and had been using drugs—crack, you know, the bad stuff, illegal stuff. Jessie, he was only fourteen—my boy, only fourteen and using drugs—wild from the start he was."

Jessica felt that this was a time she had better just sit down and listen to every word. She patted his hand and said, "Think about what happened step by step and perhaps it will clear up in your mind, little by little."

"I remember about not liking that so-called counselor now—he had slitty eyes, sneaky like, not open, above board; you know, sort of like he needed counseling. Anyway, he was the one provided by the police department through the school. It was one of those no-choice things, you know; if I didn't do it—he was out on his ear, out of the school system, completely on the street!

"But if he was bad then, he got worse, I tell you. He became belligerent, hostile, said I did it to him but wouldn't say what. One night I heard him crying in his room. The little tough guy, crying. I knocked then went in and he yelled at me, said I caused him to be used by some nut. I asked more and he yelled, 'Get the hell out!' I started to say, 'Don't you talk to me like that,' but something made me not say it. I thought about it all the next day, thinking strongly that something weird must be happening. The more I thought about it, the more suspicious I became. Could the counselor be a sicko? Jessie, you're right; it is slowly coming back!"

It seemed no time before the two of them, Martha and Debbie, had crossed the river and arrived at Lytle Place.

Debbie exclaimed, "Wow, this is some place, and my mother and her boyfriend are somewhere in there? Wow!"

"Deb, are you sure we better go in there? After all, your mom is forty-eight years old and knows her own mind. I really don't think we should disturb them."

"Well, what you are saying is true, but she promised me she wouldn't go here and here's what's happening, and from what you said, he is bad news. We need to save her from herself; past life or no past life!"

They quietly went in the lobby and asked the girl at the desk if she could locate Jessica Hastings. She seemed more than happy to oblige them. "Oh, yes, the nurse; she's in room 23, second floor, that way," she smiled.

Jessica listened carefully to Daniel, hoping to find clues to what happened with his Joey, when there was a knock on the door. Daniel looked irritated. "Who could that be?"

Jessica opened the door a crack, then exclaimed, "Debbie, Martha, what? Why are you here?" *Oh my god,* she thought as her pulse quickened. *Why? Why now?*

"Maybe you better tell me why you came over here after you promised you would not, Mother! Surely you know how we worry!"

Martha tried not to look guilty.

"Now my train of thought is broken—who is that Jessica?" came Daniel's angry-sounding voice.

Jessica took a deep breath and said, "Oh, Daniel, a surprise—my daughter Debbie and friend Martha have come to meet you!"

"What the hell for? I don't want to meet them. I'm still sick, might die—tell 'em to leave and don't come back. We don't need 'em. We don't need nobody! Get the hell out!" Daniel's mellow tone had changed to solid anger.

"Daniel, you don't mean a word of that—yes, you are still sick, very sick!" Jessica nearly screamed at him before she went out in the hall to talk to Debbie and Martha.

"I have no idea why you two took it upon yourselves to come over here," she said in hushed but very upset tones. "I am perfectly all right. All you did was upset the applecart. He was on the verge of recalling a very bad thing that happened in his life and you may have stopped all of it, because it is a painful memory.

"I am sorry he acted like that. He wouldn't under normal circumstances, but it has upset me, too. I cannot stand to have anyone talk to my family like that or my best friend!" Jessica was clearly shaken. "I don't know what to do! Yes, I do. I'm not staying here now. I'm going to give him some time to think about what he's said to you, Debbie, and you, Martha. He can't do that. He is sick in more ways than a virus and believe me, that is all it is biologically, so I have been in no danger."

Jessica put on her hands on her daughter's shoulders before she spoke. "Debbie, I am so sorry I broke my promise to you, but I guess I do love him in spite of it all."

Jessica continued, "Perhaps, you'd better wait here while I get the few things I brought, okay?"

"Of course," said Martha looking at Debbie. Debbie nodded, speechless.

Jessica entered the apartment without looking at Daniel and proceeded to get her nurse bag and other things together. Daniel said, "Just what are you doing? Didn't they leave yet?"

Jessica faced Daniel squarely and said, "I see no reason for me to stay here now. If you can talk to my daughter and my friend as you did, you are strong enough, well enough to care for yourself. Just think about it and I want you to think about it very deeply. You told my daughter to 'get the hell out.' My daughter! Part of me. How can you say you love me when you speak to my daughter that way? How? Tell me how? I don't belong to you. I am not your property. I am my own person. Yes, I confess I do love you, but even with love, people are individuals. 'No man is an island unto himself.'

"Continue thinking about what happened with Joey, but you need help, Daniel. If your Joey had been alive, would I have talked to him in the way you talked to my daughter? Think about that. I'm leaving now and when you consider you can act civilized, and be civil to my family and friends, perhaps give me a call, but only then."

Jessica opened the door, slipped out, and quietly shut it.

"Jessica!" Daniel yelled at the top of his voice. "I'll write you a song!"

CHAPTER THIRTY-THREE

Jessica, Debbie, and Martha stood outside in the cool of Lytle Place in silence. Jessica finally spoke. "You don't know him. How could you have followed me here? I'm embarrassed for both of you! Do you consider yourselves sleuths or what?"

"Mom, don't blame us, blame yourself. You broke a promise. As far as I know, in my lifetime you have never done that; and naturally we were worried, and I see our worries are well founded! That guy is trouble paddling down the river at full speed! No one has ever talked to me in such an angry, hostile way, and if I have any say in this matter, no one will again!"

Martha's silence permeated the night air; she put her hands behind her, nearly biting her lips to keep from saying anything, but her expression spoke volumes.

Jessica turned on her heels. "It's late. I'm very tired. Let's go."

Martha hugged her and said, "We will talk about this; perhaps we shouldn't have come. I'll call you."

"Uh huh," said Jessica. Not bothering to look right or left, she made her way to the car, got in, turned on the engine, and headed for the river bridge, crossing it and thinking how wonderful it would be to be home and think only about work in the morning, forgetting today, be only normal, think only normal thoughts. But that wasn't possible. Ever since Daniel had come into her life, normalcy had ceased. Turmoil had begun. She had even broken a promise to her daughter because of him. No wonder Debbie had been concerned and Martha a key witness to the drama. Martha's silence said, "I told you so!"

But no, I can't blame Daniel for my breaking a promise. I had the free will to do that. I chose to go there; to be there with him. Daniel, who has a very loving side to him, but also a side I do not understand, especially if he is who he is, or I think he is who he is. I am so mixed up. What happened to him in the interim? If I don't figure all this out in my own mind, I am going to be as crazy as he is. Turmoil is not good for anyone with a chronic illness, and with Daniel, just the fact that I never know when the lid is going to fly off is too much stress for anyone. I know it can't be good for me. A calm life with just my family is so much better; I almost yearn for it. I'll just be a grandmother to the twins. I'll sit in a rocking chair and read to them, give them a grandmotherly love, and forget about Daniel. But what will Daniel do? He needs me at least to find the perfect medicine for his particular kind of illness, then I'll tell him, "Bye." Sure, you will!

Crazy. I called the man I love "crazy." Only in the mental wards have I heard the nurses throw that word around so blatantly, but Daniel has many sides, many personalities, and one of his sides can be definitely crazy! The way he talked to Debbie and Martha, will they ever accept him when or if he straightens up now? He must see Dr. Jerold as soon as possible! Now how do I arrange that after what I said to him? His having the flu doesn't excuse his behavior now, the kind that's reared its ugly head before!

Too many thoughts besieged Jessica as she took a long shower, then slipped into bed. After lying there twisting and turning about for an hour or so, it became evident if she were to sleep this night, she needed help. She got up and went to the medicine chest to look for a sleeping pill when the phone rang. *It can't be Daniel. I am not ready to talk to him; it's late.* But she picked up the phone anyway.

"Jessica," said Martha softly, "I know it's late, but I've been thinking about how we should not have butted in on the two of you tonight—I'm so sorry. Don't you think, though, we need to talk?"

"Yes, perhaps. I've some sorting out to do, but first I need to go to bed. You are my very best friend, and yes, I want to talk later. I'm about to take a sleeping pill."

"Okay, bye, but don't please get into the habit of those things," said Martha before she hung up.

Good advice from my good friend, as there were only three left. *When have I taken that many sleeping pills? I guess since I met Daniel; an obvious conclusion.* Drinking down the pill with a half glass of water, she made it back to bed and closed her eyes to await the blissful feeling. The last thought she had was *I must make it right with Debbie—I can't have conflict in my sweet family, no, none.*

The alarm chiming its church bells was a rude awaking for Jessica, who didn't stir the whole night long thanks to the sleeping pill. She hurriedly readied herself for work, then drank down a Boost before she called Debbie. "Debbie, we need to talk, honey. How about coffee in the usual break room after work?"

"Mom, I've been worried sick. I was awake all night it seemed. We've got to talk. Mind if Becca comes? I feel this is a major family upset or trauma unlike any we've ever known!"

"Debbie, please don't be so melodramatic. Daniel needs help. He would not have said those things if he didn't, believe me. Look, I gotta go. See you both then." Jessica dropped the phone and hurried out the door. The ride to work wasn't nearly long enough for her mind to quietly think of how she would explain Daniel and Daniel's moods to the girls when she didn't understand them herself!

The day was over too fast, the problems solved smoothly, nothing to make her late for the appointed hour. Both girls were waiting for her when the elevator deposited her. *These are just my daughters,* thought Jessica, *not dragons, not judge and jury. Debbie looked most like a judge!*

"Hi, guys," said Jessica sunnily. "Glad you could make it, and right at the appointed hour. You've been brought up well!"

"Let's get down to it. We are so worried about you! Who or what is this guy?" Debbie spoke nearly in tears. "I, uh, we would like nothing better than for you to find a wonderful man; you deserve that, but you don't deserve what I heard the other night. I think you must rethink this!"

"I don't believe I should have to remind you that I am forty-eight years old and have a right to come and go as I please, but I also know I broke a promise to a family I love more than life, and that takes precedence. Daniel has problems and his actions are what we might call extraordinary—certainly something we are not used to." The words just seemed to flow from Jessica's mouth as if she knew exactly what she had planned to say.

"Extraordinary, I'd say so!"

"Let me go on," said Jessica. "Anyway, as you recall, I went through a regression and I feel most certain Ulysses in that life, my life as Elizabeth, is Daniel, because even though he has a type of mental illness, I cannot turn my back on him until I help him get well. If he calls me, I want to arrange a session with Dr. Jerold, who could help him sort out his life and perhaps give him some meds to find himself."

Becca piped up, "Sorry, Mom. From what Deb tells me, you are taking on a zoo animal."

"Now that is unkind, but of course, we are definitely not used to being talked to in that manner, and you're right; he was extremely rude to Martha and Debbie, and I'm so sorry for that. But that same man can be sweet and charming—he is very talented, he can write music, he sings beautifully—"

"Don't make excuses for him. He was horrible to us; you know it, Mom," broke in Debbie.

"Right, okay, he acted horrible, I will admit it; but neither of you were born yesterday. Both of you have heard that some people have problems through no fault of their own. He has, I guess, although I don't know enough about it yet, what you might call a split or borderline personality. It's a disorder that is chemical in nature. I've read about it—he can't help it. He didn't ask for it. Just like I didn't ask for MS. We just play the hand we are dealt. Something happened to him along the way. But girls, it's the sweet, charming part I fell in love with; believe me I wanted to dump the other part a long time ago but something wouldn't let me; something George said, and then this thing with Dr. Jerold made me know why. It may be the Ulysses part from years and years ago that clings to me, I don't know. The way I left it was that when he could be 'civil to my family and friends' give me a call. After that, he may not call, I don't know; but if he doesn't, I will be very sad."

Debbie said rather sarcastically, "Could he be civil?"

Jessica answered, "Deb, were you listening? We don't know all the skeletons he has carried around with him in just this lifetime and until he meets with the doctor, we can hope a lot of the bad experiences will be erased when he is put on the right medicine. I don't know much about mental illness or what causes it other than a brain imbalance, so I want to give him all the help I can give him because I love him. I know you can't understand how I can after the way he acted the other night, but please try."

Jessica's chair scraped loudly as she rose; others followed suit and the three took hands and left the room. Becca hugged her mother and said, "Please, please be careful with your decision making and realize with the kind of mental illness he obviously has, his mood could turn on a dime. If anybody hurt you in any way, I don't know what I would do!"

Debbie just shook her head.

The night before Daniel had waited quietly, oh, so quietly in his bed, waiting for the merest indication that Jessica had not meant what she said and would be opening the door to his room, but he could have sat on the edge of his bed all night. *No Jessica. Just who did those people think they were anyway? Trying to barge in on us, they did! Like they owned the place or something! Why did they?*

Owned the place? Like me, heh! I've gotta get out of here. This place is costing me a fortune and then some. Things are not working out like I planned. I am in a kettle of fish and this kettle is about to boil over!

How could she? How could she just leave me like that? Oh, I get it; she's pulling the friend act on me, when it's obvious that we mean more to each other than that!

Daniel got out of bed and headed for the bathroom, but slammed the wall with his fist on the way. Still lightheaded, the motion threw him backward in a circle and he stubbed his toe smartly on the chair. "God damn it to hell!" he yelled, and hobbled the rest of the way to the bathroom holding his damaged toe. "Now, if she wouldn't have gone that wouldn't have happened—I think it's broke!"

Finished in the bathroom, he shuffled back to bed. *What did I do that was so terrible to cause her to leave me and go with* them*? Something about if Joey had been alive would she have talked to him that way.... Well, Joey ran with a rough crowd—everyone including him was tough—so how would I know? But no, of course, Jessica would not have talked to him that way. Jessica is Jessica. Jessica is a lady, so obviously*

Jessica's daughter would expect her to know someone decent. Well, I'm decent. I'll show them just how decent I am! I'll write her the best song she has ever heard, that ever pierced her eardrums, and I'll sing it for them, too, and they find out just how decent I am!

Daniel put both feet on the floor and massaged his toe. Aside from the toe, he was beginning to feel almost himself again, like the fog had lifted. He looked at his guitar over in the corner longingly. He reached for the robe Jessica bought him—*I don't want to get chilled after the plague*—and walked gingerly over to reach for his guitar. Sitting forward in the chair, he played a few chords, then up and down the frets, waiting, hoping for that special song to come into his mind. "Jessica, oh Jessica, my lady Jessica—the warmth of you against my heart—you bring my days joy complete with your desire for me."

Now h*ow completely stupid can that be! If she wouldn't have gone and would be sitting here beside me, I could find a song for her; it would be in here in my head. Why did she go?* Daniel climbed into his bed and curled himself around his guitar. *I know it's in here when she comes back...,* he thought. He made a cocoon of himself and his guitar—finally casting aside the guitar and drawing his legs up tighter and tighter. "I'm sick, I'm still very sick—how could she leave me like this?" He repeated this over and over until he began to rock in the bed and the "she" became a generational "she," not particularly Jessica, just "she." Before long he began crying softly, "I've lost her, I've lost her again."

Sleep came like a shadow of little visions in the darkening night. The quiet hum of the air conditioner made all seem peaceful in the haze of trouble that permeated the room.

Dawn came early for Jessica, and since she couldn't get back to sleep she went out the back door, simultaneously pulling her robe tightly around her shoulders. She sat down on the glider locked in thought. The sun had just begun its trip for the day and she thought of the lines from an old poem, "I met God in the morning, when my day was at its best...." Somehow, she couldn't think of the rest of it. Her mind, of course, was on Daniel, not God. But still, she prayed, *Please God, let him call, but not just for me; I need to help him find himself and I know it's possible....* Jessica had always felt it wrong to pray for anything for herself and now she wasn't even sure what she believed. Oh, for the simple faith again!

Daniel awoke with a jerk, nearly knocking his guitar on the floor—his feet hit the floor and he jumped back in the bed, forgetting his hurt toe. "Oh ouch, damn thing, ouch!" He gingerly made it to the bathroom. Standing there, his mind skipped at once from his toe to Jessica. *If Jessica had stayed with me, I never would have broke my toe. I know it's broke, but how can I get her back? They shouldn't have come; I wouldn't have talked to them that way, would I? She talked so definitely to me—as if she really meant what she said. I know I have a problem, but I took a pill. When was that? I don't know ... I DON'T KNOW! If she really loves me, she will have to love me for what I am and stick by me. We don't NEED her family or anyone. I will have to let her know that, but first what do I say to her? My trying to write a song didn't work, but she got me so upset. I've got to be calm.* Daniel realized he was still standing at the john while all those thoughts tumbled in his head. He finished with a shower and got dressed in his baggy jeans and a bright shirt.

I'll write her a letter. That's what I'll do—my words on paper will tell her how I feel and I won't get so emotional, and maybe, just maybe I can later put the letter to music, if it comes out right. I can't talk to her now. It won't work for me.

Daniel put his pen to paper and began to scrawl:

Jessica, beautiful Jessica
My sweetheart
Your dark curls
Silk their way
Around my fingers
Like threads
Ready to be spun
In an array of hope
My heart aches for you
Jessica, beautiful Jessica
My sweetheart
Come back to me
Before life's ultimate
Mystery takes me
Without you
I am nothing
Come back my Jessica
Come back!

Ultimate mystery ... where'd that come from? Well, it won't win any prizes; wonder if I could make up a tune for it, modified a bit. Then he wrote:

Dear sweet Jessica,

I am so sorry I was rude to your daughter and your friend. I don't know what comes over me. I guess I think of us as inseparable, and it just hit me the wrong way when they came over here. Please, please forgive me, my darling. You know how I love you—more than life itself—more than this paper would hold my words.

Remember how it feels to be close together, warm, as close as we can get, not letting go. If you could only see the storm in my heart, like pounding rain on a tin roof—let's throw out this friend thing. It's not for us.

More love from above
along with mine,
Daniel

Daniel folded the letter as neatly as he could and put it in one of the envelopes someone had conveniently left in the desk. He thought, *I will mail this on my way to breakfast and she will get it tomorrow. This romance, this heartache I express to her maybe will help, and I just can't talk to her about it now. If it doesn't help, I'll kill myself or go back to Galveston. Killing myself might not be the best choice because I don't know what is on the other side, although here is sometimes worse than what I can imagine!*

He put the letter in his shirt pocket and put on his light jacket and quickly left the building, not looking anywhere but straight ahead. In the first mailbox on the corner, he deposited the letter. *Oh, Jessica, if you can feel the love I'm sending on that piece of paper!* Daniel knew he would break down if he heard her voice—he pictured her efficiently at her job getting a call from him. *No, not this time. I will keep control. I am in control.* He headed for his coffee and sausage biscuit—a long and brisk walk that kept his body taut and made many of the opposite sex look admiringly his way. He knew it and he liked it, but no one would do for him but Jessica. Jessica was his woman....

Then he remembered the ring and Maria. He went back to the apartment and packaged it up as best he could – he would mail it tomorrow. No explanation, just so she gets it back.

CHAPTER THIRTY-FOUR

It seemed strange to Jessica that not one ringing phone produced a mellow voice she so sincerely wanted to hear, although she did not know how she would handle Daniel calling her at work this time. Oh yes, she had handled it before, but this was different, so different: she was very angry at him, so loved him, so wanted to help him all in a messy package—certainly not neat at all. Had it ever been neat with Daniel? No, never! So no wonder her girls thought she needed her head examined. Yes, possibly, even if Daniel were her soul mate or whatever. How she wished George were still here and she could talk it over with him. George, toward the end, had not seemed like her stepfather; more like an old and trusted friend. How she had wasted precious time with him. She had loved him much, much too late. Now she loved him very, very much.

I know more than ever what a foolish young girl I have been. It is never right to carry grievances, and what's so awful I held against him—the fact that he tried to be my father? Was that so terrible? But I was young. No excuse, though, for carrying it into adulthood when I had two grown children. I would say I was an emotional brat! I was still lost in adolescence. Poor George and poor me. What a loss!

Elizabeth wasted her opportunities as well, by standing by the door waiting for Ulysses. She could have been helping others. *Elizabeth is in me, and one would think souls would learn their lesson! Elizabeth said she would not waste time waiting for a man, but I do believe there is a parallel here.... I am waiting for Daniel to call, and I so believe Daniel was Ulysses. So I am waiting. It would be different if Daniel and Ulysses were not the same soul, but am I helplessly tied because of Ulysses?*

But how do I know anything? I am going nuts with this. If Daniel calls, and I know he will, the next step will be to get him over to see Dr. Jerold to help him with his mental problems and just see if he won't consent to being regressed. First things first, though; he needs to be on medication, and Dr. Jerold has a good reputation of helping mania, depression, and other such ills. Of course, he will have to be willing. I can't plan his life for him.

That should be my cue, though: his willingness. If he's not willing, I will realize Ulysses or Daniel, whatever; it makes no difference. It's personality this time around that makes the difference. I must develop some strength in my makeup here and now and tell him we just cannot be an item. No, it won't work for either of us. I then must realize he cares much more about himself than he does about me or ever did! I will then make three people happy—Debbie, Becca, and Martha.

Bea poked her head around the corner and said, "Jessica," softly. Seeing she made no headway, she repeated more firmly, "Jessica, Mrs. Lewis in 04 is pretty low; her pressure's 68/42. I'm not sure she'll last much longer!" Jessica quickly snapped out of her reverie and went down the hall. Mrs. Lewis, a favorite of hers, might indeed be ready to cross over, and since she apparently had little family, Jessica wanted to be there.

"Bea, please try to get in touch with her daughter—I guess she is the only one Mrs. Lewis has!"

"Mrs. Lewis, it's me, Jessica."

Mrs. Lewis's old cataract-glazed eyes looked at Jessica and said, "Nice of you to see me off. It must be time…." She smiled at Jessica and said, "They seem to be waiting for me—some fine people I've known. I'm old and I hope I go with them." She squeezed Jessica's hand, a faint squeeze but definite. "I'm afraid, though—what do we really know?"

"Mrs. Lewis, God will watch over you, now and then. God created us. We are children of the creation, so don't be afraid, although I know the unknown can be scary. I'll hold on to your hand and won't let go. Your daughter is on her way."

"I would like to see her before—before I have to leave, you know." Her voice trailed off. "She is always busy, though."

Her breathing became labored and Jessica wasn't sure she could hold on until her daughter arrived. She knew she had a living will in her chart. Jessica was thankful for that; she had seen so many resuscitations of old people that really were ready to go on. Although she was unhappy to lose this sweet person or any other sweet person, she didn't fear death anymore. Death for Mrs. Lewis would be just a transition to another place, another journey to make up her mind what she wanted to do next. Really, it could be thought of as exciting.

Jessica just did not fear death anymore, hers or anyone else's. She patted Mrs. Lewis's hand. "I'm sure your daughter will be here any minute. Would you like to say a prayer together?"

Mrs. Lewis sighed, "That would be nice, but honey, I've been praying all my long life; if God's not with me now, I'd be very sad about it. Of course, you can't see God, but these others are here, and you, my dear friend, too; but it's late...."

Her breathing became very labored and Jessica knew it would be any minute that she would cross over. Laura Lewis came rushing in. "Mother!" She nearly knocked Jessica out of her chair in her haste, although she hadn't been to see her mother, at least here at the hospital, very many times. "Mother, I'm sorry, I do love you so much!" she said and put her head down on her mother's chest. Mrs. Lewis smiled and put her hand on Laura's head, just as the machine announced that her heart had stopped beating. Tears began to flow down Laura's face and she demanded, "Bring her back, bring her back! There wasn't enough time. I need to tell her things, lots of things; please, please bring her back!"

"I'm so sorry, ma'am, but her orders were not to resuscitate. We can't bring her back," Jessica said as gently as she could.

"You medical people are all alike. Always think you have the upper hand; well, you don't! I'll sue you and the hospital. I'll show you who has the upper hand!" Then she put her head down by her mother's again and cried her heart out until it seemed there were no more tears. Jessica tried to comfort her, but she pushed her hands away.

Jessica wondered how such a fine person as Mrs. Lewis could have had a daughter who seemed hostile to the world around her, but everyone has their story; Laura Lewis no doubt had an interesting story.

"Let me know when you need us to help," said Jessica. "I will be at the main nurses' station, but stay with your mother as long as you need to."

It didn't seem more than ten minutes before Mrs. Lewis came to the nurses' station.

"Mrs. Hastings, I'm ready to call someone now. Here's my card. Could you have someone call this undertaker for me? I'm sorry I fell apart. May I talk to you?"

"Yes, yes, of course, but let me make this call for you and I'll be right with you." Jessica noticed Laura was visibly shaken.

Jessica quickly made the necessary call and then ushered Mrs. Lewis into her office.

"Your mother was a very kind and wonderful person. I know you will miss her."

"That's just it—I know that now. I always thought she saw the world through some special glasses she wore; even when my father left us, she forgave him right away. She never saw the world as it really is. I'm not like that. We had several arguments because she refused to see, or rather, I got so mad at her because she just was so unrealistic. But something funny happened to me in there when I wanted her to be alive so much. It just seemed like there was a warm glow around her and I heard her voice say, 'Everything is all right, Laura. Peaceful and bright.' I know I must have imagined it, but it seemed so clear, and her voice and everything, but it couldn't have been."

"Laura, I think it could have been; just believe it. I've worked here for a long time and sometimes unusual things happen to people at the point that someone dies. Your mother was a wonderful person and if anyone could give you a consoling message, she could. Just believe it, Laura, and remember it; don't think you were imagining."

Laura Lewis's expression changed and she simply said, "Thank you, Mrs. Hastings. I won't ever forget and I'll try to be more like my mother would have wanted me to be. I wouldn't ever sue this hospital. You were always here when I should have been." She hugged Jessica and left. Jessica really had never heard of anything like that, but she felt she told Laura what she needed to hear.

With so much going on, she had nearly forgotten her own problem, but it was okay; life does definitely go on. Problems are minute in the whole scheme of things.

A new shift had been on for quite some time and she needed to get on her way. She especially needed to call Martha when she arrived home. Martha hadn't called, probably didn't know what to say after their posse spied on the two of them. Oh well, she could see that they were worried, and probably for good reason, but it was only after Jessica began her trek home that her mind really focused on Daniel. *Why, I wonder, did I not have to cope with a call from him? He typically would cry, be upset in various degrees, and my heart would break for him. But he did not call! Did he leave me again? With Daniel, always a guessing game, never anything sure; he would never be a true and loving mate. My husband had been that until ... I was diagnosed, then where did true love go? Life is never a certainty.*

There would always be trouble—unless, unless somehow he could be cured. And what kind of a man would he be cured? There are certainly no guarantees. Would he be the sweet, romantic Daniel or a zombie on drugs? I know he would hate hospitalization from the stories he has shared. Perhaps if he had a stable home environment for a while as an outpatient—one where it could be seen that he took his meds. Oh yes, Jessica, I know my girls would be tickled pink about what I'm thinking, but I haven't even heard from the "love of my life" or who I think might be.

Jessica pulled into her driveway, got out of the car, and turned the key in the lock just in time to hear the phone. Her heart leaped into her throat as she nearly dashed to answer it. "Hello—oh, hello, Martha."

"Well, I know you are mad at me; your enthusiasm for my voice is shattering, but put yourself in my shoes. Wouldn't you have done the same if you were worried about me?" said Martha.

"Yes, probably. Oh, of course, after I thought about it for a LONG time, and what hunk have you been seeing lately so I can burst in on your nest? Anyone's a risk, you know, and as far as my risk is concerned he may be in Alaska for all I know!"

"Maybe we should rejoice and be exceedingly glad!"

"Martha, you don't know him, and therefore, you don't know of whom you speak, and this isn't his usual behavior. If he loves me like he proclaims from the rooftops, I would hear from him, especially after my edict of the other night."

"Jess, you are right. I don't know him, but after the little I heard he is not the type of person you need in your life, ever. I know I shouldn't judge the whole person by that one episode and he may be licking his wounds, but Jessica, honey, use your head!"

"I have, you know, I have, Martha, and you know why I can't turn my back on him now. We have a story together and somehow, we are meant to be together, even if it seems to you he isn't my type at the moment. I know he was very ugly to you and I know that part is hard for me to explain, because he has those moments. He was very angry and I'll have to admit I didn't think too well about you or Debbie then either; but of course, I love you, and I wouldn't ever speak in such a way to you. But it all points to background. Daniel did not grow up as you or I did. I don't know the full story but he had a very deprived (*maybe even depraved,* Jessica thought) background. He didn't grow up in the best of neighborhoods—not everybody does, you know. I'm sure he is very sorry for what he said. I just haven't heard from him yet and that worries me greatly."

"Jessica, what can I say? Maybe you are right and I don't, or didn't, have the right to be a butinski … time will tell, I guess. But honey, please be careful. I don't want you getting sick again. You gained your weight back when he stayed away for a spell and you look good now. I would hate to see you lose ground again just because of a jerk like him. Sorry, Jessica, but the way I see it, in this life, that is what he is! Maybe something happened to him that didn't happen to you between lives or something. Just maybe. I just thought of that."

"You just might be right. I hadn't thought of that. If he ever calls, maybe Dr. Jerold can see him! Martha, you are brilliant to think of that one! I thought it would be interesting to find him with Elizabeth as Ulysses, but I didn't think of the possibility that he might be a more interesting soul than I am! I basically just wanted him to get some help with whatever is bothering him, whatever illness he has; he just isn't normal sometimes. At least he isn't some suave hypocrite—he is what he is!"

"Yes, but I think our bursting in on the two of you could have been handled in a more, shall we say, friendly way to his lover's daughter and her best friend! And as your best friend, I feel just awful that we ever put that ad in the paper—that's the worst thing I have on my conscience and again. It was my idea. Jessica, I'm so sorry I ever thought that bit of devilment up, and you are the one that has paid the consequences of something that shouldn't ever have been done! The way I see it, whatever happened to Daniel's personality in whatever lives he had, he ended up as a sleazebag in this one and it will take a lightning bolt to convince me otherwise—sorry, honey…."

"Martha, you've made your point. You are my best friend always; however, we've both got to go to work tomorrow."

"Yes, and he just might call tonight and you want me off the phone—bye."

CHAPTER THIRTY-FIVE

Daniel tossed and turned in his bed—finally got up, turned on the light by the bed and began pacing the floor—back and forth, forth and back—until he swore, "Damn it to hell! Why don't she call me? Guess she doesn't care about me anymore!" He hit the wall with his fist, knocking a mirror to the floor. Amazingly it didn't break, but Daniel kicked it, in revenge, with his foot. Then he crouched down on his knees and looked in the mirror. There were only the faintest traces of the surgery on his face. "Well, it can't be this. I'm the handsome devil I've always been! All women love me, but Jessica—she won't call. Guess she was serious about what she said, but she is pushing me around. Women don't push me around!" He looked again intently in the mirror. This time his face seemed to change. He was himself, but his eyes looked hostile, strange, immobile, not like previously. He hit the wall again with his fist—it hurt him. He threw the mirror at the wall; it broke in two pieces. "Why? Why did I do that? I'm a lunatic!

"But Jessica made me do this—she did this!" He put his fist in his mouth, letting the saliva act as a salve. Oh, how it hurt! It seemed to him suddenly that he saw Jessica's face on the wall. Shadowy, unclear, but there. The small light in the background gave it a glow. "Jessica? I didn't mean it!" He reached out to touch the wall and the Jessica of the wall was gone, but not before she had smiled at him. He fell to his knees and began sobbing. "What's happening to me? She was there, but she couldn't be; that would be too good—too good to be true."

Why? Why would I see Jessica on the wall? That's crazy! The sobs subsided and when he got control of himself, he lay down on the cold floor beside the two pieces of the mirror, still gently crying; the tears dried to a crust forming a gentle mask until he finally went to sleep on the cold, hard floor.

He awakened the next morning, shivering and stiff as a board. *How did I get on the floor? I'm not getting sick again, am I? I'm so cold.* Daniel stretched his arms and legs, then, horrified, he saw the broken mirror and remembered—remembered how he got there. *Oh God, I took one of those pills; why didn't the damn thing work? They worked when Bonny made me take them. Maybe they are old, not potent anymore.*

But I sure am! I know I can't be sick; I've got to get help. Jessica knows I need help. Surely, she will respond to those words I wrote her in the letter. She will get it today. I handled it right. I know I did this time.

I remember last night; it seemed I saw Jessica's face, her image on the wall. It was—it was. I can't be crazy. I'm as sane as anybody; but I wish I wouldn't get so sad that I cry. I'm a man. Men don't cry like that. It is like there is a big hole in my heart because I can't remember things. Joey things. They made me think I killed—killed my own son. They set me up. I know that now, and then that awful place they put me for who knows how long. That's the hole—the big black hole that brings crazy things to my mind. I couldn't have seen Jessica's face in the wall. That's all crazy stuff. They did something to me!

Maybe Jessica will help me find the answer ... maybe that is why I saw her face on the wall. I know there is a reason for that and for the dream and for the time I couldn't stop writing her name. That was too weird: made me think I was weird!

I wonder, though, if I could write like that again—weird as it was—maybe, just maybe there would be some answers at the tip of a pen! How does that go? "There are more things under the sun," or is it "Eyes have not seen, nor ears heard, the wonders God has bestowed." But that is biblical; seems I learned that when I was made to go to Sunday school and all the kids made fun of me. It wouldn't be a biblical thing; more like devilish.... I know it scared the fool out of me! Who's to say what is of God and what is devilish?

I had the dream of the beautiful lady and then wrote Jessica—the answer. Maybe there might be an answer to the puzzle of Joey. Maybe the answer comes from something unknown or from God, who people say they know, but do they really? God, I don't know if I even believe in you, but I did call you by name and I guess I have called on you a couple times. Does He have helpers? I'm scared to try.

I need a hot shower on my neck. It feels like a crooked ton of bricks. Then I'll get some breakfast and then ... be nice if I could find a quiet place in the park where Jessica and I went, Eden, and take my paper there—close to God—like on a mountaintop, even though I think He's not up there anywhere, but maybe part of me, part of all creatures, part of everything.

The Daniel of today appeared quite lucid. *Of course I do; of course I am. Nothing at all wrong with me, no, sir!* Daniel kicked up his heels before he got in his still-clean car. He began to sing in his best mellow tones, "Off to the junk food joint I go, joint I go, joint I go…." It felt so good to be out in the sunshine, his fever finally gone; except for that stiff neck, he didn't feel the slightest bit dizzy from his days of fever. *I must be ready for a new life. It seems like I was sick forever. How long is a forever anyway?* He pulled up at the fast-food place where they knew his voice as soon as he opened his mouth.

"Hey, glad to see you back! The same, sir?"

"Yeah, two sausage and egg biscuits, coffee with lots of cream." He thought Jessica wouldn't approve of his usual breakfast, but he sure did like it and he was sure hungry!

He crammed two bites of the sausage-egg biscuit into his mouth, dropping biscuit in his clean car, and slowly sipped the coffee on his way to the park. It wouldn't do to burn his tongue on top of his other injuries. His toe was as broke as broke can be. He had noticed in the shower it had turned interesting shades, from purple to near black, but what was a broke toe? He was well!

When he arrived at Eden, he looked up at the sky. It was almost turquoise blue, and the cumulus clouds looked like huge feather beds. He imagined what it would be like if they were and he and Jessica were making love in the sky. *Well, she would get my letter today. My words will sing to her and she will call; she has to. If for some reason she doesn't, I will have to break down and call her. I can't stand being without her.*

Whatever happens with us, though, I'll have to move from here; this place would skin a cat after very long and this cat can't handle it—if stepma could see where I live now, she would think I hit the big time. That was the one compliment she ever give me. "Your voice, Danny, may take you far, if you don't act too crazy."

Now, why did she have to throw that in—I weren't a crazy kid, was I? I don't remember being crazy. She was probably just jealous. Her kids couldn't sing a lick. Or it might have been those dreams, or because I liked to play with a pendulum. That pendulum knew its stuff, though; it made the other kids take note of me. If it weren't for that, I would have spent more days under the porch, playing marbles, with no friends at all. They did like my singing. There wasn't an operetta that I didn't have a part in, and I'll have to give Ma credit; she always scurried for a costume.

Why does life have to throw us so many punches? I might have made big time had it not been those punches. If there is a God, why all the challenges, the unexpected deaths, the turmoil? But at least here, we don't have to scrounge for food every day like some poor people. Even though I grew up poor, we always had enough to eat. And talk about injustice: if God is God of all, what about those third world countries and the children that have to be prostitutes just to be able to have enough to eat? What would it be like to be a child in the Sudan?

Maybe there is a chosen people, or are chosen people. That's not fair! I'm going to blow my mind asking all these questions no one knows the answers to. And I'm also going to blow my mind trying to use correct English all the time. Jessica would want me to always be the proper gentleman, so by God, I'm going to try!

Daniel sat down at one of the tables in the park and got out his pencil and paper. He looked at the sky again and tried to calm his mind; then in his mind he asked a question. "Is there a God?"

At first, nothing; but then very, very slowly his hand began to, on its own, in large script, at first draw large circles all over the page, and then wrote "God is No beginning, no end." *Well,* thought Daniel, *guess I could have thought that up myself, but it seemed to come from outside me. I'll ask something else: Where is heaven?* Again his pencil took off with many scribbles and circles until the words "No place—no suffering, no pain" came out. *Well, that's nice,* thought Daniel, *but what about hell? Is there a hell?* The pencil took off wildly to the top of the page and then down in his vision field and wrote first in small letters then getting larger before it finished with these words:

"Form is reborn and reborn and reborn and reborn and still does not see the LIGHT."

Daniel dropped his pencil. *Now, what in the hell? I know that didn't come from me! I'm getting out of here ... there's something around me giving me answers. I'm some goddamn Ouija board!*

Daniel scrambled from the table into his car, revved the motor, and took off with grass and gravel flying behind him. *What did that? Who did that? It seemed like the pencil had a mind of its own! I shouldn't have tried it again—am I bewitched or something?*

What is that about being reborn and reborn? Is there something out there that knows more the heck than I do? His heart was beating fast. He hadn't even finished his sausage and egg biscuits that had somehow lost their taste. *I'm going home to lie down; I might still be a little sick.*

He entered the lobby and the girl at the desk looked up and said, "Mr. Cummings, may I see you a minute?"

"No," said Daniel, "I'm busy."

"But this is about your account, sir," she said.

"Oh God, girl, can't it wait? I've been sick, you know."

"It's behind five days, so I don't see how it can wait."

"Okay, let me go get a check for this place, and believe me, it's the last money you're getting from me—you guys are bandits!"

"Do you want to give notice?" she said.

"Yes, I will be out of here in less than a month; you can count on it, baby!"

Daniel hurried to his room and quickly sat at the desk and wrote a check for the tidy sum. *Oh God, now what? Jessica, please call me, baby—we've got to work something out between us. I've gone and done it, now!*

He literally ran it down to the lobby.

"Here you go, sweet thing—made to order!" Daniel knew how the girl wanted to go out with him, so what did a little flirting amount to, even though she could never get to first base with him and knew it.

"Thank you for your promptness," she said icily.

Back up in his room, Daniel raised the window a little to let in the beautiful day. He pulled off his shoes so that his hurting toe could get some relief from the pressure. *Ahhh—I know they don't do anything for broke toes, so, old toe, you have just got to mend—so heal up, you hear? Darn thing. Considering the job done on my face, the meds sometimes know what they are doing.*

Now, what the deuce is all that pencil stuff about? I bet if I sat in that park with that pencil and kept asking questions I would keep getting answers. Darn spooky. It seemed like it was outside myself. Especially that reborn, reborn, reborn stuff. Do you suppose that is how it is? I've often thought that, but it would get downright tiresome after a while. Hey, now wait a minute—since I've often thought that, it's possible my subconscious may have been coming through. I just plain don't know. The only thing good about it I can think of is they didn't teach that in Sunday school. Sorry, Ma.

He laid down on the bed, hands underneath his head, thinking things over ... *maybe when Jessica calls me ... she will call me today when she gets my letter, I know she will.*

He rose up and saw the broken mirror. *Oh God, I can't tell her about that. I really had a spell last night. I thought I was better, but—but something, something sometimes does go wrong with me—like a loose circuit or something.* He looked over to the desk and thought about the pencil lying in the drawer. It was calling to him just like the refrigerator does sometimes when there is a good leftover on hand. This makes anything about the refrigerator seem mundane. *Maybe I'm the thirteenth, lesser disciple!*

He put his hand on the bedside table. *I wonder if they have a Bible in the drawer there. Do those Gideon's still do that? Maybe if I read a little of that Gideon stuff, whatever is wrong with me will go away.* Sure enough, there was a Bible in the bedside table. *I wonder why I didn't notice this before:*

HOLY BIBLE

King James Version

I wonder if that's the Bible they used at the graveside service of Carlos the old man. I know it made me think. They were beautiful words. If I ever find Joey, I'll have a service for him. Everybody needs a service. If we take the trouble to live in this chaos, we should go out with a little fanfare.

Daniel fingered through the Bible, reading verses that meant little to nothing to him, except the beginning of Genesis, God's creation of the Earth. It read beautifully to him. He finally got drowsy and fell asleep, the Bible on his chest. When he awakened, still sleepy, his hand on the bedside table looked strange. *What is going on? My hand on the table is outside my real hand! Outside my hand?* He felt so light, and suddenly his complete self, all that is of him, raised up from his body and floated around the room. He looked down at the bed and his body was there in the same supine position, but the real part of him, the thinking, knowing part was floating around the room. He felt no bodily pain; amazingly his toe did not hurt. *What is this? Why am I up here? Am I dead? But why? Why am I dead? I didn't feel sick again; maybe I have had a severe relapse and didn't know it.* He began to hear beautiful music—so beautiful he could hardly stand it. Not the kind he played—not rock—but almost heavenly. *I must be dead! Did I have a heart attack or something? No pain—I suffered no pain. I thought if you were going to have a heart attack, you clutched your chest and it hurt like the deuce! Too bad I paid that rent! Maybe I can float out the window and see Jessica once again. She would be at my funeral, and her family, too. Why was I so mean to them? I want gobs of people at my funeral.* Seeking all of this, he floated out the window and came upon groups of people—he tried to talk to them, but they ignored him. *Maybe I'm not ready to be dead or why don't they talk to me? They are dead for sure. I know they are!* Some of the groups were laughing and having fun—a few groups seemed mean. *I'm not ready for this!* The beautiful music played on and on, the most wonderful music ever heard by him. *I must go to the music, see Jessica; it's my funeral, I know.* The music became almost deafening, when "POP"—he came back—back to his body. *What happened?* He felt his body through his clothes; there—all right. He felt from head to toe, checked his arms and legs—yes, all of him intact, for sure. *God, I didn't die. Thank you. I wasn't ready, but for some reason You gave me a glimpse. We don't really die.... We transcend.* Daniel grabbed a box of Kleenex and tried not to cry. *I for some reason know a little of the mystery.* He got up from the bed, trembling, feeling himself over and over. “I am back! But I was really gone....”

CHAPTER THIRTY-SIX

Across the river, Jessica picked up the mail and put it in her purse and her key in the lock. For some reason, she shivered. *I wonder if Daniel is all right—and I wonder if he wrote a song for me like he hysterically said he would; but that would hardly make up for his terrible behavior the other night. Why I even tried to explain him to Debbie or Becca—wasted words. I don't understand him myself. Daniel needs help and apparently, for reasons of the past and present, I'm still in love with him—an impossible situation, unless he disappears from my life again, and if he does it will be the best for both of us....*

Entering her home, she put the mail on the kitchen table and the kettle on for a cup of tea, a routine she could do in her sleep. This daily procedure proved so restful when she got home from work. Today had been particularly trying with the death of Mrs. Lewis, who had not only been a patient but a friend as well. She wondered if the spirit of Mrs. Lewis had gone straight on to that place, that cosmic place where Elizabeth had gone and if she would stay there for a little while with loved ones that had gone on before. That's a question that wasn't answered on the tape. *I guess it would be an individual thing, different for everybody. I know Mrs. Lewis would go to a good place; she had been such a sweet woman, but this whole thing is so confusing. It's not cut and dried like it used to be for me. I wonder what happens to someone who is really an awful person? Certainly the awfuls aren't grouped together. I've got to go to the library again and see what I can find on cosmic consciousness.*

Jessica shivered again. *I've got to get hold of myself and get my mind off such things as this.* She picked up her tea and her mail and went into the living room, sat on the couch, put her feet up on the hassock, and began the near daily sorting of the mail: "the throwaways" and "the keeps." She came upon a scribbled letter that had a familiar feel. Daniel—it had to be from Daniel. No phone call yet; maybe this was his song, or who knows what it was? She held it in her hands for a minute, contemplating. *Maybe he is saying an abrupt "goodbye" again—who knows?* She held it close. *Whatever. This is a "keep."*

Tears came to Jessica's eyes when she read his words: "Without you, I am nothing" and "Life's ultimate mystery takes me." A large lump came up in her throat as more tears flooded her eyes. *I had been thinking about that very thing. It's like we are on the same wavelength, even though he says things I wouldn't dream of saying. I have to call him and we have to see that doctor, Dr. Jerold. I have to know where he has been along the way as well as help him find himself now, this time, and bring out the goodness in him.*

He can express himself beautifully—like a poet. And then there's that other—that part that can scare me. But he's never been violent. It's just that it's inside him, in his words that hurt. I'm not used to such things; I have to call him and I have to call him now!

She punched in his number. The answer was not the strong, mellow-toned voice she expected.

"Jessica, you had to call; you had to." His voice shook with emotion. "If I died would you come to my funeral? I haven't been the best person, you know—I'm afraid you wouldn't come … nobody would come." His voice trailed off.

"Of course, of course—but why are you thinking of death? You're all well now and hardly had been close to death; just sick with a fever, that's all. Honey, has something happened to make you think those things? We do need to talk, but not about death. We are both too young for that!" said Jessica.

Jessica went on, "I got your letter—I, I know whenever people, or you say something you later regret, it's hard to put into words how you really feel. So sometimes, or I guess you felt writing me was the best avenue. Daniel, it is not what you said that really bothers me, it's the almost venomous way in which you said those words. Daniel, you don't own me! It's like in *The Prophet*. I feel we belong together somehow, and we stand together to hold up our temple, but those pillars can stand apart. We have to have periods of apart-ness. But I would like for you to like my family and my friends and for them to like you, and with what happened the other day, that might never be. Daniel—I have two daughters, a son-in-law, and two grandsons. They are part of me. They are part of my life and always will be as long as I am alive. You will have to take giant steps to undo the harm done by the words you lashed out at my daughter Debbie. You somehow have to realize you need help. Most of us do not think the world is after us, Daniel. You need to see a doctor. Would you do that for yourself and for me?"

Daniel, listening to Jessica, had his hand over his eyes, trying with much difficulty not to sob an interruption, but finally said quivering, "Yes, anything.

Things have been happening—maybe some kind of sign. There's something out there, Jess; not things, I didn't mean to say that. It's like there is another, uh, dimension or something out there and I saw it!"

Jessica's answer came quickly. "I'll be over, or would you rather come here?

"If it's okay, I'll come there. I would feel safer. I don't think I want to be here—things are different here."

"I'll be waiting." Jessica hung up the phone and collapsed on the couch. *Now what?* she thought. *What is he talking about?*

It's all been a dream, thought Daniel as he quickly showered, *But then again, it was too real—too real to have been a dream. Jessica will help me with this or think I've completely lost my mind. Or maybe she will think I'm like the man in* A Beautiful Mind. *Only—only that guy was sick or a real weirdo! An intellectual sick. Well, I'm intelligent—so what else is new?*

He dressed quickly, wearing the turquoise sweater he knew Jess liked. He glanced down at his bed and saw the Bible lying there. "No," he said aloud. *That didn't have anything to do with my flight or whatever it was.* He put it back in the drawer nevertheless.

He was quickly on the road in his still-clean car, though it was marred now with the crumbs of biscuit; inside he still felt shaken. *When will this shaky feeling go? I'm on the way to the home of the love of my life, and no matter what happened to me, with her I can be content. With her, I've changed considerably.*

With her, I am safe from whatever is out there, perhaps in another dimension or from me—who knows? If it's from my unconscious mind, the unconscious knows more than I do. Would I expect that? He reached down to pick up the particle of biscuit and flung it out the window. *Bonny never cared whether the car was clean or not. Well, Bonny's not here. Bonny's not here, no more, no more. Wonder where Bonny went when she died? If that wasn't a dream, it's a lot more complicated than anything I had ever imagined! I've got to stop thinking about it. Jessica might not even buy it, and if she doesn't I'll just take the experience with me for the rest of my life. When I do die it's bound to be interesting. I know now, or at least I think I know, the light just doesn't go out. The strongest evidence is at first my hand left—and I saw it leave. I did—I saw it do it, so I know, I know!*

He pulled up in Jessica's drive and took a deep breath. *My beautiful Jessica is inside waiting for me. I wonder if this will be my (our) home some day, but I have some fence mending to do. And I have a lot to tell her. I know I must get it straight or she may not believe it happened.*

Jessica opened the door before he even had time to knock. He put his arms around her and pulled her close. "Jessica, I don't think I'm like other people. I probably do need to go see that doctor because of the weird world I've been living in."

Jessica took his hand and led him to the couch. "Tell me about it and we'll see if it's strange. Things have been a little strange for me as well."

Daniel started with the writing and with special emphasis on the reborn aspect in his writing. "You know, Jessica, that may have been in my subconscious mind. I have thought all along in a way that either we die for real or we may somehow come back. I have no idea, of course, how it works, if we are in control, or if there is a God, or even if that is a learned name for the Life Force or explosion that brought life. Maybe we are not supposed to know. Maybe that heaven-hell idea has just been used by the organized church to control people, uh, to control the masses through the ages. You know, I think all religions in some way are used to control—that is why I never liked the organized church. For instance, Hindus may think, if you are not a good person, you would come back as a lower animal, so you better watch your step.... Protect those cows, one might be Aunt Charlotte! Actually, Jessica, I don't know much about religions, just that I don't like them. But when I wrote that without any conscious awareness, or it seemed to be from without myself, it made me think that someone was telling me what to write, since it seemed I had no control over my hand. It was just put there, told to me, so I would start thinking about it.

"Then—this will really blow your mind—this is what really made me think I am a weirdo. I lay down on the bed, and I know this doesn't sound like me, but thought I might see if there was one of those Bibles in the bedside table; you know, like those Gideon people sometimes put there. Well, there was. Thought maybe there might be a verse or verses that would cheer me up; wrong about that. I did like the creation story, though. Anyway, that Bible made me sleepy and I guess

I dosed a little. When I woke up—now I really was awake, Jessica—I could feel the hardness of my hand on the table. Then, all of a sudden, I realized my hand on the table was outside my real hand! It really was, Jessie, and then the rest of me just kinda floated out of my body, up to the ceiling, and then floated around the room. Jessica, I looked down at the bed and I saw my body there, lying there, but the knowing, thinking part—me—was floating around the room. I broke my toe and it hurts like the devil, but when I floated my toe did not hurt.... I decided I might be dead, but why? Maybe had a relapse and didn't know it. Honey, I heard this unbelievable music—not rock but almost heavenly, it sounded. I decided I must be dead! Did I have a heart attack or something? I suffered no pain if I had a heart attack. I had thoughts; like, too bad I paid that rent! So typical of me, and I wondered why I sounded off mean to your family and I wanted gobs of people at my funeral. I thought why stay around, and floated out the window and came upon groups of people. I tried to talk to them, but they ignored me. I knew they were dead for sure. I know they were! Some of the groups were laughing and having fun—a few groups seemed mad, angry. I know I shouldn't be one of them and was not ready for this! The beautiful music played on and on, the most wonderful music ever. I knew I must go find the music, maybe see you at my funeral. The music became almost deafening, then with what seemed like a 'pop,' I was back! What happened, Jessica? I felt myself all over and over to be sure."

"Daniel, I have never heard of such a thing—how frightening for you! No wonder you sounded so unlike yourself when we talked on the phone. I couldn't believe it when you talked about being dead, but with that on your mind, of course, you were completely disoriented and probably didn't know whether you were here or there! Honey, that's so strange, but strange things can happen to people; it just shows we only know a minute particle of what there is to know. But I certainly believe in an afterlife, and Daniel, I believe now in a before this life, too." Jessica said rather timidly, "That does make it easier to believe the regression that happened to me. We evidently are ourselves, us, what we are, whether we have a body to live in or not. You were not ready to die, but you had an experience that sounds to me like what death would be like, but you weren't ready for the end mystery. At least I think that is what happened to you. I don't know why, though; why would that happen unless for a reason?"

"I don't know, Jessie, I really don't know. All I know is that it scared the fool out of me—but in a way it was reassuring, I know now that there is something or some part of everybody that lives outside the body, but I also know everybody, no matter how good or bad, has a place. There were groups of people, or souls, that I knew were not good. I guess if we are good, we have to get past that part. I wouldn't want to get stuck with those suckers or any bad group. As I said, it scared me, too. What if I couldn't raise myself out of a bad group, and I bet I couldn't if I don't change some of my ways. Something is wrong with my head sometimes; I know that, and I need to change that, whatever it takes—a ton of medicine or what. I don't want to die and land in a place I don't want to be. I want us to be together when we die—I have got to get a hold on that—that part that sometimes goes off, you know, Jessica?

"That doctor you mentioned, I'm ready to get the help, or the medicine I need to not go on an anger binge or whatever it is. I know I have been that way even to you sometimes, and still you stuck by me, no matter how I acted, and maybe if I can get well, really well, completely, I can find out what happened to Joey. I've got to find out the truth about that or I can't be content or ever be myself!"

"Daniel, maybe I can call Dr. Jerold at his home and make an appointment for both of us. I think after that strange experience, we should probably make an appointment as soon as we can," said Jessica.

Jessica really felt this was not one of his "crazies" since he sounded more sincere than she'd ever heard him and was clearly shaken up.

"Don't you think we had better wait until morning? Doesn't he have a secretary or someone?" Daniel remarked as he realized his reluctance. "We can do it first thing in the morning—it's too late now to call, don't you think?"

"You're right," said Jessica when she looked at the clock. "It's after 9:30. We'll wait until morning. I feel sure he can help with his wealth of experience. I'm, of course, not positive but I bet he'll know what happened to you and be able to make you understand it and feel better." Daniel's presence had made Jessica completely forget the time.

Daniel pulled her close to him and said, "My sweetheart."

Jessica felt her heart skip a beat. She looked up at him; his chest was warm and comforting against her shoulders. She pulled his chin down to her lips and gave him a gentle kiss.

Daniel picked her up and carried her to the couch, where he bent her back and laid her down on the many pillows and kissed her as if he was finally home. He crawled in beside her, cuddling, saying, "I know you don't want me to stay, do you? I'd like to."

"Of course I do." Then she murmured, "I don't, Daniel. We have many problems to work through, I feel, and I think the doctor can help us do that." She didn't move. "I want things to be complete this time; we dove in last time without really knowing each other—without first being friends, and I feel we should be completely honest. As you know, I left something out about me and now I need to lay matters on the table. We need to find out who we really are, don't you see?" Jessica, while saying all of this, held her arms tightly around Daniel as if she couldn't let him go.

"Okay, but I don't believe it and I don't want to hear it!" Daniel blurted. "I'll go, if that's what you want."

He sat up abruptly, loosening Jessica's grasp. "Let me know when you hear from ole doc—but he better not want to give you an examination, though; you're mine and there's nothing wrong with you." Daniel nuzzled her on the nose. Jessica felt the saltiness of his tears on her face. But then, with a little laugh, he kissed her again, longingly, and then carefully opened her blouse as he moved his kissing down to her breast, then moved back and buttoned her up.

Daniel had definitely pulled himself together, but his face looked a little stricken. "You understand, we are together? You are so beautiful, but it's more than that. It's like our destiny or something. I don't think I would have trouble getting just a girlfriend, but you are more than that to me."

Jessica signed. "And you are more than that to me. When I was regressed by Dr. Jerold, I found that out and I know why, at least I think I know why—because we have been together before. That's why after I met you, I began having disturbing dreams but it was at another time, Daniel."

"Were we on a couch?" Daniel asked.

Jessica laughed. "Not exactly a couch, but you're close to the picture. But we need to have everything explained to us, so we'll both understand. We both need life tapes to see if I'm right; then we'll know we belong together—belong together to love and help each other now, in this lifetime."

"Reborn, reborn, reborn," Daniel's voice trailed away.

"We don't know anything for sure, honey, until you see Dr. Jerold as well."

"You know I'll do it now, even though it sounds very weird!" Daniel got up to leave. "You know I think I'd do almost anything you asked except maybe jump off a bluff!"

Jessica felt her legs go numb and wondered if she could get up, but she managed to move herself around and put her legs to the floor. They had done that before, then recovered in a little while. "I'm not sure where the nearest bluff is," she laughed, then said, "I am so tired, would you mind letting yourself out?"

It seemed to Daniel that Jessica changed the subject rather abruptly.

"Sure, I'll lock you in—are you sure you're okay?"

"Yes, I think so—rest is all I need."

Daniel gave her another kiss and headed for the door, then slipped out quietly. Jessica remained on the couch.

CHAPTER THIRTY-SEVEN

As Daniel drove home he felt better having talked to Jessica as far as his concerns, but he was still worried about it. *Am I strange or what? Yes, until I get help, I'm strange. Jessica has the right idea, so I guess I must see that doc for my illness—whatever you call it—and start taking those damn pills. As I remember, side effects—sick at my stomach and stuff. When Bonny died I stopped taking them; when I went off I had the sense to take one or two. Then that place, that fake hospital, changed everything for good. Talk about nightmare, that was a real one—they might have burned my brain.*

He noticed the biscuit crumbs in his car as he pulled into the parking garage. *I've got to get this heap washed and cleaned before my lady rides with me. It must be a chariot again.* He compared his "chariot" to the others in the garage. *If I have a winning song someday—maybe those stuck-up cars won't look down their noses at me!*

I wonder, though, about Jessica; she looked pale when I left. Could she really have MS? I won't believe it! Why would she say she had it? She wouldn't lie about a thing like that. Why would she? Especially now, she wouldn't lie unless she wants to get rid of me. Well, I've got news for her; I'm not leaving on any account. Not this time. No, never. I love her too much! If she is ill, we'll face it together. After Bonny, I never thought I would think that!

Jessica rubbed and rubbed her numb legs, as she had done before on another occasion. She felt like she still had strength—strength enough to get to the bedroom and do the necessary grooming for bed, but why do they just do like that all of a sudden? Rubbing didn't help. Rest would. It had before.

She raised herself slowly and made her way to the bedroom. Oh, they felt so strange. *Stranger than before? I really don't remember. That was quite some time ago. Those were some of the first symptoms. Oh, I know the ABC's of MS, and thank goodness I haven't had to start that yet. I hope I am just tired. Daniel did lay a lot on me this evening. He must be what they call a sensitive. So interesting. I wonder what Dr. Jerold will think of that. I've got to get to bed and hopefully in the morning these numb legs will be back to normal. It's hard to lift them. I'm just tired, that's all. I may have to call both doctors in the morning if they aren't better. Please God, You have laid enough on me. You have played hardball long enough—now I'm ready for kindness! We always learned about a loving God, but bad things continue to happen to many people—I haven't been singled out.*

Jessica threw her clothes on the floor and carefully got in the shower stall. She turned on the water and let it cascade on her face before she washed her hair. *I just don't have the time to take off my makeup; the shampoo will have to do it.*

As she dried off she began to think back, as she had too many times, to the sin, the very wrong thing she had done as a teenager. *Not only do we have many lives, but we also have lives within lives. I have changed since then, but I am not the flawless individual people take me for—my wild affair with Daniel is a good example.*

She put a towel on her pillow, knowing wet hair at night might cause a pain in the neck in the morning. Tomorrow was a workday and she had to get to bed. She prayed again silently, "God, let's work together with this."

She thought of the first time she had sex and how awful it had been. *I was only fifteen, and what happened? Pregnancy. My miscarriage saved me or my life's path would have taken a completely different turn. Were you with me then, God?*

Now what? Since she had that awful flu, she had only had the injections every three months for her illness. The steroids were given for a short time only to get her over that flu, thank goodness. Steroids nearly always have awful side effects. This must just be a fluke like I've had before. A hymn came into her mind. "Mine eyes have seen the glory of the coming of the Lord" *Why that? I don't even like that! Daniel is not the only one that has strange things happen in the mind.*

Neither Mother nor George knew how scared I was or what happened. God, I was only a fifteen-year-old kid. Oh, that resolved itself before either one found out, although I think Mother suspected something. If I don't stop thinking about this, I will never get to sleep. "Prove it if you want to be my girlfriend." Well, I did prove it finally, and then—then tears came to Jessica's eyes. *I was really dumb to let him talk me into it and it hurt so much. Nobody knew unless Greg told somebody and I don't think he did. I can still see his face—the disbelief. He had his life all planned, he said, never mind about mine. He said I had a problem! Well, that put the fear of God into me and I never did it again! That is, until I married and it took a great while for me to enjoy making love. But I was in love! It could have been the perfect marriage until—until this and he left. Said he just couldn't handle it. I know he's had second thoughts. Too late now.*

Jessica laid there for another fifteen minutes until it was evident she wasn't going to sleep this night. She got up and took an Ambien, sat up in bed, and looked at a fashion magazine for a little while. She had to think about something else. Her numb legs and her sins bounced around in her mind until she began to feel the effects of the medicine. She put the magazine on the floor and scooted down in the bed, glasses still on, and flipped off the light. Her legs were feeling better. *Yes, it may have been just a fluke. God doesn't punish people for sins. In fact, it seems like after creation, God has moved away from the lives of people. God is inside us; that is the way He knows how we move and think. How else could it be? But I still wish I hadn't done that—it's on the record, my record for this time. How awful. Since God is inside, we punish ourselves I guess; at least I think that is how it is....*

The alarm rang and Jessica quickly put both feet on the floor and wiggled her toes. One foot was perfectly fine, okay, but the other still felt a little strange. She tried it cautiously, afraid of the results of foot to floor. Oh *God, still strange, but not as bad as last night.* She stood up, realizing immediately that it was dragging, just like it had when Daniel had left her.

Remember, it got better, but now Daniel is here. Or is it a sign that he might leave again? Oh, stop it!

I can't believe it; this time, I've told him the truth and he doesn't believe me, but he does know now. Thank God, now there is nothing to hide. I've told him how it is with me and my heart is relieved. But I'm not myself. She put her face in her hands to catch her tears. *I've got to get help, if there is some.*

I can't be negative now. It's not awful, terrible; I can go to work. In fact, I must—I must, but will that day come when I cannot? Everyone will notice again and, of course, say nothing. I hate being patronized—I can't kid myself about that! I'll have two calls this morning—Dr. Amish and Dr. Jerold. Later, when I get the appointment with Dr. Jerold, I'll call Daniel right away.

She had no trouble driving to work, and she tried to ignore the eyes on her when she got to her floor. She talked with Bea briefly about her obvious setback. When she got to her desk, she called Dr. Amish, who agreed to see her as soon as possible. Later when not so busy, she called Dr. Jerold's office. She told the secretary she and her friend would like to make an appointment together. He could see them next Monday after work. Jessica guessed there were many persons waiting to see him. She would have gladly taken time off from work, and she knew Daniel was chewing on nails.

Dr. Amish, in his usual manner, sat back and sighed after seeing Jessica walk. "Jessica, let's wait and see before we start any of those ABC drugs. As you remember, this dragging foot might go back to where it came from. We don't know enough about these apparent relapses, so let's just see what happens—give it a little time. And as for you—plenty of rest—put your feet up, even at work when you can. I know you need to work; besides, it's good for you. I cannot emphasize enough: rest, rest, rest. Get someone for the housework—no vacuuming for you. Use your good sense. I wish you had a live-in!"

Jessica blushed at that and then said, "I'll see what I can do."

She made it back to her office, trying with difficulty not to drag her foot. *Oh, why does this have to happen now? I guess Daniel has no choice but to believe me. Will he leave me now? His mood can be so manic, then depressed; it's difficult to tell what he will do next or how he will react. This is something that may cause him to go out of his gourd. Why am I concerned about him? I am the one this is happening to—I am the one that should be screaming. Have I ever screamed because of this? No. Perhaps I should and get it out of my system. Screaming won't make it go away—no matter how loud I scream. Unless a miracle happens, it will still hover in my being. I've seen so many horrible cases and I am so lucky, so far. Yes, I am lucky. I'll always keep that in my conscious mind no matter what.*

I should have called Daniel about Dr. Jerold before this, but I just didn't have the time!

"What's wrong with that doc that he can't see us sooner, now that I've made up my mind that I wanna go?"

“Sorry, Daniel. I didn’t pull any strings with him—I’ve gotta wait my turn and so do you, and now I’ve got to get back to work, honey; we’ve been especially busy today.”

“Hope I’m still here by Monday,” Daniel growled.

“Now you don’t mean that—think about it.” Jessica spoke firmly—she had about had it for the day. She wasn’t going to treat him with white gloves and party manners.

CHAPTER THIRTY-EIGHT

Earlier, Daniel had slept in quite late—stretched, laid back in the bed, and thought, *Voices of the heart—voices of my heart.* The contemplation warmed Daniel. One idea he was sure of: he would never, never leave Jessica again. *What a fool I had been to ever, ever do such a thing.* Love, his heart was so full, so full of love for her. *I don't know why these crazy feelings come over me—but I'm going to get to the bottom of it and get help—get help now. Then, if I can get her family to forgive me, maybe even become friends with me, things might work out like I want them to. As Jessie said, I don't own her—we need space sometimes, like the pillars of the temple, she said. Wish I could be as wise. Jessica is definitely that.*

When his sore toe hit the floor, a change of mood entered Daniel and the space around him. *I've waited this whole morning, no breakfast, no phone call! I'll give that woman fifteen more minutes, then I'm leaving, at least for food. What does she expect? I'm not calling that hospital. They don't like me. They're not friendly to me. They zero in on me. It's obvious. I don't know how she can put up with them. When we get married, I'll make her quit!*

Daniel paced around for the next ten minutes until his stomach emitted a long growl. "That's it, I'm out of here!"

He showered, dressed quickly, went downstairs, and winked at the girl. "Hey, cutie," he said. She ignored him, or at least tried to, with difficulty.

He made his usual breakfast round, then drove to the park. It was a beautiful sunny day. After breakfast, Daniel left the park and ran his car through the car wash. It felt good to, in small way, be what he knew Jessica would want him to be. Then he hurried back to the apartment.

It's late for Jessica to call now, he thought, but when he entered the apartment the phone was ringing. He dived to answer it and got there barely in time. *Oh damn, I was not too kind during the conversation.* In his hurry to the phone, he hurt his toe again. *Ouch! That is the very behavior I am trying to avoid. There are two of us. She could decide to leave me! I can't do this ever again.*

I'll call her back even if I get one of the hostiles. He called her quickly. "Jessica, honey, I'm so sorry I talked to you that way. I don't know why I do that except that I hurt my toe again and I thought you would call sooner."

Jessica in her usual calm way said, "I do think you need to work on that, because I don't particularly like it. Would you like it if I talked that way to you?"

"Well, I know I didn't like it when you laid down the law with me and I don't really know why I would treat the one I love in that way, and I do love you, Jessica, and I wouldn't want to lose you. You are my life."

Jessica melted as she always did when he put on the charm and used the mellow voice that made her think of his beautiful singing voice. "Daniel, I love you, too, and I want to hear you sing to me again. Our appointment is not until Monday—we will have to get together before then."

"I have no doubt, sweetheart—tonight?"

"Tonight would be good for a talk, and could you bring your guitar? I want to hear you sing again," Jessica answered.

"Of course," he replied.

"I remember 'Roses in the Moonlight.' I'd love to hear that."

"And I love to sing it for you, sweetheart—see you around seven, okay?"

"I'll be waiting," said Jessica.

Jessica had some difficulty getting ready for Daniel's visit; not only was her foot numb and dragging a bit, but it also was occasionally painful—it hadn't done that previously. *It will go away, I know it will; it's got to,* she thought. She ironed an old '70s caftan, thinking her limb would not be so noticeable. It really looked pretty good as it zipped up forming a turtleneck. Vintage clothes seemed to be back in style, although this wasn't exactly vintage—close though. She wore her sapphire bracelet that she had received for Christmas, and in that apparel she felt like the tragic Bronte character Catherine waiting for the disturbed Heathcliff. Although she was sure that was not quite how the story developed. Her own story now had twists and turns, and what a story—not at all like she had previously envisioned! She looked in the mirror—pretty good, though pale. She reached in her makeup drawer for a color of blush that would match her dress. *There. Better. I guess I will be putting on a face when*

I'm eighty-some in a retirement home, assisted living, or worse. Everybody has to face that or something as they grow older. My girls have always said they would take care of me, but that depends—I wouldn't want to be an albatross around even my family's neck! It's difficult to predict how this story will turn out now that Daniel is in the pages.

Well, the blush helped. How will Daniel feel about me now? He may bolt!

Jessica opened the door as soon as she heard the doorbell.

"A princess," said Daniel as he entered and hugged her simultaneously. "How beautiful you look!" He carefully brought in his guitar.

"Oh Daniel, it seems you've been away from me forever. Let me look at you."

They stood back from each other. This time the one that was emotional was Jessica—tears ran down her face, although she had told herself she wouldn't cry.

"What's wrong, Princess?"

"Your princess has lost her glass slipper, dear; I put this on for a reason. I cannot walk as well as I might. I've had a little relapse, but these things often go away."

"Where?" questioned Daniel.

"Here, in this foot."

Daniel reached down to touch her extended foot. "Does it hurt? So you do have it. I didn't want to believe, but it doesn't do anything to my love for you—you know that don't you? You are part of me. We belong together, no matter."

Jessica put her head on his shoulder and regained her composure—she was determined she wouldn't cry anymore. They walked together to the kitchen; Daniel didn't try to help her.

"You look to me like you are walking just fine; you only have the slightest limp. Let's just say you are fine and perhaps it will go away sooner," Daniel remarked.

"Yes," Jessica smiled, "positive thinking—it's bound to go away sooner."

"And if it doesn't we'll deal with it." Daniel bent down and rubbed her leg again, then he kissed it and lifted her up and carried her to the bedroom and sat her on the bed.

"I was going to make some tea," she said.

"I was going to play a tune," he said as he went to get his guitar.

Jessica sat back, propped up on pillows, while Daniel, sitting at the foot of the bed, played and sang right to her many songs—songs he had written, including her favorite. *He is so talented,* she thought. *He could have gone far, if only ... if ... that thing that happened in his life had not taken it over.* "Honey, your voice is just beautiful and your writing talent is amazing! It's not too late to do something with it, you'll see."

Daniel remarked, "Well, it's a little late now, and I just enjoy singing for you anyway and maybe a small group someday. I just don't know about it anymore. I started out with great energy and enthusiasm, but with all that's happened, it just went down the drain."

"I have faith in you; anybody that can sing and compose like you do should be discovered again; but of course, none of us knows what the future will hold. I'm very interested in what Dr. Jerold will find out about you, since you are so talented. Maybe if you are a good subject for regression all kinds of avenues will become clear. I certainly went under easily, and it really surprised me. I had no idea I could be hypnotized, but it seemed just around the corner for me."

Daniel laughed a funny laugh. "Does it hurt? I'm afraid all kinds of weird stuff might come out about me, because I'm weird, you see."

"Oh Daniel, you've had some interesting things happen that's all—think of it that way." Jessica began to become a little uneasy....

"I'm going to try to push all of it out of my mind and put you into it, or I might put myself into you." He grinned and slid off the bed, carefully holding his guitar, and put it in its case. He slid back into the bed and put his arms around Jessica as he scooted her down in the bed. "Are you tired?" he said as he touched her right cheek.

"Not too much, but it is getting late," she said as she put her arms around him. All that romantic singing had made her want to love him in the worst way. So what if she were tired? So what if anything!

"Well, if you are tired, I guess I better get you ready for bed. Where is your nightgown?"

"In the top drawer, sweetheart, on the right side," she smiled.

He got it out. "This it?"

"Yes, but I can't put it on until I take a shower, and you are welcome to take one, too." She started to take off her caftan.

"Wait." Daniel came over and helped her with it, and then slowly took off the remainder of her clothes, stopping and kissing her with each item, exciting her almost to the limit. Then she went over and turned on the shower, getting the temperature perfectly right.

"Daniel, your turn," she said as she peeled his clothes off, shoes, socks, baggy jeans, stopping and kissing him where and when she desired, until they were both in the shower lathering each other with Jessica's special body soap and making love passionately and continuously. They were both laughing, and Daniel was singing. Jessica was thinking, *I hope this lasts forever.*

They dried each other off, got in bed, and made love until they went to sleep. Somehow Jessica had forgotten all about the phone ringing and one of the girls needing her. They slept through the night. The next morning the phone did ring. It was Debbie.

"Mom, is everything okay? Something just told me I ought to check on you," Debbie said. "Mind if I stop by?"

"Oh, uh, yes, that will be okay, honey, just give me an hour or two. I have a few things I need to do, okay? Say, 10:30 or so?" replied Jessica, holding onto her side of the blanket.

"Right."

"Daniel, honey, my daughter Debbie is coming over. Remember, you and she didn't get off to a very good start, but I would like her to meet you. But I don't think it a very good idea that she finds that you spent the night. I think she should meet you under different circumstances. Why don't you go now and come back later and meet her then, like you have just pleasantly dropped in? It would make me more comfortable, honey, please," Jessica said almost pleadingly.

"Oh, so you don't want you daughter to know we have a relationship—okay—I'll go pleasantly," Daniel quickly put on his clothes, went to the bathroom, stalkingly went out, and turned to leave.

"Daniel, please, I want you to come back and meet her; she knows we are a twosome." Jessica reached for Daniel's arm.

"It can't always be the way you want it, you know." Daniel ignored her hand, went to the door, and left.

Bewildered, Jessica shook her head in dismay. *Why does he have to be like that? He's like night and day, but his night doesn't even have a sliver of moon shining through to light his way. I don't understand him at all. We had a wonderful night and then, well, you would think I'm a stranger. Surely he would like to make it up to Debbie. Well, it is plain he doesn't care one way or the other. He just doesn't seem to care about that, when a normal person would have feelings of guilt. He just has bi-polar or something. He says he loves me, though loving people don't act like that!*

He'll just have to learn to incorporate "love" for me to my family or it just won't work.

Jessica was taking out her frustrations by fluffing up the pillows on the bed, making it look as neat as if Daniel had not spent the night. *Of course, all of this would not have happened if I had not let him spend the night, but then something else might have! Who knows! What else? I can't go on like this! But last night was a dream—it truly was! One thing is certain about Daniel. In every way he makes me refocus. I haven't even thought about my worsening leg, but Debbie will!*

She just finished straightening up when Debbie gently knocked on the door. "Hi, honey," Jessica said as she gave her a big hug. "I guess there's reason for you to be thinking about me. I should have called you and let you know." She backed away from the door.

"You mean you are worse?"

"Well, Dr. Amish thinks it might go away as quickly as it began; you know, kind of like it did before, but he doesn't want me to change anything I'm taking, just kind of a 'sit-back-and-wait' approach."

"Did you tell him you were dating a dragon and that you are waiting on him to change?" Debbie said sarcastically. "Truly, Mom, I think emotions have so much to do with health, and I hate this so much!"

"Well, we'll see about that. Daniel does have some problems, but he knows it as well as I do. We are both going to investigate the avenues that may get him that help and that is all I have to say about it, at present. As for the MS getting worse because of him—that is nutty; it has gotten worse then better before I even knew there was a Daniel. Debbie, this is nothing that I will let push me away from my family; if it begins to, I will sense it and do something about it, okay? Meanwhile, let's have a cup of tea, and guess what? I have more shortbread—my subconscious knew you were coming over this morning."

"Hey, great! And Mom, I would like nothing better than for you to have shortbread with me, a stable relationship, and a wonderful guy. I know how difficult that has been for you, and it's terrible, a beautiful woman like you. But I know the world out there can be heinous and some of us don't get to keep the hands we were dealt. It's been so hard on you. Hard on us. Dad treated you rotten—acted like a scared rabbit, but I guess he had a hidden core. I know he regrets it. You look just as good as ever and that is some men's only concern."

They sat at the kitchen table sipping their hot tea and nibbling on their shortbread, which had become a ritual for Debbie and Becca with their mom. Jessica could not imagine not being with her girls. Daniel seemed to be so possessive—did not want to share her in any way. Well, that couldn't happen. If they were to have a true relationship, he would have to join and be part of her family, not shove her in a corner alone with him. Her girls and she were too close for anything like that to happen. Debbie was commenting on the degree of her illness when there was a soft knock at the door.

She looked at Jessica as if to say, "Should I?" Jessica nodded.

Debbie went to the door and there stood Daniel. He had that friendly grin on his face. Debbie didn't feel like letting him in at all, not at all. She called to her mom and said, "We have company."

Jessica got up from the kitchen table and slowly walked to the door. Daniel gave her the look that exhibited solid charm. She took his hand and said, "Daniel, I'd like you to meet my younger daughter, Debbie, all over again. Debbie, this is my friend Daniel. Daniel, this is Debbie."

"Debbie, I'm truly glad to meet you again and I am very sorry for the way I acted the other evening. I can't even say it was because I'd been sick. I have no excuse for it. I've been searching my soul as to why I act that way sometimes and have come up with zero. I just don't know. What I do know is that I love your mother and I should never act like a horse's butt to someone she loves. In fact, I shouldn't act like that, period. Jessica is a beautiful lady and I need to be the best I can be. Probably it will be difficult for you to forgive me and think of me as your mom's boyfriend after my explosion of temper, but Jessica and I are going to try to get help for me when we go to that psych doctor. I haven't taken medicine and I need it. I have some kind of problem I wouldn't want to go into now, but Debbie, please, just meet me halfway, please? I'm really not a bad guy. The other night it seemed like it, but I'm really not. Please, Debbie?" Daniel looked close to tears, but his charm and handsomeness was getting through to Debbie.

"Well, I just don't know what to say at this point other than I will try very hard to forget the other night, but the scene is still fresh in my mind, and believe me, it was a scene! I can see the reason Mom is nuts over you, though, and she always goes to bat for you, no matter what you have said or done; so if she sees a lot of good stuff in you, I guess I will have to find it as well. Glad to meet you, Daniel," Debbie said in a rather stiff voice.

"I left my guitar over here last night, honey," Daniel said to Jessica.

"Oh yes," said Jessica, "would you mind playing something for Debbie, Daniel?"

So the rest of the afternoon was taken up with Daniel playing and Debbie thinking more and more of Daniel. Debbie liked country! She tried to still be angry with him, but it was next to impossible with his singing and playing talent. She couldn't wait to get home and call Becca and Jon.

CHAPTER THIRTY-NINE

Monday after work seemed to Jessica to come in a twinkling of an eye and it was time to go to Dr. Jerold. Daniel had agreed to meet her at the restaurant nearby, have a quick bite, and go on to the doctor's, which was close to the restaurant. The restaurant happened to be the same one where they had first met for their tea and french fries eons ago; Jessica had been so impressed that Daniel knew Macbeth's soliloquy. Well, they had traveled many miles since then and she hoped that he could be helped by seeing Dr. Jerold, and that from then on, all of the miles would be happy ones for them. If she had anything at all to say about the matter, they would be! But Daniel had to do his part as well.

Daniel put his arm possessively around her shoulder and helped her to the back of the restaurant. He ordered, "Hot tea and double fries." He looked at Jessica with a twinkle in his eyes. "I'm sorry, honey; that might not have been what you wanted."

"Daniel, for this particular evening, that's exactly what I wanted, thank you," replied Jessica. "You read my mind," she added with a returning smile.

Even though Daniel made an effort to appear of the utmost of stability, it was evident he felt nervous, even his hands shook as he picked up his tea. Finally he said, "Why did you get me into this? I am not going to like being hypnotized. I am not going to like it at all!"

After he put down his tea, Jessica put her hand on his shaking one and said, "Honey, for one thing, you might not be a good subject and can't be hypnotized.

Fortunately for me, I happened to be a good subject and I found it quite interesting and helpful; in fact, fascinating, very fascinating. I stopped having those troubling dreams, so it proved extremely helpful to me.

"Furthermore, as far as you are concerned, remember, you will not say anything under hypnosis that you wouldn't say normally, so please don't find it scary or anything. It isn't. I heard myself talking, only in a different way. It was me, just at a different time and place. That is what's so interesting.

"Another plus: the doctor may find out why you have trouble now and give that his first priority. One way would be giving you meds. He's an M.D. and a psychiatrist and can put you on exactly the right medication for your particular type of trouble. Just have faith in him. I did, and I do, or we wouldn't be sitting here talking about this right now. I sincerely doubt if when you came back from Galveston, I would have had faith enough in you if it weren't for Dr. Jerold."

"Then," said Daniel, "guess I should bow down to the great guru!"

"Honey, I mean every word. Please give it a chance."

"I'm not sure I have any more faith in doctors than I do the police considering what some of them did to me. That's the trouble: I can't remember the blanks (the little deaths). I can't find them. I can't find those blanks!" Daniel covered his eyes with his hands.

Jessica thought it would be better to get out of there before his emotions got the better of him and he might not go to Dr. Jerold's at all.

"I didn't realize how starved I was," said Jessica as she started jamming the fries into her mouth. "Okay, I'm ready, are you?"

"Are you tense or something? I've never seen you eat with such vigor; this little piggy went to market!" Daniel looked at Jessica strangely.

"Let's just finish up and go; it's always better to be a little early than a little late, don't you think?"

"I'm finished then, if you say so. Let's go and get this mysterious saga over with," said Daniel as he wiped off the table with his napkin, got up, and put his arm around Jessica to usher her out. "I do hope, especially for your sake, I'm an okay guy, a 'normal.' This has gone on far too long; longer than you'll know, longer than even I can remember. I guess my stepmother might know. You know, the wicked old stepmother. Everybody has one of those, don't they?"

"I hope you're kidding, honey," said Jessica.

"Well, stepmother, yes—in the wicked sense, no. I guess she tried and it kinda turned out wicked. She did tell me I had talent once. I believe my guitar was the only real friend I had and it was an old one left in the corner by my uncle who gave up tryin' to play."

"When did you start to play?" said Jessica, who was trying to keep the conversation light.

"As soon as my fingers could stretch around the frets, it came naturally. I forget how old I was. I sang at school first," Daniel reminisced.

"There's so much we don't know about each other, Daniel, and here we are at Dr. Jerold's office to learn even more, and I realize now we don't even know our own histories this time around; we let our attraction, our chemistries take over without knowing that much about each other. I had no idea you had a stepmother. So many things can affect how one thinks, how one interprets ideas. We should have known more about each other, but no, we just dove in!"

"What's wrong with having a stepmother?" Daniel said in an abrupt manner.

"Nothing, nothing at all ... oh, here's the secretary. Oh hi, I'm Mrs. Hastings. Mr. Cummings and I had an appointment at 6:30 with Dr. Jerold."

"Oh, yes, he's ready for you—the patient before you cancelled. I'll get the info on Mr. Cummings later," replied the secretary. Jessica had explained ahead that she doubted if Mr. Cummings had insurance because he traveled around a lot. *Now that is the truth! If the medicine is really expensive, we'll pay for it together.* Jessica's conversations with herself had become frequent since Daniel had come into her life.

Dr. Jerold opened the door for them. *He has such a winning smile, surely Daniel will like him.*

"Jessica, Mr. Cummings, come in—you may sit over there. Mr. Cummings, I understand you and Jessica are close friends, but on this initial contact would you rather we just talk alone?"

"Absolutely not—I have no secrets from Jessica."

"Well, I'm sure you feel that way, but later on you may change your mind and wish to talk with me privately. We'll see how our sessions develop. Are there any particular issues you'd like to discuss?"

Jessica blurted out, "He had an unusual experience—something unlike anything I've ever heard!"

Dr. Jerold looked at Jessica with surprise. "Let Daniel tell what happened—uh, is it all right if I call you Daniel?"

"Of course, do you think I'm an old man or something? Jessica knows what happened; let her tell it. If she forgets something, I'll fill in the blanks."

So Jessica set about telling Daniel's experience of leaving his body and floating about the room; how he thought he was dead, the floating out the window, the coming upon groups of people who would not talk to him, the heavenly music, and then arriving back.

"Jessica told my story pretty accurately. The only part she left out is that I'm a little crazy! And, oh yes, I do weird writing. It seems like it comes from outside myself, I think I could become addicted to it. Where's a pen?"

"Oh," said the doctor, "that's what some call automatic writing. I believe there have not been any studies proving that it comes from outside oneself, but the assumption is that it is the unconscious mind, a product of dissociation. I believe that is what came out of one of the parapsychology departments at a prestigious university."

"Prestigious or not, it knew more than me. How could that be?"

"The unconscious mind holds many secrets, Daniel, you will find. And I think you are right; it can be addicting. Better to leave it alone. Has Jessica told you anything about her regression and how it made her stop having nightmares?"

"Yes," said Daniel stiffly.

"Well, I would like to do the same with you to see if we can find the source of your problems."

"Now I'm not going to spend one dollar to have some shrink find out my secret information," Daniel said sullenly.

Oh no! thought Jessica. *He's starting it.*

"Okay, one dollar. Is it a deal?" Dr Jerold reached his hand out to Daniel.

Daniel smiled broadly. "Okay then, if I think you're worth something, I might make it a dollar and a half."

"Great! Now as far as the out-of-body experience goes, that is not so unusual. Some people have them in a dream state, but others do as you did and are completely aware of what is going on. Another name for this is astral projection. It may be the sensation of consciousness outside of physical body."

"Don't give me that crap! This was no sensation. I'll tell you what—you do it, then come back and tell me all about those groups who wouldn't talk to me—those mean groups—you tell me what you experienced!" Daniel's agitation was pronounced and Jessica put her arm around him.

"It would be my guess that you are somewhat clairvoyant, especially since you have had that automatic-writing experience; but of course, that remains to be seen. Some people practice trying to have out-of-body experiences and think it is something to be attained. In fact, there are a few books on the subject. They actually want to do this," said Dr. Jerold.

"Well, not me—no, sir! Who would want to do such a thing again? I hope it never, ever happens to me again!"

"Daniel, it probably never will, but you can relax with it and not be a stranger to it if it does." Dr. Jerold's calming voice seemed to make the experience just a ho-hum, everyday occurrence.

"Now, aside from that, would you tell me what is troubling you most, then what you would like to change about your life? I might find it necessary to regress you under hypnosis because many times problems start early in a person's life and are hidden from the NOW."

"I guess it would be all right," said Daniel haltingly.

"Good," said Dr. Jerold. "Another thing, Daniel; some patients we find go back into a life before this one that would prove interesting. Is that okay with you?"

"Like Jessica did, yes, that would be okay, but it would be strange, very weird; but if Jessica did it, how can it be so weird? Jessica and I may have known each other—fantastic, but she seems to think so!"

"That's a good answer, Daniel; if Jessica did it, it can't be weird. Do you know of anyone who has her feet so firmly planted?"

"Well, except for that one foot that I'm worried about," said Daniel.

Dr. Jerold looked at Jessica.

"I've just had a little flare up—I'm okay. Would you rather I leave?"

"Perhaps it would be better," replied Dr. Jerold.

"No," said Daniel. "If I say something about Joey, I want her to hear it."

"Let's just talk for a while, Daniel."

After Daniel filled the doctor in on what happened with Joey as far as he could remember, gave a description of the place he was taken, and told of his mental problems, his wife's cancer, etc., nearly all three were ready for sleep. Dr. Jerold was amazed at what Daniel told him.

"Daniel, in order to hopefully get some answers to the questions we have and perhaps find out what may have happened with Joey, I would like to give hypnotic suggestion. Is that all right?"

"Don't leave," he said to Jessica.

"I won't. I'll be right here."

Dr. Jerold told Daniel to look at his thumbs and gave the usual hypnotic suggestion, and it wasn't long until Daniel's head began to sway and then go down.

"Daniel, I want you to find yourself in a significant time in your life. Where are you?"

Daniel proved to be a good subject and chose a time in his life right after Bonny died.

"I had to buy a black suit; there are the kids, Mac and Betsy. They are dabbing their eyes. Why were you not here when your mother needed you?

"Oh, here comes Joey.

"He's ignoring me. Why does he do that?

"Come over here." Daniel appeared to be motioning. "Mac, Betsy, why doesn't he sit with the family?

"God, he has on a T-shirt and jeans and is slouched way down in the pew. Can't he show some respect? Oh no, they are motioning for us to go past the casket. I can't stand it! Go, kids. Oh, no, no, no, no—Bonny please don't be dead. Son? Son? Be my boy Joey, don't cry, honey, please, don't—she was awful, awful sick, you know that. She couldn't get well. Son … maybe if I put my arm around him, he'll stop. Oh, okay, I understand; you would rather be by yourself.

"No, no graveyard. We're through. Bonny, when she was so sick, said she wanted to be cremated, so Joey, if you had been home more, you would have known. My fault? Cancer isn't anybody's fault, Joey, it just happens. Joey, Joey, please stay with the family for a little while. What do you mean I don't want you to? You know I want you. Everything is MY FAULT? After what I did to you? Whatever can you mean? Not here, Joey, not here. All right, go on—GO—but it is not my fault. What are you talking about? Betsy, you're not leaving, too? Please stay with your dad for a while; I need you now. You will? THANKS, honey, THANKS. Let's go to the house—Mama would want us together now. You know she would. Mac, spare a while for your dad, okay? We'll go get chicken and have a meal. Your mother would want that. She always wanted us to be a close family. Things just sometimes didn't work the way she wanted. Things got a little crazy. I know I worked too much and wasn't home enough for you, Mac. Mama loved picnics. How 'bout a picnic on the front porch? Maybe some of Bonny's friends will come over. Bonny made friends. I'll get enough chicken and stuff.

"Spread out the cloth, Betsy. Here come Joe and Bea. They are loyal—look at the butterfly that keeps alighting on the table—pretty isn't it? Strange—notice that? It won't go anywhere but here."

Dr. Jerold spoke up.

"Daniel go away from there, back in time, several years back. Back in time. Where are you?"

Daniel began speaking in a childish voice. "With Grandpa on the farm. Grandpa is making Bobby beat me up," he choked out.

"How old are you?"

"F-f—I'm four."

"Who wins?"

"Bobby—he's eight. Bobby al'ays does. Granpa likes fight—he's sit on step cheerin' an' drinkin' that stuff dat smells bad."

Daniel's face gets red; he starts to cry.

"No, don't hit Granpa, I'm big! NO, DON'T!"

Daniel cried harder and pushed his hands away from his face as if to push a stick or cane away. "I can't hel' it!"

Dr. Jerold said, "Daniel, run away from there. Now, we are going back further in time, far away from your mean Grandpa, far back in time.... Now, where do you find yourself?"

Daniel frowned repeatedly and finally said, after his face seemed calm again, "On the porch swing with Sis."

"Oh, on the porch swing—what are you doing?"

Daniel looked happy, and still in a childlike voice said, "Pushing with my feet. She likes to swing. I havva watch her, always havva...."

"What's your name?"

"Ernie. She's Rosemarie. We're watching those funny machines go up the pike. There's lots of 'em now—more than the buggies."

"What year is it?"

"Dunno—1913 maybe. I'll look on calendar—gotta watch her now, so you'll havva wait. Who are you?"

"A friend. How old are you?"

"Ten. I remember that—that's easy. Ma said, 'No party for me.'"

"Why?"

"'Cause we was poor, she said, but she didn't havva tell me. We have enough to eat; she cans and stuff, but I know since I was little we was poor and that Ma loves Rosemarie more than me."

Then Daniel reached out his arms as if to catch something, and shouted, "No, no, Rosemarie, stay here.

You can't cross the pike now, too many machines. NO, oh NO, LOOK, COMING, YOU CAN'T, OH MA, OH MA! He lunges and falls forward.

"What happened, Ernie?"

"I pushed Rosie away from the machine; it missed her." Daniel started mumbling, "Thank God, Thank God, Thank God...."

"What happened to you?"

"I saw myself be hit. Ma came running out and picked up Rosie. She was okay. The folks carried me into the house, but I wasn't there, er, in my body."

"What happened then?"

"I didn't stay around long; there was a place for me. I HAD to go. Some nice place, a bright place—many bright forms. One helped me."

"Do what?"

"I don't remember except calmness and waiting, waiting ... then I remember I had someplace to go and got in queue."

"Anything else?"

Daniel stirred in his chair. "No, just here."

Dr. Jerold looked at Jessica, who looked disappointed. Then he spoke again to Daniel.

"Daniel, I want you to search again in your mind, back before you were Ernie. Where do you find yourself?"

Daniel's eyes twitched many times, then perspiration broke out on his face. When he spoke, his voice was quivering.

"We're behind rocks with muskets waiting for men in blue. I'm so skeered—it's very hot, flies all around. We can't bury our dead—the enemy—too close. We're in the mountains. We s'posed to sneak attack, but it's not going to work; I'm skeered and they're coming! I hafta hide! We're s'posed to shoot now—so many of them. I run to a cave—all for naught. One of ours sees me—calls me yellow belly—I am—" Daniel clasps his chest, moans, and slumps over.

Dr. Jerold seemed as disappointed as Jessica, nodded to her, then said, "Now Daniel, I want you to go again back in time, way back as far as you can remember. Be very calm. Go back, back in time, back in time—see if you can find yourself in another time, another place. Go away from the war, back in time, to a different, maybe happier time—back, back in time…."

In Daniel's mind, men walked single file through the dense woods as quietly as they could, trying to avoid standing on or hitting sticks that might snap. Daniel envisioned home—his home among many other log houses in a circle—the fort. He saw Elizabeth and John there. They had looked so apprehensive when he left. The tears glistened in Elizabeth's eyes. This was no ordinary hunt. He knew he had the sight—that special vision. His Ma had said "Ulysses, thou art born with a cull on your face. You see things others do not see. Frighten you it may, but it is a gift."

"Yes, I am Ulysses. That is our fort; we always hunt for meat for winter. Something is different this time—I feel uneasy." He heard himself say, "Brothers, spread out and get what small game God allows us, then we dig the trap. Spread out, brothers." Daniel put his arms in rifle position as if to shoot. It appeared he shot many times in this position. Then he got up and it looked like he might be digging in the soil with others, but he talked so quietly they could not hear.

Dr. Jerold said, "Where are you now?"

Daniel replied, "I'm in the very, very dense woods of the Lord, but digging this trap will get the meat from Him to feed our fort all winter. We already bagged some squirrel and muskrat. I am missing my wife-mate, Elizabeth, though I must hunt for the good of the brothers."

Dr. Jerold perked up. "Who's your wife-mate?"

"I'm grateful for Elizabeth, my beautiful lady. God gave her in wedlock to me. I prayed and prayed and now she loves me back. God granted us a son, John. Amos, a brother, calls me to help, so I must!"

"What did you say your name is?"

"Ulysses—my dear Mother named me. They laugh at my name, though it be from the *Iliad*. You're a friendly voice, whoever you are—one of those I guess….

"Amos, what are you doing? Don't point that at me—never point at brothers—might hurt somebody. Amos! Amos! You don't want to do that! Don't!" Daniel holds onto his chest and slumps over, saying, "AAAhh, Amos, you've killed me."

"What happened, Ulysses?"

"Couldn't you stop him … guess not!"

"Again, what happened?"

"I saw my brother Amos drag then hide my body in some brush; he's hurrying but he's covering it so well they'll never find it. Oh Elizabeth—I loved her so—she's my life. What will my angel do? Though we have all sinned, she is close to an angel for me. Amos should be shackled—she'll know, she'll know!"

"Why did Amos shoot you, Ulysses?"

"I saw it, I knew it. He wanted Elizabeth, and when we had a son, he seemed to hate me. But we couldn't help it. Some women are given sons by the Lord."

"Where are you now?" said Dr. Jerold

"Just in the woods, hoping they will find my body. I don't need a body to think, but I know I'm dead."

"Will you be going somewhere?"

"No, just to find Elizabeth. I just don't know—I don't know what will happen to her or me...."

Dr. Jerold looked at Jessica. who was holding back her tears.

"All right, Daniel, I'm going to clap my hands together and at the sound you will awaken—wake up!" Dr. Jerold clapped his hands together gently. "You're here in the office with Jessica and me, and you've been on quite an interesting journey. Wake up!"

Jessica went over and sat beside him.

"Wake up, honey. I'm so happy, I can hardly stand it. I thought I might be wrong, but I was right—we have been together before! We have, we have. Oh, Daniel!"

Daniel finally rallied around and smiled at Jessica.

"I heard myself talking—I knew it was me, but it was like in a dream. I did hear what I said, but it was different. I talked different! And I was a kid, and I couldn't control being a kid; it is so weird but it makes sense and I know it's true."

Jessica hugged him so hard that he gasped.

"I can't breathe! Sweetheart, I lost you then—that is why we can't lose each other ever again. That we got together at all is just amazing with all the people out there in this old world!"

Jessica said, "It seems we were led to each other, but it is not without problems. My stepfather, George, made me aware and to stay aware; then I was so afraid I may have been wrong since you had other experiences. Then you suddenly go back and zoom in on Ulysses—you've been much more interesting than I was. All those lifetimes—but poor Daniel, dying so early."

Dr. Jerold said, "There may be an undercurrent in that—we'll have to see how that affects your problems in the present."

"Do you really think they might? God, I was a traitor once!"

"But you saved your little sister," Jessica put in. "That was wonderful!"

"The fact that he died so early—there is a message there. His personality may have strongly been Ulysses looking for Elizabeth. These puzzles are difficult," said the doctor, who looked at his watch.

"Pay at the door?" remarked Daniel. "I heard myself, so why do I need it? I was both good and a traitor—and I remember Grandpa. How could I forget? Do you suppose he was my punishment? I wonder why I went to Nam. That was certainly significant and I weren't no traitor."

"I don't know," said the doctor. "It may have been too painful. These sessions don't tell everything.

Grandpa had a lot to do with your problems since they were early year happenings. I would like to run some tests and make a definitive diagnosis and go from there. With the correct medication you should see a great improvement in your complaints and not have so many highs or lows—just have a stable mood, which is what most patients want. How does that sound?"

"Don't make me a zombie; neither one of us could stand that!" Daniel blurted out.

"I find your past lives very interesting, Daniel. So interesting that I would like to do a case history, that is, if it is all right with you.

"How much will that cost me?" snarled Daniel. Jessica took his arm as if to hurry him out.

"This one will be on me," said Dr. Jerold. "We, that is, the faculty need to get out a paper or so every year or we might lose our jobs. I think Ulysses, the soldier, Ernie, and Daniel might have a lot to say about how the past leads to the present. You, Daniel, are a very good subject, and there seems to be a kernel of sensitivity twining throughout these personalities."

"Well, in that case," said Daniel, "there's more stuff for later, but we are going."

CHAPTER FORTY

Daniel worked with Dr. Jerold for several weeks. The nurturing Daniel should have had as a small boy was sorely absent since his real mother died early and then no warm human being took her place. Instead he had been placed with his grandfather, an alcoholic whose greatest thrill in life was to see a fight. In this case, the fight passed between small boys instigated by the grandfather. Most days were the same. The grandpa would get drunk and insist that Bobby fight with Daniel. Bobby had a mean streak and liked nothing better than to beat up on his small cousin; and so it happened—day after day after day.

Case studies have shown that if the first seven years in a child's life are not loving and stable, the child grows up to be a troubled adult. Daniel was no exception, but he remembered the good times—those times he eventually had with his father and his early musical talent, being smarter than his stepbrother, and other little joys. Then his father was taken away. Although Dr. Jerold didn't tell this to Daniel or to Jessica, in his opinion if Daniel had not had those few positive years, his diagnosis would have probably been made in prison.

The doctor decided it would be better if Jessica and Daniel didn't see each other even briefly until Daniel's meds were worked out. Jessica thought it probably a good idea. The idea of Daniel being on his medicine and perhaps a new person certainly appealed to her. But she told the doctor, "Leave the wonderful part alone, okay?"

This would be a good time for Martha and me to check out a group we read about in the classifieds that believed in reincarnation. They did, and were sorely disappointed. The group didn't seem of this world, so to speak, but were donating all their time to who they might have been. Some even dressed the part. Jessica couldn't believe that just for the meeting there was a "Marie Antoinette," clothed in the appropriate costume, who had been told such by her Ouija board. The Ouija board was honored with encasement in an embroidered canvas bag with handles. Jessica wondered how long it took the "Marie Antoinette" to do the embroidery. There were many others fascinated by their other worlds. Could these people function in the real world?

They had such faith in the medium that it made Jessica want to throw the whole idea out—the baby out with the bath water. The so-called "medium" had no real answers to anything and was rude when asked a tough question. Surely the group would eventually see the light and quit paying this person. She began to wonder if she had been Elizabeth at all in just this association with these people! She told Debbie and Becca, who seemed to think their mother might be coming back to their world. Of course, she assured them she had never left it!

Maybe Dr. Jerold knew of a group that were true scholars—there had to be, after all. There are parapsychology groups in many universities. She knew of Duke, especially. Funny how her interests had shifted!

Martha knew of a psychic person who occasionally had visions. She realized she had a gift of sorts, but certainly didn't advertise it. She just knew she had been here before because she came into this world loving horses. She started drawing her horses at age two, then by age six she began to read and she copied pictures of horses from equestrian books. To own a horse was not easy in the city, but she would not rest until, at the age of eight, she had a horse of her own. Every weekend she would go to see him, until, as a little girl, she had him broken in and before long became an avid rider. Her parents marveled because neither one liked horses, but they were grateful they had enough to give their only child what she wanted most in this world. When grown, she married a man who shared her passion for horses and they lived on a small ranch in Kentucky. Martha and Jessica went to see this woman, who appeared to be around their age. She was very gracious and hospitable.

She told them the horse story and then added that during those years, however, she noticed certain people didn't seem like strangers. Something about their eyes told her she knew them, and there was something else.

"Jessica," she said, "I sometimes dream about people. I know dreams are supposed to be about the dreamer, but in my case that is not necessarily so. I may dream about you or Martha when you have gone. Usually they are harmless dreams, though; but sometimes they are not. Sometimes I feel it is necessary to tell the person what I dreamed. I have to make that decision. I never want anyone to call me, asking if I got anything in a dream or such. That would wear a good soul down!"

Martha said, "I think we have found our normal believer in reincarnation, don't you, Jessica?"

Jessica smiled her answer, "Most definitely."

Martha said, "Is this ever a burden for you, I mean the visions and dreams?"

"I don't let it be; there always has to be a balance in life. Sometimes I will meet someone I have known before, who is obviously on a different level; then, it's best our paths don't cross much."

"I think I have learned a little about levels," said Jessica.

"Yeah, that boyfriend you have!" Martha responded.

"Martha!"

Right before they left, the lady took Jessica's hand and said, "Does this boyfriend have psychic gifts? I keep getting in my head 'GI Joe'—does that mean anything to you?"

"Maybe he has some psychic-ness, a little. I don't know about any GI Joe."

"It may become clear," the lady said.

Meanwhile, Daniel told Dr. Jerold more about his experiences with automatic writing and how spooked though intrigued he was by it, and the out-of-body experience, which made Dr. Jerold more certain Daniel was a psychic "sensitive." This may have started with Ulysses, his mother, and the cull on his face. Maybe, just the suggestion—who knows? A cull was no more than the afterbirth, a superstition. The other evidence that Daniel was a sensitive was no joke! However,

Daniel's mental health was fragile, and taking Daniel back to further lifetimes might be risky. His goal: stability in the now. It wouldn't hurt him to be psychic as long as his brain chemistry remained normal. No doubt his soul psychically looked for Elizabeth, lived and died until he found her, but so interesting and so strange … a good paper.

Dr. Jerold tried a combination of medicines that seemed to slow Daniel down too much. He took away one, and one day Daniel came in and said, "You know, Doc, I feel great, terrific! I haven't felt the slightest bit troubled for days now. You must have hit the nail on the head with these medicines!"

"Daniel, I feel I have made a correct diagnosis. It is my professional opinion that you are not a borderline personality. I would diagnosis you as bi-polar, and if you take these medications without fail and have blood levels drawn every month, I believe you will do just fine. And I would like to borrow you for another week at least to finish up my paper, and as long as you feel great, I see no reason why you can't see Jessica. I know she is worried about you."

"I've been calling her every other day because I am worried about her. First I wanted to deny it, but she does have MS, Doctor, she does."

"We have to look these things straight in the eye, Daniel, and I think you are definitely strong enough to see it for what it is." Dr. Jerold looked very solemn.

"Bi-polar is almost better."

"It is, if you continue to take your meds," said Dr. Jerold.

Daniel left the office, but picked up his cell phone immediately to call Jessica. The old Daniel never would have spent the money for a cell. "Sweetie, let's go see *Harry Potter*. I've always wondered what all the fuss was about; and then tomorrow I've got to move, or see about moving somewhere. I've already overstayed my welcome with that little cutie downstairs!"

"Sounds fun, Daniel, but just to be with you is enough. Also, I hope we can park up close," said Jessica.

"We will, or we won't go to that one; we'll just neck. How would that be?"

Jessica replied, "Anything, honey, just anything—and I mean it! We will talk about moving later."

Jessica cuddled up to Daniel in the car, but to Daniel she seemed no better, but no worse either. She glowed with her usual beauty. Why, why did she have to have this torturous monster that held with it a huge question mark? It seemed to Daniel he had been through this before, but with Bonny they both knew she was not long for this world. He thought with shame how he sometimes treated her sharply, when she certainly hadn't asked to be sick, hadn't asked for the cancer that finally took her to the other world. This, for Jessica, for him, was somehow worse. He really, really loved Jessica. Through time he had loved her! He had found her at last, and would support her as long as and whatever it took.

They both enjoyed *Harry Potter*. Daniel had always liked movies about fantasy, and even though he had tried to forget his strange experiences, the strange held a fascination for him. He took one look at Jessica and saw how tired she appeared to be. "Honey, I know it's been a long time since we've been together—really been together—but tomorrow is a workday for you and I have to find a place to move. Let's call it a night, okay?"

"I'm surprised, Daniel, but I think it a good idea. Meanwhile, I'll see if I hear of any apartment close by and we can plan on this weekend."

Daniel walked her up the walk and inside. He kissed her until it seemed like he had changed his mind, but then let her go. "'Night, my sweetheart. Please get a good night's sleep."

Daniel walked to his car deep in thought. *I wish she would mention or at least think about my moving in with her; but it is her family, I know. At least she has a family....*

Daniel awakened the next morning with a picture in his mind. It seemed he knew what happened to Joey, clear as a chiming bell. *Oh Joey, why did you ever get started with that stuff? But now I know—I know who did it!*

It was the school's counselor! The counselor, since Joey was a truant, was provided for him by the police department. The school insisted; they had no choice in the matter. Bonny and he had taken him that first time and then he went by himself after Bonny got so sick. When Bonny died, Joey spent less time at home, but he made sure he went to school, and after school the school made certain he went to the counselor.

Daniel sat bolt upright in the bed. I remember now how I found out! *I was driving home and something strongly told me to follow the car taking Joey from the school. I watched as he was dropped off, and then waited a good ten minutes before going up to the counselor's office. The door was shut and I got this eerie feeling—something was wrong in there. I put my hand on the door knob; it was locked tight. I put my shoulder against it and broke it open! There was all kinds of drug paraphernalia on the desk—bag after bag of what I felt sure was cocaine. Two cops were standing there watching the "counselor" hit "Joey," and he cried out when he saw me, "Daddy, no!" but I rushed that counselor son of a bitch. He threw a paper weight or something at me. The cops beat me down. I felt woozy. When I came around I was lying by Joey's unseeing eyes. I turned on my side and felt his still-warm body and cried out. A cop said, "You killed him, see, you killed your own son. The gun's in your hand." I didn't! I didn't! I blacked out again and the rest I remembered—but Joey's death, so horrible, I blocked it out! I gotta call Jessica. No, maybe not. She is having a rough way to go. Maybe I should just tell the doc, but I gotta tell him now.*

"Doc, they killed my Joey—that son-of-a-bitch counselor killed my Joey. Joey must have been somehow in on helping them sell. I walked in on them beating him. They doped me, killed my boy, and put the gun in my hand. That's what they did! Then put me in some kind of weird funny farm and kept convulsing me out so I wouldn't remember what they did. I know it now, but how can I find Joey's body? I'm not out for revenge. He was in it, too, but must have wanted out—always, always a problem! Guess he picked a dangerous business—who knows what. Maybe he didn't bring in enough money—I don't know. We have a murder, and then all I know is they hid me away. As far as any authorities are concerned, my son and I left shortly after the death of my wife. The other kids were out of the house by then and didn't care about me after Bonny died—didn't care enough to file any missing person's report, so that's it. Either the counselor or those cops did it. Like I said, though, I'm not out for vengeance—I just want to know what they did with him so I can give him a proper burial. That's all that is important to me. A burial like Maria gave her Carlos—it spoke to me."

"Now you are talking about people we haven't talked of before. Who are Maria and Carlos?"

"Uh, Maria, the woman in Galveston who bought me my GI Joe for Christmas," Daniel stammered.

"And who is Carlos?"

"He died—he was her husband."

"I don't think you are giving me the full story here, Daniel."

"Maria was married to Carlos and he died and she gave him a beautiful graveside service and I was there," Daniel said softly but firmly.

"And Maria gave you a GI Joe for Christmas?"

"Yes, I guess part of me will not forget her for that."

This didn't sound like the old Daniel. This Daniel was caring and compassionate. Dr. Jerold gave a thankful sigh and said, "We need to talk some about that in our next session, and as far as just giving Joey a burial, are you sure, Daniel? Those crooks might still be selling, you know."

"I'm definitely sure—I know I want out of any mess. I've had enough, though we might have to bring the counselor down—to find Joey."

"Well, what's your next step then?" said Dr. Jerold.

"The only way I am going to find Joey's body is to get to that counselor. I know Jessica hasn't been feeling too well, but I think she will want to go with me. She hasn't had a vacation day since I have known her; I need to first talk it over with her. If for some reason she feels she cannot go, I'll go myself. I think she'll want to, though; it is not that far to Illinois from here."

Dr. Jerold marveled at the change in Daniel. Thank goodness for modern science! "Right, Daniel, not much over 200 miles I would expect. I think Jessica would probably want to go, like you said, but I haven't seen her lately. I hope her health is stabilized."

"Well, yes, I would say it is stable, and I know she will be very happy to hear I have had total recall about Joey. It's sad, very sad for me, but also like a weight has been lifted from my chest; you can't imagine!" Daniel said quietly, "I will call her as soon as I hang up with you."

"Oh yes, she will be so happy that you remembered. I don't know why it finally came to you, but there could be many reasons." Then as an afterthought the doctor said, "Have you shown her your GI Joe?"

"Well, no, not yet. Maybe I will."

Jessica took the call from Daniel at her desk. "You remember EVERYTHING, Daniel?"

"Yes, everything! It came to me like a bolt out of the blue. Like it was just given to me. I am so happy, though sad, too, if that makes any sense."

"Honey," said Jessica, "I can't imagine anything making any more sense—of course, it does. It's like being relieved when someone very, very ill dies and they find peace. That makes you happy; losing them makes you sad. It's a mixed emotions sort of thing. That's not a perfect analogy, though."

"Right—it's a very bad thing I had to remember, but remembering, finally, made me happy, as it was causing me such turmoil," Daniel agreed. "Now, the only thing I want is to give Joey a proper burial—that's all. So all we need to do is to get that counselor louse and the cops, and that should lead us to Joey, if everything falls in line like I see it. I don't want any vengeance; just a resting place for Joey."

"Oh Daniel, you are taking this so in stride—you are being so strong about it. I am really proud of you." Jessica could hardly believe the new Daniel—even a new Daniel might be shedding some tears.

"I'm so relieved that I can see it happening like I want it to, Jessie—that's all."

"I have many other nurses under my supervision, but you come first. I'll see what I can do about taking off, honey; I certainly have the time coming. I'll call you as soon as I know something, and it should be this evening, okay?"

"Illinois isn't far; you shouldn't get overtired or need a lot of clothes, okay? Don't be packing a lot of stuff you don't need."

"Okay, talk soon."

Jessica had three weeks of vacation coming—it just was not always easy to get it on the spur of the moment, but she didn't want to let Daniel down for anything. He needed her support in the worst way, no matter how strong he sounded. It was amazing, though, the change that had come over him since Dr. Jerold and the meds. Her calmness around him seemed to be the way things always had been. Of course, she remembered his other behavior, but it was remote, distant, far from her now. *I will always see to it that he takes his medicine; if I notice he forgets a prescription or even a pill.... Well, it looks like the rest of my life has been mapped out. He's been over-solicitous of me, and my concern for him will never end. It certainly would not take three weeks to track down that counselor. I'll just take a short leave; but if it takes three weeks, I'll have it.*

It didn't take long to arrange the leave with her supervisor, who simply said, "Jessica, I'm glad to see you take a little time away; you work too hard." So, that was that. Almost too easy. Hmmm, almost scary easy! Jessica worried too much.

Debbie and Becca had forgiven Daniel. He had charmed them completely. Debbie realized he had an illness, just another illness, only this one had a mental illness name. Since his diagnosis, she understood his outburst of that night, even though she hated the thought of it when she remembered it. Now, though, both girls dearly loved to hear him sing and play his guitar. It seemed any request they had, he could play.

After leaving work, she called Daniel back saying she could leave on Sunday. She planned to pack a few things Saturday morning and see her girls Saturday afternoon.

Daniel had other ideas. "Of course, sweetheart, you will want to see your girls, but if they could come to your house to see you, I could stop at the barbeque joint and bring supper. That way I could see them as well. You know how fond I've become of them." Daniel still had not found a permanent place to live—he knew Jessica wanted him to move in with her. He just somehow knew these things.

Saturday morning, Jessica awakened with her usual tiredness. "Day by day," she said aloud. "You learn to cope." Still her limp had not gone away, but that wasn't so bad. The weariness she felt was almost like a fever. It seemed weekends might be a gift—a gift to stay in bed. That is why she thought of having someone in to clean the house. Daniel had helped her many times. *I don't think it wise to get married even though he wants to. What a drag I will be if I get worse. I have three bedrooms, plenty of room—more than enough room. I wonder what the girls would think. They are modern-thinking young women and they would understand why I don't want to marry.*

But they would hardly think Daniel just ran the vac! *Debbie I think would understand, but I'm not sure about Becca. Jon is completely religious, and then there are the little boys to think about. It seems my life is wrapped around whether I might hurt someone else all the time, but that's the way life is ... complete love of family makes me merged with family. I have to be sure that there won't be reverberations.*

Traveling with Daniel will bring out the real Daniel, but he seems fine, wonderful; almost too good to be true. I'd like to offer that we drive using my car—it's only two years old and less likely to fall apart. She laughed aloud! *I don't want to insult him. Oh well, Illinois isn't far, and at least I won't be traveling with apple cores.* She laughed again. *I seemed to know in those early days things would somehow turn out all right.*

After filling her train case with her cleanser, makeup, etc., she packed a couple of wrinkle-free dresses, pj's, stretch slacks, two blouses, and a sweater. She planned to wear a travel outfit that didn't wrinkle. It was reversible and would give her another option. Everything was packed and ready when she heard a knock at the door.

Both girls hugged their mom and wasted no time making themselves comfortable by sprawling out on the couch. "Well, Mom, so you're taking off with a dude—a Daniel dude, to be precise. I declare, you never know what mothers are going to do in this day and age. What is this world coming to? Got to watch these matriarchs!" Debbie was her usual self, though she had come to like Daniel a lot.

Becca said, "Hmmm, traveling together. I guess that means you will be staying in the same motel—separate rooms, of course, would be the proper thing, as we know our mom is always proper." She gave Jessica a look and a wink that insinuated that she knew Jessica and Daniel were quite close and she doubted they'd be "proper."

Jessica thought that maybe this might be the time to approach them with the possibility of Daniel moving in, although she hadn't even said anything to Daniel.

"Becca, uh Debbie, you know Daniel and I are close, uh, in love, even though it was touch-and-go there for a while. Well, he still hasn't found a permanent place to live and I was thinking he would be a great deal of help to me if he just moved in here. You know, the guest room has a bath adjacent to it and why could he not move in here? I haven't said a word of this to Daniel because I wanted to kind of get a feel for what the two of you would say or think. I guess I mean that.

"Anyway, I need to think about it a little longer myself. One thing I know for sure, and I hate to tell you this—I could use his help. I don't have the energy I used to have for some reason and he would really be a help to me now that he is well."

Debbie was the first to speak up. "Well, Mom, he seems like a completely different person than the one who talked so mean to me that night, but I hate it that you are losing energy. Does this happen all the time or just some of the time?"

"I guess I used to look forward to Saturdays so much and now I feel like I have a fever most of the time. Through the week, still the feverish feeling, but I know I have to go to work and the momentum at work and the patients' troubles make me forget. I know I probably just need to go to another level of treatment." Jessica tried not to sigh and tried to look upbeat.

Debbie continued, "Perhaps so. Please see that stuck-up doctor as soon as you get back. But thanks for at least letting us know this time. But as far as Daniel is concerned, I guess you are old enough to make your own decisions about what you want to do, but why don't you just marry the guy? We like him; you have the seal of approval of this committee of two." She hugged her mother like she might be a carton of eggs.

"Yes," said Becca, "it would be better if you would just marry him; we could explain that better to Jon and the children."

"But," said Jessica, "since I'm old enough to make my own decisions, what if I don't wish to get married, at least at this time? I would like to see how it will work out. I want to see if, on his own, he consistently takes his medicines, and I want to be sure this darn MS doesn't get any worse. I don't want to be a drag on him—I love him too much to do that to him. Surely, Jon will understand that."

"I see what you mean," said Debbie. "Lighten up, Becca, will you? It's not Jon's life. Mom can do what is best for her. I completely understand."

"Besides, he is like Ulysses again, I can feel it. It is like the happiness that was cut short so very long ago…." Jessica's voice trailed off.

"Whatever you say, Mom—whatever. We are still not sure about that. Jon wonders why you ever went to that doctor in the first place," Becca remarked.

"As for the other doctor, I don't think he is stuck-up at all, but that he knows his stuff, and please get yourself over there as soon as you can!"

"You tell Jon Dr. Jerold put my life in order—I have no more nightmares, and a miracle has happened finding Daniel, when you think of all the people in the world; we finally got together again after centuries. Tell him, and tell him to just have faith in me and my judgment; or let me talk to him. You know how I love Jon; I don't want to be misunderstood! And yes, I will see Dr. Amish as soon as possible."

"I think I would have to be very sure before I would ask anyone to move in with me. Are you sure this is what you want? He's not from our same background, and those things become screamingly clear when you're under the same roof," Becca added.

"Well, Mrs. Wiseacre has a point to be taken into consideration, but she can put herself in the corner of the stuck-up doctor!" said Debbie.

"I guess you realize what you two are doing—taking my decision and making it yours, well, again, I think I can do this, but I appreciate your input, really I do." Jessica smiled at her two daughters. "As I said, I haven't asked Daniel yet. I am 'taking it into consideration,' so thanks a lot."

"Well, he has a way about him that has gotten under my skin, especially when he sings. I just wish he were twenty years younger," said Debbie.

"Jon is just as cute."

"Beauty is in the eyes of the beholder."

"All right, you two, since I must again remind you that Daniel doesn't know about this, I feel like it's disrespectful to him talking anymore about it. Now you know my thoughts. I wanted you to know them. Now the ball is in my court, okay?

"Okay," said Debbie, "my mouth is now sealed—like you said, it's your decision."

"I understand that," said Becca, "I'll just tell the boys their granny has a roommate."

"So what's in the fridge?" Debbie, no matter how serious the conversation, could somehow switch it to her stomach. How she stayed so waiflike was a mystery to all who knew her.

"Not a lot," replied Jessica. "Besides, Daniel wanted to see you before we left and he's bringing barbeque for dinner. There may be cheese in there, though, if you're famished, but it is five o'clock. I would expect him soon."

"He's coming? Yum! I mean yum barbeque." Debbie started doing exercises. Becca glared at her and then started thumbing through a magazine as if she could care less.

Jessica put a red and white plaid cloth on the table and moved a small plant from the living room for a centerpiece. She set the table, just for a diversion, with her grandmother's antique crockery dishes.

"Can I help you, Mom?" Debbie realized her mother's condition was more important than her exercising.

"No, it's done now, but thanks, honey."

It wasn't long before the familiar knock of Daniel's came at the door and all three went to greet him.

CHAPTER FORTY-ONE

Daniel and Jessica were heading west the next day, surprisingly in Jessica's car. He had asked her last evening if it wouldn't be a good idea since her car was a later model, almost as if he could read her mind. Jessica was not at all uncomfortable with this, like she might have been earlier. It was not as if he were taking over or anything; it was as if he had always been here—here at her side. Her thoughts regarding "getting to know a man better traveling" seemed silly, superfluous, and perhaps had been a product of the earlier Daniel. Well, they looked the same, except the Daniel that drove her car, carefully, and had a barely distinguishable hairline scar on his right temple. From what he had told her of his accident, he fixed up well!

They held hands and sang folksongs—"when they weren't laughing and talking"—nearly to their destination. It didn't seem like they had a grim task to accomplish. Daniel went out of his way to keep that part of the trip quiet, at least while they were traveling. He soon pulled into a nice-looking motel.

"I think we should stop here tonight and then drive into the town in the morning. My plan is to first go to the school, and hopefully they still use the same gruesome counselor," said Daniel. "You know, Jessica, I'm glad you decided to come with me. First, just because, and second, you're so classy; you'll lend credence to my story. Without you they might not believe me and I'd have to approach them on bended knee, or they might think I'm some bum! You know, I'm not exactly the humble type." He gave her a quick squeeze, then a kiss.

Jessica said, "I brought my swimsuit, although this is a business trip. I'm envisioning how a hot tub might feel—I hope they have one. Did you bring your suit?"

Daniel replied, "I brought everything I need and then some," as he reached in the back seat and dug his swimsuit out of a pillow case. "Let's go, baby!"

Jessica had a feeling Daniel may have known about this motel, as it proved to have all the amenities. She stayed in the hot tub for a long time while Daniel went for a swim. The tub felt so soothing and healing. There seemed to be nothing like warm water to make her feel like she didn't even have MS at all; she felt rejuvenated! When Daniel got back in, she pulled him to her and said, "Sweetheart, don't you think we need to get a little rest before tomorrow?"

"And a little food? Jessica, we haven't had dinner yet, but actually I'm not very hungry. Let's just see what there is in the dining room. I'm not going to let you go to bed without something to eat."

The dining room had closed, but they were served anyway. They both got low-carb rolled sandwiches and herb tea so they wouldn't be any trouble. Daniel said, "We can make up for this in the morning," and then to the waiter, "Don't you have a gigantic breakfast buffet?"

"Yes, sir, the best. People drive from town to come here!"

With this Jessica knew Daniel knew about this place. Daniel opened the door to the room and said, "Milady?"

Since they had just come from the pool and tub, they took off their robes and damp suits and dove into one of the double beds. It felt wonderful being together again, skin against skin, and then making love as if it were the first time all over again. Before turning off the lights, though, Daniel said, “Got to down my medication. Do you have any you need to take?”

“No, not this time. I take it with breakfast.”

“Oh, Jessica, I forgot to tell you—who guards my medicine and makes sure I take it?”

She said a sleepy, “Who?”

“It’s my soldier friend here, GI Joe, see? He sits by my medicine bottles.”

“Oh, GI JOE?” Jessica remembered what the psychic lady had said but was too sleepy to question him any further.

When Daniel got back in beside her, Jessica was practically asleep and slept contentedly until morning. Daniel told Jessica the plan again he had for zeroing in on the counselor. She put on her no-nonsense-looking dress softened by the strand of pearls. “Does this look all right, honey, for your classy lady?”

“Jess, you, as always, look beautiful, and as far as the dress goes, it looks very professional. Guess I can’t wear jeans.”

“Guess not.... Oh Daniel, you haven’t packed up your GI Joe yet, have you? Let me see him please. Oh, he’s a handsome gentleman, and young, too. You haven’t had him for a long time. I thought maybe you had him since you were a little boy and that you saved him all these years.”

“No, sweetheart, I wasn’t blessed to have had one when I was little. All the other kids did, but not me. Anyway, I don’t really want to talk about this much except that Maria, that woman in Texas, gave him to me for Christmas. I insisted. I was being my usual tormented self. So my inner child is here. Now, I've told you about it."

Jessica realized this was a sad subject that had a happy ending—one better left alone.

They were in the small city before Jessica realized it and pulled up to the school. Jessica could feel the perspiration beginning to make her hands sticky. *Come on now, Jessica,* she said to herself, *it will turn out okay. Daniel has always said the truth from the very beginning. He did not remember all of it and now he does. Thankfully, now he does!*

She put her damp hand in Daniel's. He looked down at her and said, "I'm nervous as well, but you're supposed to hold me up! Let's go. He's got to be the same principal." They went in the door and up the well-trod steps to the second floor. Classes were in session. That was a break. They went to the door marked "Mr. Bishop, Principal." Daniel nodded, indicating to Jessica that this, indeed, was the principal they sought. Daniel knocked gently and to a hoarse, "Yes?" turned the knob, opened the door, pushed Jessica in before him, and followed behind.

"May I help you?"

"I do think so. May I introduce Ms. Jessica Hastings, my friend, who has come with me to witness what is said today."

"Mr. Cummings!" Mr. Bishop stammered. "I must say I'm surprised to see you. I thought you and Joey had left the area some time ago. Are you back for a particular reason? I noticed your house just the other day. It looked well kept, like someone had been living there, but Joey never came back to school. I didn't know what happened. Early on, we sent the truancy people to find him, but no Joey, and we couldn't find you either, so we figured you and the family left town." He appeared shaken. "You, uh, you may have heard about the scandal and came to see about that?"

"Oh, you have a scandal, all right. You tell me yours and I'll tell you mine," Daniel nearly hissed at him. "If you have had a scandal, I hope it ties in with that evil so-called counselor you, yes, you recommended for Joey. Joey is dead, dear Mr. Bishop, and I hold you partly responsible."

"Oh my God, you cannot mean it—Joey dead! How did it happen and what do you mean *responsible*?"

"A few years ago by the people you recommended—they killed him."

"Joey was killed? This is worse than we imagined. You cannot mean this!" Mr. Bishop's face became gray.

"Yes, the counselor recommended by you and the school as one to help get him off drugs was using him as a supplier for quite a network, it looked like to me. Yes, Mr. Hampton from the police department, the counselor you recommended to us for my Joey, killed him or had one of his goon cops do it and I suspect worse crimes than supplying illicit drugs were committed against minor children. Use your imagination. At that time all I remembered was that they tried to make me think I had killed my own child. Then they took me someplace and gave me shock treatments to wipe out my memory—but it's back now, clear as a sunny day!"

"Don't you think we ought to call the police department if this is true?"

"So you think it might not be true? Well, it's true all right and I want that so-called 'counselor.' I wanna know what they did with Joey's body. I want to put my boy to rest. Do you realize what a crooked police force this town has?"

"It's not the force; it was Hampton and two policemen who have disappeared. The three of them were running a drug operation using kids in trouble. Their suppliers came in at night on the freight. They kept them addicted so that they would have to meet the freight, undercover, and threatened them if they didn't. Maybe Joey was trying to break away, stop using, and that's what happened—they killed him. Oh, I'm so, so sorry. Joey was trying—he was trying, and then we sent him to that heinous criminal. But you have to believe me, Mr. Cummings, we didn't know, we had no idea—he had falsified credentials. The department didn't know, believe me, but he must have had some sort of a conscience...."

"What can you possibly mean?" said Daniel.

"He hung himself before they went to arrest him."

"Oh no." Jessica put her arms around Daniel, so afraid she would have to calm him down

But instead he said, "It's all right, honey." But to Bishop he snapped, "The scumbag couldn't face the music, could he? How 'bout a note, a last goodbye?"

"Everyone knew the reason; he was in it up to his neck and, uh, he knew it—although in this day and age, I find it unusual that he hung himself," Mr. Bishop nervously replied.

"Were there survivors?" Daniel said. "I don't care about the way he did it; it's just that he did it. I wanted that man alive so that I could find out what happened to Joey's body."

"Only his wife, and she found him hanging there in the cellar," said Bishop.

"When?"

"Last week." Bishop fell into his chair.

"Is she still in town?"

"Yes, she is, but under a doctor's care for severe nervous strain. She's preparing to leave as soon as she can get his business matters in order," Bishop replied.

"Well, I have news for her: things are not in order, and you—you don't plan on leaving, or going anywhere." Daniel's temper flared. Jessica put her hand on his arm.

"We'll have to remember, Daniel, she didn't do anything."

"I'm not sure about that! She might know a hell of a lot; Bishop, where does she live?"

"I'm afraid you'll have to get that from the police."

Daniel approached Bishop's desk, went behind it to Bishop, who was still in his chair, put both of his hands on his shoulders, and shook him until his teeth rattled. "Perhaps you didn't understand me. I said where does she live?"

Bishop put his hand in his top drawer, pulled out an address on a piece of paper, and handed it to Daniel. "Perhaps you'll find Mrs. Hampton here—this is her address," he said in a barely audible voice.

"And as far as you're concerned, Bishop, you have not seen me; I wasn't here." With that said, Daniel took Jessica's hand. "Let's go, Ms. Hastings."

Back in the car Daniel looked at the address, at Jessica, and quoted:

I am the master of my fate.
I am the captain of my soul.

"I've always loved that, honey." Jessica patted his hand. "And it can be true; my hope is we do not get into trouble with the authorities without calling on them with this information."

"The 'authorities' gave no help to me in my time of trouble when I needed it in the worst way," replied Daniel.

"It was a cover-up, and from what Bishop said only those three were involved."

"That is what that mealymouthed excuse for a person said, but I think we may be in time," Daniel said with a look of determination on his face.

"Well, onward we go, and thank goodness the wife is still around, uh, we hope."

CHAPTER FORTY-TWO

Daniel drove down Mallory Lane to a better part of town and up Bradford Blossom Boulevard to quite a large house. They parked the car in the ample driveway and he helped Jessica out of the car. They hurried up the long walk to the impressive double doors and knocked. A woman in uniform came to the door and said, "Miss Hampton ain't home."

"Yes, I think she is. Tell her some old friends have come to see her." Daniel spoke in his most positive tone.

The maid left and Daniel whispered to Jessica, "This is it—this is the place, the house they kept me in for who knows how long, and you might say the drug business paid mighty well! That woman is guilty as sin!"

"How do you know?" Jessica whispered back.

"The smell. I'll never forget the smell. I would get a whiff of it when they would take me from one room to the shock room."

"Oh Daniel, that was a horrible crime against you and needs to be reported. We can't just let that go. I've never heard anything described in such a way. You've remembered everything." Jessica could feel her excitement mounting.

Mrs. Hampton started down the stairs and wavered, holding on tightly to the railing when she spotted Daniel. "Oh," she uttered.

"Oh yes, and don't worry, Mrs. Hampton, come on down." Daniel's mellow tone convinced her and she came down, looked straight at him, and then cast her eyes down.

"What is the matter, Mrs. Hampton? Do I hurt your eyes? You can look at me, and as of right now we won't tell, but I'll not making any promises. I understand your husband met an untimely death by his own hand; could he not stand himself? Or what he had done? Or was he just a coward? Yes, you had a great time keeping me prisoner in one of those massive rooms!

"I just want some answers and I want them now! It was upstairs, wasn't it? Where you tried to knock me out of my mind, pretending to be a nurse?"

"No, no!" quivered Mrs. Hampton.

"Yes, yes! Mind if I look around? Jessica, you stay down here in case there is something that would be hard on your eyes. Oh, by the way, this is Ms. Hastings, Mrs. Hampton. Now, Ms. Hastings is a real nurse, not a psychotic one!"

Mrs. Hampton's expression stiffened. "I'm a nurse, I'm a nurse—I was a nurse for years on a psychiatric ward; in fact, I was head nurse!"

"Figures—but your license expired years ago, right? All you kept in your mind was how to do shock treatments for your late husband. Yes, I remember you as much as a zonked mind can remember." Daniel toured the many upstairs rooms. "Yes, here's the room; it smells the same. At least you knew when to turn the shock mechanism off. I'm not here for the crimes against me, though. Tell me, I want my son! What did you other-world creatures do with my son's body?"

Mrs. Hampton broke down and cried, nearly becoming hysterical.

"Stop it! What did you do with him? What did you do with my Joey?"

"He, my husband, couldn't stand what he did. The s-s-shame of it. Floyd dealt drugs, not d-d-death. It was an accident. He got sicker and sicker, almost insane, and then—then … I found him…."

"Some accident—I saw him beating Joey and who knows what else he did to him! Now, listen up—where is Joey? What did they do with my boy?"

"I think they put the body in that other house, but I don't know," she cried.

"Is that, by the way, the house on Elm? My house? And why it was kept up so the police wouldn't get suspicious?" Daniel's face was very close to Mrs. Hampton.

"I don't know! I don't know!"

"Look, Miss Innocent, if I find the body, you won't be arrested as an accessory. Be thinking! If I don't find the body, I'm going to the police. You stay right here. Don't think of leaving this town—do you hear what I have just said?"

"I will stay here, Mr. Cummings, a-and th-think!"

"Oh, you remembered I have a name. You do that. You think!"

Daniel looked at the distraught Jessica. "Let's go, Jessie."

As one driven, wordlessly Daniel drove to another neighborhood. Jessica could feel her heart beating in her chest. *What if we find him? What if we don't? I know if the body of Joey is in that house, it will just be skeletal remains. Can Daniel stand the shock of finding it? Up until this time, he has been Sir Galahad. It has been unbelievable how he has handled this and himself, the new Daniel. But will he be able to control himself when or if we find the remains of his son?*

They pulled into the drive of a fairly middle-class neighborhood. The grass needed mowing and the shrubs were covering the windows. "Well," said Daniel, "they had the grass mowed, the least possible thing so people wouldn't get suspicious, but forgot the shrubs. I would say it's been about a week since the grass was mowed, wouldn't you, Jessica?"

"In my poor judgment, yes, it looks it—whoever was keeping it up has gone," answered Jessica. These were the first words she had said since the drive from one neighborhood to the other.

"Well, I made my money honestly; hence, the poorer-looking house. I didn't think of getting into drug racketeering—I missed my chance. Joey did, though—smart kid!"

"Honey, please don't. It's over now, and please don't blame yourself. Peer groups oftentimes influence others to do the wrong thing."

"Yes, but in this case I'm afraid Joey became head peer.

"You know, Jessica, I must have been really discombobulated when I got out of the 'funny farm.' I must have been like a man without a country, without a home. When I was dropped in Cincy, shaken and confused, I didn't want to go back. I didn't know who Daniel Cummings was for quite some time."

"And you don't want to press charges? I would think the right thing to do would be to tell the authorities just what happened to you. They would somehow find those policemen, and the wife is still alive. Mr. Bishop is right here in this town as principal of the school. It seems to me that justice should prevail!"

"No, I came for one reason and one reason only. If we find the reason in this house, there will be no reason for us to go to the authorities. I'm not even sure of the date. You know how they do in trials."

They pulled in the drive, got out, and hand in hand went up on the porch. Daniel tried several keys before one fit the lock, then he turned it and they went in. There was a strange, musty smell that gave Jessica the idea of death or that they may be walking into a morgue. *Maybe we will find something that will lead us to Joey's remains. It's possible!*

If we find Joey's remains here, it will be over. I want us to, and I don't want us to. I'm afraid of how Daniel will react, but he's been okay; he must continue to be okay, although now that he remembers, it has to be a terrible shock to him. He is holding up so well; when I remember how he used to cry at the drop of a hat. This is now, Jessica; this is the Daniel who is well. Forget the other!

The house looked to be about forty years old, as it had hardwood flooring and was built of brick. "Well," said Daniel, "looks like the older kids made at least one trip here. A picture of Bonny was above the fireplace and we had a few antiques; they seem to be missing. A lot of junk here. Let's go up the stairs. I know you're scared. Don't be. Whatever we find, we can deal with it. I don't know if Joey's remains are here, but they might be. Come on."

Daniel took Jessica's hand and practically pulled her up the stairs. She didn't like being where he and Bonny had lived together as married people, although she knew how silly that was; worse, she felt they would not leave that house without some clue as to where they would find Joey. Daniel seemed perfectly competent to deal with just about anything. She wondered if she could. It was all so eerie. There were three bedrooms upstairs, sparsely furnished, each with the same musty, empty smell.

"I don't think they used my house for anything—drugs, anything. They just kept everything mowed so no one would be suspicious. I never knew the neighbors. Bonny may have spoken to them. Not seeing me or Joey around would be no skin off their backs," said Daniel rather bitterly. "People are just not neighborly anymore. I wonder who the ghouls got to keep up the lawn."

"But not the shrubs," said Jessica, as she looked straight out the upstairs window and saw where it was nearly covered with vines. "I wonder how long it was, Daniel."

"I would guess around three years now; but you know, I don't really know the time frame. I don't know how long I was at the funny farm and how it messed up my head and my life. We're both glad I'm back again, aren't we?" He drew Jessica to him for a long hug.

"Honey, let's get out of here, soon, can we? You didn't like the smell of the big house—this house smells so musty. I don't like the vines that have crept up to these bedrooms. It reminds me of a Hawthorne novel. Let's go!"

"As soon as we can. We need to visit the downstairs; we just looked around, that's all." Daniel was determined to go over his house with a fine-toothed comb. Jessica was remembering the mysteries she had read as a child and young adult, and she felt weak kneed.

"Okay," she said weakly. She also needed to sit or lie down, but not here.

They walked all over the downstairs, looking in closets, etc. Daniel even took the upholstery out of some overstuffed chairs. He shook his head. They were about to head out the back door when he noticed a squeak in the hardwood in front of the fireplace. "I don't recall that ever squeaking before." He walked back and forth. Still the squeak. He took out his Swiss Army knife.

Jessica said, "Daniel?"

"There might be something here—right here." He began working on one of the boards with the knife. It was loose. He worked some more, using all the strength he could muster, and the whole board came loose. He removed it. "Jessica, I think their might be something down there. Stay here. I'm going to the car and get a flashlight. I don't know whether you noticed but this house is built on concrete blocks, not a slab, and I think those other floorboards may be loose as well.

While Daniel went to the car, Jessica found new energy and tried the next board—she pulled it with all her might, bruising her hands, and it came to her. Two boards loose from the hole into the crawl space—her heart began to beat excitedly. *Flooring should not be this loose,* she thought, *not hardwood flooring; it should be sealed!*

Daniel came back. "Pretty smart, aren't you, sweetheart. Don't ruin those pretty hands—let me try some more with this knife. It's obvious that they've been disturbed then put back." They worked until they had a sizable hole, enough for Daniel to drop down into the crawl space. Then he saw dirt that was very disarrayed, apparently mounded a bit, but certainly not even.

"Jessica, I may be down here a while; if you would be more comfortable in the car, maybe you had better go there."

"No, I'm staying with you. I can lower myself down there, too," replied Jessica.

"No, sitting in one of those chairs would be better. I don't think you should be down here would be my guess."

"I'll pull one over."

Daniel started digging wildly, using only his hands as tools in the loose dirt. He couldn't understand why the dirt would be so loose. The grave turned out to be very shallow, no more than two feet, and he found what he was looking for lying in the earth. He dug some more—an almost perfect skeleton that had been bent at the torso made him gasp and nearly vomit.

"Jessica, I found him! I found my Joey!"

"Daniel, I don't want to doubt but how do you know it's Joey?"

"There's no doubt. I'll show you." Daniel pulled himself up with an object in his hand.

"What is it?" Jessica was thoroughly shaken and about to cry. The whole discovery had been frightening and almost too much for her.

"It's his—it's Joey's ring. Bonny and I gave it to him when he managed to graduate from the eighth grade. Joey must have been proud of it because he never took it off." Daniel put his arms around Jessica, dirt and all, and broke down for the first time. "How could they do that to him? A young boy, only fourteen years old. I'd like to believe what Bishop hinted, that he was trying to get out of it, get out of drugs, come clean, and that's why they killed him. But Jessie, he would not confide in me. Then I remember his last words to me: 'Daddy, no!' He knew what I had come upon and he didn't want me bruised by those animals. He must have loved me even though he acted like he couldn't stand me. He had to act the big, tough guy. And you know, I think I loved him best. The other kids sensed that and that's why they could care less now. Oh Jessica, what was my Joey has been reduced to mere bones." Again, he broke down.

Jessica felt so sorry. "Our bodies, or bones, are not who we are—were, thankfully; that is, who Joey was, when there is no more life, becomes just that: an empty shell. This is all terrible, Daniel honey, but don't beat yourself in the head about the other kids now. Life is long and there is still time for reconciliation with them.

"Surely you want to press charges? The evidence is right here in this house. We know it's Joey."

"No, I don't. I stubbornly don't! I just want to give him a proper burial, out away from this damned town. I really hate asking you to do this, but now that I've found him, I don't want to leave him, even though I know how crazy it sounds; you, Jessica, of all people know I am not crazy."

"I understand how you feel. What should I do? I'll do whatever," said Jessica, who had no idea what Daniel wanted.

“Will you drive to the middle of town to Byrd’s Hardware and get something to put him in? Use your own judgment—something nice, if you can find something. I just can’t leave him. I hope you understand, please, Jessie?”

“Of course. Would it be around the square, the park being the middle of town?” inquired Jessica.

“That’s it. It’s on the east side at the corner. It’s quite a large hardware place and they carry all kinds of things, not just hardware. It would be a fun place for you just to shop if it weren’t for what I am sending you for. Meanwhile, much as I hate this, I’ll make certain I have everything together in this crawl space,” Daniel said sadly. “And, don’t worry, you look great. Somehow I didn’t get any dirt on you.” Daniel leaned forward and kissed her, this time making sure he didn’t touch her with his grubby hands. “Now, go on.”

Jessica drove to the center of town until she saw the large “Byrd’s Hardware” sign and pulled into a spot. *It doesn’t look like they are having much business this day. Good, or maybe bad. If they have a lot of business I could get lost in the peopled place—this day I will be remembered, probably. Oh well, be cool, Jessica. Yes, I can be very, very cool, but my only disguise is my sunglasses. No large floppy hat. I’m easily recognizable with this limp. I must not limp. If I use one of those shopping carts, no one will even know that I limp. Thank you, God, for giving humankind the ability to think up the good old shopping cart. That was a good one!*

CHAPTER FORTY-THREE

Once in the door of Bryd's, she grabbed a cart as quickly as she could but didn't escape from "May I help you, lady?"

"Actually, no, I just want to look a little. I hear this is a fun place to shop."

"Well, yes, you've come to the right place. We get our merchandise from everywhere, as far away as India," the clerk said proudly.

"I hope you don't mind if I just see what you have. This is certainly not just a hardware store," smiled Jessica.

"People from out of town are usually interested in our imports. They are in the next room."

"You're right—that's my forte. Thanks so much. I'll head on in there," said Jessica, who seemed quite agile with the shopping cart—no limp in view. It indeed proved quite an interesting place. She walked the aisles slowly, looking, touching, picking up some objects, as any interested shopper might. *I know if I find it, I'll have to buy something else or look suspicious or strange. I feel like a criminal. I'm acting like a criminal. If we bury a body without letting the police know, we are criminals! Oh God! Maybe I can talk to Daniel. Maybe I can let him know we shouldn't do this, this way, but he is so determined! But I can see why—there will be all of those questions. Maybe they won't believe him and with all the publicity that would ensue—it won't work! We will just be breaking that one silly little law. You should have some say about where your loved ones are buried. Why, take me, for example: I might like to be buried in my own back yard.* She stifled a laugh.

Look at this aisle! This whole next section has different sizes of trunks. I can't believe this! They are so unique and so beautiful. It's like all of this is planned. They are just what I need. What Daniel needs....

I'll go pick something else out first. I don't want it to look like I just came here for a trunk! That clerk is very aware of me. There's a lovely tapestry over there. Maybe I should get two of them—one for each of my girls. Then the trunk. It has to be long enough for the longest bone. Oh, this is close to ghoulish. That would be hip to knee. I don't like this at all! I'll pretend it's a puppy!

Guess that bronze-looking one will be okay. Jessica the nurse with anatomy courses. Do you suppose that's why Daniel wanted me to do this chore? It should work, and the inside is lined. A trunk for bones. Joey's. This means so much to Daniel! I'll act like I am going to keep the tapestries in the trunk. That should make the clerk less curious about me and satisfied.

Jessica went to where the cash register was located and the eager clerk. "I believe I'll take these. I can't wait to show them to my family. They are just beautiful!"

"You've made expensive choices, but they are fine quality. Now with tax, that's $411.91. Pretty high, Missy."

"Well, here is the cash—I don't like to charge such things; luxury items, you know." Jessica smiled to put herself at ease.

"I certainly thank you, Missy; my best sale of the day. Let me help you to your car."

"Oh, I'll just take it in the cart and you come get the cart, okay?"

"Sure, good idea!"

It seemed to Daniel that Jessica had been gone a long time. He had carefully laid out all of Joey's body, grieved some more, and was just waiting. He thought, though, *How can I grieve over a pile of bones?*

I realize she may not even have found a large enough box at the hardware store, but I know they carry trunks and such. Then the door opened.

"Daniel, are you still down there? You wouldn't believe the beautiful trunk I found. It looks like bronze. Shall I lower it down and you can see if you like it as well as I do?"

"Sweetheart, it doesn't matter; we just need it and we need it now. Thanks so much for going out and doing that gruesome chore."

"Any way you look at it, it is gruesome. What you had to do is very, very sad and awful compared to my just picking out a trunk. But I think the sooner we get him in there, the better we will both feel."

"It is very nice," said Daniel. "It will just take me ten or so minutes to get it done and then I will just push it up to you. I think we should leave everything as we found it. I'll flatten over this grave and come on up. Then we should put the boards back the best way we can. It would be good if we had some sealer, but I don't want to take the time. They didn't, or I never would have noticed the squeak and found the body."

Jessica, as always trying to be helpful, said, "There are some old magazines in the trunk of the car. Would you need those to put in the corners of the trunk to help pack it in there?" Then she thought it sounded like sacrilege. She, of course, had never been faced with anything like this before.

"Honey, no, I think the trunk you bought is just perfect and I really wouldn't want to put anything else in here, you know?" Daniel had a melancholy tone to his usual mellow voice.

"Of course. I don't know what I was thinking of—I just wasn't thinking … but I do think we should hurry, don't you? I will feel much better when we are out of here—out of this town. What if that clerk starts talking about the lady from out of town who bought the trunk?"

"I'll pass it up in a minute; I'm nearly through."

When Daniel had everything done, he passed the trunk up to Jessica. *I will just try not to think about what we are doing,* thought Jessica as she moved it over to the fireplace. Daniel, no dirtier than he had been, came up and out. "Don't worry, Jessie; it will be all right. Let's put this floor back." Putting the floor back proved strangely easier than pulling the boards loose. Jessica was so thankful for that. Everything looked almost as it had before.

Jessica carried the tapestries and Daniel carried the trunk out to the car. If anybody was looking out of neighboring windows, it was all very innocent-looking. After putting Jessica's purchases in the trunk of the car, they got in the front seat and drove away. Jessica started to breathe normally again. Thank goodness most of the trauma was left behind them; but unfortunately, not all of it. *I don't know why I am worrying so; after all, this is Daniel's house.*

"You are right, Jessica; this is my house except that I haven't paid any taxes on it for the last how many years? A big mystery to city hall and to me. They didn't know where I was and neither did I for a while. As soon as I can, I will pay the back taxes and put it up for sale, and that should give us a nice lump of money. I don't want anything to do with a house that housed my son's body."

"Daniel, you are reading my mind again. But what about this—how did city hall leave well enough alone? They knew you weren't there; there may have been a larger conspiracy than we will ever know now. And I believe you are right. If we reported this, there would be a trial and no doubt a long and drawn-out one; but since we would win with the evidence we have, don't you think it better that you go to the authorities and make sure everything comes out?"

"With city hall on their side, I don't think so. My poor little Jessica, the likelihood of them finding those guys is next to nil. You've lived a sheltered life, honey; you don't know the real world."

Jessica retorted, "But what about Mrs. Hampton and Bishop? Are they just going free?'

"Bishop's only crime was not knowing, we might say—stupidity. As far as she goes, yes, she committed a terrible crime, but she was one of those namby-pamby women that was afraid not to do her husband's bidding. Bonny was like that—but that's another story. One I'm ashamed of, but I'll tell you some day." Daniel's conversation rolled right along with his careful driving away from town.

"Are we just going to forget those cops who might be selling someplace else then?" Jessica again persisted.

"Yes, we are, because we have what we came for in the trunk you so deftly picked out without my help for the end of Joey's chapter. Perhaps he was supposed to live only fourteen years—I had short lifetimes for two of mine that we know about. I apparently came right back, uh, that is, my soul consciousness did, looking for you. I didn't seem to speak of a layover bus stop," Daniel laughed.

"No, you didn't. You may have popped right back, unlike me, Elizabeth. I thought it odd that I saw you but realized most of you had gone back and you weren't really Ulysses as I had known you. You were just a shadow of what you had been and I, as Elizabeth, intuitively knew that. Elizabeth seemed wise when she was in the holding place," Jessica laughed back.

"Although I hope I don't ever have another astral travel experience, it does seem that I know what you are thinking now, more than ever. Maybe I just know you so well. I'm not doing anything spectacular; it just happens, that's all. It doesn't make you uncomfortable, does it?"

"Well, no, it's not that I have to be careful what I think, because what I think is usually about us, for us—you know, sweetheart?"

"Well, we accomplished our mission, sweet one, and I couldn't have done it without you by my side. You are my stabilizing influence, my rock, my girl—I love you."

"And I love you so very much and I am so proud of the way you handled this. You really didn't need me," Jessica answered, putting her hand in his.

"I will always need you—my soul searched for you and finally found you, but didn't realize it at first because I couldn't find my soul or find myself. I'm afraid I hurt you deeply, Jessica, and I'm so, so sorry for that. If you'll have me, I want to be with you for the rest of this life. We should grow old together. I have far-life memory now and I know we belong together. Please forgive me for the wrong I have done."

"Of course, I forgive you; that is the easy part. But if, Daniel, you are proposing, I love you for that but I can't marry you, and that is because I love you too much. My—no, I will not own it. This illness won't let me. I want you to feel free to leave if it becomes intolerable. I want you with me with no strings attached. I've thought this through carefully. If we want to live in my home together, that would be wonderful. I'm not a prude anymore."

"Now that I've finally found you and myself, I'll never leave you, Jessica, no matter what. Perhaps together we will be strong for each other," answered Daniel.

Their silence spoke their feelings for a mile or so, and when tears came to Jessica's eyes, Daniel touched her cheek and said, "Fifty miles or so out of town there is a wonderful wooded area. Years ago, I purchased half of it with another musician. We used to come out here with our families and play and sing. We shall come upon it soon. I guess you know we are not quite through with our mission. When we bury Joey, could we have a little service? That's why I brought that Bible even though I've never been very religious."

"I didn't know Joey, but I think he would like a service as a memorial." Jessica clasped his hand and held it firmly.

"You didn't know that I put a small shovel on the floor of the back seat. It's brand new so it wouldn't get your car dirty."

"I wondered how we were going to dig. Oh Daniel, I'll be so glad when this is over with! We're breaking the law you know."

"Yes, and you know why. We have got to do this ourselves, law or no."

They pulled the car into a densely wooded area. It was covered with vines of all sorts, hiding it from view. There were beautiful pines all around. A fine, tall pine, the most beautiful, seemed to call to them. *This is the spot.* Daniel dug the grave and then buried the trunk. Jessica looked around for something to mark the grave, a cross maybe.

"Can we mark the grave with rocks in the shape of a cross? The forest is so dense—how can we mark it?" said Jessica.

"We'll recognize the tree. But the little service is most important, and I guess I better hurry because the sun is going down. Could you help me look up something?"

Jessica thumbed through the Bible until she came upon John 14. She was glad it was the poetic King James Version.

At dusk in an eloquent voice, Daniel read the passage from John 14:

Let not your heart be troubled: ye believe in God, believe also in me. In my Father's house are many mansions: If it were not so, I would have told you. I go to prepare a place for you. And if I go and prepare a place for you, I will come again and receive you unto myself, that where I am, there you may be also.

A cool wind came up in the darkening forest and lightning made an intriguing pattern across the sky. They both looked up as a storm suddenly gained momentum. Jessica began to feel a renewal as the wind blew through her hair and then a strange feeling came over her. She reached out to Daniel.

"We know there is definitely life after death, don't we Elizabeth." And with those words Ulysses took Elizabeth's hand and said, "Now our John is with the Lord, may he rest in peace. I am back now with thee, my dear Elizabeth. I will never leave thee. We can build a new cabin over there." Elizabeth smiled and said, "How did thee know I thought that, my husband, my friend, my dear Ulysses?"

Printed in the United States
57632LVS00001B/1